On Such a Tide

Bryan Webster

For Mary,

my wife, counsellor and best friend

Bryan Webster

Copyright: Bryan Webster 2005

Bryan Webster asserts his right to be recognised as the author of this book.

Second edition: 2019

ISBN 9781691612888

All characters in this book are fictional. Any resemblance to persons living or dead is co-incidental. Similarly, all organisations in the book are fictional.

Note: This second edition enters the story later than the first edition. It omits earlier management efforts to save the plant at York.
I would like to thank Lynne Dickinson, not only for suggesting the adjustment but also for her corrections and comments.
BW

Bryan Webster
Fair Havens
Houndlaw Park
EYEMOUTH
TD14 5DA

On such a tide as moving seems asleep,
Too full for sound and foam,
When that which drew from out the boundless deep
Turns again home.

Crossing the Bar: Tennyson

Other Books by Bryan Webster:

Aida and the Soothsayers (2011) Kindle

Time, Hens and the Universal Significance of Fiddle Music (2013) Kindle

Wrapped Together in the Bundle of Life (2019) Paperback and Kindle

Eyemouth and Hecklescar Stories (Short stories from the 1960s) (2018) Kindle

CHAPTER ONE

On his journey south to see The Chairman, John reflected on the turbulent week he had endured and the terrifying decision he now had to make.

John was Managing Director of Pinkerton-Loyalty, a subsidiary company of Loyalty based at York; The Chairman Walter Radleigh; he headed the board of the parent company Loyalty plc; the top man.

They had met just over a week ago. John had been summoned to the Holy of Holies: the Executive Suite at Guildford. He had found that meeting disconcerting. This one could be devastating.

When he had arrived for the meeting last Thursday, he had found The Chairman accompanied by The Knight.

The Knight! Frank John Wantley had first been elected in 1988 to represent the citizens of Kingsbury and Gudley having tired of helping his brother run the family livestock auction business. In 1990 he was wise enough to back John Major against Michael Heseltine in the Tory leadership election, and reaped the reward of a Junior Ministerial Post in the Overseas Trade Division of the Department of Trade and Industry. The job consisted largely of touring the world drumming up trade for British Companies and cosying up to dubious heads of state. His coarse sense of humour endeared him to some, but offended enough of the others to make sure he moved no further up the ministerial ladder. (The insult to the wife of the Taliman President was particularly clumsy; the consul reported that Wantley was lucky to get out of the country with both hands still attached to his wrists). But it wasn't all bad. With a mixture of guile and ingenuity he had been able to smooth the way of several large contracts in the Far East. This stood him in good stead, for when the electors of Kingsbury and Gudley decided they no longer wanted him, the House of Lords took him up.

Although he was now a knight and rubbed shoulders with the rich, Sir Frank was not rich, at least not in his own estimation. The fishermen of Birsett, whom we will meet shortly, would have been delighted with the £18,000 a year for life that Sir Frank was given on demitting his office, but for the lord it was not enough. He therefore fished about for a non-executive directorship or two to supplement his income.

At a meeting between industrialists and peers in London, late in 1998, (the purpose of which is not recorded) he happened to run into JP Marwick, a financier and JP had recommended him to the Loyalty board. They were flattered that a knight of the realm, albeit a temporary and uncouth one, was willing to serve on the board and appointed him at a salary of £30,000 for a nominal five days' work a month. The arrangement suited both sides. It gave Sir Frank a well-paid hobby and, to their gratification, the Loyalty directors discovered that their new colleague had interesting contacts amongst the greedier power brokers in the Far East.

You must not think that Sir Frank did not work for his money. He took an interest in everything and interfered in most of what interested him. For reasons that were not apparent at the time, he took a special interest in Pinkerton-Loyalty. John heard more from Sir Frank than he did from Anthony Mortimer, his nominal boss. He could reckon on a phone call from The Knight at least once a week and a visit every couple of months. When Sir Frank visited, he made a point of talking to each of the senior managers, and always joined them for lunch on the days he was in the plant. An accomplished and witty raconteur, he entertained them and, although his stories were often crude and uncomplimentary to the distinguished names he dropped, the managers came to enjoy his visits. John remained suspicious of his interest, But the senior managers, with the exception of Mack, John's friend, soon felt they could talk freely to this friend in high places and they did so with increasing confidence.

For some years now the York plant had been overworked and underfunded. It needed big investment to equip it for a stream of new products now nearing production. Mack, John's Engineering Manager, had designed a comprehensive manufacturing and assembly system that would fit the factory for the new product range. But it would cost well over £5 million to implement. Sir Frank had shown a great deal of interest in these plans and had persuaded John to keep them under wraps until he, Sir Frank, could complete the Resource Study he had persuaded the Board to conduct into the company's manufacturing capability.

Last Thursday. with his normal courtesy, The Chairman, Radleigh, had welcomed John warmly, asked him if he had enjoyed the Easter break and apologised for dragging him down to Head Office. John basked in the attention of the Chief Executive. Normally he sat in an audience with Radleigh a remote figure at the front, behind a lectern, addressing his remarks to the company in general, and John a mere spectator, not expected to ask a question and only once asking one. Or, rarely, in a group sitting round a table in the conference room with Radleigh semi-detached at the head, listening patiently to the interchange without comment, or addressing the group in that low pleasant voice that bespoke authority and certainty. If Walter Radleigh had a personal life, John was unaware of it. Like our teachers at school he emerged fresh and powerful on a Monday morning in the building and disappeared on Friday night into oblivion. He embodied the soul of Loyalty and the spirit of authority; in the subconscious of the lower Loyalty managers he was the exalted one, the Holy Father, the king. They may moan about him, but there is no doubt that they regarded themselves as his vassals. And here he is, the king, now, sitting over the table from John, giving him his full attention. John felt lifted above the common life at Pinkerton and the petty business of managing a manufacturing plant. The factory at York seemed remote and insignificant. He felt part of something greater and much more important.

What was the York Managers' Meeting with its routine reports compared with this intimate discussion of corporate strategy; what the significance of a shortfall of twenty-three machines on line three compared with these great affairs of state; what the monotonous loyalty of Mack and George and Sarah compared with the confidences of the industrial nobility? The king had a mission for John.

"We are planning to move manufacturing off-shore; we need your help to do so. We have identified a location in Bainan, on the outskirts of Kalamandi, the capital. The finances are in place and the plant purchased but we need to act quickly to have it fitted out ready for the new CF controller.

"Oucha!," John heard himself saying, "This is rather sudden. I expected the Supply Research Group to report first."

For a moment John thought the Chief Executive looked puzzled, then The Knight broke in.

"Time is short, the decision has been taken, Kalamandi is the best option. You must forgive us John; we had to keep things under wraps; it is market sensitive."

Mack had said that The Knight was stringing them along. He was right, wasn't he? John glanced at Sir Frank as a wave of resentment swept over him. But he mastered it and spoke quietly.

"What about York?"

"We need to run it down," said Radleigh, "planned final closure, when? Say, end of year. But we need the output until then. You could help us with the timing."

"Closed? All of it?"

"Yes, I'm afraid so. We are negotiating with a developer for the site; apparently it is a prime housing area. It's hard on the employees, but we're head to head with the Japanese now and they have a plant in China. We can't compete."

Had he left it there, John may well have stormed out of the meeting, full of righteous anger at the closure of his beloved plant. But The Chairman did not leave it there; he had more to say,

'We'd like you to join the project team as Operations Co-ordinator. Sir Frank, here is project leader.

'Me? Co-ordinate the move?'

'Yes, head up the team on the ground.'

John could think of nothing to say. He sat staring at The Chairman.

Then Radleigh smiled and asked the question that had haunted John all week, that had robbed him of his sleep, had plagued every waking hour, had induced him to deceive those who trusted him,

'Are you with us, John?'

'Take a few days to think it over. We'll meet again on Tuesday at 11, Ok?'

CHAPTER TWO

Back in York, during that week, John had parried all questions about his visit to the big boss, saying only that he was to see him again on Tuesday. He was more forthcoming with Mack, but only to admit that the future of the York Plant was 'under review.'

John had joined the company when it was Pinkerton, twenty years ago. The company had grown rapidly, due to the inventive genius and flair of the then owner, Flambert Pinkerton. An electronics engineer, Pinkerton had developed all sorts of ingenious solutions to problems in the controls industry – switches, gauges, displays. For each product developed, Flambert set up a production unit to make it, believing, like most inventors, that any contractor would make a mess of his lovely piece of equipment. When the original industrial unit filled up, he took over the one next door, then the next and so on until he occupied most of the estate. At this point the local council suggested that he didn't understand the purpose of Industrial Estates: they were for little struggling businesses that had difficulty with the rent. Flambert then built a factory for himself on a piece of reclaimed land they offered him on the outskirts of York.

As the factory neared completion Flambert set out to recruit a Production Manager. He appointed a recruitment agency but rejected all the candidates they put forward on the grounds that either they didn't understand the products or wore beards. John had contacted the agency but had decided not to proceed when he realised the job was far from his stamping ground near Glasgow. In desperation the recruitment agency offered John an all-expenses paid trip to York if only he would talk to Flambert. *'Just talk to him; listen to what he has to say; you'll like him, he's a fun guy; if you don't want the job, tell him; the trip's paid for anyway, without obligation; your wife (Marion, isn't it?) will enjoy the trip; you can't lose; you can say no if you want to'*.

They knew John was a rare breed – an electronics engineer who understood production. He had chosen to leave the security of the research labs of his current company, McLelland Electronics, to dirty his hands-on contract control. This meant steering the contract through the various stages of design (what precisely is to be made), production engineering (how it is to be made) and production (making sure it is made within cost on time).

Even before he met Flambert, the office at York disconcerted him. At McLelland's, the offices, particularly on the shop floor where John lived, were ramshackle affairs. They looked like what they were – box-shaped afterthoughts with a fake wood desk, two metal chairs and a badly painted filing cabinet. If, on the wall, there was a picture of a gear wheel or a bottle of lubricant that was a bonus. Here on the first floor of the new Pinkerton building there wasn't a box in sight.

More like a garden than an office, it rejoiced in flower tubs, shrubs, sculptures, wrought iron screens and pictures so aesthetic they resembled nothing but themselves. All around, scattered in tasteful unconformity, were desks, filing cabinets, photocopiers, conference tables with chairs and overhead projectors at the ready, armchairs and sofas. All the admin staff were accommodated here. Flambert called it Arcadia.

When Flambert eventually appeared, he looked more like a folk singer than a businessman. He wore casual slacks and a checked, open-necked shirt. (John only once saw him in anything else – at a reception when he appeared in evening dress, but he discarded the tie halfway through dinner). Flambert had taken an instant liking to John and offered him the job on the spot. John, at first, had refused and put up a whole flock of objections, Flambert shot them all down.

"I thought this was just exploratory".

"I've found what I'm looking for."

"I like my present job."

"You'll like this one better."

"I'm on a high salary."

"I'll double it." (He didn't; but he did increase it substantially)

"My home is in Glasgow."

"Make it here"; (he shouts to Gladys, his secretary, who is sitting among the shrubbery) *"get the estate agents to pick up John and his wife to-morrow morning to show them houses. There're the new ones, at Poppleton. You'll like Poppleton."*

"We have a small child."

"We have two of the best schools in England in York."

"When can you start?"

John did start, over twenty years ago now. His task was to consolidate the little production units into one productive system. He relished the opportunity. Flambert, on the whole, let him get on with it. The company prospered, hindered only by Flambert's occasional enthusiasm for expensive solutions to non-existent problems. He and his backroom team produced and designed systems, John made the product, adding and integrating them into an effective productive plant.

There were disputes, but Flambert could be generous as well as forceful and the two men got on well.

Then one day Flambert appeared in John's office and told him he had appointed him General Manager. He, Flambert, had become tired of routine success. He enjoyed struggle, so he was launching a new consultancy company; just him, a girl to man the phone (his words) and a couple of graduates. He would keep control of research at Pinkerton and of Marketing. As well as Manufacturing, John would control Materials and Production Control, Product Development, Design, Personnel, Engineering, and all the rest - the whole shooting match. John noticed an omission.

"What about finance? Are you taking that?"

Flambert paused; there was something he hadn't told John, something he didn't want to tell him.

"We have a new chairman," he said. "Part-time; UKi have put in JP Marwick. You'll take accounts, dotted line to Jim Arkwright, the Financial Controller; Jim will report to JP"

JP was a financier and looked like a financier. In his early fifties, he was taller than medium height, well built, with a round face and thinning grey hair. At work John did not see him dressed other than in a smart dark pinstriped three-piece suit and sober tie. John soon found out that JP was no clone. Inside the suit was a confident man who needed no props to support him; a quiet, pleasant man with a generous nature. If he had ripped off investors and ground down the poor it didn't show. John learnt to trust him. He was shrewd but honest; if he made a promise, he kept it.

During the two years of JP Marwick's chairmanship Pinkerton enjoyed an Indian Summer. He kept Flambert's inspiration alive but on a leash, so that new products came on stream but fewer of them failed. JP enrolled John on the Wentworth Senior Management Programme, and then encouraged him to apply what he had learnt. Management at Pinkerton became more professional, leaner, fitter. Costs were cut by 15%.

"You can move up to Arcadia if you like, or stay; whatever," Flambert said as he left John's room."

John stayed, and created a precedent. Gradually other senior managers abandoned Arcadia and set up home in their departments with their secretaries and staff, and Arcadia became a showpiece used only for important meetings and, of course, by Flambert whenever he came in, and JP.

This, John recalled later, marked a watershed. When Flambert withdrew something went with him. At the time John detected no dramatic change. He found it exciting, demanding, stretching – General Manager! Responsibility, power, opportunity, BMW. But Flambert had sensed the shift; the glory had departed; the dead hand of management accounting lay on the company now. Before the company had been prosperous; now it must be profitable.

Almost immediately John made two appointments. The first was to promote George to Production Manager. George, a tough but pleasant Yorkshireman, was one of a now rare breed who won through without preparation or qualification. He had started as an operator and made it to Supervisor. Now John gambled and brought him into management. He never regretted it.

John also recruited his friend, Ian McIntyre, as Engineering Director. Ian is compact, thickset, with wiry hair, steely eyes and a disposition to match. He has come up the hard way. John recruited him from their mutual old firm of McLelland's in Glasgow where he had served his apprenticeship before taking his Higher National Certificate (HNC) on day release. Then he went one better and graduated B.Eng. on a sandwich course at Strathclyde University. He wanted to advance but his way was blocked by younger graduates with purer degrees and more acceptable speech than his thick Clydebank accent. He wears his Scots tongue like a badge, but uses it sparsely. He prefers action to words; a quality that gets things done, but gets the backs up of those who expect him to be subservient. He has a habit of playing with a compact Swiss Army knife, flicking it through his fingers, opening the tools in turn, in turn snapping them shut. This combined with his nationality gives him his nickname: Mack the Knife. He is married, lives happily in Rawcliffe with his wife and three children. His wife, Fiona, also from Clydebank has been and still is a close friend of Marion, John's wife. Mack never mentions John and Marion's separation to his boss but it broods in the background of every conversation. Now 43, Mack wants to move on, but will, for the moment, stay loyal to the man who gave him his big chance. That is the way he is made.

It was this man, this friend, this unfailingly loyal lieutenant that he must now deceive if he were to keep The Chairman's confidence. But Mack had news for John.

'Martin Purves has been in touch.'

'Martin Purves, at Group? Facilities Director? What did he want?'

'Me!'

'You? What for?"

"He buttered me up. Said that The Knight was very impressed with my plans for this site. They want me to set up the plant somewhere out east."

As he said this, he fixed his eyes on John. John held his gaze and replied,

'That is what they are looking at.'

'He made it sound like a done deal. They're stringing you along, John.'

John parried the thrust.

'What did you tell Purves?'

'I told him to get lost'.

Again, Mack stared at John. Again, John evaded his friend's intensity.

"Was that wise?' he said. 'Think, Mack, it's an attractive offer: a greenfield site, start from scratch, set it up the way you want it."

"That plan was for here - Pinkerton, York. It wasn't for.... where is it? "

"Kalamandi, in Bainan."

"You see, I don't even know where it is. But you seem to."

"The process is transferable; it'll work there as well as here. Better, perhaps, with a new workforce. Opportunities like this don't come often. You should think about it."

"I have, and I don't like it."

"There's a possibility you could head up the operation once it's set up. It's there for you if you go for it. It's a great career move, think about it; talk to Fiona."

"And what would Fiona and the bairns do in China?"

"It's not China, Bainan."

"Wherever! What will they do there? What kind of life will they have there?"

"It can be a great life abroad. They'll supply a house, choice of car, maybe cars, living expenses, private schools for the children, servants, no income tax. It'll set you up for life."

"I like my life the way it is," said Mack pointedly. 'They're not on.'

"Why, Mack? Why so certain? We could all be out of a job in a few months' time, maybe sooner if you rough up board members. It's a great chance."

"No! For two reasons. One: stick with the friends you have. Two: don't trust The Knight. I don't know what he's up to John, but it has a nasty smell coming from it. I'll stick with the ship for now. I'm young enough yet."

Then, guessing precisely what was passing through his friend's mind, he added, "You do whatever you think is best for yourself."

He stuck out his hand. John smiled, took Mack's hand, shook it – but did not look him in the eye and instinctively unclasped quickly as if he might infect his friend if he left his hand there for long.

Infect him with what?

Shortly after Ian left, John. trying to settle his agitation through routine, was disturbed by a phone call. It came from Jacqui Boutelle, a consultant who had been working with Sir Frank on the Supply Research Group. When first introduced John had been wary of Jacqui, but her grasp of logistics, her honesty and her willingness to listen to what John and Mack had to say had persuaded John to lower his defences. The fact that she was young, open and vivacious added attraction to her more prosaic credentials.

But why did she want to see him now, in between his crucial meetings with Radleigh. Was that co-incidental, or did she have information or advice? Or, could it be . . .. No, it couldn't be that! She certainly knew that John was separated from his wife, and might be available, but she was happily settled with a partner of her own, wasn't she? No! Why then did she suggest dinner tomorrow evening?

CHAPTER THREE

If you had met John you would wonder how he could think that someone of Jacqui Boutelle's class would find him attractive. Besides, she lives happily with a commodity dealer from Geneva, whose name is not Boutelle, but Guigou, and who is not, like her, French-Canadian, but Swiss. He works weekdays in Geneva and comes home to London and Jacqui at weekends. How this makes for a happy partnership I do not know, but that is the way it is and it seems to work for Jacqui.

John has never been much to look at, and whilst middle age has added something to his waistline it has added nothing to his appeal. His hair is thinning on top and growing grey round the sides. A man, however, does not make it to Managing Director by being modest. I have seen many a bald-headed podge of much lower rank chat up a bright young thing in the office and go away with hope in his heart and steam on his glasses simply because she didn't tell him to get lost.

Jacqui had chosen Stavarinos in the West End for the meal and was waiting when John arrived at eight. She had booked a secluded table in a dark corner. She welcomed John with a peck on the cheek. His thoughts were not on the contorted descriptions of the food on offer. He rocked between a pretended nonchalance and a galloping desire to be finished with the whole thing as soon as possible – whatever the whole thing was.

They ordered wine, John nodding sagely when the wine waiter showed him a label he had never seen before and giving a passable imitation of a mouth wash when the waiter poured a little in his glass to sample. They ordered; the food came. When he discovered that Jacqui was French-Canadian, he steered the conversation to French-Canadian separatism, then she introduced Scottish devolution, and did he have any folks still living up there and, when she heard that John's father was battling cancer, expressed her concern, but did not mention her own happy domestic arrangements and thereby led John on.

Here we see a man picking his way towards the unknown, drawn powerfully to the excitement and awakening opportunities of the future yet afraid to step over old familiar boundaries. John's moral framework had been built in the home of his parents, kirk folk in the small village of Birsett just over the Border on the East Coast of Scotland. There he had learned a simple code of 'right and wrong', and had seen it more or less lived out in the lives of his mother and his father.

That lay in the past. Over the years that framework had been modified, adjusted and shortened until it had become what might be called 'uncommitted respectability'. It had not been nourished in any way. He had long abandoned the family habit of church-going and had given little consideration to his standards of behaviour.

Recently, due to his father's failing health, he had spent more time in the old place, and had been reminded of the old principles, but they sat inert in his mind. In business affairs he had always behaved decently and more or less honestly, bending only slightly to do what he had to do to protect and advance his interests and those he conceived to be important to the company. He respected his managers and treated his employees fairly and as generously as company circumstances and finances permitted. His life would have sailed on in the same general direction were it not for the sudden winds of change that had now blown up. He could not stay on familiar territory and he had glimpsed a wider horizon where the big boys play and he wanted to play with them. He was fifty, he told himself; if he didn't do it now, he would never do it.

John tucked into his Beef Bourginon and tried to work out what would arrive next, and in two minds about what to do when it came. Then he noticed a family party moving into a table just over from theirs. In the party was a girl, aged about seventeen, dressed in her best for her night out, fresh and innocent and lively, a young girl like…. Rebecca, his daughter. The sight of her brought John up short. Jacqui noticed.

"You have a daughter?" she asked.

John now had to talk about Rebecca and about Robert, his son and what remained of the father in him asserted itself and gained strength. Then, in train, what remained of the husband in him. He thought of Marion, his wife - and what would Rebecca think if she knew that he was toying with the idea of sleeping with another woman?

This question did not resolve the matter for John. It may have prevented him from making the first move but would it have been strong enough to condition his response to a move in the other direction? We will never know; for that move will not come. Not for the reason we know. John eventually left the scene with the nature and strength of his morality untested. But before that we must take the sweet, Crème Brulee for John, Lime and Orange Sorbet for Jacqui, then serve the coffee. Jacqui sat back in her chair and eyed John in a way that discomforted him.

"Can I speak to you as a friend?" Jacqui said, and John gulped before he replied.

"Er. yes, of course,"

'I hear you have been offered a role in this move abroad.'

'Ah, you know about that?'

'Yes, well, some of it. And a lot about what lies behind it, or should I say, under it. Watch Sir Frank. He has convinced the Board that moving production to Bainan will open up markets for the company in South East Asia. It is all very political; government ministers appear to be up to their necks in it, and Sir Frank seems to understand how it works; he has a lot of contacts out there."

"It all sounds a bit nebulous,"

"It is, but Sir Frank has convinced the board it is worth the risk. I suspect……." she stopped for a moment, and lowered her voice, "I suspect it has all been lubricated."

"You mean from Loyalty to ministers in Bainan."

"That too, but that is not unusual in these places. I mean from Bainan to Sir Frank."

"That's a serious charge."

"Not really, it happens all the time."

"But the company has a policy on gifts…."

"For the troops, yes, but this isn't gifts; it's arrangement fees."

"Are you certain? Does Walter Radleigh know?"

(Like many minions, John had a touching faith in the integrity of the man at the top.)

"No, I'm not certain, and no, I'm not sure whether Radleigh knows."

"Why are you telling me all this?"

"I don't like being manipulated."

"Manipulated, in what way?"

"Well, I put a lot of work into this Supply Research Group, but the report never got to the Board. Sir Frank summarised it himself."

"The Board accepted that."

"Of course, he's a director, I'm a hired hand; hired by Sir Frank."

"It seems very elaborate, what has he been playing at?"

"I don't know but I can guess. This is the way I see it. He is negotiating with Bainan when he learns of your plan to upgrade the York plant. He recognises it as viable. If the Board hears about it before he is ready, it may well scupper his ambitions in South East Asia, so he decides to head off your approach by setting up this Supply Research Group."

"But he couldn't have known about our development plans so early, I only spoke to him.... when? - first week in February. I invited him up, on the first Tuesday in February."

"He knew about it well before then. I started a good fortnight before that. Somebody must have tipped him off."

"Jim Arkwright! Finance! He reports to Head Office. He's a snake!" mumbled John.

"Whoever," said Jacqui, "he knew. Then he asked me to come up and see you. I was very impressed with your plan – and with Mack – he knows what he's about. But when I reported back to Sir Frank, he was keen I should find for South East Asia. Then I tripped over his involvement with Bainan."

"How?"

"At that stage I had not realised I was just a front, so I was doing the job properly. I went to the Bainan embassy for information on wage rates and development grants and discovered they knew all about Sir Frank. They were really much too forthcoming about him; they seemed to think I knew what was going on."

"What did Sir Frank say when he found out?"

"Nothing, because I didn't tell him."

"Why are you telling me?"

"Because," smiled Jacqui, "you strike me as being a straightforward sort of guy. I don't want to see you get hurt."

"So, this job I'm being offered is a buy-off - to make things easy for them at York."

"Not entirely. There is a job there, and if you can believe it, Sir Frank quite likes you and thinks you can smooth the transfer of the work to Bainan. He's pushing for you quite strongly with Radleigh."

"I thought you were trying to warn me off it."

Jacqui laughed. "Oh, no, not warn you *off*, just warn you about what you'd be getting into. You must make up your own mind."

"Arrgh....what a decision!" said John trying to sound light-hearted, "It sounds sordid – Loyalty bribing government ministers, Sir Frank stuffing notes into his back pocket, closing the York plant, opening up at the other end of the world, where, from what you say, everybody'll expect a back-hander. Do I want to be involved in all that?"

"That's the game. If you want to play, 'thems the rules'. Somebody's going to have to do it, why not you? The rewards could be tasty. Not only for the project - from what I've heard, if you went the right way about it, you'd be in line for the Operations Director's job at the end of it. Anthony Mortimer is talking about retirement next year."

"I'd have to sell my soul for a seat on the Board, is that it?" smiled John.

"Don't be a cynic, it doesn't suit you. If you go into it with your eyes open, it's not so bad" chaffed Jacqui, "We're all for sale but I charge twice as much for dubious jobs. That's where the money is. If you feel badly about it – you can always leave your pile to charity when the final promotion comes."

"Do you not feel Sir Frank used you? Do you not feel angry?"

"Of course, but it cost them - £20,000 for 15 days work; you can buy a lot of cats to kick with that. But we're letting Sir Frank come between us. Let's have another cup of coffee and slip into something more comfortable." coaxed Jacqui, smiling and John thought at that moment she looked particularly vivacious and inviting. "Tell me about...."

John never found out what the more comfortable subject would be, for just at that moment the waiter arrived with a message for him. Would he ring Helen Paulin: urgently?

Helen Paulin was John's cousin in Birsett.

CHAPTER FOUR

Helen's call, as John expected, concerned John's father, Willie. Helen had found him lying as pale as death on the bathroom floor when she came to put him to bed. The doctor thought it might be internal bleeding and had sent him immediately to the Borders General Hospital. They had given him a blood transfusion but he was seriously ill and was drifting in and out of consciousness. Margaret, John's sister, had come from Edinburgh to be him. If John wanted to be sure of seeing his father he must come immediately.

For all the comfort of a limo from the restaurant to King's Cross and first-class carriage from King's Cross to Edinburgh Waverley, John did not have a comfortable journey. Too many discordant thoughts jangled in his mind. He tried to read the Financial Times, then to do the crossword, then to sleep, then to do some work from his brief case, but nothing gave him relief from his anguish.

Added to his natural concern for his father and his disconcerting assignation with Jacqui, there lay the dubiety of the move to Bainan and, above all, his frustration at having to postpone his critical meeting with Radleigh. He felt like a juggler with all the balls in the air and no hands to catch any of them. Incessantly too, along the long corridor of his mind, a question banging on a distant door: was it right to accept The Chairman's offer to head up the move to the East? Not shrewd, not career-wise, not appropriate, but right? When we are tired and frustrated signs and portents prey on us. What worse then, than John, starting out of an uneasy doze, to see York Minister glaring at him in the carriage window. York! Just passing through.

John was met at Waverley in Edinburgh by Alex, Helen's husband, a fisherman, and entered a world strangely different from that he had left behind. As he rattled down the A68 in the Aurora's van he became more comfortable than he had been all day. Helen had taken the family car to the hospital and left Alex to put the bairns to bed and then go to Edinburgh to meet John's train.

The Aurora is a boat that fishes out of Birsett; its van something of a public property. Anyone who needed a vehicle in distress borrowed it, as Alex had now done. Not far out of Edinburgh they had to stop to secure the passenger seat. It had taken to throwing John into the windscreen whenever Alex braked. The van had not been built with a removable seat, but corrosion and ill-use had modified it and convenience had preserved it. The seat could be removed to accommodate a few more boxes of crabs or to stow a couple of craves. It was then re-fitted using two metal bars, a nut and bolt and a length of orange nylon rope. The rope had come loose so it had to be tightened. While Alex dealt with the problem, John helped himself to the coffee Alex had kindly brought along. The seat fixed, they drove on more or less in silence. John would have preferred conversation but he knew Alex well enough not to expect it.

There are two types of silent men. One broods in his fortress and when he comes out, he comes out fully armed looking for a fight. Alex is of the other sort; they sit at ease in their own house with the door open; come in if you wish, but be peaceable and don't expect to be entertained. Alex lay opposite to John in almost every respect. John tallish and beginning to fatten up, Alex 5'4" and as wiry as ever; John rich, Alex poor; John driven by ambition, Alex content with his lot. John fitted people and things around his plans; Alex planned his life around other people and the unplanned movements of the sea and crustaceans.

Alex, however, had more children than John and still had a wife. He promised nothing he could not deliver, could be trusted and had a reputation for never being out of temper, which, given Helen's volatility is quite an achievement.

'You should live with him,' she replied when people commented on his placid nature, but she didn't mean it. If she went over the score, he took a walk down to the harbour until the storm blew over. They had lived with each other long enough to know each other; had known each other well enough to love each other; and loved each other deeply enough to depend utterly on each other. It wasn't something they spoke about it; they articulated it in the detail of their ordinary days.

John found the silence oppressive. He tried to engage Alex in conversation. He ran through the normal gamut in few seconds.

"How's Helen?"

"Fine"

"And the bairns?"

"Fine"

"Louise is in what class now at the school?'

'Third year'.

'She's quite an entertainer, I hear.'

"Aye, she keeps us all going; yer fither dotes on her."

"David is in sixth year at Hecklescar, isn't he?"

"Aye,"

"Exams this year, what is it, Highers?"

"Aye,"

"He should be alright, he's a bright lad."

"Doesn't work; his head's full of lasses."

That stopped that topic in its tracks.

John tried holidays, the price of fish, the idiocy of the EU fishing policy, and football. Alex agreed with him on everything. Then Alex had two questions of his own: about John's family.

"How's Rebecca and Robert?"

"Fine,"

"And Marion?"

"Fine."

Now John reached for monosyllabic.

They arrived at the Hospital at half-past five, and found that Willie had left intensive care and was sleeping peacefully in a room beside the nurses' station on Melrose Ward. Helen had gone home, but Margaret had stayed behind to see her brother.

"A burst ulcer, they think. It was touch and go. But they think they have it under control and have given him transfusions. He's stable now – he was speaking to us before he fell asleep. They'll keep an eye on him here for a couple of days, then send him to The Bield."

"And after that?" asked John.

"He can't be left on his own," said Margaret, who had had the night to think about it, "if Helen hadn't found him when she did, he would have……. he wouldn't be here now. We'll have to persuade him to go to The Bield…. unless…"

"Unless what?"

"Well, I was thinking, Marion has always been very close

to your father. I know you two aren't getting on, but I'm sure she would come if we asked her. Roddam thinks so too. You don't need to ask her. I will."

"She has a job, and I don't think it's a very good idea anyway - and it's using her."

Margaret side-stepped the second point.

"I didn't know she was working. Well, I can't do it. I've got the shop. I mean we don't know how long it could go on for. It could be months; the business would be ruined. Oh, I know this may sound callous, but it isn't that. I'm not putting the shop before father; no, no, it's just, that we can't all just throw up everything. I do love him. I don't suppose Helen would think of moving in for a few months, do you? She could take Louise with her; the rest are old enough to be left now. I left Abigail when she was younger than... What do they call Helen's oldest?"

"David,"

"Yes, David."

"We can't ask her to do that; she's done far more than we could expect already."

"We could ask her."

"I don't think we should, it's an imposition."

"Well, it's all very complicated," pronounced Margaret huffily, "There's nothing else for it. He'll just have to go to The Bield. We will pay half."

"Is this what father has come to?" thought John; 'a complication?'

CHAPTER FIVE

Willie had never before been a complication. Independent from the age of fourteen, he had taken a berth in his uncle's boat, worked hard and, by the time he was twenty-eight, had a boat of his own. He had prospered at the fishing, married a local girl when he was thirty, bought the old manse, and produced a family of a girl, Margaret and a boy John and had steered them to prosperity.

With his children making their way in the world away from Birsett, Willie sold his boat and the old manse and bought the house on the brae which he renamed Braeshiel in a fine disregard for Gaelic definitions. There he and Jane, his wife, lived for twenty happy years.

Most mornings he walked down the brae to the harbour to give advice to and take stick from the younger fishermen. Jane kept the house, took care of the garden, knitted and sowed, went to the Women's Institute on a Tuesday evening in the Village Hall, and visited her own and Willie's relatives. Every fine afternoon saw them walking, to Fairnieside, up round Fairnington, along the cliff top to Hecklescar. In the evening they sat and read their books, in winter by the coal fire, in summer by the window looking over to the sea. On Sunday they walked down the brae to the little kirk and came back to a dinner of roast beef and Yorkshire pudding. Sometimes Willie's sister, Nell, joined them.

If this sounds dull and uneventful let me try to interest you in a fortnight every May when they went on holiday; often to the Highlands near Oban where they toured the Isles on the steamer. Here Willie showed Jane how to navigate the Sound of Mull in poor weather. He had done it once in a seine-netter. In the summer they had John and Margaret, sometimes together, sometimes separately, for a week or two, and then the grandchildren, when they were old enough, for more than a month at a time. Helen's bairns also dropped in; but more of Helen later.

Then there was the occasional rarity off the boats, like the basking shark tangled in the Braw Lads' nets, so big they couldn't lift it aboard and had to tow it in. Willie had taken the bairns from the school down the brae to see it and Bessie Spowart threw up at the smell.

There were the changing seasons. They welcomed the aconites braving the biting wind under the hedge in January, and looked for the crocuses, daffodils and tulips as winter rolled into spring. They picked raspberries at Blackhouse in July and blackberries in the lanes near Causewaybank in September. In December they hunted the quiet roads of Coldinghamshire for holly trees with berries so they could deck the hall for Christmas.

Then there were events in the village: the annual Brae Time Trial when serious cyclists from all over the Borders pedalled and peched their way up the brae from the harbour to the school house, a rise of two hundred feet in half a mile. Or, less seriously, the occasional pram race when 3 or 4 local youths attempted to push a baby buggy or a pram loaded with one of their number over the same course. Boisterous disorganisation, misapplied effort and frequent refreshment stops made sure that not many finished. There was the annual gala and the crowning of the Fisher Queen, whist drives and the sale of work in the Village Hall and, blessing the year's end, the

School Christmas Concert with mince pies and tea to follow. All these Willie and Jane enjoyed.

As well as these spectacular events, life flowed and ebbed daily through the village: babies born, sometimes in wedlock, sometimes in surprise; young folk getting into trouble, getting their standard grades, or getting married; old folk losing themselves or losing altogether; folk who were neither old nor young doing the best they could or the worst they could get away with. But we do not need to describe it all now; they will intrude into our story and, as courteous people, when their story collides with ours, we will attend to it. I simply mention them here to convince you that life can be interesting even when it is peaceable and rewarding even when little money is spent on it. If I have failed then you may find interest in the antics of the more blatant characters of our story.

Then one morning Willie woke up and found Jane lying lifeless beside him.

"Best way to go", said the village wisdom.

"Not best, not good even, not good at all" said Willie. He was 75 and alone for the first time in his life.

Of course, at the time John and Margaret came to him. John arrived the day his mother died. But he was now General Manager of a manufacturing company at York, Pinkerton Loyalty, and we know that executives cannot be spared from their duties for long. So, the day after his mother's funeral John made his way back to York.

"There is not much more I can do here," he confided to his sister, "I'll be back to tie up any of the legal loose ends once things settle down." She agreed. His father assured him that he must go; he was needed at York. He left with a show of reluctance some of which was genuine. Margaret stayed for a fortnight, but in the end had to return to her husband and young daughter whose complaints about her absence swelled as time and distance dissipated their slight initial anguish. Margaret went back to Edinburgh. Her father was left in a lonely house to his own devices, to his sister Nell, and to Helen, her daughter.

Truth to tell, Willie was relieved to see Margaret go. Much as he loved his daughter, he preferred Helen. Helen would let him grieve; Margaret wanted him to 'move on'.

Helen is married to Alex, whom we have met. Like herself, he belonged to Birsett. They have five children and Helen has spent her married life looking after them. She cared for her mother since her father was lost, now she took on the care of her Uncle Willie. All this horrified a liberated woman like Margaret. But there again, Margaret horrified Helen.

Helen had kept an eye on John's father for ten years when she broke up John's dinner with Jacqui Boutelle and summoned him to his father's hospital bed.

Margaret's plan to commit Willie to The Bield irritated John, but he had no other offer to make. He couldn't stay. He had to get back to York. He had to get back to The Chairman. Reluctantly, he agreed to speak to his father about the care home once Willie was well enough to consider it. But John did not like it. He saw it as unfair, unsympathetic, unkind, cruel almost. But what else could be done?

That first night, Willie woke up long enough to acknowledge his son, then he went back to sleep unaware that his fight for life was an inconvenience to his family.

Margaret drove herself back to her husband Roddam and her home in Morningside. John jolted his way down to Birsett with Alex and let himself into his father's house. Alex went to bed but rose at midday so he could take the boat out to haul some craves in the afternoon. They must change the bait or by Monday it would stink. His trip also took him away from Helen who was not in the best of fettles after her excursions of the night before.

Some people in stressful jobs go out like a light while others lie awake all night. They try little tricks to settle the mind before they sleep. John had learnt (from his father) to "close your eyes and think of something nice". On this night he searched for something nice.

You would think that he might recall the swish restaurant and his attractive companion as nice, or the possibility of a place on the Board hinted at by Jacqui, or even the luxury of first-class travel; but no; all of these grumbled. One event, however, did not; one memory of the day lay untroubled on his mind: standing in the lay-by in the cool evening drinking hot strong boat coffee whilst Alec fixed the seat in the Aurora's van. John smiled as he thought of it, and soon fell asleep.

First thing in the morning he rang Radleigh to explain his absence and postpone the meeting. Radleigh sounded understanding.

"Take as long as it needs," he said, "Give me a ring when you get back."

Thus reassured, between his visits to his father, John found himself sucked into the flow of life at Birsett. I will let you glimpse this life, for I would not want you to believe that only events that serve our story are important.

John went to Helen's for his lunch each day and got caught up in the lively cacophony of that family, with Louise, youngest and apparently weakest, manipulating the competing claims of her brothers and sisters to her own advantage. A stream of friends and acquaintances called in at Braeshiel or stopped him on the brae to ask after his father.

One of them is Cecil, from Surrey, almost 80, who cares for his invalid wife, Dorothy, in a bungalow on the main road. She is eighty-six, a native of Birsett, diabetic, arthritic, dyspeptic, patient, almost blind. A carer raises her from bed and dresses her in the morning and undresses and puts her back to bed at night as well as giving her a bath once a week. Apart from that Cecil cares for her. He never complains; neither does she. He hoped Willie would be back home soon.

Jimmy "Possum", Willie's old fisherman friend, told John about James Wacky bringing back three salmon from the rocks at Bennison, the largest fifteen pounds, to sell at the back door of the Restless Sole. He tried to explain who James Wacky is:

'Wacky's not his real name, ye ken, he's a Cowan, his mother was a Mitchison, lived doon the brae, but moved to Hecklescar when she married Dice Cowan; he was called Dice because he was caught making dice at the High School by the woodwork teacher. They were loaded dice, ye ken.'

John vaguely remembered Dice, but could not place James Wacky, partly because he did not want to. Duncan Johnstone, Willie's domino companion, and self-appointed industrial correspondent, reported that the freezer factory at Hecklescar had been taken over by BGrowers, a group of farmers from up the country. They were going to use it for freezing peas, sprouts and broccoli, but it wouldn't last long; none of the owners of the freezer factory lasted long. He also said that Gainslaw Globes was in trouble again and that Kate Strothers and her man Colin had had to mortgage their house to keep it going. 'Not a viable concern,' concluded Duncan the guru, who normally lost at the dominoes.

Maggie Swaz told John that Jeanie and Cissie had gone shopping to Edinburgh, but Cissie was that intent on helping Jeannie down the steps of the bus, that the bus went away with two of her bags still on it. The driver is claiming he had never seen them, which is very funny because there was only him and a lad from Gainslaw on the bus when they got off. Cissie has put in a claim.

'It would never have happened if Davie was still driving the bus; he would bring yer messages to yer hoose if ye left them.'

Helen also had a story that Marvin, who crewed on the Aurora, had fallen into the harbour at Hecklescar after coming out of the Basking Shark with his cousin but had that much drink in him that he floated and had been pulled out before he could drown. When they had got him home, he'd been sick all over the new carpet that his partner Wilma had saved up for years to buy. It's a creamy colour and she'll never get the sick marks out. She was greetin' (crying) to Helen about it at the school gate.

On Sunday, John took Mr Scott to visit Willie, and of all his visitors, Willie valued most the company of his old friend.

Mr Scott had been parish minister of Birsett in the days when it had a parish minister; that is, before it was linked with Beanston. Although a big man, Mr Scott was diffident by nature and found himself in the ministry before he realised that he had little aptitude for it. He avoided church meetings, encouraging others to take the chair. Nor did he like speaking in public. His services were unpredictable; hymns, prayers and readings were likely to be misplaced or missed altogether. His sermons jerked from topic to topic as he snatched at the thoughts careering through his kaleidoscopic mind; they generally finished abruptly halfway through a sentence.

In the village, however, he was respected as a good man and many a tired family blessed him for the respite he had given them by sitting up with a sick or dying relative. Others had cause to remember a loan given to stave off a debt-collector, or a reference that won a wayward boy a steady job, or a friend to speak for them in court, or someone to talk to when there was no one else to turn to. On one occasion, he chased all the way to London in the train to bring back Jessie Tulloch's lassie that had run away from home. By such consistent acts of kindness, he gained the respect of everyone in the village. That respect, however, did not run to enduring his services and in his time the congregation dwindled. When Mr Scott reached sixty-five, he retired and was not replaced. Mr Mordun of Beanston took Birsett under his wing.

Mr Scott was a bachelor and lived alone with his dusty books and yellowing newspapers in one of the small houses that cling to the cliff halfway up the brae. From his back windows he looked into the bottom of Willie's garden and so could visit his friend without straining overmuch his arthritic knees. He read The Scotsman and The Times every day and The Economist every week and never threw out a copy. Those who visited him (and he had many friends) believed that one day he would submerge beneath his archives and never be seen again. He had attended Heriot's, one of Edinburgh's public schools but spoke the local dialect. He had a double degree but a simple faith. He, like Willie, was well over eighty but there were few social and political issues on which he was not well informed and he had sharp opinions on all of them. He and Willie were sparring partners and kindred spirits. He came on a Sunday evening about seven and stayed to listen to 'Your Hundred Best Tunes' with his friend. Originally, they played scrabble, the word game, but nowadays the board was often left in the cupboard. They just talked and told each what they had heard or what they had read, and often, things they had heard many times before. It was the best of times for Willie, and, I believe, for Mr Scott too.

John invited Mr Scott back to Braeshiel for tea. Mr Scott agreed and afterwards he and John kept up the traditional scrabble game. The old minister won the game, thanked John for the company and confessed to missing Willie, and fearing for his future.

John stayed at Braeshiel for three days, until the Monday. By then his father was sitting up. John saw the doctor at the hospital. He said his father, although ill, was not likely to die yet. He needed supervision and nursing for a few days and he would receive that at The Bield. The Birsett doctor, Dr

Stacey, would keep an eye on him there. John saw Dr Stacey and he agreed that was no need for John to stand by. Willie said the same; he'd soon be home, and Helen would look after him. John rang George and rescheduled the Managers' Monday Meeting for Tuesday. He then rang Walter Radleigh's secretary and re-arranged his meeting for Wednesday.

CHAPTER SIX

Back in York, John sensed something amiss even before the Managers' Meeting started on Tuesday morning. He heard no banter in the outer office. The managers, Mack, George, Jim, Colin and Sarah, trooped in grim-faced and sat glumly around the table. Honest George, the production manager, spat out the question causing this unease.

"John, is it true that the work is being transferred offshore and this plant is to be shut down?"

John glanced briefly at Mack. Mack gave the merest shrug of his shoulders.

"That is not confirmed," said John, trying to sound authoritative, "but it is being discussed."

Jim Arkwright who, as Financial Controller, had links to Head Office, leaned forward and looked round the table.

"Stop wriggling, John," he sneered. "It's a done deal. It's common knowledge at Guildford."

John saw the accusation amplified in the faces of George and Sarah.

'It isn't true, is it, John? You would tell us if you knew.'

John's executive instincts, however, proved proof against such sentiment. He said nothing but stared back at Arkwright. Arkwright blinked and turned away. They all noted the defeat.

"I'm seeing Walter Radleigh on Wednesday," John said, "I'll report back on Thursday. In the meantime, I want you to stamp on the rumours. Call the briefing groups before lunch and tell them no decisions have been made. Tell them I'm going to Guildford and we'll make a statement before the weekend."

John had faced down Arkwright but he could not face down the truth. At his meeting with Radleigh he had been told what he did not want to hear and his managers did not want to believe: that the plant that provided their livelihood was to be wound down and closed. That their battle, their struggle, their cost-cutting and belt-tightening, their whipping-in of their workers, their whipping-up of optimism, their long hours and long days, their stress and anxiety, their devotion to their leader, to John, counted for nothing. The Board had decided: the plant at York must go.

John, however, had been told he did not have to go with it. He did not need to be among the dispossessed. He had been offered not only escape, but glittering opportunity.

Radleigh had squeezed John in at the end of the day so John travelled to Guildford by the afternoon train. Before he left, Mack made a point of coming to see him to tell him again to watch his back. John put this down as a good luck message. It meant much more than that; he should have listened more carefully.

John had made up his mind about the offer Radleigh had made. On the journey down, he prepared his reply strategy. He would try to persuade Walter Radleigh, even at this late date, to abandon the move offshore and concentrate production at the York plant. If that failed, he would probe the probity of the decision, asking about the relative merits of the move and in particular the suggestion that the placing of the factory in

Bainan was corrupt. John recognised this as hazardous but old principles, though now decayed, demanded some sort of indemnity. If he were satisfied on all counts, he would accept the position in Bainan on condition that everything possible would be done for the people at York by way of phased rundown, generous redundancy pay, outplacement, and early retirement.

If you think that this sounds logical and high-minded, that is what you are meant to think; Radleigh is meant to think that way too. This strategy of John's has been manufactured not only to salve his troubled conscience; it is also intended to impress the top man with the sagacity and integrity of a future main board director. At the end of the conversation he would introduce the subject of his own future once the transfer had been successfully accomplished. Thus, the fly flew towards the flowers unaware that the spider had intentions too.

And a web! For Loyalty, like all organisations, had webs that spread in every direction. By them people connected; by them they climbed higher; by them they were trapped and brought down. Such a web now stretched out for John. It had been many years in the making. Many hands had had a hand in it; those whom John had crossed or slighted: those whom he had not promoted; those he had; those who feared him; those who disliked him. Jim Arkwright, his Financial Controller had crafted part of it, Anthony Mortimer, John's immediate boss at Head Office, added a testy strand or two. Martin Purves, the executive charged with the transfer to Bainan wondering why Mack had snubbed him, stitched in a disgruntled corner. Of all the hands none had been busier than The Knight. It was he who stitched it all together.

John, although unaware of the net closing round him, instinctively suspected that this meeting might be The Knight's doing. John half-expected him to be at the meeting and that made him apprehensive. He need not have worried. When he arrived in Radleigh's office he found The Chief Executive alone.

"Sir Frank can't be with us," he explained, "But I have asked Martin Purves to sit it. You know Martin, Engineering."

John spent the time before Purves arrived to tell his ultimate boss about the rumours spreading at York about the transfer of work offshore, and the apparent widespread knowledge of it at Head Office. Radleigh expressed his disappointment but seemed more concerned about the leakage of price-sensitive information to the stock market than the fears of the workforce.

"The share price moved sharply up this morning," he said, "I wonder if they have got wind of the move."

Here we ought to comment on the cynicism of investors who think that depriving their fellow citizens of work is good news. But we will resist the temptation and when we next see the redundant workers of Loyalty-Pinkerton will try to persuade them that their sacrifice is appreciated by the stock market.

"We need to announce it to the market to-day or to-morrow. You'll have to hold your hand until we've made an announcement. We will let you know when you can release it to your people. Thank you, John."

'A good start', thought John, as Martin Purves arrived to join the meeting. He shook John's hand and settled himself at Radleigh's right hand. Something about where he sat and how he sat down; the way he took out a notepad and laid his pen beside it, disturbed John. He recalled Radleigh's words - 'Martin will sit in' What for? As a witness? Purves made no mention of Mack's refusal of the position he had offered him, and John made no connection between that refusal and Purves's presence at the meeting.

"Now then, John," said Walter Radleigh, with studied

cordiality, "Have you thought about heading up the move? We'd like you to do it, are you with us?"

Had he thought about it? Had he thought about anything else? Are you with us? 'Won't you step into my parlour?'

John flew into his spiel but quickly realised that he had no chance whatsoever of changing Radleigh's mind on the move offshore. Radleigh swept his arguments aside. He praised Mack's production engineering plans but it did not think it viable in the UK; it had to be South East Asia; it had to be Bainan. John abandoned his advocacy when he saw Radleigh's irritation rising. He also abandoned his references to the Resource Study Group when Radleigh dismissed it out of hand as something that Sir Frank was playing with - it had no implications for this move.

Had John left it at that who knows what might have happened. But he did not; the tattered remnants of his old integrity let him down. He opened up the question of corruption.

John knew that he had to 'gang warily' and did so, almost to the point of obscurity, but as he laid his suspicions before Radleigh and Purves he felt the meeting chill. Up to this point the discussions had been chatty, cordial, constructive. Now Radleigh sat stiffly, leaning back in his chair, away from John, his eyes narrowed, his mouth thinly pursed. Purves, too, retreated and sat with his head down over his notes, playing nervously with his pen. But John pressed on and, in particular, asked for clarification of the role of Sir Frank in the negotiations with the Bainan government.

"I'm sorry," he said in conclusion, "for raising these points with you, but I just want to know what I am getting into; I am not usually a political animal."

Radleigh studied him for a moment. Then turned to Martin Purves; Purves nodded. Then Radleigh spoke to John in a low measured voice.

"Let me understand you. You are suggesting that the move to Bainan is based on some sort of deal between Sir Frank and politicians in Bainan?"

"No," cried John, "I'm not suggesting that …."

"Then what are you suggesting?" snapped Radleigh,

"I am sure," mumbled John, "that there are genuine reasons for transferring the work to Bainan but…."

Purves cut in.

"Your colleague, Ian, doesn't think so. He seems to think it's a fix."

"That's up to him," John blurted, "But I can accept…"

"Accept!" cried Radleigh, "Accept! Is that all you can manage, John? Accept! Not agree, not support, not commit - only accept!"

Radleigh's cold eyes locked onto John's face. John felt the colour rise in his cheeks; he dropped his head and scrambled frantically to untangle his thoughts.

"Would you leave us for a few moments?" cut in Radleigh before John could reply. John suddenly found himself in the outer office with the door closed against him.

John had not expected this. He had expected explanations, justifications, assurances. He had expected to be told that they do things differently abroad and if you want to trade with these people you have to bend the rules and lubricate the process. He had expected to be told this, and had that been done, he would have accepted it. But he was not in control; someone else had set the trap; he had blundered into it.

The adjournment lasted no more than five minutes, though it seemed much longer. Eventually Purves opened the door and ushered him in. Radleigh asked him to sit down.

"There is no other way of saying this, John, I'm afraid,"

he said. "I have to ask you to resign from Loyalty."

"What?" exclaimed John.

"I'm sorry,"

"You're firing me?"

"No, not that, unless…… No, I am asking you to tender your resignation. It's the best way."

"This is unreal. I don't believe I am hearing this."

Radleigh made no reply but kept his eyes fixed on John. Purves hung his head.

"But…. but…" muttered John then dried up.

Radleigh filled the gap.

"Ms Waltham, Director of Human Resources will be in touch with you over the next few days. Don't go back to Pinkerton. If you need to collect any personal effects from your office contact Ms Waltham and she will arrange it."

The trap had been sprung. John felt it slam shut. His dismissal, carefully planned, had been clinically executed. He had no witnesses and the victors write the minutes.

"So that's what this meeting was about," John cried, "But why?"

"We will give the reasons in due course," said Radleigh measuring his words, "and hope to reach an amicable settlement with you, but I would advise you to say nothing more until you have taken legal advice."

He looked at Martin Purves again; again, Purves nodded.

John will never be told why he has been dismissed. He must come to his own conclusions and act on them as he thinks fit. In the meantime, he has to take himself back to York. Where to in York? A rented flat. Who to? To no one.

CHAPTER SEVEN

If you want to know how John Swansen felt in the days after his dismissal, pull a black bag over your head and jump off a cliff.

Within minutes of entering the flat at York John started work on his laptop, writing a stinging letter to Walter Radleigh expressing his disgust at what had happened to him, demanding an explanation and justifying his own doubts about the Bainan contract. He wrote and rewrote the letter; he shortened it and lengthened it; he convoluted sentences then cut them up; he heaped up lurid adjectives and indignant nouns then pared them back. But, whatever he did, by the end of the night he was no nearer having something fit to send than when he started. He went to bed at six, slept very little and rose at half past nine.

After breakfast he looked at what he had written the night before, deleted it, and typed out a few words to his erstwhile boss.

Dear Mr Radleigh

Following our meeting yesterday, I have put the matter of my departure from the company in the hands of my solicitors. They will be in touch with you in due course.

Yours faithfully

John Swansen

Now he must find a solicitor. He couldn't use the firm's law advisers, and assumed that a trawl through Yellow Pages would not track down the best advice, so he asked himself who would be likely to know a firm that specialised in handling breach of contract claims.

He picked up his address book and riffled through the pages. He found this disturbing; it brought home to him the enormity of what had befallen him. His stomach already tossing, heaved. Name after name repudiated him. Most were contacts of Loyalty or Pinkerton; they wouldn't want to be seen to be helping him. There were numerous public servants – from enterprise organisations, colleges, trade departments, local councils, etc., who communicated with a Managing Director; John Swansen the man meant nothing to them.

Equally he found names of other chief executives, directors, senior managers; they would not want to be associated with someone who had been sacked, a *Managing Director* who had been sacked, a managing director who had been clumsy enough, not clever enough, to be sacked. John recalled his own crocodile tears over departed colleagues; of standing at the bar at conferences lamenting the latest casualty, agreeing that he should have seen it coming, should have quit while he was ahead, should have been better, or wiser, or more politically astute. Whatever, the fault lay with the unfortunate.

Now he was the fallen one, the subject of hypocritical pity. Who could he contact of all these illustrious names and glittering titles? He trudged depressingly from page to page, deciding to call someone then deciding not to, picking up the phone then putting it down. Then he dialled a number but put the phone down before anyone could answer.

"Get a grip," he told himself and rang Harry; he was in London for the day. He rang Len; Len was in a meeting. He rang Maurice and heard his secretary saying, "Yes, Mr Swansen, from which company?"

"No, no company, a friend, it's personal."

"Would you hold a moment, please, Mr Swansen? I'll see if Mr Frobisher is in."

Of course, he's in; you know that. You're asking him if he wants to speak to a Mr Swansen.

('Who?' 'Swansen, John, says he's a friend.')

('Swansen, John Swansen. Can you remember him? Is he in the book?')

('Just a minute……. here's a John Swansen, MD at Pinkerton Loyalty, will that be him?')

('Could be, Yes, that'll be him. Put him through, but interrupt if he's on too long.')

"I've tracked Mr Frobisher down, Mr Swansen. I'll put you through."

"Maurice, long time no see, how are things with you?"

"Great, and you?"

"That's what I'm ringing about. Where can I pull in good legal advice on a contract matter?

A pause.

"Sales contract?

"No, employment contract."

"Not yours, I hope."

"Yes, I'm afraid so."

"What's happened?"

John heard himself blurting out an incoherent story about being in discussion with his company about mutual separation; going his own way; incompatibility; personality clash; no faith left in the board; better to get out while I'm still young; moving on; fresh challenges. Anything, anything but the truth: they have booted me out!

Maurice is not deceived.

"Are you OK?" he says. "You sound a little stressed."

"No, I'm alright. Lack of sleep, late night last night. Can you give me the name of a good brief?" says John, trying to lighten up.

"Well, we have Meldrew and Birks, but they're mainly commercial. Look, leave it with me, John. I'll get back to you."

Give him credit he did – ten days later; after ten days the incubation period would be over, the infection would have lost its virulence. Infection? Incubation? What's all this? What's the disease? Powerless disgrace, that's what. For that you are sent into quarantine. Please don't mix with susceptible executives.

After bruising at the hands of Maurice, John he contacted no more of his peers. Bruising? Maurice had been nice to him, almost friendly, has offered to help. That's what Maurice thought and we might think so too. But John felt bruised - and crushed.

Of course, he could have tried some of the previously fallen, but they had been removed from his address book, the book of life, and had entered the insubstantial after-life of the once powerful; he did not know how to communicate with the departed. Then he reached a name that cheered him: J P Marwick.

JP Marwick, you may recall had been appointed by UKi when they rescued Pinkerton from the flights of fancy of Flambert Pinkerton. Flambert had agreed provided JP accepted John as General Manager. JP had no problem with that and set to work to get to know John. He liked what he found and gave John a free hand. JP was a financier and looked like a financier. Back then, JP was in his fifties and at work John did not see him dressed other than in a smart dark pinstriped three-piece suit and sober tie. John soon found out that JP was no clone. Inside the suit was a confident man who needed no props to support him; a quiet, pleasant man with a generous nature. If he had ripped off investors and ground down the poor it didn't show. John learnt to trust him; he was shrewd but honest; if he made a promise, he kept it.

During the two years of JP Marwick's chairmanship Pinkerton enjoyed an Indian Summer. He kept Flambert's inspiration alive but on a leash so that new products came on stream but fewer of them failed. JP enrolled John on the Wentworth Senior Management Programme, and then encouraged him to apply what he had learnt. Management at Pinkerton became more professional, leaner, fitter. Costs were cut by 15%.

JP repaired the balance sheet and secured the company's financial future. John cut his managerial teeth during that early cost cutting and emerged from the two years with a reputation for toughness and a tight grip on the company. But JP had his eye on another prize and he duly landed it. One day he called John to his office to tell him that Pinkerton Ltd was being sold lock, stock and barrel to Loyalty, a UK plc growing rapidly through mergers and acquisitions. By this manoeuvre, JP gave UKi the option of cashing in its investment or of backing the new management by converting their holding to shares in Loyalty. JP himself took cash; UKi took half cash and half shares; they both made a decent profit.

JP, with an eye to retirement, decided to use some of his winnings to purchase a little house somewhere far from the madding crowd. John pointed him in the direction of Birsett and the row of old fishermen's houses at the foot of the brae. JP liked what he saw and made himself a somewhat distant neighbour of John's father.

From his stake in Pinkerton, Flambert walked away with a cash windfall, which he will no doubt squander on schemes that will benefit whoever is lucky enough to be with him at the time. Who knows whether he will make a second fortune or end up broke? He may even cross our path again. If he does, we will be glad to see him.

The company became Loyalty-Pinkerton; Loyalty to show who was boss, Pinkerton to kid the market the service would be the same. Out of the blue, two young executives, Tom Curtis and Gerald Hopkins, arrived to take over. Little notice was given of their arrival. JP heard when he protested yet again to Loyalty's chairman about the length of time Loyalty was taking to appoint a successor.

Tom Curtis came as Chief Executive, Gerald Hopkins as Director of Finance. Their careers in Pinkerton need not delay us long. They had no interest in taking part in our story. They were career managers schooled in the ways of corporate politics. Their ambition was to be rich and powerful; their intention to so manipulate Pinkerton that its successes would be credited to them and its failures to somebody else – John, for instance.

"Ah," said JP when John rang him to report his departure from Loyalty. "This doesn't surprise me; it wasn't a fit, John, you and Loyalty. I know just the woman to talk to. Her name is Belinda Boyd; she works for Booth, Blair and Brown. The number is, just a minute: 020 7324 6110. Tell her I sent you. Good luck, John, ring me any time. If I'm not here you can reach me at Birsett – but you know that. I'm up there a lot now. There's more to life than work."

These few words warmed John. Someone understood, someone would help, someone liked him. He rang Belinda Boyd immediately and reached her immediately. She spoke to him in a curious staccato Birmingham accent that made him feel he should only speak when spoken to. He explained the position and from her interrogation concluded that she knew what she was talking about. At the end of the conversation she said that she would put in writing what she thought she could do for him and how much it would cost. If he intended taking up their offer of help, he should, while it was fresh in his mind, write down what had happened with dates and times, and gather together any documents or records of conversations that might be relevant to the case. The way she asked made him promise to do it. She then asked him if he had a computer.

"Yes," he said.

"Does it belong to you? "

"Yes."

"You bought it, not the company."

"No, the company bought it."

"Then it belongs to the company. Delete anything you don't want them to know. Buy your own machine and copy everything you need. If they know what they are doing they will ask you to return their property. I will be in touch on Monday and you will come down to see me on.... Wednesday at one; you will have had lunch by then, so will I."

John went straight to the local "Computer World", bought a laptop computer and copied everything as instructed by Ms Boyd. Then he had a light lunch and felt surprisingly calm.

It was as well he bought his own computer for on Friday morning Ms Waltham rang to say that she would call for the company's computer in the afternoon; she would be accompanied by a security man. The car he could keep for six calendar months (the formal period of notice) from to-day's date. His salary would continue for the same period, but they would expect him not to speak to the press, or give any interviews until a settlement had been reached. If he wanted to collect any personal possessions from the factory, she would arrange access on Saturday morning to avoid embarrassment to all parties.

Those not familiar with the departure of senior managers from their posts may wonder at the brutality of John's treatment. How can it be that one day (Tuesday this week to be precise) he is trusted implicitly with company assets worth many millions of pounds but the next day is not allowed to enter his own office without an escort? What about legal periods of notice? What about being innocent until proven guilty? What about common decency? None of these have any force against the suspicion in the mind of his former colleagues that John is up to something:

'How do we know? He suspects us of dubious dealing in Bainan. What else does he suspect? If he probed further, he might uncover others matters we would rather not have to explain. If he is not thinking the way we are thinking, not accepting our explanations, what other malicious thoughts might he be playing with? After all, this is not a democracy. If he were left in place even for a day who knows what damage he might do to the body corporate. There's a threat, better not risk it. Isolate him, pay him off, get clear of him. He knows the score; this is the way it's done'.

John had visitors before Ms Waltham. On Thursday evening, Mack and George arrived at seven and stood on the doormat looking sombre. If they had been wearing black ties and holding black bowlers, they could not have more closely resembled undertakers. They conveyed their sympathy and talked in hushed voices about how unfair it all was. They reported that Jim Arkwright, the Financial Controller, had been put in charge.

John tried as best he could to explain what had happened, but found himself constrained by his former exalted status. In his mind they were still subordinates, and therefore should not have access to his deeper thoughts. But their visit heartened him; their friendship had overcome their reticence. They did not stay long and on leaving, George passed on the best wishes of Sarah, Rita and some of the others. He added that when the dust had settled, they would have a retirement dinner for him.

When Jim Arkwright discovered that George had been to see John, he reprimanded him. George told him to get stuffed.

When Ms Waltham arrived on Friday, John soon realised that she was not prepared to discuss his separation. She kept the security man at her side throughout. She asked only for the computer and John gave it up to her. Before she left, she said that he, or his legal adviser, if he preferred it, would be informed of any offer the company is prepared to make, but this in no way prejudiced the company's position on John's resignation.

"I didn't resign," stated John, "and I'm not going to."

"I understand your position," she said, patiently, "This is a difficult time for you. You may wish to talk it through with someone. We have contacted Shelter Executive Counselling and asked them to give you what help they can; the man you should speak to is Max Cavendish. We will meet all costs, of course. I'll leave his card." She laid a business card on the table.

She arranged for John to be smuggled into the factory on Saturday under escort to collect his personal possessions. He had last entered the factory only three days earlier yet it was already swirling out of reach in the dividing current. As he passed the gatehouse, he glimpsed a known face behind the grille but it no longer belonged to Charlie; he had become a nameless security guard. He entered the office block and walked through reception, but felt a stranger. Surely, he would feel different entering his own office; surely? No, his office had gone; replaced by Jim Arkwright's. The carpets, wallpaper, desk, chair, cabinets, computer were the same, but he felt no attachment to them. He did not need the new artefacts to tell him that it no longer belonged to him; not the ugly onyx desk set, not the garish modern painting on the wall, not the grotesque elephant's foot waste paper basket. The difference lay in his mind; he had become detached. Jim thoughtfully had packed John's own personal possessions into a cardboard box: his pens, desk set, leather executive blotter folder with matching diary, his painting of St Abb's Head on a rough day. In the box he found a framed photo of Robert, Rebecca and Marion smiling on some foreign promenade in the sunshine. He had forgotten about that photograph; Arkwright must have found it in a drawer. Under the nervous gaze of the security guard he glanced round the office for the last time. Nothing here that belonged to him.

He put the box in the boot of his car and drove out through the gate. He knew where he was going, impelled by a conviction he had had since stepping out of Radleigh's office on Wednesday evening; a conviction that had strengthened with the intervening hours - an irrational, pointless and essentially juvenile conviction. He must tell Marion what had happened.

CHAPTER EIGHT

Until Marion had walked out almost a year ago, John had thought that he balanced his work and his home pretty well. Her disaffection had come as a shock, yet he had not found it earth-shattering or life-threatening.

What was her complaint? He hadn't noticed she had changed the curtains in his bedroom! (*His bedroom! He had only moved in there temporarily to save waking her up when he came to bed!*) He didn't spend enough time with the children! (*The children! They were grown up, had their own friends; they didn't want their old father hogging their time*). They never went out together! (*Not true, they went to Robert's Prize-Giving and what about the meals out in Mauritius when they were on holiday? And the trip to Paris for the Convention?*) They were no longer a couple! (*What on earth does that mean?*)

He had been surprised at how little impact the split had had. Not only surprised, but half-guilty for it half-proved Marion's point: he had not cultivated their love and friendship; he had let it die. Not only guilty but half-frightened. Had he caught the cancer he had seen destroy other top managers? The cancer that consumes everything in their lives except work, ambition and the firm; the cancer that, in its progress, destroys all alternative feelings.

Such questions had grumbled in the back of his mind,

but he has been so busy, so preoccupied with the future of the company, and lately, so teetering on the edge of a cliff, that he has never addressed them. Now, that he has both motive and opportunity, he will do so, will he not?

Marion was not surprised to see John. Mack had told his wife, Fiona, what had happened and Fiona had told Marion. It would be wrong to say that she had stayed at home thinking he might come, but normally she would have been at the shops at ten on a Saturday morning. This morning she had sent Rebecca off on her own; she had reasons of her own for wanting to see John.

She made a cup of coffee and listened to her husband, her estranged husband, complaining about his bad treatment. She offered no advice and asked only those questions that were supportive and reassuring. This was not mere diplomacy; she could appreciate his distress and regret that his toys were broken.

"What are you going to do now?" she said when he had run out of words.

"I'm going to take them all the way." he stated. "I'm going to expose Loyalty, and I'm going to expose Sir Frank if it's the last thing I do."

"And then?"

"What do you mean?"

"Are you going to look for a job or retire, or what?"

Strange as it may seem, this question had not occurred to John. He had been secure for so long that it had not dawned on him that he had not only lost his job, but also his livelihood. Like many professionals he had assumed he was paid for what he was, not for what he did. Now he would learn that that is not the case. It will be a painful experience. In the meantime, Marion is waiting for an answer.

"I'll take a couple of months off," he said, trying to

sound as if it were planned, "then I'll have a look at what is available."

Marion nodded and smiled - sadly, I would say. Still he tilted at windmills. In case she is misunderstood, let me add that Marion is not sad on her own account, playing the role of the little woman waiting at home for her erring husband to return. She is not sorry for herself; life is less fraught and less complicated than it has been for years and she has put her freedom to good use. She is sorry for John.

"I had a letter yesterday morning," she said, "and I wondered whether I should tell you about it. Now that you're here you may as well see it. It's from your sister Margaret."

"From Margaret, what does she want?"

"I'll let you read it."

She fetched the letter from the bureau and handed it to him. For Margaret it was a long letter, three pages; a scribbled notelet was more usual. But she had difficult matters to discuss.

Dear Marion, (it read)

Roddam and I think you should be acquainted with the circumstances surrounding my father Willie's illness, for we know you were always very fond of Willie. Your father in law is not well and the doctors believe that he will soon be in need of more intensive care. I do not mean intensive care in the usual hospital sense, but in the sense that my father needs someone to be with him at home.

At present he is recuperating from his most recent bout in hospital at The Bield, but this is unlikely to last much longer than about a fortnight, after which time decisions need to be made about his long-term care. We have discussed the matter with John but he seems to be reluctant to accept any of the solutions we suggest.

Setting aside the impossibility of myself or John being able to give 24-hour attention due to our work commitments, we did think that Helen might be asked to sleep overnight at Braeshiel until such time as the matter is resolved one way or other, but John is reluctant to ask Helen to do this, and we appreciate that she does have her own family to consider, though we would have thought that David is at an age when he could be left with the younger children at night, except Louise who could go with Helen. We have also suggested bringing in a full-time nurse, but this would be hideously expensive and we doubt if father's resources would be sufficient to afford it.

Which brings me to the point of this letter and I hesitate to write. If it were not for Roddam's belief that you would want to know what this suggestion is, I would not put it to you. I remember how very grateful my father was when you cared for him after his prostate operation. We were all very grateful, in fact. Would you not consider some such arrangement at this juncture? We are sure it would not be for long and would give my father the love and attention he needs during his last few weeks. And, of course, it would lift a great burden of anxiety from both Roddam and myself and from John. Please let me know your reaction to this suggestion as soon as you have time to consider it properly.

I trust you and the children are well. Roddam is very busy at the moment with a development in the New Town and Abigail is off on a two-week study trip to Paris, so I am left to run the shop by myself which makes life very hectic. Please give our love to Robert and to Rebecca. Abigail, I'm sure, wants me to send her love.

Your loving sister-in-law,

Margaret.

PS: We have not told John we are writing this letter to you.

"I told her this wasn't on." snapped John when he had read the letter, "She has no right to ask you to do this. I told her you had a job and I told her that Rebecca was sitting her A levels. She has no right to ask you. I'll speak to her. I'm very sorry. We must find a solution ourselves."

"Yes, you must indeed," said Marion,

"There's no need for you to reply. I'll sort it out."

"No need, I've replied."

"By letter?"

"No, I phoned."

"What did you say?"

"I said it was time the Swansens stopped treating other people as door mats."

"How did she take it?" said John, missing most of the point.

"Surprised, I would say. But I think I can see a solution to your problem."

"Oh, what?"

"You go to be beside your father. There is nothing to stop you now. You can use the couple of months you are taking off."

"Me?" said John, "but that's impossible."

Marion could have replied that it was not impossible at all. She could have said that it wasn't even difficult. She could have said that the only difficulty lay in his own sense of priorities. She could have given him the reply that he so often had given her in the months before their separation: 'make it happen, Marion, make it happen'. And this when she was pleading that her life had become bleak and pointless as the children no longer needed her, that he was always absorbed in his work, that she was plugging the gaps in her husband's life at the expense of her own. She could have pointed out that, had they still been together, John would not have thought twice about asking her to go, indeed, would have expected it. But she said nothing because she loved John's father, and hated to think of him as a burden or bone of contention. In her heart of hearts, she wanted to go to Willie, wanted to see him through his last lonely weeks. The job! - pushing papers over a desk, would have been sacrificed for him. But something strong and insistent in her mind told her she must not give up the ground she had so painfully won. Equally strong, but undefined lay the conviction that John must go.

John's protest went unanswered. He would speak to Margaret; they would sort something out. Then he returned to the subject most on his mind and filled in some of the details he had not previously covered and repeated some of those he had.

Then he returned to the flat and spent the rest of the weekend and the early part of the following week writing an autobiography to give to Belinda Boyd when he met her on Wednesday. By then had had laid out his life story, from the moment he met Flambert Pinkerton, through the steady management of JP, via the Loyalty take-over and the manipulations of Curtis and Hopkins, to his own reign as Managing Director. Towards the end he concentrated on the machinations of Sir Frank, the treachery of Jim Arkwright and the deceit of Walter Radleigh. It makes such riveting reading that I would have included it as an appendix if I did not think it might overshadow my own poor tale.

I can't imagine that Belinda Boyd has had any training in outplacement counselling; it's not her style. But her direction to John to write down the sad story proved more effective than anything Ms Waltham's Executive Counsellors might have done. It did not cure the injury but it identified the spot and focussed the anger. By the end of the narrative, John knew what hurt him. It lay not what he had claimed before; not deceit, corruption, or Loyalty's desertion of the factory at York. It proved much simpler than that: he'd been knocked off his pedestal. He had been sucked in, strung along, outplayed, outfoxed, wrapped up in pink ribbon and dumped on the front steps. He was expendable; Jim Arkwright could do the job; in that lay the sharpest pain.

When he arrived at Booth, Brown & Blair for his appointment with Belinda Boyd he thought he knew what he wanted. Belinda proved as formidable in the flesh as on the phone. She resembled what we imagine a lady vet should look like: close on six feet tall and built like a rugby prop forward. Her hair is short and straight and she wore a long loose floral dress with a white collar. Set in this bulky frame lay a large but flexible face. When serious it made you want to plead guilty without extenuation, when smiling it encouraged you to believe that God herself was on your side. JP was right; she would serve John well – if he would take her counsel.

John thought he knew what he wanted so he outlined his vision of Walter Radleigh and Sir Frank in the dock, squirming under questioning; being shot from fox-hole to fox-hole; the press scribbling down lurid details; questions asked in the House; the share price of Loyalty plunging. Of course, he didn't paint in the details for Ms Boyd, nevertheless she got the picture. She let him run on for a while then brought him up sharply.

"It's all about money, Mr Swansen; how much will they have to pay to shut you up. Have you a sum in mind?" she said.

"No, no, it's not about money."

"You don't want your job back, do you?"

"No"

"And you don't want to work for such a set of bandits, do you?"

"No"

"Then it comes down to money."

"Money's not important; it's the principle."

"Millionaire, are you?" she said rather than asked.

"No, but I have enough."

"Enough for what? How old are you? Fifty-one, two, and what are you going to live on the rest of your life? You're married with children – you have to provide for them. Mr Swansen, money is important. We'd better work out how much we can lever out of Loyalty. That's how we'll settle this in the end. We may as well start now."

John saw there was no point in protesting further and her demeanour disinclined him to keep trying. He went along with the calculations: notice under contract: compensation for loss of employment: payment in lieu of tribunal award for unfair dismissal: payment for the distress caused: dislocation costs: legal costs.

"Say, £200,000," concluded Belinda, "with an option of early retirement at £35,000 a year indexed. Agreed?"

"Agreed," replied John, feeling diminished. He didn't want money; he wanted justice. However, like many people with a cause, by justice he meant revenge. And his cause, as we know, is not untarnished; it is alloyed with his own grubby contribution. This, however, increased rather than decreased his passion for revenge; he would polish up his own role by blackening theirs. But none of this he admitted to Ms Boyd.

"I'll read your stuff and let off an opening shot next week. They'll take time to reply. I'll chase them up if I don't hear by …. when, (she fished among the flowers of her frock and drew out her diary), …. by the middle of next month. I'll be in touch." She scribbled an entry in the diary and replaced it in the drapery. Take a holiday, Mr Swansen, get it out of your system; life's too short for spite."

He stepped from the offices of Booth, Blair & Brown into the late spring sunshine of a London day in a black mood. Spite? It is not spite! But for the moment he couldn't find a better word for it.

CHAPTER NINE

Only a week had elapsed since the fateful meeting with Walter Radleigh, yet the waters had largely closed over events for everyone except John. Even at York life had returned to near normality, for however much special events might excite us, it is the routine of life that carries us forward. John now had no routine, and the autobiography that had occupied him in the few days since his dismissal was complete and in the hands of Belinda. He rose on Thursday morning with nothing to do. Nothing to do but to make breakfast, and that only a bowl of muesli, a cup of coffee and a couple of rounds of toast.

He recalled the question Marion had asked a few days earlier and asked himself what he was going to do now. He answered it the way any wage slave would answer it: find a job. But how?

He did not know. He rejected out of hand the counsellor, Max Cavendish, that Ms Waltham had offered. He would take no help from Loyalty; he didn't want it and didn't need it. Yet the thought of trawling through Situations Vacant in newspapers appalled him. There must be a more dignified way for executives of his calibre. He remembered the odd occasion when he had been flattered by an executive research consultant asking if he would consider an appointment they were trying to fill. John had followed up some of them but never very far and in the last few years, since he had turned fifty, he had not been approached at all. Surely, those consultants must still be beavering away and might be interested in finding him another position. He searched through his business card collection and found a name and number. The call failed; he tried two more with the same result and had he known why; he would have stopped his search right there. The reason such executive search consultants had moved on simply demonstrated that they had found proper jobs, for many of them were in the same position as John: out of work executives looking for work; until it arrived, they would try their hand at recruitment consultancy. At his fourth attempt John hit the more enduring variety of the species and spoke to a Mr Zack Mallinger of Mallinger Associates, 17, The Headrow, Leeds, who listened patiently and politely to his request then suggested they meet.

Zack confided that, at this moment of time, he did not have any particular position in mind, but he could offer their Counselling and Placement Service that would set John on the way to finding the position of his dreams as he had just the sort of track record much in demand at the moment. Something about Zack grated but John agreed to an appointment the following week. In the meantime, he had work to do; Zack wanted him to compile a CV, a Curriculum Vitae; your life distilled into three A4 sheets. A slick CV was the first step on the way to a new future, Zack said. On Friday morning an information pack from Mallinger Associates arrived; it included a brochure praising the merits of Zack Mallinger, Search Consultant to the Blue Chips, a framework CV for John to follow, and a note on the fee: 10% of starting salary, or, £2,000 if the candidate turned down more than two positions offered within six months. Zack knew what he was doing.

I have no wish to drag readers through the jungle of Executive Search and would have prevented John from venturing into it if I could; Orpheus travelled more comfortably through Hades. I will keep you in touch with his progress but not bore you with the details. For it is not Zack or Belinda that will lead John towards a new life; it is his father Willie, and he will do it without fee or paperwork.

It started with a phone call from Helen who did not yet know of John's fall. A social worker wanted to visit Willie's home to make an assessment of what care he would need if and when he returned home. She had persuaded the social worker to come on Saturday morning and had contacted Margaret; could John come too? Of course.

John packed a case and travelled north. That is how he came to leave York. He would only return to it once or twice after that. No forward plan produced it, no great change programme, no big decision, no acute analysis of pros and cons. Life, as so often happens, had backed John into a corner; Willie needed someone to stay with him; it would be his son, John. John agreed, but assured himself that it would be temporary - because it happened to fit in with his plan to take a couple of months to think about what he wanted to do next.

Embarrassed at John's dismissal, Margaret told anyone who asked that he had resigned over a matter of principle. Helen sympathised with him and told him he was well out of it. Willie grieved for his son. And John, to prevent more grief, told his father that he welcomed the change and had intended taking the summer off anyway.

Of course, John's fall excited the grapevine in Birsett and Hecklescar, but not for long. The news that the Bold Venture from Hecklescar had fished up a human skull in its nets off the North End of the Tillies (and had the whole catch confiscated because of it) and that the Birsett Inn was up for sale again pushed John's minor problem off the verbal front page. That is not to say that some of the locals did not salt it away to use later as an illustration of what happens when somebody gets too big for their boots.

John collected Willie from The Bield on Tuesday, the last day of April, and tried to establish some sort of routine for his father. In the morning, Helen looked in after she had taken Louise to the school, and came in the evening to see Willie into bed. Willie usually rose not long after Helen went away and contrived to spend his days happily and without too much inconvenience to his son. A home help (Janet from the council houses, two classes below John at the school, Agnes's lassie) came in two mornings a week, and a nurse (Mary from Prior's Cross, married to Norman Forest) looked in once a week and could be sent for if Willie needed medical help. But the burden of caring for Willie fell on John. He bought the groceries, prepared the meals, washed the dishes, made the beds, tidied up the rooms, weeded the garden and generally made himself useful. He did what he did thoroughly and without complaint but he resented every minute of it; he felt out of place, trapped, humiliated and diminished.

One prospect that could have given him most comfort lay off-limits. He could not wish for a quick release, for that meant wishing that his father dead. He could not wish it but he nevertheless entertained it and it added to his discomfort. He faced inevitable failure. He had faced failure before, of course, but his favourite recovery strategies were no use here. Flaccid managerial jargon offered no help; this descent offered no "wake-up call", could not be "turned around", could not be "put to use next time".

Two things made his suffering (John's not Willie's) bearable. First, the people who broke up the monotonous days with their visits. Alex called virtually every day usually on his way home from the boat. Delightful, skipper of the Aurora, also breezed in from time to time with a crab or a fillet of fish, and would have brought a lobster but for the fact that Willie disliked them. Jimmy Possum came on Tuesdays as well as bringing Willie the Fishing News on Friday morning. On Wednesday, Duncan Johnston and Sandy Donaldson arrived as they had always done, no longer for a game of dominoes, but they came anyway and brought the lottery ticket for Willie to check, for, in spite of his afflictions, he had not given up gambling. Willie, when well enough, managed his Monday afternoon visit to old Bessie Raeburn and took her, as usual, the Berwickshire News. Mussent Grumble, the newsagent from Hecklescar still called with it on Thursdays and brought the gloomier sort of news from Hecklescar and, by way of cheering Willie up, never failed to describe any ailments or medical disasters that he had heard about.

Then Helen's bairns would tumble in, unannounced and boisterous. David and George, the older children, didn't come much, but Morag came, usually with her pals, to borrow something from her grand uncle that she dare not request from her mother. Calum popped in, usually on his way up the brae after pottering about the harbour and sometimes brought a poddlie he had caught. Willie had never cooked one of these coarse fish, but always accepted them as if they were prime salmon. Then, of course, little Louise came. She had always come on a Wednesday; now she came almost every day as if she were checking up on her grand uncle; as if she had caught something in the wind, something she did not like.

John's other solace was his work. What work? He doesn't have any work, does he? Well, no! But he has to have work, just as he has to breathe and eat. He has found himself a table and set up on it his laptop and a note pad and pens and his mobile phone and there, when he has a moment, he does his work. What work? Well, there is the Financial Times to read each day, and, you may remember, his CV for Zack. He is on the third draft. Then there is his case for loss of office which allows him to use a spreadsheet to work out the possible compensation he doesn't want, and in connection with which he sends Belinda regular e-mails with more evidence of the perfidy of Loyalty, and anecdotes illustrative of the behaviour of Sir Frank. When these immediate concerns fail to keep him busy, he turns his attention to something he has always wanted to do – to sketch out his plan for setting up a company from scratch; the way it should be. You see, he has work!

But such work did not offer him a way of escape, a way out, a way back even. Like a yachtsman who has fallen overboard, John watched with terror his old familiar life disappearing rapidly over the waves. He ls still attached, however; if his lifeline holds, he may climb back aboard. And to what is the line attached? To Belinda Boyd and through her to Loyalty, and to Zack Mallinger and a business future.

Oh, and to one other: JP Marwick. John has met him once or twice on the brae and stood for a few minutes talking about matters much weightier than the lengthening days, the changing winds and the spring exploding life in garden and hedgerow; they talked big business. JP spent two days a week in London and kept his ear to the ground. He brought John up to date with life in the city, with trends in the economy and with the antics of his former company and colleagues: Walter Radleigh, Sir Frank, and, from way back, Tom Curtis and Gerald Hopkins the get-rich-quick kids of early Loyalty days. And, from further back again, our entrepreneurial friend, Flambert Pinkerton. Apparently, he was into handheld network systems now and had approached JP for advice on finance. ("He seems to know what it means," laughed JP). This flow of news, although it concerned some people he did not like, let John glimpse a broader, busier thoroughfare than the pedestrian traffic of Birsett.

Willie occupies the same space at the same time but he lives in a different world. John is camped in the wilderness for the night waiting for the morning so he can move on. Willie is at home and has reached that stage of life that younger people find incomprehensible. He has accepted that he did not have long to live and, in a sense, is relieved that the daily struggle with pain and sickness would soon be over. Yet he enjoys his days. This thin joy is a pale shadow of what he had known when the family was growing up and the days were overfilled with activity and exhilaration. Nor could it be compared to the substantial contentment and pleasure that Jane and he had known in their years at Braeshiel. But memory is gracious; it allows us to recall the high times of our past without robbing the present of its more mundane happiness. Willie likes the house he woke up in; the house that he and Jane had made home together. He likes the view from the window out over the sea and the sweet and exciting memories of days spent on it. The chat and banter of his friends warmed him and catches him up in the flow of life of the village. He relishes the quiet philosophy of his old friend Mr Scott and loves to rib him for using long words and quoting from the poets. He delights in the garden, trees, flowers, birds, airs of the countryside. He takes pleasure in the children's stories and exulted in their vitality.

We know that these are not new experiences; they have been cultivated for years. Now the pretentious human claim of being different has fallen dumb; he takes his given place amongst all living things, understands that the stream that runs through him, runs through them and ran through his beloved Jane and runs yet through his children and all children. He is caught up in the same cycle of life and death; he shares their life and their death. This belonging brings the consolation of knowing that he is not alone, but part of a great company under heaven. The blackbird singing in the crab-apple tree may well be silent before he is, but still it fills the air with music on this evening. Willie will sing for as long as he can. After that let God make of it what he will.

John did not understand any of this, and Willie had no way of telling him. He simply told his son that he was all right, and he should not to worry about him when John told him he had to go down to Leeds to see a man about a job.

He is off to see Zack Mallinger. Mr Scott will father-sit for the day.

CHAPTER TEN

The offices of Mallinger Associates were up an unprepossessing stair above The Leeds Equitable Building Society. Once inside the door they took on a pleasant tubular and blue ambience. A beech wood desk with tubular legs decorated with blue and silver silk flowers framed a blonde receptionist. She fitted the room so harmoniously that John would not have been surprised to discover she had tubular legs. Her name bar tastefully proclaimed that she was Michelle and she greeted John with a broad smile. John introduced himself; Michelle handed him a badge and tapped the time of his arrival into the computer at her side. Michelle invited him to take a seat on the low blue sofa below a large reproduction of Monet's Water Lilies. The sofa was plainly not meant for sitting on for when John eventually collapsed into a sitting position his knees came up to his chin. He struggled to his feet and was standing looking at the Monet when a small broad-shouldered man in a black and white checked double-breasted suit and mauve kipper tie strode out a door with his hand outstretched and declared in a loud London-American accent.

"Hi, I'm Zack. Have a good journey? Come in, come in, good to see ya."

The sight and the sound confirmed John's worst fears but he followed Zack through the door. He found himself in a room similar to the one he had just left, except that there was more of it on a bigger scale. Zack motioned him to a tubular and blue armchair and sat down in its replica on the other side of a coffee table. On the table lay a folder. Zack flipped it open with a practised flourish and settled himself into his chair.

"Now," said Zack, "Tell me about yourself. I've read the CV, now I want to meet the man."

John felt his hackles rise; nevertheless, he picked up his CV and began to expand on what he thought were the most important features of it. Zack paid acute attention, asking detailed questions about the companies, the responsibilities John had carried, and the people he had worked with. He scribbled the answers onto a sheet of paper in the folder. Then he asked the question John had dreaded.

"And why are you leaving your present position?"

John expounded on 'mutual agreement', and gave just enough detail to back his version of events. Zack saw through it and scribbled, "*Fired*" in his folder.

He had another lame duck on his hands. Disappointing it was; every time he thought he had laid his hands on a hot property, it turned out they were over fifty and damaged goods. But Zack was a professional and John noticed no change in his attitude.

"What sort of vacancy would you be interested in?" he asked. John had prepared for this one.

"Chief Executive of an autonomous medium-sized company; or a board level appointment with a larger company, maybe Operations Director; but it has to be line, I'm not interested in support, not engineering, finance, or materials or anything like that."

Zack made a point of writing all this in his notes. He had an annoying habit of flicking the cap of his pen off and on with fingers of the hand in which he was holding it.

"Consultancy?"

"No."

"Must it be manufacturing or would you take something in services?"

"What kind of services?"

"Retail, financial services, telecommunications, logistics."

"Not financial services."

"It's a booming sector. Are you sure?"

"Pretty sure, I know nothing about Financial Services."

"Doesn't stop some I could think of. The other services, OK? Even retail?"

"Yes, if it's big enough and the top job"

"I only deal in top jobs." said Zack grandly, "General Manager level in those?"

"I'd consider it." Zack flicked open his pen and wrote, '*not fin, GM rest*'.

"Statutory agencies?"

"Such as what?"

"Health, enterprise, environment, even education, the government is keen to recruit industrial managers."

"I'm not a political animal, but why not." Zack scribbled *'Not applic'* in the folder.

"Charities?"

"Not my scene."

"Are you sure, there's some big jobs with decent salaries in charities now – lottery money, I expect. Sure?"

"Sure…. unless at national level and something I was interested in."

"Such as?"

"What?"

"Such as what charities are you interested in?"

"Well, anything, really, I'm not sure what there is. Something along the same line as I've been in." Zack wrote, 'No'.

"What package are you looking for? Salary indicator? (John now realised Zack was working through a list). You were on £100,000 plus a possible £20,000 bonus, right?"

"Car?"

"Mercedes."

"Options?"

"In parent company."

"Pension? Personal or company?"

"Executive scheme"

"Private health care?"

"BUPA"

"And what K" (salary) "are you looking for?"

"Better; must be six figures."

"Would you come down on the overall package? A BMW for instance?" John wondered if Zack was laughing at him. "He's all patter," he thought

"I'm not interested in anything less." Zack wrote down *'Unrealistic aspirations"*

By now I am sure you realise that we have dropped in on a fairy story, and one with all the makings of an unhappy ending. Zack has nothing on his books that will suit John and will not be able to sell him to anyone for anything like the money he is looking for. John will not lower his expectations (yet) so there is nothing Zack can come up with. John doesn't really believe that Zack can do anything for him. He doesn't even like the man. But these two are not dealing in reality; executive fantasy is what brings them together.

For Zack there is the fee, but we do him an injustice to label him a mercenary. He likes wheeling and dealing in men's (and occasionally women's) destinies, casting himself as fairy godmother or wise old owl depending on the result of his efforts. At the Human Resources Conference at Harrogate he brags about the top managers he has placed and the poor boys and girls he has made rich. He also shakes his head sagely at companies who have rejected his candidates, appointed a dodo and gone under because of it. He mourns crocodile fashion the candidates who have turned down appointments he has procured for them only to come crawling to him after six months looking for a second chance.

"I say to them: 'there is a time in the affairs of men when you have to jump aboard or miss the boat.'"

We can understand Zack's game but what about John. Surely, he is looking for a job? No, not yet, he isn't. We know that what he really wants is revenge and for that he has to nurse his injury. What better way than to confirm to himself, and demonstrate to the world, what an asset Loyalty have thrown away? The world, of course, isn't interested, but Zack makes his living out of injured pride.

"Location important?" asked Zack.

"No," said John, "Anywhere in the world, anywhere. I have no ties," Zack ticked the international box. Now he's dealing in magic carpets.

Michelle brought in the coffee, in a silver jug with a blue handle and poured it into blue cups with silver rims. Zack introduced John to the rest of the counselling and placement service. They'd done the placement bit. Now he expanded on the counselling. To John this sounded like a concoction of amateur psychology (you are grieving over your lost job; you feel unwanted and unloved; you need to deal with your resentment; we can help you work through it) laced with dollops of corny advice. John thought the best of this was that 75% of all jobs are not advertised, and he thought it best because he didn't want to demean himself by replying to recruitment ads.

Then, much to John's relief the proto-counselling was over.

"If you need an ear, mine's here," concluded Zack. "If you want to talk, I want to listen."

Zack then said he'd run John's details through the database and would be in touch shortly about suitable vacancies. He sounded confident of success; John wanted it to be difficult.

John driving back north felt strangely better for the experience. Why? He is little nearer getting a job than when he set out. Why? Because he has checked the lifeline to his former greatness and busy-ness; it still holds. For all his contempt of Zack, the little man has reassured John that he is still in the game.

On this same day, back in Hecklescar, Clarissa, sixteen, of the great tribe of Mitchison, dressed in her party best, clomped on her platform shoes into Gordon Swinton's office at SeaNorth, the fish processors. There Gordon interviewed her for one of the vacancies in the crab processing department, and once Gordon had worked his way through her application form and had assured himself that for all her qualifications, she would be able to scrape the meat out of the carapace and claws, gave her a job, starting Monday.

"You look very smart, m'dear," he said, as he shook her hand at the end, and thereby convinced Clarissa that her dress sense had got her the job.

****

"You're an auld hypocrite," chaffed Mr Scott, softly and

kindly.

Willie laughed and accepted the label. He and his old friend were sitting late on a lovely May evening in the sea window of Braeshiel waiting for John's return and watching the sea turn from silky ultramarine through liquid silver to burnished pewter as the light faded. They sat without lights so as not to disrupt the mellow mood in which they drifted. Willie had risked a glass of sherry along with his pain-killers and was momentarily relaxed and free of pain. Mr Scott's glass of whisky had had the same effect on his aches and stiffness. Willie had been trying to explain to his friend (he could explain it to no other companion; they would laugh at him) what we have already heard explained – his kinship with all living things.

"You must have slaughtered millions of fish in your time; do they not count in the fellowship?"

He did not say this to contradict Willie, but to save his friend embarrassment. He could see that Willie had strayed into unfamiliar territory, possibly due to the sherry. Clearly what he believed ran deep, but he didn't have the words to convey it. Maybe banter would help; it formed the normal currency between them.

"That's what fish are for," retaliated Willie, "to be caught and eaten."

"I don't think they would agree," said Mr Scott.

"You don't get to choose your fate," replied Willie.

Mr Scott having no answer to this, lapsed into poetry:

"And I have felt a presence that disturbs me with the joy
Of elevated thoughts; a sense sublime
Of something far more deeply interfused
Whose dwelling is the light of setting suns
And the round ocean and the living air,

And the blue sky, and in the mind of man:
A motion and a spirit......."

"I like that", murmured Willie, "Ye see, it's not just me. Who wrote it?"

"William Wordsworth."

"The daffodil man?"

"That's him."

"Say it again."

Mr Scott said it again. He had scarcely finished when the door opened and John walked into the room.

"Sitting in the dark," he said.

"Not really," replied Mr Scott.

CHAPTER ELEVEN

At six o'clock on Saturday morning Andrew Douglas, the postman, put a basket of homing pigeons on board the train at Gainslaw, bound for Belgium. By Sunday night one of the pigeons, Border Dancer, had flown back to its loft at an average speed of 68.7 mph to take second prize in the National Championship.

At nine o'clock in the evening of the same Saturday little Johnny Armstrong, nine, from Birsett doon-the-brae, didn't come home. His mother, Susan went looking for him and found his woolly hat lying on the shingle near the Crumbly Brae. His pals said they had last seen him dodging the waves on the rocks.

Susan's expedition to Newcastle for love of a wayward Geordie ended two years ago when she reappeared on her mother's doorstep with two children and a sickening distrust in men and dreams. Now this.

I relate these events to remind you that other things are happening in Birsett. They are all important and they are all connected.

Willie was not able to attend church on Sunday, but insisted that John went; Louise went with him. Helen attended with George, Calum and Morag, but Alex didn't go; he had taken out his boat to help the lifeboat look for the young lad;

Delightful took his boat too. By nightfall they had found nothing and the search was called off.

On Sunday afternoon, the warm sunshine and sumptuous green of the garden persuaded Willie he must drag himself out to see whether the woods were yet lined with bluebells and the lonnens with red campion. He asked John to take him for a run, and would he invite Mr Scott? John protested gently and asked his father if he felt well enough to go, but Willie insisted. They set out on the now familiar run along the A1 to Beanston, up the Langton road, turn left to Whiterig, down into Foulden and through the village, then up Chester Law by St John's and Bastlerig. At the top of the hill, stop a little while to take in the view. Then down through Cocklaw to Beanston and home.

It wasn't far; 10 miles in all, but it provided all that Willie wanted. You must judge for yourself whether your gruelling journeys of hundreds of miles to places with strange names provide more interest and enjoyment than these ten miles to him. As they went, he pointed out old sites and told old stories. Here, where the railway crosses the A1 the wheel came off Nicholson's bus; the bus hit the parapet and stopped the trains for the day. At Beanston Park, behind the hawthorn hedge just coming into mayflower is the only group of elms that escaped Dutch Elm Disease in the 1970s, and there's the honeysuckle just beginning to spread through the hedge – in another month the whole hedge will be a fragrant feast. Beanston church, built by the laird in 1865, has gargoyles on the tower and the best organ in the district; here it was that Willie and Jane were married because Jane's mother came from the country and wanted to laud it over the neighbours. At Whiterig, lang syne, the farmer gave his hands their orders for the day:

"Them that hes wellies, ye go an' muck out the byre; them that disn't have wellies, er...ye....ye....er....ye go an' help them."

Here, in the scrub at Hag Wood Willie and Jane once saw a redstart, and a whinchat, and a little further on you can pick wild raspberries in July. There, up the bank on the edge of the wood, is where the badgers were, probably still are. Here is the old tithe barn at Foulden where the ministers used to exploit (is that the word, Mr Scott?) their parishioners by gathering in their share of the harvest. St John's up on the hill there is as old as history, and why St John's? Some connection with the Knights Templar, d'ye think? This wood here on the left is always carpeted with bluebells, yes, there they are, and this lane here, look at the campions, red, they're called, but look at them, all shades of pink, and there's a white one; the white flower in front is stitchwort. It's going to be a bad year for Sticky Willie; see, it's halfway up the hedge already.

"Stop here, son, at the top of the law, this is where yer mother and I aye stopped."

He fell silent at last and drew his two companions into his devotion to the beloved landscape. The whole of Coldinghamshire presented itself to them, from the Lammermuir Hills to the sea, from the Eye Valley to Bunkle Edge, from the sweet green fields of Beanston to the high dark moor of Coldingham. They drank in the blessing of the lovely May day.

As they wound slowly down the hill, John saw a young woman walking up the road. She had a stick in one hand and a dog's lead in the other. As the car approached a black Labrador broke out of the hedge and bounded into the road. The woman grabbed it by the collar and hauled it onto the verge.

"Pull in, John," said Willie; "I want to speak to her."

The woman watched anxiously as the car drew up opposite to her. But her face brightened when Willie greeted her from his open window.

"Kate," he shouted, "I see that dog's no better!"

"Oh, it's you," she cried, " I didn't recognise you in the

posh car." She came across to Willie's open window

"This is my son, John, d'ye mind him?"

"Oh yes, the big shot," she smiled.

She bent into the car to take John's offered hand. John immediately warmed to her. She had a fine open face, lit by large brown eyes and a welcoming smile, framed in a cluster of dark curls peeping out from her anorak hood. Aged, John supposed, about thirty.

"Not that big," muttered John, then hoped he hadn't sounded condescending.

"Kate is Danny Strother's girl, ye ken, from Beanston. In your time he was a teacher at the high school. I think he went to, where was it? Kate, Livingston?"

"Yes, still there, but planning to come back here when he retires. At least mam is planning - he'll do just what he's told, as always."

"How's the business?"

Kate straightened up, grimaced and shrugged her shoulders.

"Struggle as usual." She looked at John and laughed. "We could do with some help from somebody that knows!"

"Well," smiled John, "If I can…"

"No, no, " laughed Kate, "We'll manage, we couldn't afford you!"

Then she dropped into the vernacular to speak to Willie.

"But how are ye, Willie? I haven't seen you up here for a bit, I heard you'd been no' weel."

"Now our secret is out," laughed Willie, "Ye'd promised not to say anything!"

"But you've no' been right?" insisted Kate.

"A wee bit," admitted Willie; "That's what happens when you're auld."

"Ah weel, take care o' yersell."

She stood away from the window and let the struggling dog go; it bounded away up the road.

John drew away but saw Kate waving and stopped until she reached the car.

"Have they found the boy yet? I know Alex was out looking."

"Naw," said Willie, "Nothing yet."

Her face clouded.

"Poor lad, poor Susan."

"Does Kate have children?" asked John as they pulled away.

"Naw," said Willie, "they say she wants children, but Colin needs her in the business, so they're stuck. That's the way it is nowadays; it's called family planning. She'll be too old if she waits much longer."

"I like her," said John.

"Most people do, she's a fine lass, as genuine as they come."

"What's the business?"

"Gainslaw Globes"

"What on earth is that; a souvenir shop?"

"No, it's a little plastics company on the industrial estate at Gainslaw. Her husband Colin runs it; she does all the paperwork, I think they employ, what, five people, something like that."

"What on earth is a plastics company doing here and with a name like Gainslaw Globes?"

"Ye ken the plastic floats for the nets, ball things, globes, ye see, they used to make them. They make one or two other bits and pieces, I think. She did tell me what, but I can't remember what they are now."

"Do they make money?"

"Naw, they don't seem to. They seem to stagger from crisis to crisis. Her husband's fither set it up, but he died a few years back and Colin took it over. He's a canny lad, works all the hours God sends, but I don't think he knows what he's doing."

"Sounds wrong," said John, "They're miles from the markets, I don't see how they can compete, and they're not big enough."

You could help them out, couldn't you, son?' said Willie.

'Of course,' replied John offhandedly, thinking his father was simply making a comment. But Willie intended more than that.

'You'll ring her when we get home, eh?' he insisted, and John agreed to do so. When he rang, he heard an answer machine promising that they would call him back.

Willie was tired when they arrived back at Braeshiel and went to bed for a few hours. This proved his last trip up the hill. He went out only once more, down to the harbour for a few minutes to see the new winch that Alex had had fitted. When he next left home he would not return.

The ambulance took him to The Bield where he lay in bed for ten days looking, out of the window at the broad blue sea, and talking, when he had breath, to his visitors. It is bad enough that he has to die and suffer its attendant indignities, so we will not stand and gawp any longer at our old friend.

We have the right to two incidents only during those

last days. One day he was surprised and delighted when Marion walked in. They embraced each other and cried and said nothing that if written down would convey any significance. But it carried the love they shared and bore the hopes the one could not reveal to the other.

Margaret visited every day, but one evening Willie waited until she had gone then said to John.

"I've left the house to Helen; you mustn't let Margaret take it from her. She'll be disappointed, I know, but she'll get over it. It's in the will."

This was the first time Willie had admitted to John that he was dying; it proved the only time. On the last day of May, with the sun uncertain in the sky, the sea restless among the rocks, and a low mist blurring the horizon, Willie Swansen slipped anchor and set sail where we may not follow. At least, not yet.

CHAPTER TWELVE

Willie left no elaborate instructions for his funeral, just that he wanted it old style and to be laid beside his wife Jane in the kirkyard at Beanston. (There is no burial ground in Birsett). Old style is a simple service in the house followed by a short committal at the graveside. The undertaker, Gabriel Orkney brought him back to Braeshiel for the last time and placed the coffin in the room Willie had slept in for thirty years.

First thing on Wednesday, the appointed day, the furniture in the sitting room at Braeshiel was removed or pushed against the wall and its place taken by plastic chairs carried down from the village hall by Alex, and his two crew members, Dod and Batman. At quarter to eleven, friends and families shuffled solemnly into the room and occupied the chairs. Margaret and Roddam sat in the front row with John: their daughter Abigail had promised to come but had not yet arrived. Helen and Alex brought David and George but left the other children with their aunt. Mr Scott found a chair beside the door along with Jimmy Possum and Willie's two dominoes companions, Duncan and Sandy; relatives and friends filled the remaining spaces. Others just stood in the doorway.

Although John had not invited them (he had left it to Helen to ring Marion) he hoped that his own family, or at least Marion and Rebecca, would turn up. He wanted them to be there, but they had not arrived by the time the Parish Minister, Mr Mordun, pushed his way through the throng to start the service. He placed himself with his back to the fireplace facing the congregation. He drew the words from the service book, except for a few of his own in praise of William (as he called him) and an informal prayer in which William was mentioned twice and the family once.

The undertaker's men then carried the coffin from the bedroom along the short path and loaded it into the hearse waiting on the brae. At the gate, a group of men, dressed in dark suits, watched this manoeuvre; amongst them Dod and Batman off the Silver Cord, the skipper of The Boy Peter, Dave Pallin, and Del and Kit off the Aurora. Marvin, the other member of the Aurora's crew, had said he would be there but had not yet arrived. The undertaker waited for the company to spill out of the house and to find seats in cars,

"You come wi' me." "Naw, I'm full up, Dod'll tak ye." "There's a bus at the top of the hill, for those that don't have transport," announced Roddam, and the locals wondered where the "hill" was. Eventually the confusion cleared and the cortege moved off along the A1 to Beanston.

At the kirkyard a large crowd had gathered; men mostly, (not long ago it would have been only men). They attended not only from Birsett, Hecklescar and local villages, but from Port Seton on the Firth of Forth, from Anstruther, Pittenweem and St. Monans in the East Neuk of Fife, from Peterhead and Fraserburgh in the North East and from Gamrie, Buckie and Findochty along the Moray Firth; old fishing friends from many years back; Englishmen too, from Seahouses and North Shields in Northumberland. A party had travelled from Mallaig, the old herring port way, way up by Fort William in the Highlands.

The good folk of Beanston that built the Church of Dionysius in the 12th century clearly believed that their beloved dead should be kept close for the kirkyard clusters round the walls of the now ruined church. The new kirk, however, built in more civilised times, turns its back on the kirkyard, soaring up through a screening belt of trees as if it were trying to shake off its erstwhile parishioners.

The squat old kirk welcomes us on this sad day. The kirkyard is a contented honest place, quite unashamed of what it is. It lies peacefully on the banks of the river from where it looks over to the wooded bank rising up to the baronial pile of Beanston Castle. The surrounding trees on this sunny day in early June are decked in their loveliest green dappled with drifts of may blossom, strands of yellow broom and mauve bouquets of rhododendron. The grass is carpeted with daisies and, in the hedge bottoms, buttercups echo the sun's cheerfulness.

The minister and the undertaker walk slowly out of the shadow of the short tree-lined avenue that leads from the road to the kirkyard. The coffin follows, borne aloft by six of Gabriel's men drafted from their joinery duties for the occasion. The mourners follow: family first, close behind the coffin, Margaret holding the hand of Roddam, then Helen and Alex with David and George uncomfortable in their best shirts and breeks (learning this solemn duty which they, if they continue to live in Birsett, will continue over the years until, eventually, in their turn they will lead the procession). Then John, bereft of his family and feeling it, walking beside the hobbling Mr Scott. This group walks in silence. Other mourners, in a murmuring black tide, spread across the green grass and lap around the grey headstones to where Jane lies and now makes room for her husband.

The coffin is placed on poles over the dug grave, and the solemnity of the occasion at last silences the crowd. Gabriel quietly calls out the cord numbers, "Number One"; John moves forward to the head of the grave and takes the cord; "Number Two" and Margaret glimpses at the card she holds in her hand and moves forward (Willie would not have approved of this; this is men's work); "Number Three" should be Robert, John's son, but Alex steps forward, then David, then a couple of cousins, then old Mr Scott, and finally Jimmy Possum. The coffin is lowered, the cord-holders step back and Mr Mordun takes his place at the head of the grave and opens his book.

Then a commotion at the back of the crowd: two people running out of the shadows; a man and woman; a young, slim, beautiful woman in purple top and black trousers, a flabby forty-year-old man in jeans with a yellow shirt barely covered by a denim jacket. Abigail and friend! Mr Mordun waits as they make their way to the front. But as they move through the assemblage, John catches sight of another group standing a little off the back of the crowd; sedate, smart, silent: a tall slim young man, a shorter younger girl, and .... and Marion; his children and his wife. He puts up his hand, catches Marion's eye and waves them forward. They look at each other then slowly they walk towards him. The crowd catches the drama and lets them pass through until they are at his side. Rebecca finds her father's hand and grasps it. Marion stands by his side. He senses the presence of his son behind him. Instinctively he feels that something that had been lost has been found.

This is the second miracle accomplished by Willie through his suffering. The first was his son's homecoming.

Mr Scott, as we have heard, has always disliked speaking in public and, since his retirement from the ministry many years ago has successfully avoided taking any part in any church service. But this day he has determined to do something for his old friend. For days he has worked on a short tribute to Willie and has asked for and received Mr Mordun's consent to read it out at the graveside.

"I am the resurrection and the life...." Mr Mordun announces and continues until he scatters the crumbs of earth into the open grave.

"Forasmuch as it has pleased Almighty God to take unto himself the soul of our dear brother here departed, we therefore commit his body to the ground, earth to earth, ashes to ashes, dust to dust, in sure and certain hope…"

Once he has pronounced the words, he stops and nods to Mr Scott. The old minister takes a pace or two forwards; a sheet of paper trembles in his hand; he coughs nervously and starts.

"I want to pay tribute to my friend Willie Swansen… for…he, I mean, I, have…known."

Here he stops; the paper in his hands shakes so much he cannot make it out. His lips tremble. He tries again but he cannot make sense of what he has written; he is going to fail his friend. He turns in despair to John and hands him the paper.

"Read it for me, John, if you will."

John takes the paper and reads it.

"It is normal on occasions like these to talk about a man's accomplishments. But we cannot claim for Willie that he changed society, nor that he leaves some creative work of genius, nor that he made a fortune, nor that he carried out some notable public work. There will be no page in history that bears his name, nor any plaque that points out where he was born or where he lived. For Willie Swansen was a not a politician, a poet, a tycoon, nor a public servant. He was a fisherman, an ordinary man living an ordinary life in an ordinary way. He was a generous good man, but his generosity did not consist of spectacular acts of charity nor of grand public expressions of beneficence. It was made up of "that best portion of a good man's life, his little, nameless, unremembered acts of kindness and of love".

"Willie wasn't perfect and most of us could, if we wanted, remember times when he exasperated us with his obstinacy and argumentativeness. But he was what I would call an entire man. He was, I like to think, what God had in mind when he made man. (What he had in mind when he made women, I have never fathomed!)" A ripple of laughter ran through the crowd and Mr Scott glanced nervously at Margaret and Abigail and smiled. "Willie took from this world no more than he needed and gave back much more than he could afford. He was good in the details of life - a good husband, a good father, a good grandfather, a good uncle and a good grand uncle, a good skipper, a good counsellor and a good, good friend. Goodness with him was not an attribute, or an accomplishment; it was what the man was made of."

"Nowadays, it is fashionable to pretend that no great tragedy happens when someone dies. We are told not to mourn the loss, but to celebrate the life. I am sure that is a worthy sentiment, but I mourn Willie's passing; for me it is a calamity; what I have lost cannot be replaced; I know of no one like him. He is one of a rare breed; a man who, in all circumstances of life lived well, who was always what we expected him to be. God keep you, Willie Swansen."

John finished reading and handed the paper back to Mr Scott who nodded his thanks. For a moment the whole crowd stood silent in that sunlit, quiet, green place. This natural sequence of respect was broken by a movement amongst the family group; Abigail wafted to the open grave and threw into it a single red rose in a plastic wrapping. ("It's what we do in Edinburgh," explained Margaret to her cousins later.) I'm sure Abigail meant well.

Then Mr Mordun pronounced the blessing and the undertaker's men lifted the tray of family flowers and placed it over the grave. Del came forward and shook hands with John, Robert and Roddam, and kissed Margaret, Rebecca and Marion. Kit followed, then others, including John's banker friend, JP Marwick, who had passed the time of day with John's father over the years and had come to pay his respects. Cecil from Surrey, too; he whose life is caring for his sick wife, took

John's hand and asked to be excused from the reception. By the time the sympathisers had finished the crowd had dispersed and the small family party drifted out of the kirkyard leaving it to the breeze, the birds and those who have a right to be there.

And I reckon that, if you have to wait somewhere for the last trump and the stars cannot accommodate you, you could do a lot worse than Beanston kirkyard.

(If, my materialistic friend, you find this sentimental, do not fear; no doubt you will attract to yourself others of like mind. Who knows; if you leave instructions, they will consent to dump you in any old hole without any ceremony at all?)

The reception would not be held at Braeshiel where Willie would have wanted it. It could not accommodate those who had travelled a distance to take refreshment, so John had arranged to welcome Willie's friends at the Red Bull in Beanston.

CHAPTER THIRTEEN

The reception at the Red Bull brought everyone back to earth. At first people sought out John and Margaret to express sympathy and recount their memories of Willie, but slowly the conversation turned to mundane matters such as failing health, the falling school roll at Birsett, the lives and follies of neighbours and the whereabouts of little Johnny Armstrong. Alex, Del and other fishermen stood round the door talking fish, boats, prices and the pig ignorance of the Fisheries Minister.

Marion, Robert and Rebecca shared a cup of coffee and a sandwich with John but left within half an hour to make their long way back to York. John wanted them to stay but found their presence disconcerting. Rebecca tried to inveigle her mother and father into conversation but did not succeed. They were too conscious of their separation to appear to be together. Margaret scarcely spoke to Marion and patronised Rebecca. Roddam sought out the minister and complimented him on the service,

After they left, Abigail, prompted by her mother, introduced her man friend as Jude. He must, John thought, be almost as old as I am.

"What is it you do?" John asked Jude by way of opening a conversation.

"Is that important?" said Jude, pleasantly, in his anglicised Edinburgh accent.

"Pardon?" said John, not sure he had heard correctly.

"Is it important what I do?"

"Well, no," said John, "not if you don't want to tell me."

"I'm a painter, as in pictures rather than 'and decorator', but I do some work at the University, I lecture on the Philosophy of Art and lead a tutorial. That's how I met Abigail. Is that what you wanted to know?"

"Yes, thank you," said John

"And you," said Jude, "are something big in business, I hear; what is it, 'Managing Director' (he pronounced it rather than spoke it) "and divorced."

His pushiness irritated John.

"Not divorced, separated."

"Me too, several times," laughed Jude, "I even tried marriage once, when I was young and foolish. Better open-ended, I think, if you pardon the expression."

"And Abigail?" threw out John, deciding this was a verbal contest and as an uncle he had an interest.

"Nothing serious," laughed Jude again, "Just good sexual buddies."

He's playing games, thought John.

"Are you deliberately trying to shock me?" John asked bluntly.

"Are you shocked?" asked Jude looking John in the eye and smiling expressionlessly.

Abigail butted in to save John from having to answer. Abigail took in the scene and understood what had been happening.

"Judy, you've been playing games again," she chaffed. "Uncle John, you'll need to forgive him. He has this theory that if you don't assault people when you first meet them, you never get to know them. The first words he said to me were, "Are you a virgin?""

The pair then left John to look for entertainment elsewhere, and found it by holding court in the bar, impressing the younger folk with orders for exotic drinks the barman had never heard of. For the first half-hour they preserved a decent sobriety but steadily the noise and turbulence increased until the older people began to look disapprovingly in their direction. Eventually Margaret sent Roddam over to bring their daughter to heel but she rebuffed her father for being stuffy.

"Granddad Willie knew how to enjoy himself; he wouldn't mind," she said. Roddam retreated; Jude aimed comments at his back he did not pick up.

Helen had allowed David and George to attend the reception and they made the most of it. They helped themselves freely to the sausage rolls, sandwiches and coke; anything stronger was off limits (David, the oldest, you'll recall, is barely seventeen).

After a while Helen came up and asked John if he'd seen David; he had disappeared. John set out in search of him and found him with Abigail and Jude in the bar. David was sipping a drink from a clouded bottle. When Jude saw John, he snatched the bottle from David's hand and held it in his own.

"What's that you're drinking?" John asked David.

"It's not his; it's mine," answered Jude.

"Is it?" snapped John, "In which case tell me what it is?"

"It's a breezer," said Abigail, "Everyone drinks them."

"David doesn't," said John. "He's under age."

"Is he really?" said Jude in mock surprise, "You naughty

boy!"

Abigail smirked and two other girls sniggered.

"Your mother is looking for you," said John. David, abashed, rose and went with him. A wave of laughter followed them. Alex was levered away from the fishing party to drive David home in disgrace; George went with him.

Kate Strothers came up to thank John for the reception and to tell him she would need to get back to the factory. Her eyes filled with tears as she talked about Willie.

"I'll miss him," she said, "He wasn't anything like as old as his age." She smiled at her own unconscious wit and her smile again surprised John with its warmth and simplicity.

"I'm sorry we haven't been in touch about the factory," she said, "It's not that we wouldn't like your help. We didn't want to bother you with your father being so ill. I expect you'll be going back south now. We've missed our chance."

"No, no," said John, "Not yet, there are things to do, I'll be around for a couple of weeks yet. Ring me to-morrow and we'll fix up a meeting."

"Are you sure? There's nothing much we can do for you. It would help us, but…."

"No, no, I want to come, it'll keep my hand in. Give me a ring – at Braeshiel."

The guest mourners departed until only the family, Mr Scott, Del and an unsteady Marvin were left. Each leaving guest took away a piece of Willie. For a few hours he had been held together by the sympathy of his friends; now he was dispersing in wisps of memories to Port Seton, the Moray Coast, to Mallaig. It is not a bad fate for a fisherman, but it left behind a bleakness in the Red Bull so the small party there dispersed too. Del put Marvin in the Aurora's van and drove him home. Helen and Alex followed them along the road, taking Mr Scott with them. Then John, Margaret, Abigail and Jude were ferried back to Braeshiel by Roddam. Margaret had stopped speaking to Abigail; Roddam never spoke to Jude anyway.

Braeshiel felt cold without Willie so, although it was a warm day, John lit the fire in the sitting room and went off to make a cup of tea. The others waited in silence for him to return. Jude helped himself to the Financial Times from the magazine rack whilst Margaret prowled round the room examining ornaments. Abigail laid back on the settee, closed her eyes and affected sleep. Roddam busied himself with a small notebook and a pen as if he were doing some sort of calculation. Just at this moment they were more dysfunctional family than John's but at least they were dysfunctional together.

When they had drunk the tea and eaten the biscuits and said how pleased they were that such a large number of people had turned out for father, John walked to the bureau and produced the document they had all been waiting to see. It was not the will; that was still somewhere in the offices of Cockburn Heath, the solicitor in Hecklescar. (He hadn't lost it, he said, but he couldn't quite track it down; give him a couple of days and Mrs Somerville, his patient secretary, would find it.) The bureau document was an informal letter from Willie explaining what was in the will. John asked Jude to leave and he did so.

The letter contained little in the way of greetings or sentiment. It set out what Willie owned and what he wanted done with it. He had written it barely a month ago.

Willie reckoned he had about £15,000 in savings.

"Is that all?" exclaimed Abigail.

"He's been retired a long time, and his pension was very small." explained John.

"That doesn't include the house, of course," added Roddam

Willie had a life insurance policy for £5,000, to cover funeral expenses.

"That should be more than enough," commented Roddam.

Willie had then listed what of his possessions he thought might have value. They weren't many and they weren't worth much. There was a small collection of porcelain figurines that had belonged to Jane (she had once said she liked them and ever after she received one or two from the family for her birthday): he would like Margaret to have those. There was a gold pocket watch and a chain, a present from Jane: he left that to John. He owned a painting of The Mary and Jean, his father's boat, painted by a local fisherman. He didn't think it would be worth much: would Roddam like it for his office? Roddam accepted it with good grace but it never graced his walls. There were a couple of old local history books, Thompson's "Prior's Cross: Priory and Village", and Scott's "History of Gainslaw" that John could have if he wanted them. To Abigail he left his only extravagance: the eternity ring he had given Jane on their fortieth wedding anniversary, in gold, diamonds and rubies. It would become hers on the day she married. (What an agony had gone into this bequest. In his heart he had promised it to Louise but for one last time he reached out to his prodigal granddaughter.) The rest of his possessions were to be disposed of as John and Margaret thought fit.

"Does that include the house?" interrupted Roddam, not realising John hadn't finished.

"No," said John, without reading the letter, "The contents, but not the house. He has left the house to Helen."

"What?!" exclaimed Roddam,

"Is that what is says?" asked Margaret from the edge of her seat.

"Yes," said John, "I'll read it, "Please forgive me, John, Margaret, but I want Helen to have the house. You both have your own houses, Helen doesn't, and she has been very good to me. I don't know what I would have done without her. I hope you understand."

"What is this you're reading?" puffed Roddam, "Is it the official will?"

"No," said John, "The will is with Heath, the local solicitor; he's looking it out; we'll probably get it to-morrow."

"Then I think we need to wait to see what that says," said Roddam tightly, "No point in getting into dispute before we need to."

"What dispute?" said John; "You've heard what he said."

"He may have been unduly influenced," snapped Roddam. "We'll need to see the will."

"You will see the will," John spat out "as often as you like. I'll get you a copy. But it will make no difference. Father told me himself that he wanted Helen to have the house, and I will see she gets it."

"His immediate family have rights…."

"It really is a disappointment," Margaret broke in trying to calm the storm, "Abigail had her heart set on it."

"What on earth does Abigail want it for?" cried John, staring at Abigail. Abigail brazenly held his gaze.

"We had thought dad would leave it to both of us, to you and me. We were then prepared to buy out your half and make it into a holiday house. We could have come down here at weekends and for holidays. Abigail could have had it in the summer and brought her friends."

"The best laid plans…." said John flatly, "Dad has given it to Helen."

"It's no use to her anyway," put in Abigail. "It's not big enough; there's only two bedrooms, not counting the box room. They have four bedrooms in the council house and David said, even then he can't have a room of his own. So, what they are going to do with a two-bedroom house I don't know."

"I would think," said John in exasperation, "that he had in mind what he and mam did when the family grew up. They lived in the Old Manse until we left home then they moved down here. I'm sure he thought that Helen and Alex would do the same."

"She's schemed for this," said Margaret bitterly. "She didn't care for father at all, she was just after…."

"That's enough," snapped John as if he were in an unruly business meeting, "No more discussion. Helen gets the house. That's what dad wanted." He stood up and walked to the door.

"We'll see about that," said Margaret almost to herself; Roddam nodded his head vigorously.

John walked out, not sure where he was going; he just wanted to be away from his close relatives. He walked down the brae to the harbour and along the road that snaked along the foot of the cliffs. This road ends where a sheer rock face cuts off further progress and here John turned and walked back. As he walked, first the sound then the sight of the sea surging and sloshing amongst the rocks penetrated his mood and made him aware that the world is wider than disputes; wider than father and sister and brother-in-law; wider and more generous.

When he reached the harbour on his return journey Del, Kit and Marvin had arrived to prepare the boat for fishing. Birsett is a tidal harbour so for two hours either side of low tide the Aurora does not have sufficient water to enter or leave it. They had missed the morning tide due to Willie's funeral and would now use the long evening to haul and set their craves. If it did nothing else it would sober Marvin up.

"Good turnout for Willie," shouted Del, then, when he had John's attention, added, "Willie's left the house to Helen, I hear,"

Now Del had heard no such thing. He is fishing. But it let John know that the house is a matter for village as well as family, and the village thinks it ought to go to Helen. John felt angry at this interference but he concealed it.

"I haven't heard that," he shouted, "But when I do, I'll put a notice on the board."

Del laughed; John smiled weakly.

When he walked back into the room at Braeshiel, the family had obviously discussed tactics and had decided to humour John for the time being. Jude had returned to the house and they were making preparations to leave for Edinburgh.

"I'm sorry," said Margaret who only made strategic apologies, "We'll just all have to work together to see what we can do."

John decided to leave it at that. Shortly afterwards, after polite goodbyes and formal regrets, they drove away leaving John alone in Braeshiel.

Friends, if you would be a consolation to the bereaved, visit them on the evening of the funeral: it is a desolate time for them. For John, it was Helen who came down and warmed the room. Later Mr Scott arrived and stayed for supper with them both.

Before she went back to her family, John told Helen about the house. Helen feigned surprise and protested that it wasn't right but John suspected that she had anticipated that the house would be left to her. He wondered whether his father had mentioned it to her. To his relief he elicited no evidence that she would give it up easily. She could fight for the house with a clear conscience because she had gained it without deceit. She had looked after Willie because she believed it was right to do so. Virtue had been rewarded; as it should be - but seldom is.

CHAPTER FOURTEEN

John devoted most of the morning after the funeral at the table he had dedicated to work. By midday he had rung the solicitor, Cockburn Heath, about the will and had fixed up three appointments for the following two weeks. The solicitor promised to have the will ready for inspection by the following afternoon.

The three appointments were with Kate and Colin at Gainslaw Globes on Monday morning first, with Zack Mallinger a week on Wednesday at eleven in Leeds, and with Belinda Boyd the day after at one-thirty in London. (He would stay overnight in York on Wednesday and collect some more of his belongings from the flat). In preparation for the meetings he wrote briefing notes setting out the background, listing questions and subjects to be covered and "desired outcomes". You may not think that this is much for a man of John's calibre to accomplish in a morning, but it is enough to convince him he is still making things happen.

Seven weeks had elapsed since he lost his job, but he had not had time to brood on his misfortune, nor to feel the emptiness of days without work. His time had been employed in looking after his father; and his emotions filled with the pain of seeing him decline and die. John accepted all the consolations offered by friends; that his father was an old man; that we all have to die sometime; that it was good that he had been able to spend so much time with Willie lately; that Willie had lived a full and fulfilling life; that John had done the right thing by his father. Nevertheless, he felt his father's loss acutely; more acutely than he had anticipated. For within his natural distress lay that discovery that strikes many people in their fifties: that our parents walk between us and death and screen us from it. When they go, we see with some alarm that we walk towards it too.

This apprehension added to John's insecurity. He felt persecuted. It added up: the loss of his job, the break-up of his marriage, the death of his father and the conflict with Margaret were not separate events but a campaign against him. Not able to identify any one persecutor, his anger floated free and settled on anything and anyone that happened along. Helen ran into it first and had a trying afternoon helping to sort out Willie's things. What she wanted to throw out, John wanted to keep; what she thought might be kept, John thought useless. When she started to ask John about every item this irritated him even more. In the end she welcomed Louise when she arrived from school.

Louise had come to her own conclusions about Willie's disappearance, and these would surface from time to time over the next few months. For the moment she said nothing but attempted to adopt John as a replacement for her great uncle; he was, after all, in the same house, and, in her eyes, about the same age. John, in no frame of mind to indulge her, answered her chatter with grunts and monosyllables. Then she delved into the discard box and pulled out Willie's old slippers. John snapped at her and told her to put them back and not to touch anything more. Her lip quivered and her eyes filled with tears.

"Now ye've made the bairn greet with yer ill nature," said Helen, taking Louise in her arms. Then she put down what she had been doing and took Louise home. She didn't appear again that day. John was left alone and, for the moment, that suited him. He worked on into the evening, and for relaxation, read The Scotsman without taking anything in and attempted The Financial Times crossword without completing it. Then he went to bed and didn't sleep.

The next day he had Margaret and Roddam to cope with. Originally Margaret had planned to come for the weekend to help John with the disposal of their father's effects, but the dispute over the house had turned the visit into a trip to the solicitor to see the will. They arrived for a lunch they brought themselves; and ate it more or less in silence. John asked Margaret to look through the house to see if there were anything she thought they should keep, and in a great effort of charity, he also offered her anything she would like from the house that had not been included in the will.

Cockburn Heath had his first name visited on him by his father, who had set up the business in Hecklescar. This father admired Lord Cockburn, the Lord Advocate at the beginning of the nineteenth century, so decided to call his son after him in the hope that he might emulate the great man and rise to high office in the law profession. Cockburn had no such aspirations. True, he qualified as a lawyer and true, he went into the family firm, but that exhausted his ambition. Neither did he continue the dynasty for he remained unmarried. His interest lay in yachting and he spent more time pottering about on his boat in the harbour than in applying himself to land searches, wills, conveyancing, deeds, trusts and petty disputes in the County Court. He spent most weekends afloat, even in the winter, and several times clients had turned up for appointments only to find their solicitor still negotiating with the wind and water somewhere off St Abb's Head.

Tall, thin and stiff, he wasn't built for sailing; he looked as though a decent breeze would snap him at the waist. Now in his fifties, his hair still long and black dropped over his eyes when he bent forward at his desk. And bend forward he did, to within a few inches of the desk top, for he was short-sighted and could only read documents in comfort if he were uncomfortably close to the page. But he was a genial man and liked nothing better than to chat to his clients - particularly if they were able to discuss boats, harbours, sea, weather - or anything else of a nautical nature.

His offices occupied the first floor of an old Victorian building that dominated what passed for the Market Square of Hecklescar. It had been built by an old clipper captain who had decorated it on the outside with stone symbols of his occupation. Ropes snaked round the windows and under the eaves; a sea monster glowered over the gutter along the roof; two chunky looking masts served as pilasters either side of the door and between the two upstairs windows a carved clipper ship still sailed the China Seas.

Whilst the outer office gave the impression of being up to date, with computers, fax machines, and photocopier, Cockburn's office made no concession to modernity apart from a telephone, if you count a phone modern. It was a large room with a large fireplace placed between large wooden-doored cupboards and was lit by large curtainless windows. An old glass bulb hung in an old glass globe from an elaborate plaster rose in the middle of the ceiling; the ceiling had faded to a dirty cream and was soot-smudged where it overhung the fireplace. The paper that covered the walls must have been expensive when new, but now the red and gold flock had faded where many years of sun had bleached it; round the doors and light switch greasy fingers had converted it to dirty grey-brown. A threadbare faded Axminster carpet largely, but not completely, covered the floor. Cockburn's desk stood by the window, while a table surrounded by four old horsehair padded chairs occupied the inside corner of the room. The wall facing the window held an open bookcase and another, glass fronted, sulked against the window wall. Two old khaki-coloured filing cabinets completed the furnishings. Above the fireplace a large Montague Dawson print of the clipper Thermopylae reminded clients that this was once the old captain's drawing room - and Cockburn that he was wasting sailing time by sitting in his office.

But none of these furnishings made half so much impression on visitors as the general clutter of the place. Every horizontal surface had something piled on it; the desk, the table, the chairs, the bookcases, the mantelpiece, and, in the corners, the floor. There were legal papers, folders, files, document boxes, magazines, newspapers, wads, wallets, packets, bundles tied with grey ribbon, overlapping, flopping, falling. In fact, so comprehensive was the general confusion that if you could give the room a clever enough title you would have a fair chance of winning the Turner Prize.

"Do not concern yourselves with the apparent chaos," said Cockburn, in a deep purring voice, as he came to greet them. "I know where everything is. I can lay my hands on anything I need within two minutes." He beamed and ushered them to the table with the chairs, cleared the contents of the chairs onto the floor under the table and invited them to sit down. Then, like an attentive waiter, he cleared a space in front of each of them, by adding its contents to the pile already occupying the centre of the table.

"Now then," he said, when he had finished his excavations. "What can I do for you?"

"We're here to see my father's will."

"Ah, yes," said Cockburn, glancing nervously towards his cluttered desk, "The last will and testament of William John Swansen. I believe Mrs Somerville has tracked it down." He stood up, walked to the door, opened it and bellowed into the space beyond it.

"Mrs Somerville," he shouted, "The Swansen papers please." A distant voice from along the corridor shouted back. Cockburn, looking guilty, shut the door and made for his desk in a kind of slow, stiff lope.

"It seems," he explained, "That she has put them on my desk. Efficiency, that's what it is, efficiency." He scrabbled among the papers on his desk, muttering "efficiency" which, as his hunt progressed, became less distinct until it descended into a low rumble. Then he grabbed a bundle, let out a cry of triumph and brought it to the table.

"Efficiency," he glowed, "Less than two minutes, I think."

("And seven days," said John to himself.)

"Now then," said Cockburn, trying to look grave. "Let us see what it says."

He then started to read it in a kind of running summary.

"...last will and etc. etc. of William......Swansen... of Braeshiel, etc. etc. in the County of dum-de-dum-de-dum, and being of sound etc. etc. I appoint.... executor. (that's me).... dum-de-dum...I hereby will and be.... dum-de-dum-de dum..."

"Look," snapped Roddam, "we want to hear it.... all."

"Ah, sorry," said Cockburn, pleasantly, "legal gobbledegook; you don't want to hear all of that, we just put that in to impress the client and raise the fee." He laughed at his own wit. Roddam frowned.

"Here's the nub: 'I leave my estate jointly to my son John William Swansen, of, de-dum..' (Roddam glowered at him)'......York, and Margaret Jane Craig, of, 14, Merchiston Heights, Morningside, Edinburgh EH10 2DA' (he read this out in full even to the post code with one eye on Roddam) 'except those items and amounts which I will specify in other instructions under my name.'

"What does it say about the house?" snapped Roddam.

'I leave my house, Braeshiel, Birsett, in the County of Berwickshire, to Helen Paulin, my daughter, of 21 Upper Birsett, Birsett, Hecklescar, ………'

"What did you say?" demanded Roddam

"I leave…."

"Not that, who does it say?"

"Helen Paulin!"

Read on, read on, who, who?"

"Helen Paulin, my daughter…"

"My daughter! My daughter! Helen isn't his daughter, is she?"

John anxious to hear the name Helen, had missed the mistake; as had Margaret.

"It's a mistake," said John.

"No, no…. we're getting at it now," said Roddam, excitedly.

"Not at all," snapped John, "It's a clear mistake – it's Helen's name and Helen's Address. It's a mistake."

John became aware that Cockburn Heath was watching this spat as it if were no concern of his. John explained the problem to him.

"A mistake, obviously," Cockburn said, "It doesn't affect the will."

"Oh, doesn't it?" put in Margaret fearing her husband might be outnumbered. "Helen isn't his daughter."

"It's a mistake," fumed John, "a mistake. He clearly means Helen."

"It's not clear at all," rasped Roddam. "If that's a mistake, what else is a mistake? The will is invalid."

"Oh, I don't think so," purred Cockburn in an attempt to quieten the party, "A typing error doesn't invalidate a will."

"We'll see about that. I'd like a copy please. I want to

take it up with Rennie Murray in Edinburgh. Roddam intended this to impress Cockburn; Rennie Murray are well known, respectable, intimidating. Cockburn showed no sign of intimidation. If they had owned an ocean racing yacht he would have been impressed, but they were criminal and commercial; he knew more about petty wills than they did.

"You can certainly have a copy, but Rennie Murray will charge you the entire estate just for reading it. I think we should sort it out between us. I'll speak to Mrs Somerville and see if she can throw any light on it. She'll know the parties involved."

Without waiting for Roddam to reply, he went to the door and bellowed down the corridor. In a few moments Mrs Somerville arrived. She was a small, neat, busy woman in her early sixties, with gimlet eyes, sharp nose and short straight grey hair. If you had wanted someone to play the part of Churchill's secretary in The Second World War you couldn't have chosen better. She looked the sort of woman who didn't make mistakes.

While Roddam and Margaret glowered at her and John leaned back in his chair and stared at the ceiling, Cockburn explained the problem to Mrs Somerville, verbally mincing round his secretary rather like a mongoose tackling a cobra. Mrs Somerville listened intently.

"What date is the will?" she demanded.

Under Mrs Somerville's gaze Cockburn leaned forward and searched for the date for a few moments. Then his nerve failed him and he handed the document to his secretary.

"Five years ago, in January," she announced, then froze her face as she searched her memory banks. "I was in Australia, visiting Raymond, my son; you brought in a temp from one of those Edinburgh agencies; I recommended Gladys Horsburgh, if you remember, but you brought in a temp." With one bound she was free, and Cockburn tied up and delivered for sentencing.

"Ah," he said, "Was that when it was?"

"Yes," said Mrs Somerville, "I know fine Helen Paulin is not Willie's daughter. It's a mistake." Here she looked at John and Margaret.

"I've known you all since you were bairns."

Margaret didn't want to be known by Mrs Somerville since she was a bairn and refused to look at the woman.

"We wish to reserve our position." she said grandly, and stood up. Roddam also stood up.

"It is probable," said Mrs Somerville, "that the will was altered then. I'll see if I can find the notes Mr Heath would make when taking instructions. As you see (she glanced round the room) we throw nothing out. Sometimes that comes in useful."

"We still want a copy," demanded Roddam of Cockburn.

"You shall have a copy," said Mrs Somerville without reference to her boss, "Follow me please. Do you want a copy, John?"

John nodded. Roddam and Margaret followed Mrs Somerville along the corridor. Cockburn looked at John, shrugged his shoulders and smiled.

"Very efficient, Mrs Somerville." he stated, then, after a second or two, added, "The banker with the holiday house down the brae is a friend of yours, isn't he? He has a Bavaria 44. Lovely boat."

CHAPTER FIFTEEN

Around this time John began to think more about Marion that he had done for years. This was to be expected for we have all noticed that when things go badly for a man at work he looks to his home for comfort.

John didn't have a home; he had sacrificed it to his job. But he still had a wife, or, as we have seen, he believed he still had a wife. But did he? We need to know and have been remiss in not paying attention to Marion. We have been as careless as John, treating her as if she were merely pattern on the wallpaper. We hardly know anything about her and should now seek to make her closer acquaintance. It will not be a disagreeable task; she is an attractive and interesting woman.

Marion had never been a beauty in the Abigail sense of the word. She is dark-haired, small and neat but has now put on a little too much weight to be considered chic. Originally, John had been attracted to Marion the same way he had recently been attracted to Kate Strothers - her smile. When Marion first smiled at him, he thought her hazel eyes were the loveliest he had ever seen. They have darkened with the years but they still reflect the pleasant personality that lies behind them. For Marion is blessed with that happy disposition that takes the good in life and fights the bad instead of complaining about it. But that has not made her a doormat. She served early warning on John when, on their third date, he turned up late. When he arrived at the appointed place she had gone and only contrite apologies and persistent attention persuaded her to give him another chance. Her other fault we already know about - she is forthright. This endeared her to Willie who shared the same trait and liked nothing better than to bait her. "Are poor people feckless (Willie) or luckless (Marion)?" provided a bone they often chewed on. They went at it hammer and tongs but they both knew the rules and arguments generally ended in laughter at their mutually intransigent positions. Their encounters had nurtured their friendship.

A relatively trivial incident convinced Marion to call a halt to her exploitation by John, for that is how she had come to see it. She had borne years of disruption and inconvenience playing second, then third, then no fiddle at all to the demands of her husband's job. What started with delayed homecomings and cold meals, grew into cancelled holidays, postponed outings and discourtesy to visitors, and matured into broken promises, arrogant denial and disappearances without explanation. He had started stalking out of the room whenever Marion attempted to rein him in or to talk about their deteriorating friendship.

Marion, as we have said, tended to push on in life rather than moan. In response to John's increasing indifference she had developed a life of her own. This centred on her growing family but soon widened to other interests. She made herself a good neighbour for, unlike many in the executive housing John had chosen, she had no social pretensions and befriended anyone who wanted to be a friend. She had continued to go to church although John increasingly found it inconvenient. It had been the church at Clydebank that had brought them together. John had been brought up in the faith and had attended church when he went to work in the west. He had first spotted Marion in McLelland Electronics' factory working as a secretary to the Production Director, but was pleasantly surprised to find her seated not far from him in church on Sunday. Their love had grown from there. Now he had other occupations on Sunday morning. He either went to the factory or worked at home. Marion attended on her own with the children. She could not go regularly to any midweek meetings because of John's irregular hours, but she helped with special events, took her turn on the flower rota, and stood in when she could for the crèche on Sunday morning. She also took on the unofficial duty of making sure that anyone visiting for the first time was spoken to and made welcome; a stranger to the city welcoming strangers. Later on, when the children were at school all day, she delivered meals on wheels and made friends with her fellow 'wheels' and with some of the old people that benefited from them.

Through her church, her charity and her general sociability she had gathered a comfortable circle of friends. Once a week she and Fiona, Mack's wife, met for a cup of coffee, one week at Fiona's, the other at Poppleton. Even when Fiona took a part-time job at the school they still met and helped each other through the shoals and reefs of family life. Marion also liked books, and read them whenever time allowed, light fiction mainly, but sometimes she'd try something stronger, like George Mackay Brown, Longitude or the Bronte novels.

But better than this list of doings and interests one incident from their early marriage demonstrates what Marion is. Jane, John's mother had been visiting them and they had taken her to a variety show at the King's Theatre. They came out of the theatre just after ten and walked to their car parked in a street not far away. They were about to drive off when a lad of, perhaps seventeen, came lurching past in a sort of staggering run. His jacket and trousers were dirty and torn, his shirt covered in the blood that oozed from his mouth. They could hear close-by the cries and commotion of a gang of youths intent on violence. The running lad collapsed in a pile on the pavement then frantically tried to get to his feet.

John's instincts were to drive away as fast as possible. But Marion stopped him.

"He needs help." she said

"He's drunk," said John, "and that's a gang after him. We'd better get out of here."

"He's hurt and they'll kill him," she cried already half out of the car.

She ran to the youth, then dragged and pushed him into the car. John drove away as fast as he could. The gang spilled round the corner of the street as he drove off. Although injured, the lad in the back seat refused to be taken to hospital or to report to the police; he would find his own remedy when he could. They dropped him off at the door of a tower block in Townhead.

You can see then what Marion is made of. Whether she drew this compassion from her father, I don't know. (He was one of the old trade unionists, more passionately attached than politically attuned). Her sympathy went deep and never varied. John, on the other hand, as he rose through the ranks, lost touch with his roots. By the time he had settled into an executive chair his interest in working people had refocused to a general and (slightly suspicious) benevolence.

Marion and John's paths diverged. John retreated into the narrow world of Pinkerton and Loyalty, Marion ventured into a wider world of family, friends, fiction and society. They were, as it were, walking along parallel paths with a hedge between, keeping each other in sight, glimpsing each other in the gateways. For a long time, Marion believed, believed and hoped, that soon the hedge would end and the paths re-merge.

When it did not happen of itself, she decided to force it. If she took a stand, she thought, a really firm stand, she could call John back. She picked her ground carefully: Parent's Night at Rebecca's school; the night when parents talk to teachers about their child's progress. Rebecca had been struggling for a while, particularly with her maths, and Marion feared that she might not gain the 'A' levels she needed for her university course. Marion told John she wanted him to attend. He refused. She insisted. He objected. She said that she had had enough of trying to bring up the children on her own. He said he couldn't be expected to do everything; he said (as he had often said) that he bankrolled everything. (How she hated the phrase.) She said that if he didn't come to Parent's Night she would walk out; she had had enough. He said, (and remember now he is a Managing Director, used to deference, not used to accommodation) that he would try to make it. Marion had said that wasn't good enough - he had to be there. He repeated that he would try to make it. Marion replied that that wasn't good enough - he must be there. He refused to promise. The day, the time arrived. She waited. He didn't turn up. She went on her own. He didn't follow. When he came home that night, he found a note. She had gone and Rebecca had gone with her.

That Marion grieved scarcely needs saying, and she had the added burden of Rebecca's distress. Rebecca didn't want to leave and could see no reason for leaving; it was just the latest silly row. She didn't mind her father not going to Parent's Night; she didn't want to be the reason for the split. But her mother would not be persuaded. Marion had convinced herself she must make a stand. But what comfort are convictions when you have made your daughter cry.

Marion had thought that John would be jolted out of his apathy and make an attempt to recover what he had lost. But John felt no such pangs. At the time he welcomed the relief from the tension between job and home, particularly a home that no longer offered him the relaxation to which he felt entitled. This added hurt to Marion's injury as she discovered how little John valued the home she had created.

She had had no grand strategy when she planned her stand. She had gambled on one throw and she had lost. She did not know what to do next. In character, she went straight forward. She negotiated a settlement with a surprisingly distant John that gave her the house and a decent allowance, she found a job and started out on a new life. Her friends, particularly Fiona, had been uncritical and supportive and now, eight months on, her new life, her new independent, uncomplicated life had taken the edge off her pain. A collection of activities now filled her days; activities largely devoid of substance. Yet something might be made of it, if only John would go away. But he kept coming back looking for the mother in her. If only he had not lost his job, if only he had gone to the Far East, if only he would go, disappear, obliterate himself from her life, she could then accept that their marriage had come to an end.

But Rebecca would not accept the demise of her family, and John intended visiting her when he came to see his temporary - and utterly inferior, counsellor, Zack Mallinger.

CHAPTER SIXTEEN

Before Zack Mallinger next week John has Gainslaw Globes this week. The company plied its trade on a unit in Gainslaw Industrial Estate and John could tell, before he entered, that someone cared for it. The car park looked clean and clear of the debris that typically litters such estates. A pot of flowers either side of the door brightened the entrance. The small reception area proved equally bright and bore on its walls the framed achievements of the workforce, both individual and corporate. Among them, John saw that Kate had taken several courses in software applications and that the company was certificated for ISO, the quality standard. He found this encouraging; the externals, at least, were in good condition. He rang the bell and signed the book. Kate arrived immediately and took him into the office.

As he stepped inside, the office assaulted him. Its walls screamed at him in an astonishing shade of yellow. Motivational posters shrieked from every wall. "Go for it" yelled one; another cried, "You can do it"; yet another, this one with a climber almost at the top of a mountain peak, "Achievement is the next step".

"It's Colin's idea," sighed Kate when she noticed that John had noticed. "Yellow is inspirational."

Kate apologised for the size and untidiness of the office,

but the office looked neat and tidy apart from an area at its far end. There, a desk littered with papers, folders, files and plastic parts rose from a jungle of boxes, bags, directories, manuals, binders, tools, and other flotsam that had failed to find a place on the desk or had fallen off it. This, Kate explained, was Colin's patch.

Kate sat John down at a table in the middle of the office and brought him a cup of coffee. Referring occasionally to a loose-leaf binder she told him about their little enterprise. When John attempted to make notes, Kate told him that she had written a summary that he could take away with him. As she talked, she glanced from time to time at the door as if embarrassed by the absence of her husband. She assured John that Colin would be along shortly.

After about half-an-hour Colin bounced in, looking uncomfortable in a suit that, John suspected, Kate had persuaded him to wear it in honour of their visitor. He was mid height, wiry, and though he claimed to be younger than Kate, looked much older. Drooping shoulders, greying moustache, balding hair, and a drawn face portrayed a tired and worn-out man. The most striking thing about him were his eyes. No doubt when Colin looked in the mirror, he thought he saw drive and determination; John saw stress, or panic. Kate noted John's reaction and felt impelled to say something by way of explanation.

"Colin had one of his poor nights last night." she half-laughed. He half-smiled.

Colin gabbled the explanation that they had an order due for despatch on Tuesday, tomorrow, and it wasn't ready. It could only run on one machine, the NB150, and that had broken down in the middle of last week and was out of production for two days. He had worked the weekend in an endeavour to meet the delivery date and had finished his shift at seven this morning. He had had a couple of hours in his bed before turning up to meet John.

"Will you make the delivery?" asked John.

Colin deliberately tapped the wooden table in front of him. "Yes, of course; if you must you will" he said. John hadn't noticed that slogan on the wall but was sure it would be there somewhere.

"Do you set the machines?" said John

"Oh, no," said Colin, "I'm the Managing Director." He said it with an attempt at humour, but it held an edge that prevented it being funny. John saw Kate put her hand gently and reassuringly on his knee when he said it. He didn't draw his leg away, but John noticed that he stiffened against her touch.

"Colin sets the machines out of hours," explained Kate, "we have two setters on day shift."

That led them into a general description of the business. The company employed eight people: Colin and Kate, two setters, and four operators who did any assembly that needed doing. In addition, there were two or three people that they could call on if orders demanded it, but that wasn't a problem at the moment. Sales were low. Two major orders had been cancelled, one in November, the other in February. In the latter case, the customer had decided to source from Eastern Europe where labour costs are cheaper, but to protect continuity of supply had not told Colin until the last minute. They paid their arrears and took the tool out within a fortnight. (The tool is the mould that makes the parts and usually belongs, as in this case, to the customer not the supplier). The cancellation of these orders had lost them over 30% of annual sales: a crippling blow to an already weak company.

Gainslaw Globes had drifted far from making net floats and now made nothing at all for the fishing industry unless you count the little plastic forks they made for fish and chip shops. They turned out seed-trays for plants, plastic knobs for flat-pack furniture, boxes for foodstuffs (100ml, 250ml, 400ml), caps for thermometers, retainers for insulation, toggles for tarpaulins. In the past year or two they had manufactured brackets, plugs, clamps, caps, handles, holders, clips (double pitch clips, 4-pitch clips, 6-pitch clips), escutcheon plates, spacers, corner buffs, pins, and many other necessities of our plastic dependant society. They made them in thousands, tens of thousands, and hundreds of thousands; the forks they made in millions.

They made all these in all these quantities but they didn't make money. Before the cancelled orders they had scraped along; now what they earned from sales each month barely covered what they spent to make the components they sold. Other expenses such as VAT, maintenance, insurance, rent and rates, professional fees and interest on loans largely went unpaid until the creditor threatened action. As far as John understood the figures, the company was being kept afloat by the forbearance of their creditors and the goodwill of the bank. God help you if ever you find yourself in that position for, like Kate and Colin, the bank will demand your house as collateral. To spell it out: if your company goes down, your job, your income and your home go with it.

Colin talked incessantly, words tumbling over each other until, at times, they became an almost unintelligible gabble. John, who always took notes at any meeting he attended, couldn't keep up, and afterwards could scarcely read what he had written. Eventually the torrent ceased and John asked how and when they thought they would escape from the bind they were in.

"We'll trade ourselves out of it if we can make £40,000 sales a month," he said with forced enthusiasm. Kate shook her head.

"And what sales per month are you doing now?"

"About £35,000."

"£33,000." put in Kate. Colin shook his head and smiled at her pessimism.

"What, for instance," said John, "Did you do in May and April, the last two months?"

Colin motioned towards Kate. Kate opened a folder and replied,

"May, £32,451, April, £27,654."

"April was a short month – with the Easter Holidays." protested Colin.

"But that means in two months you have made £60,000 sales, say, against a target of £80,000. You're light by £20,000. When is your year end?"

"September."

"So, you will need to do £5000 better than your target in each of the next four months to make £40,000 a month overall. That's provided you're on target in June."

Kate sighed. John pressed on. He relished this hunt over familiar territory, for he is not the prey. No, don't blame him. We know these two young people are in deep trouble, but John is trying to help them and is entitled to derive some satisfaction from that. I have known men who enjoyed disinfesting a basement of rats.

"What chance is there of doing £45,000 a month for the rest of the financial year?"

"If we land an order we're chasing, we could do it," said Colin, glancing at Kate.

"And how would you rate your chances of getting it?" asked John suspecting a difference of opinion.

"Very good, I would say, eh, Kate?" said Colin. Kate didn't reply; her face remained expressionless.

Colin then explained. "There is a company in Glasgow, a

design company called Caledesign Solutions, they don't make things; they just design them. Then they have a tool made and place it with a plastic moulding company like us. They can steer a lot of work our way. At the moment they have designed a new range of products for Scotia HomeFlair (they make kitchen fittings and gadgets), and they're looking for a plastic moulding company to make them. We'll not get all the product but if we won half of what we have quoted for it would add £200,000 to our annual turnover."

Throughout this forecast, Kate sat looking at John, doubt in her eyes.

"That's good business," said John, looking at Kate.

"Yes, it is, it is." enthused Colin. At last Kate spoke.

"But unlikely," she said. A look of betrayal flashed into Colin's eyes.

"Think positive, Kate, come on."

John intervened.

"Look at it this way - what percentage confidence?" asked John, "Where a hundred is certain and ten is not at all likely."

"Eighty percent," said Colin slapping his hand on the table and looking at Kate. John followed his gaze.

"Kate?" he asked quietly.

"Twenty," she said sadly, "They're stringing us along." Then she blushed.

"The chief designer fancies her," teased Colin, "We can't keep him away!"

"But we won't get the work," said Kate, firmly reining in her husband.

Colin stood up.

"Must dash," he said, "I need to be in Glasgow by two."

"You do sales too?" said John.

"Put it in front of me and I'll eat it," said Colin, grandly, "Nice to meet you, John." He strode to the door, then stopped.

"What happens next?"

"I'll let you have a short report," said John, "But I'd like to see around the plant."

"Yes, fine, Kate'll show you around. Make sure you point him at Charlie." said Colin, then added, "and make sure you wipe your feet." Then he was gone, driving out of the car park like a man possessed.

"Wipe your feet?" queried John.

"He's having a dig at Charlie – and me, I suppose. He thinks we're too tidy."

She paused as if to continue then fell silent. She obviously wanted to say something, wanted, perhaps, John to adjudicate between her and her husband, but in the end, she said nothing. John understood and kept quiet.

Kate took John out onto the shop floor. It was warm, airless but immaculately tidy. Nine moulding machines paraded along the shop in neat rows, small ones at the front, large ones at the back. The floor around them (well, all but one of them) was clean and uncluttered and painted with a soft maroon non-slip paint. Bold yellow lines delineated the aisles, and white lines at the front of the machines encircled bags of materials on pallets as they awaited their transformation into components. At the other end of the machines similar white boxes housed cardboard cartons of finished product. A clean orange fork lift truck driven by a close-cropped young man in a smart blue boiler suit scurried back and forward along the aisles, from store to machine, from machine to despatch, lifting, carrying, lowering, in a sort of mechanical line dance.

Most of the machines were not only clean but also,

sadly, idle. One of them, however, a 100-tonne machine (that's the force it delivers to lock the die, not its weight) was doing what it should, spurting out door knobs every seven seconds with a hiss and thump and clatter. The operator, a young woman in a neat blue overall and pale blue mobcap, smiled at Kate and went on watching the machine.

At the back of the shop and behind the largest machine, the NB 150, they came across a small tubby man of about sixty, dressed in a brown boiler suit. His eyes darted about in a red face and beads of perspiration ran down his cheeks and dripped off his chin. He was engaged in fitting a tool into the machine and, clearly, was not happy at his work. Kate introduced him as Charlie. (Had Colin deliberately stuck a poster behind Charlie's workstation that proclaimed "Inspiration, not perspiration"?)

"Do you know what's going on?" he whined at Kate in a high-pitched voice. "Do you know what he wants next? He's run the 250ml boxes, now he wants 400ml, but there's still 50,000 of the 250's yet to make, so why are we taking the tool off? Do you know?"

"What did he say?" soothed Kate.

"He said he'd finished the 250s but he hasn't – there's still 50,000 to run. But he said to take it off. So, I'm taking it off. Why? I don't know. I don't know anything. Nobody tells me anything these days."

"What does the schedule say?" asked Kate looking at a document bulldogged on a board at the end of the machine.

"It says nothing that makes sense," spat Charlie, "It says seed trays, but that's not what he says. He says 400ml food boxes. That's rubbish, that paperwork, rubbish."

Kate tore the schedule off the clipboard in obvious frustration.

"If he said 400ml food boxes, you'd better do them."

"I am, but why? I don't know. There's 50,000 of 250s to make yet, so why is he taking the tool off. We're wasting time. It's change, change, change; put this on; no, take it off; no, stop that, here put this on. This is no way to run a moulding shop."

This last, John suspected, was aimed at him - and he understood what Charlie meant. Nothing disrupts production like a tool change. It can take up to five hours; if it's a new tool, days. Charlie wanted to run the 250ml order until completion, but Colin had decreed that he should switch to 400ml, no doubt to meet another order, yet another order that was running late.

"This is John Swansen," said Kate to Charlie.

"Charlie's the production manager," she added.

"Production dogsbody," muttered Charlie.

John put out his hand. Charlie wiped his hand on a cloth and took John's in a surprisingly firm grip. John looked into an earnest honest face.

"Come to see how it shouldn't be done?" said Charlie.

"No, just how it is being done."

"And what do you think?" said Charlie, waving his hand round the workshop.

"I am quite impressed; it looks very organised," said John, smiling

"I'm glad you think so," said Charlie, "and what about that?" He nodded towards the mess of a machine we noticed earlier. Its belly lay open and its innards, tubes, clips, rods, hydraulic hoses, and the tool itself were scattered on the floor around it and on the bench beside it. John fell into the trap.

"Is it under repair?" he said

"Don't ask me," said Charlie, "What do I know about it? Ask the organ grinder, he's repairing it – has been for three weeks." He then dived back into the NB150. Kate smiled sadly at John and led him back to the office.

In the car on his way back home John tried to make sense of what he had seen. The little factory impressed him; somebody had it under control, but who? He was sure it wasn't Colin. Could it be Kate, or Charlie, or both? And what part did Colin play apart from rushing about, sticking up posters and causing confusion? Clearly, the company was in trouble; it needed money to survive but was losing, not making, it. Gainslaw Globes was caught in a familiar bind: if it quoted profitable prices it couldn't get the work; if it lowered prices it wouldn't make a profit.

It only takes twenty minutes to drive from Gainslaw Industrial Estate to Birsett, but by the time he arrived at Braeshiel John had reached a gloomy conclusion: Gainslaw Globes has no future. Without decent orders they can't make money, without money they can't survive; without money soon, say in the next six months, they will go broke and the bank will pull the plug. What he should say to Kate and Colin is, "shut it, get out while you can, save your house, your business has failed". But how can he put that into words that will not break their hearts? They have poured their lives into their little company.

Another thought, though not so much a thought as a sensation, stirred somewhere in the labyrinth of John's being. He had enjoyed being with Kate, enjoyed her company, her conversation, her coffee, but most of all had enjoyed the light in her eyes when she smiled. None of this surfaced in his consciousness, but something flickered that had long lain dormant. Marion had a lovely smile too.

Before he prepared his report, he would leave it a few days to let his thoughts crystallise.

CHAPTER SEVENTEEN

His visit to Gainslaw Globes depressed John. He had staked on it more than he realised. He had hoped to find something stimulating to lift him out of the trough into which he had fallen. His visit had confirmed what he already believed, that everything around Birsett was small beer, small, flat and futile. Gainslaw Globes held out no hope for him. He must transfer his hopes to Zack. You can see the man is clutching at straws.

Not that Zack had been inactive. Scarcely a week had gone by without an envelope from Leeds with details of a job for John to consider. Each one came in a "Zack Mallinger Search Consultant to the Blue Chips" glossy folder and was always several pages long, for Zack believed, like many in his profession, that quality is directly proportional to bulk. A page described the searching company, a page set out a summary job description, two or three pages amplified the summary, a page specified the preferred candidate, a page listed the salary indicator and conditions of employment and three pages praised Zack Mallinger for his expertise and success rate.

Would that the jobs matched the folders. John rejected

them all, except one. They were, in his estimation, well below his level: running a call centre in Huddersfield: temporary project director for a small civil engineering company: production director for a tuppenny ha'penny metal basher in Sheffield: fund raising director for a charity for the better treatment of animals. The one exception was Managing Director of a Warranty Repair Company with headquarters in Altrincham, Cheshire. It did not meet his aspirations in either content or reward package but he thought it worth a trip to Leeds to follow up.

Zack received him with diminished enthusiasm and explained that he wasn't sure of the status of the job at Altrincham. By dint of close questioning John unearthed something like the truth. Zack hadn't actually been commissioned to fill the position, but had seen it in The Guardian and thought John might be interested so he had rung the company to see if he could propose candidates. Reluctantly they had agreed to look at what he had to offer and he had sent off John's details. He had not had a reply, but he had contacted them that very morning and they would be prepared to interview John if he could get him over to them a week on Friday. They had set aside that day for their preferred candidates; they would squeeze John in at the end of the afternoon. John recoiled at the thought of being hawked around and squeezed in, and at first refused to go. Zack was finally honest with him.

"You don't have a lot of choice," he said, softly. "It is difficult to place someone of your ...er ...maturity, particularly in the light of the circumstances of your departure from your last position. I have had some difficulty in persuading clients to consider your details - and your salary aspirations make it difficult...."

"Would you stop saying "difficult,"" snapped John, but the consultant's message had gone home. He agreed to be squeezed in on the Friday afternoon. He had no high hopes of the job. It would entail a long drive, but he had to start somewhere. He left The Headrow feeling diminished and grubby, inferior goods on the shelf, hard to sell. He drove back to York too fast; a speed camera on the A64 near Tadcaster flashed twice in his rear-view mirror.

The flat in York felt stuffy and unwelcoming. He opened the windows and made himself a cup of tea, but had no milk, so drank it black; he didn't like it black. He rang Marion to tell her he intended coming over to see her that evening as the phone started to ring out, the prospect of talking to Marion lifted him. The phone, however, kept on ringing; Marion wasn't in. She'd be at work; he'd forgotten. She had turned off the answering machine so he couldn't leave a message. He wouldn't bother to ring her back; he would just go over there. He went to the shops and bought himself enough groceries for three days: to-morrow he would take the train to London to see Belinda Boyd and return to the flat. Then on Friday he would sort out what he wanted to take with him and take it back to Birsett.

Just before seven, he parked the car a little way from the house in Poppleton and walked up the path of his old home. He rang the bell and waited. While he did so he noted that everything seemed more or less the way it had been the year before, except, perhaps, there were more lupins than he would have wanted; he disliked lupins and over the years had persuaded Marion not to plant so many of them. For a while he thought that no one was in but then he heard a noise behind the door and it opened to reveal Marion dressed smartly in a summer dress and short jacket.

"Oh, hello," she said, obviously disconcerted, "Come in. I'm afraid I'm going out."

He followed Marion into the lounge and sat down on the settee (he had always avoided his "own" chair since he had left last November). Marion sat down opposite to him.

"Rebecca is out," she said, nervously, "she's round at

Chloe's; she'd been revising every night, so she's gone to Chloe's for a couple of hours for a break. Even then she's taken her books. But next week will see the end of it."

She stopped and looked at John, waiting for him to tell her why he had come. He then realised he had not come for anything, except a welcome.

"I had to come down so I thought I'd pop in and bring you up to date.... with what's happening." he blurted out. Marion listened patiently as he recounted what had happened since his father's funeral.

He had scarcely finished when there was a ring at the bell and John realised that someone had called for Marion. He half expected it to be Fiona, but it wasn't. It proved to be a man of John's own age and height with a handsome open tanned face. He was dressed for a warm summer's evening in a light, casual shirt and smart trousers. He looked surprised at the sight of John.

"This is John," she said by way of explanation, "John, this is Malcolm."

They shook hands and muttered embarrassed greetings. Then John stepped out of the house and Malcolm stepped in. A wave of indignation, of indignation and ...... (what else can we call it?) .... jealousy, swept over John as the door closed behind him. Such was the impact that he actually staggered off the pavement as he walked to his car. Then he fumed in his car like some tormented teenager and stared at the door with a terrible intensity. So suddenly and completely had his emotions swamped his reason that he opened the car door intent on charging into the house and confronting Marion and.... (what did they call him?) Malcolm! But before he could put his intention into action the door opened and Marion and Malcolm came out. They walked to a parked car, got into it and drove off. John made to drive after them, then reined in his galloping emotion. He drove back to the flat with his mind awash with anger and resentment. Yet still he did not blame himself for his distress.

John spent a miserable night at the flat, but he is tough and self-disciplined and had recovered enough to catch the mid-morning train to London for his meeting with Belinda Boyd. On the way he refreshed his anger with the sights and sounds of his dismissal - not only the cold calculated coup de grace itself, but the face of Ms Waltham (Human Resources) at the door of the flat, her stuttering demand for the laptop, the sweating peak-capped face of the security man, the box of his pathetic belongings, carrying them himself because the guard had to keep his hands free to escort his elbow off the premises. But what rankled most were the bleatings and whinings from the twisted features of Jim Arkwright, now crowing from his chair in his office.

You can guess what his feelings were when he entered the lawyer's office. His accumulated hate now bore on Loyalty, Walter Radleigh and above all, the stinking, slimy, sleazy Sir Frank Wantley. They were to blame for the whole sorry mess; there were to blame and they would pay for it.

Belinda had been diligent and had procured from Loyalty a statement detailing the circumstances of John's departure (they still had not admitted to dismissing him). She handed it to John; it ran to three pages. She gave John time to read it.

"It's a strong case," said Belinda, when she saw he had finished, "Let me run through it…."

"It's rubbish," John fumed, "Unadulterated rubbish."

Belinda poised a pen over her notepad.

"Shall I write that down?" she snapped, "It'll sound good in court."

She waited for an answer. John shook his head.

"Right then, I'll summarise," said Belinda, "Their case

is threefold: One, that you made accusations of corruption against the Board of Directors that were neither substantiated nor appropriate. Two, that you encouraged other managers of Pinkerton Loyalty to undermine board policy, Three, that you manipulated the accounts of Pinkerton Loyalty to hide expenditure that should not have been authorised."

She stopped and looked at John.

"Now," she said, with just the trace of a smile, "How do you plead?"

"It's rubbish," repeated John, violently.

"Is it?" said Belinda. "Did you accuse the board of corruption?"

"No!"

"That's not what you told me before."

"I only asked a question."

"About corruption?"

"But you believe there was, is, corruption."

"Yes."

"What corruption, precisely?"

"I'm sure Sir Frank received a backhander from the government of Bainan to locate Loyalty manufacturing in their country. Maybe other members of the board, even the company...."

"You can prove that?"

"Yes, I think I could."

"I'm the judge," said Belinda, sitting up straight, "Try me."

John launched into his opening statement.

"First, Sir Frank deliberately blocked plans we had for developing the plant at York. He told us they were conducting a study, a study that Radleigh seemed to know nothing about. Second, I know that when he served in the government, he visited Bainan and made a lot of contacts. Third, he visited Bainan at Easter with the Facilities Engineering people from Loyalty. The engineer that went with him, Daffy Jenkins, they call him, said that Sir Frank seemed very thick with some of the government ministers there."

"Daffy Jenkins, Facilities Engineer, Bainan ministers, very thick," repeated the lawyer and wrote it down. John felt he was making progress.

"Jacqui Boutelle of Sumner and Frieburg, virtually admitted to us that money changed hands."

"Virtually?"

"She said that all expenses had been taken care of; lubrication, she called it."

"Did she say when, to whom, how?"

"Well, no."

"Continue," said the judge.

"Then she went out of her way to warn me about Sir Frank and what he was up to."

"And what was he up to?"

"She didn't say."

"Does she have evidence – records of conversations, documents, tape recordings?"

"She might."

"And, if she had, would she let us have them?"

"She might."

"And would she tell us what she knows if we brought her into the box?"

"I don't know, but she might."

"Might, might - and might not! No, not might not - will not. She wants to go on working, so she will not."

"But it happened, it happened, it happened; he's a crook, they're probably all crooks." exploded John.

"Perhaps," said Belinda, bluntly, not at all intimidated by his violence.

"Now then, the company's other two points. Do they mean anything to you?"

John explained that in his attempt to save the factory at York and get a head start with Mack's new manufacturing system he had used operating expenditure for capital purchases.

'And that is against company policy, I take it?'

'Well, strictly speaking, yes, but ....'

Belinda cut him off.

"And how did the board find out about it?"

"That's easy," said John, "Jim Arkwright, the Financial Controller, would tell them."

"Why him? Were there not others who knew about the plan?"

"Yes, all of the management meeting."

"So why pick on Arkwright?"

"Because he disagreed with what we were doing."

"Did he? Did he say he disagreed?"

"Yes, he warned us…."

"He warned you?" she emphasised the "warned".

"Yes."

"And you ignored him?"

John could see where the questions were leading and tried to head her off.

"It was my job to decide what to do, and within my remit."

"Was it? And what was Mr Arkwright's remit – to ensure financial rectitude?"

John didn't reply. Belinda dropped the pose.

"We wouldn't win," she said, "We'll settle out of court. They'll agree to our terms, more or less; they don't want the expense, or, the publicity."

"But I do." rasped John, "That's the point. People should know what is going on."

"Then go to the News of the World, and don't waste any more of my time." said Belinda, firmly and closed the file. "And your money," she added.

She had grown used to dealing with angry clients. She would let him stew for a few weeks then ask him if he had any further instructions.

CHAPTER EIGHTEEN

If you have stumbled into depression and felt solid ground turn to sludge beneath your feet, you understand that no matter where you look there is no path out. You just want to sit down and cry.

As he retreated north in the rain, John found himself in such a place. He had staked more on his trip south than he had reckoned and one by one the tracks that offered a way forward had petered out. For all his bluster, Zack Mallinger had made it clear that he saw little prospect of finding John a job close to the one had lost. Then Belinda Boyd had impeded the way to his day in court. Worst of all, Marion had turned from him to another man.

The Mercedes no longer offered the assurance it used to give; now it did not carry a top executive going places, but a fugitive running for cover. Hemmed in and spattered by vans and lorries, he felt helpless. He had been in command; now he was scratching around for attention. His managers and staff, Ian, George and the others had looked up to him for their roles, for answers to their questions, for decisions; had depended on his leadership. He had been the embodiment of the company; its life force surged through him to them. He had put down the fullness of his life, its strength and significance to his own virility, wisdom and ability. Now, disconnected from the sources of power, he had collapsed into a puny, insignificant moaner dependent on charlatans like Zack Mallinger. His soul screamed at the wretchedness of it all.

Calling on his dwindling fund of self-belief, he determined to ditch the Search Consultant to the Blue Chips and consent to be more vile: he would apply for advertised positions. He would also research and cold call companies that might be interested in his skills and experience. This last idea he had gleaned from Zack who had told him that only twenty-five percent of all available jobs are advertised. Such decisions offered a small cold comfort. However, he rejected another of Zack's suggestions - to network - contacting people you know to tell them of your needs. He could not abase himself so far.

Belinda Boyd had sickened him. He wanted to believe that he was a special case, not a typical example of decisive management. She had told him told him that his crusade against Loyalty and Sir Frank was futile and her arguments had battered down his defences. But huddled in the bunker of his despair he still held out. He could not accept, would not accept that he should sell out, pocket the money and walk away. Recalling his dismissal had reinforced his sense of disgrace and his desire for revenge. Drowning in instinctive resentment he clutched at Ms Boyd's facetious suggestion of going to the press. In desperation he thrashed around grabbing at whatever came within reach.

'The News of the World would be best; they'd lap it up, or the Daily Mirror. No, not them! They're rags. No-one that counts reads them. The Times, that's more like it; The Times! Or the Financial Times? Who was that reporter who interviewed me last year? Brewster, was that his name? I'll look it out.'

But as soon as he grasped these life-savers they sank. He knew that going public with his complaints conflicted with his plan to work in top management again. He knew the rules; he had said it many a time of others who were badly treated:

it's a big boys' game; don't whine; take the medicine and gripe in private.

These thoughts sickened him, but the recollection that came near to breaking him, that burned like an ache in his heart and from time to time welled up into shattering agony, was that Marion had dressed in her summer best to await this man and to smile at him when he arrived. They were going....... where? He did not know and did not want to guess. Try as he may he could not keep his mind on the A19, the A1(M), the Western Bypass and the rolling roads of Northumberland. Music, news and debate on the radio went unheard. The thought would not go away; he was losing Marion.

Braeshiel felt cold and dark when he entered it that dreich Friday evening. So unwelcoming it was, that he could not settle in it. In desperation, he walked up to Helen's house ostensibly to tell her he was back in residence. Helen had given him supper; Alex had listened to his complaints and the bairns had jostled him with their shouts and squabbles. And pushed him through the door of his emotional memory. He caught again the breath of what it was like to be home, of being wrapped up in the lives of your own folk.

Leaving them and feeling disconsolate, John stepped out onto the brae at Birsett. The light had faded and the clouds that had made his journey miserable had splintered and scattered over a clear sky that shaded from silver in the northwest through burnished copper and duck egg blue until in the east and south it darkened to soft ultramarine. The clouds, still grey and substantial, were decked with dazzling hems of pink and red, and bright linings of gold and orange. A diffusing light clothed the trees, lit up the verges and borders, touched up the brighter flowers, glowed on house walls and warmed the bare red rocks of the cliffs above the road. The light came from nowhere yet was present everywhere, hanging in the air. A soft light wrapped around him, a quiet warm light, magical and ethereal, the light, perhaps, by which God walked in Eden.

The light drew John's attention to the silence. Certainly, he heard the rush of the occasional car along the road and the distant rumble of the waves on the beach. The sparrows chattered in the hedges, jackdaws chuckled on the rooftops, swifts screamed overhead and a blackbird or dunnock now and then burst into song; but intrinsically the land lay silent.

If you do not understand how it can be silent with all this racket in your ears then you have spent too long in the city. For these sounds were distinct; they could be heard separately and a name could be put to each of them. They did not merge into the murky hum that makes silence unknown in towns.

John is not a sentimental man but so obvious and impressive were the light and the silence that he stopped at the gate of his father's house to try to take it in. With the light and with the silence there came the thought that this was much, much better than the glare and the din of cities; that the folk of this place were more substantial and had a grasp on life unmatched by the cheats, chancers and charlatans amongst whom he had moved these many years.

In this last he is traducing many people; good people, the Macks and Georges and others, who had shared his industrial life, but for the moment he ignored these good people to brood on his disillusionment.

And snatch at straws. He was sick of the deceit of big business and big businessmen. He would quit the charade. He would cut his losses and settle in Birsett.

Such a fragile consolation fed him his supper and got him into bed. But he slept little, plagued by the recurrent recollection of Marion leaving the Poppleton house with Malcolm.

His restless night and dull morning clouded the bright influence of Helen's home and golden evening on the brae. His resolution to cut and run weakened and; in rekindled determination, threw himself into the task of job-hunting.

Working furiously, he despatched letters and his CV to half a dozen large companies. He explained that he was available immediately, but did not explain why. He combed the appointments pages of the Financial Times and Times and applied for several positions he thought might be suitable. He then set up a filing system and a register to keep track of his progress. There were columns for company, job title, name of contact, date sent, acknowledgement date (for their initial reply), jog date (when he should ring them if he had heard nothing); interview date; interview rating (how likely it was to lead to appointment (marks out of ten)) and, at the end, a column for the result.

You must not think that he gave much thought to what he was doing. He went through his tasks meticulously but mechanically. The glimmer of expectation that had caused him to start the exercise soon spluttered out. Discipline and routine alone kept him at his work. He did it not because he wanted to but because he must.

Over the coming weeks, the acknowledgements column would become spotted with "none" and the jog column would have to be extended to record the frequent and frustrating calls for information. The interview column would remain consistently blank and the end column would soon fill up with "rejected", and, when that word became too hurtful, with "abandon".

Such actions and such words sapped what little resilience John had mustered. As it dwindled, his frustration increased and with it his addiction to his frantic pursuit. Since his father died, he had been in the habit of taking a walk at least once a day, and occasionally dropping into the shops at Hecklescar. Now these refreshments became rarer; he spent more and more time cooped up with his computer, papers and letters in his front room. Even there he seldom looked out to the high sky and wide sea. He became taciturn and bad=tempered and even the scampering Morag could not shake out of his depressing decline.

But we are ahead of ourselves. There is one interview he does have, in Altrincham, with International Warranties.

Everything conspired against the success of this interview: late on a Friday afternoon is no time for either party; the interviewers are amateurs; John is in no mood to answer silly questions, or any questions at all for that matter. The interviews are in the lounge of Royal Spa Hotel at Altrincham and the three young executives entrusted with the interviews have made full use of the bar throughout the day. When John's turn comes, they are slouched in armchairs with their papers spread across a large low coffee table in front of them. John recognises one of Zack's startling brochures amongst the clutter. He is seated in an upright chair on the opposite side of the low table.

They are, like many interviewers, on an ego trip. They feel superior to the candidates and make no secret of their arrogance. Had they been trained in stress interviewing they could not have done better. They take turns to talk but scarcely listen; they interrupt the answers of the questions they have asked; they prod, poke and sneer patronisingly at anything John claims to have accomplished.

John suffered half-an-hour of this before exploding.

"Tell us why you left your last job?" lit the fuse.

"I had a disagreement with the board."

They all smirked at once.

"Come, come, Mr Swansen," said the arch-tormentor, "Do you not mean that they had a disagreement with you; they disagreed with you being Managing Director. Isn't that it?"

John detonated. "You can stuff your job!" he shouted, and in one majestic heave threw over the coffee table and sent their papers, pens, personal organisers, coffee cups and glasses sprawling across the floor. For a moment they froze, then each independently but in concert pulled their knees in front of their chins and tried to make themselves as small as possible. John stalked out.

And would you believe it, they reported to Zack Mallinger that they thought Mr Swansen emotionally unstable?

CHAPTER NINETEEN

I begin to wish we had chosen a different hero. His life seems to be bogged down in misfortune. We might have been better to follow the busy and boisterous career of our friend Delightful.

And I think it is about time I introduced you properly to this, er, delightful, man. He is skipper of the Aurora; whose birth name is Laurence but has been stuck with his by-name ever since Mr Macdonald the itinerant music teacher used it to describe Laurence's 9-year-old voice thirty years ago. Unfortunately, his mother repeated it around the village and the name stuck. Fortunately, for the last twenty years it has been shortened to Del on all but officious occasions. Laurence's second name is Paulin, the same as Alex, Helen's husband, who is a cousin. Delightful is small, slight and tanned with bright dark eyes and a bushy moustache. Imagine a happy Mexican; take off his sombrero; there you have him. He owns the Aurora along with Kit; Kit Black, a refugee from up the country who lives with his wife and family down the brae at Birsett. The third member of the crew is Marvin. He lives with Wanda and their two young boys, supports Rangers from a distance and is much too fond of McEwan's export for his own good.

It seems, however, that the modern hero must agonise and although Delightful does agonise over his lottery numbers and whether to go inshore for lobsters or offshore for crabs, he is much too happy a man to be taken seriously in literary circles. We'll have to stick with John and hope his fortune improves.

There is hope for him already for the Saturday that dawns on him, the last in June, is Coronation Day at Birsett and he is destined to play a leading part in this happy occasion. The coronation is that of the Fisher Queen who is chosen each year from the top class of Birsett Primary School. She is crowned on the grassy terrace that has been levelled above the village hall and, after she is crowned, she opens the gala; a sort of country fair with stalls, games and other innocent pursuits for young and old. Traditionally, Lady Flemington crowns the queen and she would have done so this year had she not stuck a pitchfork through her foot when feeding her horse on Friday night. Mrs Mordun, the minister's wife and secretary of the Coronation Day committee therefore had to find a replacement at short notice. She settled on John as a former pupil made good and rang John first thing on Saturday morning to ask him to stand in. John, without thinking, consented and agreed to turn up at half-past one to do the honours.

He should have first checked with Helen. Morag, Helen's girl, had been firm favourite to be this year's Fisher Queen until she was rejected at the last moment in favour of Stephanie Burns on the trivial ground that Stephanie hadn't thrown Mrs Murray's cat into the harbour to see if it could swim. Unfortunately, Morag committed this offence the very week the headmaster made his choice and he knocked off just enough points from Morag's "Kind to Others" assessment to put her in second place. Helen let fly at this injustice and, after failing to overturn the decision, had fought a guerrilla war against the Coronation Day committee. John, unfortunately, knew nothing of this and went off at quarter past one to do his civic duty.

We should not let this minor misunderstanding spoil our enjoyment of Coronation Day, for there is something here for every palate. Everyone has come ready to make the best of the afternoon, even men deprived of their golf and bairns prised from their computers. In the warm sunshine, the whole ground is bright with colour and expectation, so breathe in the glad noise and bustle of the place, the general buzz of gossip and banter, the waves of adult laughter and the shouts and screams of excited children.

Visit the stalls. As you go in there is Cake and Candy, where, if you know what you are doing you will choose one of Mrs Murray's cream sponges, or buy six pieces of paradise slice for £1.50, but will avoid Wanda's shortbread which is more paving material than tea-time treat. Next along is Bric-a-Brac where you will find figurines, mock crystal bowls, cups, saucers, and plates (some of them matching), cruet sets, toasts racks, coasters, souvenir egg-cups (pic'n'mix, choose from Peterhead, Lowestoft, Llandudno, Salou), pictures, model cars, miscellaneous toys (not all of them broken), water jugs, glasses, soft bears, soft whales, soft dolphins, soft frogs, soft tigers, soft horses, donkeys and monkeys, toasters, radios, record players, scores of old LP records and audio tapes, hundreds of paperback books. You will find them all here, but you will find out something more – you will find out what junk your neighbours have been storing all these years, for Jessie who organises the stall will be able to tell you with some accuracy who handed what in (provenance, I think it is called in the trade). Don't be tempted by the ormolu clock at the back; it's a fake, made in Taiwan and brought back by Norman Stott when he was working in Hong Kong ten years ago. His wife wouldn't give it house room and put it into the jumble sale at the EU Church at Hecklescar. Since then it has done the rounds of stalls and sales and has been a raffle prize at several different coffee mornings. Everyone hopes that eventually a visitor will buy it or win it and set it circulating in some other part of the country. Yes, by all means, take a miniature lobster creel; they're genuine; old John Peterson makes them in the shed be-

On Such a Tide

hind his house and hands in a few to every charitable function in the area. Put it in the back window of your car to show you belong to fisher folk.

See where the fish kites swallow the air? That is Melinda, the local artist, dressed like an earth mother in flowered straw hat and flowing smock. She is painting Morag's face - a tiger; Morag asked for a vampire but Melinda refused, saying it offended her sensibilities.

This next stall is a Birsett speciality; what would be called a seafood deli in more auspicious surroundings; here it is called the Poo Stall. Poo is the local word for crab and here you can buy it in any form that suits your taste. You can have it whole, you can have it dressed, you can have the meat in a jar or in a tub or in a sandwich, you can buy a claw and suck the meat out yourself, and if you ask the lady behind the stall she will sell you a live one; she might also supply you with a lobster, live, boiled or reduced to a jar. This lady is no other that the other half of Delightful, by the name of Dot and her companion is the wife of Kit and she is called Spot. That, of course, is not her real name (I can't recall what that is; everyone calls her Spot) but it rhymes with Dot and thereby perfectly describes the harmony in which these two live; they seem to prefer each other's company to that of their husbands. These women have been up half the night preparing the produce for their stall so it would be ungrateful not to buy something from them. Yes, a pair of kippers will do nicely, they were cured only yesterday in the smokehouse of Weddell Carter in Hecklescar and collected fresh this morning before you were aware another day had dawned. Where, you might wonder, are the men folk, Delightful and Kit? They are here certainly but not obvious. We will come across them later.

Here is the lifeboat stall: buy a model lifeboat for the bairn or a pack of Christmas Cards. (I know it's early, but Christmas will surely come.) Helen normally runs the knitwear stall, but because of her dispute is not on duty today. But, in a subtle strategy showing that she is not against Coronation Day, only the committee, she has provided for the stall some lovely little baby's jackets that you could give to a new baby of your acquaintance. Take a ticket at the tombola stall and try to win a bottle of something or a box of biscuits. What's that? You have drawn ticket number 57! Look, you've won a bottle of Australian Red Wine. Well done!

When we have run through the stalls, we'll take a cup of tea at the tea tent and sit outside at a plastic table on the same chairs that were carried down to Braeshiel for Willie's funeral. Here we'll enjoy fresh scones baked this morning by the Skipper of The Boy Peter, Dave Pallin who, by popular acclaim, is the best scone maker in Birsett and would win first prize at Beanston Flower Show if he wasn't from Birsett and there wasn't an all-woman judging panel. Jeannie "Gospel" will serve us, or rather, will wave a teapot around as she expounds the gospel truth on Birsett gossip. We will also pick up the skits and quips of her fellow workers who despair of her ability to do any serious work. We'll hear gales of laughter coming from the backroom washing-up girls as Batman, who fancies himself as a ladies' man, retreats from them in bashful confusion. And we're pleased to see that Wanda laughs there amongst all those respectable women. She has brought along Susan, little Johnny's mother, ye ken, the lad that was lost on the rocks. Susan walks along the beach every morning and evening looking for her son. Others, too, look when they are down there, particularly after a storm.

Drink up and eat your scone; we mustn't spend too long here for the British Legion Pipe Band has struck up and we must move nearer to hear them. They play The Old Rustic Bridge by the Mill, Bonnie Galloway, then Blue Bonnets O'er the Border to finish their first spot; then Pipe Major Peter breaks off to accompany the Hecklescar Dancers. Ruth, Aileen, Clara, and Erica, and some little ones, walk onto the platform resplendent in tartan and lace to charm us with the Highland

Fling, the Sword Dance, and Skean Trews. Then the band again with slow airs finishing with Highland Cathedral that draws an extra round of applause, because Jennifer Pallin (niece of the scone maker) from Birsett played the solo. After that, tricks by Chip, the Wonder Dog that doubles as sheepdog Kip up at Black Topps on Coldingham Moor during the week. Chip should also have starred in a demonstration of geese herding and may yet still if they can round up the geese that somehow escaped from their pen. Suspicion has fallen on Morag.

As the band plays, we can try the games. David, Helen's oldest, is showing off at the Golden Goal but George his younger brother is matching him shot for shot as they try to tally up the highest score by kicking the ball through numbered holes on a large board. Have a go at quoits and hoopla. Yes, I know, the hoops never do go right over the plinth, but look upon it as a contribution to… (what is it for this year?) ….. Romanian Orphans.

Here's an old favourite: Splat the Rat. Here, I'll show you how it works. See that short length of sloping tube and see, under its bottom edge, a block of wood. Well, pick up that mallet. Now, here goes! James here will drop a potato into the top of the tube and it will shoot out the bottom. What you must do is to splat the potato when it shoots over the wooden block. Try it. Go! No, missed it by a mile. Try again; it's five goes for 50p. Missed again, and again. Look; try anticipating when James will let it go. No, too early, no, too late. No, give up, we'll be here all day. James is always in charge of Splat the Rat; he looks forward to it for weeks. He's (what would you say?) not the full shilling, but he can drop a potato down a tube and can count up to five. What more is needed?

But we will waste our time if we do not look into the faces and lives of our fellow revellers and hear the still sad music of humanity and perhaps be surprised by joy. See that woman over there, the one with the low-cut flimsy frock; that's Avril and that's her husband, Matt, beside her; he's on the oilrigs, a month on, a month off. But when he's away, they say, his kitten's at play - with the accountant at the bank, And that's their little daughter, Jessica. What lies ahead for her, poor bairn? For a sadder, badder tale see that old couple sitting listening to the band. That's Mr & Mrs Smith, with their son beside them; he works in Glasgow and comes through every year to bring them to the gala. Last year they celebrated their golden wedding and had their photograph in the Berwickshire News, cutting their cake, a hand each on the knife. Do you know it was the first time they had touched each other in thirty years? Whatever started the paralysis, I don't know. There was a rumour that he went with another woman. For all those years they have slept in different beds, lived in different rooms, eaten different meals. They share only a roof and mutual contempt; it has shrivelled them both. Each has the sole remaining ambition of outliving the other. She looks likely to win; see, he has difficulty breathing. But look, there at the gate, a contrast! The old couple: the man pushing a wheel chair, that's Cecil from Surrey and Dorothy his wife. How on earth has he got her here? See how pleased he is, how pleased she is; she looks frail, but she is here.

Yet how does *he* get away with it, him there, that big bruiser in the yellow T-shirt, prowling round. He has come from Hecklescar looking for money from Marvin, Wanda's partner; Marvin is his cousin. His by-name is Rott, after Rottweiler, the dog; see how people make way for him. His real name is Dermot, but they call him Rott; he prefers Rott. He was bright at school, much brighter than Marvin, but chased fame as lead singer in a heavy metal band by the name of Sexy-Five, if singer is the right name for the howls he made. The band struggled on for about six years, cut a few discs, then fell out with each other and with their agent. He came back to Hecklescar five years ago, aged twenty-five, broke and spoiled for any useful work. He is registered as a singer at the job centre and has learnt to avoid anything else. His ambition is to break into the big time, his interests: racehorses, drink and women. They say he goes round to Wanda's when he can't get any other female, but Wanda is a decent girl and tries to do what's right so I'm sure there's nothing in it. He's a parasite, but a benevolent state keeps him fed, healthy and housed so he can prey on women and on Marvin and Wanda.

There's another one: McNaughton, in the cream suit and Panama hat. No, he doesn't look like a leech but no one can remember him ever working and he's what? Fifty? He is prospering now as a pioneer of the drugs revolution. I know of several young people he has condemned to misery. See there is one of his victims: the woman in the blue suit with her eyes to the ground, a respectable woman from a respectable family. No, she doesn't use drugs but her son is a customer of McNaughton. He took eight 'O' levels three years ago and passed the lot at top grade, but he will take no Highers. He lives a twilight life in the single flats on the pier at Hecklescar; lives in filth and has been fined twice for theft. He's a victim, certainly, but so is his family, his father and his sisters, but worst of all, his mother. She worries herself sick about him every minute of every day; takes him his breakfast every morning and cleans him up when necessary; she's a Catholic; keeps a candle burning for him continually.

But with their campaign for legalisation, our liberal friends will make McNaughton a hero of liberty yet. Rott claims the same prestige for freeing up sex.

Hey, loosen up! We're here to enjoy ourselves. Take in the happiness - see that dad there, with the beer belly and the Newcastle United shirt, trying to teach his bairn to kick the ball; what patience! what dreams! And Gloria there, buying ice cream for her two boys; her man left her for a Gainslaw woman five years ago. For a year she hardly left the house, but now she works part-time at SeaNorth and lives for her boys; and they are a credit to her. That group of girls there, they're enjoying themselves, all togged up in latest fashion of skimpy top, bare midriff and flared jeans. They are aware only of the group of boys they are studiously avoiding. The boys, with their black breeks, white shirts and spiky hair, are doing their nonchalant best to be noticed, wanting to have a kick at the Golden Goal but, aware of the attention, turning down such childish sports. Let us hope by the end of the afternoon they all, boy and girls, will, as we once did, merge and enjoy the thrilling uncertainty of each other's company and the delicious anxiety of awakening attraction. See, they are already spiralling mutually towards the soft drinks stall.

Now then, there's a picture fit for an artist: listening to the pipes, a new mother enthralled in feeding her new baby. And there is old Mr Scott drinking his tea and enjoying the sun; on these occasions he misses his old friend Willie and has to content himself with the schoolmaster and the minister, sympathising with the one about the falling school roll and the other about dwindling congregations. There, just by the bouncy castle, see the greeting (crying) bairn with a skinned knee whose excitement has collapsed in tears but his auntie Jean there will coax him to bounce again, I'm sure. There is Dave Pallin, of scone fame, blocking the way to the cake candy stall, bragging to Alex, Helen's man, and Batman (now well clear of the tea tent ladies) about his big haul of lobsters the week before last, but omitting to mention precisely where he hauled them. There is Billy Collie with his niece, venturing out again after the death of his wife of thirty-five years and finding in the dread world enough kind words to soften his grief. He almost trips over little Louise and her friend Ruth who have discovered a displaced and, no doubt, displeased, ladybird trying to flee from the trampling feet. Louise wants to help, but daren't pick it up, so she is protecting its passage with her own slight body. Billy, for the first time for months, finds himself laughing at their antics.

We have all been here before, have we not? Lift your eyes from the busy and noisy green terrace up over the road and railway, up beyond Fairnington, beyond the quiet trees above Redhall, over the fields of ripening wheat and barley to the low shimmering ridge of Bunkle Edge. There, I'm sure, three thousand years ago in cleared green fields beside their palisades and hut circles, ancient and unknown peoples laid down their tools and the burden of their living and enjoyed fairs and feasts and Coronation Days. Just as we do today.

But commotion calls us back to the green. Rott is Splatting the Rat, or rather, isn't, and wants to play on well past his five goes. James, red in the face has called up his meagre reserves of courage, and is refusing to drop a potato down the tube. Rott is threatening him with the mallet. The men around freeze as each one waits for some other to intervene. Then Helen arrives, yanks the mallet out of Rott's hand and shouts,

"If you're looking for Marvin, you'll find him at the beer van behind the school."

For a dangerous moment, Rott glowers at Helen, but Helen holds his gaze (and, crucially, the mallet) so he turns away. He finds Marvin at the beer van, or rather at the back of the Aurora's van that today is packed with cans and bottles. Mine host is Delightful, and Assistant Barman, Kit. We have found them at last.

CHAPTER TWENTY

Whilst we have been enjoying ourselves at the gala, John has not. He felt out of place. After he had crowned the Fisher Queen and had had his photograph taken, he had received the bouquet intended for Lady Flemington. This he presented to Helen by way of contrition for undermining her campaign against the committee. He then made for the tea tent intending only to drink a mandatory tea and cake with the committee before beetling back to Braeshiel.

Had he still thought of himself as the local boy made good, he could have enjoyed the occasion. He had been raised above the crowd to crown the queen, but his fall from acclaim so dominated his thinking that he imagined that his neighbours and friends had demoted him. He thought he detected satisfaction at his comeuppance or worse, pity, in the eyes of some of them. If such sentiments were crossing the minds of the folk around him, they passed quickly. People had not come to assess him but to savour the delights of the gala, to stroll round the stalls, to buy things they didn't need, to play games for amusement and to chat to their friends.

Although John knew many of the folk there, there was no-one he wanted to mix with. If Mr Scott had not been tied up with Mr Mordun and the head teacher, he could have gone to sit with him, but he had no wish to make company with anyone else; he just wanted to go home.

Whilst fleeing from the committee in the tea tent, he spotted JP Marwick come in, dressed as for the Henley Regatta and looking as distinguished as ever. But he was not alone. With him was a woman John took to be his wife. She looked like the wife of a merchant banker: tall, elegant, well groomed, tastefully dressed. She was accompanied by a young man of about twenty. Not their son, surely?

The reason for John's doubt was that the young man was cleared totally dependent on them. He held onto JP's wife's hand and grinned at everyone around him. His dull eyes flickered with excitement and he spoke in short sharp bursts to his mother and father. John recalled that JP had talked about a son, and of his being at school, but he had thought of Eton, or Ampleforth. It had never occurred to him that someone as intelligent, shrewd, rich and in control as JP could have a son such as this. If John had mentioned it to Helen, or Delightful, or Jimmy Possum, or Bessie Raeburn who is ninety-five and never out the house, or virtually anyone else in Birsett, they would have told him that his banker friend had a son who was 'not the full shilling'. But John's image of JP was so fixed that he had never asked. He had scarcely come to terms with this contradiction of his own assumptions when the family were in front of him and being introduced. Rachel, JPs wife, struck him as being a quiet, cultured, gentle woman. Ben, his son, shook John's hand with a controlled politeness but was straining to be let loose amongst the stalls and games. Rachel excused herself and led him away, leaving the two men to enjoy a cup of tea and a bun in the tea tent.

"I didn't realise your son was with you." said John.

JP understood the coded message.

"Yes, we like him with us," he smiled, "and I am a patron of the gala, you know, so I thought we should put in an appearance. How goes the world with you?"

155

John told him and from what he said JP concluded the world did not go well with him at all.

"Are you sure you want the hassle of top management again? You should be able to talk Loyalty into a decent pension. This is a pleasant place to live."

"No," said John, "I'm too young to rusticate; there's no challenge here, I'd go to seed."

"Better go to seed than be hacked down."

John smiled and changed the subject, or at least, thought he did.

"Have I mentioned Gainslaw Globes to you before?"

"Yes, I think so; it's a plastics company isn't it. I believe you were going to see it the last time we spoke. Any use?"

John told him about his visit.

"Sounds doubtful," said JP when John had finished.

"Hopeless, I would say," said John, "I said I'd write them a report, but I'm reluctant to pull the rug from under them. Colin works seven days a week, and Kate treats it like her baby. I'm trying to think of a way to tell them it doesn't have a future."

"That's what you believe?"

"Yes,"

"Then say it as gently as you can, but say it. If you're sure."

"Would you not be?"

"From what you say it sounds doubtful, but you might be looking at it with big company eyes. In my experience small companies always look doubtful, but they're very resilient."

"I didn't know you were interested in small businesses."

"It's something of a hobby," JP smiled, "and sometimes they grow big. If you buy in at the beginning it can be very lucrative. Is this Gainslaw Globes well managed?"

"I would say so; Colin is disorganised but Kate and the production man seem to know what they're doing."

"What, then, would you say is the prime problem?"

"There are two: orders and working capital; financially they're living from hand to mouth."

JP nodded his head as if he had expected John's reply and surprised John with his next question.

"Could I take a look?"

"At Gainslaw Globes? Yes, by all means. Do you have an idea?"

"Oh, no," laughed JP, "Just an interest. I have interests; I leave ideas to others, to people like Flambert Pinkerton. We're going away for a few weeks, but I'll contact you when I get back. We're going to try to sail to Shetland, starting tomorrow."

"In the meantime, what do you think I should say to Colin and Kate?"

"You'll never succeed as a consultant if you don't learn how to answer that question," teased JP.

John looked at him quizzically but said nothing. JP explained.

"Page One: Tell them how impressed you are with their operation; that will comfort them. Page Two: Hint at certain weaknesses; that will intrigue them. Page Three: Conclude that more investigation is needed; that will allow you to charge them a further fee."

"I'm doing it for nothing," smiled John, "and interest!"

"Then charge them interest again." quipped JP.

Then he added. "Take a holiday, John, nothing will harm for a few weeks. You need the break."

This too surprised John for he thought he had appeared to the banker as relaxed and in control. He didn't feel thus, but he thought he had given that impression. Holidays were out of the question; there was too much to be decided, things to be settled, too much to do.

Holidays were also in the mind of another young lady. Rebecca had not seen much of her father since he had come north to look after his father. She was annoyed when Marion told her that her father had called the night of the church barbecue; annoyed because Marion didn't cancel and wait with John for her, Rebecca, to return. But she had not given up on her parents. She still believed, in spite of the elapsed time, that they were in some sort of extended huff, each standing on a principle she did not understand but which she felt could not be as important as being a family once again. She believed they lacked only opportunity to talk it through. What else could she think? She watches soap operas, and the whole point of soap operas is to dump characters into a crisis to see if they can talk their way out of it. To talk, her parents needed to be in the same place. Her father seemed stuck for the moment at Birsett so Rebecca conceived a plan to take her mother north.

Her mother had promised her a week's holiday of her choice after she had finished her 'A' levels, so now Rebecca would choose. She decided she wanted to go to Birsett. But before she told her mother she sounded out her Aunt Helen. Helen had already concluded that John was miserable but had no remedies to suggest. She and Alex weren't into holidays, largely by choice. They once went to Benidorm but were suffocated by the plane, the heat, the crowds and the concrete block in which they were incarcerated. Alex did his best to enjoy it; he put on a pair of shorts and a flowery shirt (they are still in the wardrobe) but felt as ridiculous as he looked. He wanted a harbour; he wanted boats; he wanted a sea that looked like a sea; he wanted home.

Helen, unlike JP, did not consider that John needed a holiday to cure his discomfort. As prime victim of his ill-humour she stood in prime position to judge what he should do. She is no psychologist and believed that John should settle himself. He should get away from Birsett for good, or stay for good.

When Rebecca suggested that she and her mother might come to Birsett for a holiday, Helen thought it as good an idea as any other. She balked, however, at Rebecca's idea of them all staying at Braeshiel so agreed to find out where they might be accommodated.

She knew that the row of old fishermen's houses that stood defying the sea at Partan Beach were let out for holidays; all that is, apart from the two that had been knocked into one by John's friend, the retired banker. She made enquiries and discovered that our friend Cockburn Heath was the agent responsible for letting out the cottages. Well, not Cockburn himself, but the doughty Mrs Somerville. Helen went to see her. She didn't tell Mrs Somerville who was enquiring; in Hecklescar you don't tell anybody anything about your family's affairs unless they need to know.

At first Mrs Somerville said that all the houses were taken until September, but when she consulted the register, she found that, due to a cancellation, the one next to JP's was vacant for the second week in August.

"But," said Mrs Somerville, "There are restrictions on that let."

"Restrictions?" said Helen, "What restrictions?"

"No pets, no children, no teenagers, no loud music, no parties. Is it an older couple?"

"No," said Helen, "But it's two people".

"But not a couple?"

"No"

"But they meet the terms, the restrictions?"

"Not exactly, there would be a teenager."

"Ah," said Mrs Somerville as if pronouncing a stiff sentence, "Both teenagers?"

"No, Just the one."

"And the other one?"

"An adult."

"Male? Female?"

Helen could see where Mrs Somerville was headed so chopped her off.

"Both female," snapped Helen, "A girl and her mother."

"It's a shame," said Mrs Somerville, "But the client insists, "No teenagers" in that house."

"There's no way round it?"

"Well, I can sometimes swing it if I know the parties, and know they will behave themselves and be quiet. The client insists on everything being quiet. He prefers elderly couples that just want to go for walks and sit by the front door and read. But last year he did agree to a family staying – he knew the father personally."

Helen was checkmated. She didn't want to reveal more, but unless she did, she might let down Rebecca. Should she gamble?

"It would be in strictest confidence," said Mrs Somerville reading Helen's mind. Helen plumped.

"It's Marion Swansen, John's wife, and his daughter, Rebecca."

Mrs Somerville almost gasped. What a nugget!

"I'm sure that would be all right: good family, nice girl, Rebecca. I could vouch for Rebecca. Besides, Mr Marwick knows John."

"Mr Marwick! He owns the holiday houses?"

"Yes, over the years he has bought them all; he likes to keep them quiet because of his wife; she's a nervous woman, can't stand noise of any kind. But Marion and Rebecca would be all right I'm sure. Shall I book it?"

"I'm not sure," said Helen, "I'll need to get back to......... I'll need to get back."

Mrs Somerville was determined to be kind to Helen.

"I'll reserve it," she said, "until the week-end. Okay?"

"Yes, thanks," said Helen.

Mrs Somerville showed Helen out, but at the door had a message.

"When you see John, would you tell him we have found the notes about the house."

"About the house? Uncle Willie's house? Is something wrong?"

From these questions Mrs Somerville learnt that Helen knew nothing about the disputed will and her disputed right to Willie's house.

I should add, in case you should think that she is a poor legal secretary and blabs all over Hecklescar matters vouchsafed to her in confidence, that Mrs Somerville is watertight when it comes to secrets. Her interest lies not in gossip but in knowing what other people do not know; her gratification is to smile and say, "Yes, I know". Now she knows that John and Marion are attempting a reconciliation. But we know something she doesn't know; she is wrong.

When Helen gave John Mrs Somerville's message and tackled him about the will, he admitted a technicality that would soon be cleared up. Then he rang Margaret to arrange for them to come down to hear what the solicitor had to say. Apart from his belief that he could win the dispute in open conflict, he had other proposals that might settle the matter once and for all.

Thursday was agreed, Thursday at two; they would take lunch on the way; Roddam couldn't really spare the time.

CHAPTER TWENTY-ONE

Rebecca heard with delight Helen's news about the holiday let. But Helen warned her not to get too excited. Marion had not agreed to come and John had not agreed to welcome them. Precarious steps lay between her and her holiday by the seaside. Rebecca asked Helen to tackle John; she was sure she could persuade her mother.

"I doubt it," said Helen, but to herself. It hurt her to think how disappointed Rebecca would be when Marion turned her down. She would turn her down, wouldn't she?

Of course, she would, or would have done; they both would have done, both Marion and John, if they had not felt guilty about their daughter. If they had sat down and discussed it as rational adults (counting Rebecca too) it would have been argued off the table and lost in a multitude of words and recriminations. But Rebecca and Helen had outflanked them, and in the end, Marion had no defence against her daughter. Here is how the conversation went. They were strolling along the Ouse Walkway in York beside the river on a warm calm summer evening.

"No Rebecca, it is out of the question. I know I promised you could go anywhere, but you had no right to go behind my back and arrange a holiday at Birsett. You will have to cancel it. If you don't, I will."

"Well," said Rebecca, close to tears, "If you don't go, I will. I'm sick of the pair of you. You think of no one but yourselves. I wish you'd both grow up. I could understand it if you had fallen in love with someone else, or dad had, but it's silly you living here and him living there. You need to get together and talk it through." (There! I told you; too many soap operas!)

Rebecca had never talked like this before and Marion realised that all her attempts to protect Rebecca from the fallout of the split had failed. She now knew that she had to talk it through. No, not talk it through – just talk; talk to her daughter; try to explain to her what she felt and why she could not go to Birsett. And as she explained it to her daughter, for the first time, she fully explained it to herself.

"If your father had come looking for us when we left home, I would have gone back to him, for I loved him then, and I suppose I love him now in a forlorn sort of way. But love that is unexpressed and unreturned is worse than no love at all, in spite of what the novels say. To live in the same house as someone you love but not to touch them, not to interact with them (oh, that is the wrong word!), not to intermingle with them (that's not it either, but it is closer), not to share a mutual life, a life where everything is common and interfused, where the details are the same details, is to have the life slowly drained from you."

Do you understand, Rebecca? How can you?

"You feel yourself drifting away on a cold current of indifference and you fight against it, struggle, stretch out. At first you think it will come within reach again, that you will be able to reach it, touch it, grasp it, hold it. Sometimes you think you are gaining on the tide, then it sets in again and the same dismal drift continues and you are further away than ever. After months, no, after years, you grow weak and tired and no longer try to close the gap; you accept that what you once had you will never have, never enjoy, again."

"Oh mum, that's sad, very sad." said Rebecca, wiping her eyes.

"I don't want to hurt you, or to separate you from your father, Rebecca. I think your father loves you yet. Try to stay in touch with him. But it's all over for me, I can't see any way back now; we've drifted too far. I must make my way as best as I can, and I'm not making too bad a job of it, am I?"

She tried to smile.

"You mustn't give up, mum. I'm sure dad still loves you. I saw him at granddad's funeral, the way he smiled when he saw us, the way he looked at you. And he came to see you the night of the barbecue. He's been badly knocked. I think he needs you."

"No, love, he needs a mother."

"Well, can't you be a mother to him?"

"No, Rebecca, I can't; I am a wife or I am nothing."

"But you were a wife once; you can be a wife again."

"I'm not sure I want to be a wife again; there was a point to it then; I made a home for you all, for your father and for you and Robert. But that is over now; Robert will never be at home again and you will be leaving shortly."

"If I pass my 'A' levels."

"*When* you pass your 'A' levels. And what need is there then for a homemaker when there is no one at home?"

Rebecca changed tack.

"Other people seem to manage it; look at Aunt Fiona and Uncle Ian. They haven't split up, they're still together."

"No, and they won't."

"Why you and dad then, and not them?"

"I wish I knew. Ian is different from your dad; Ian works to live, your father lives to ……."

Marion stopped; the cliché too sour in her mouth. They had turned away from the river and were walking past the neat gardens of a street of houses.

"It's like a garden; you work in it, thinking the other one is working in it too, creating something, something bright and beautiful, creating something together, something gathering, growing, maturing over the years so that, when the children are grown up and away, you have a richness still to share. Then the other one stops working so much, then only a little, then not at all. For a while you keep on working, believing they will come back when they are not so busy, then hoping that they might come back someday to join once again in growing something together, believing that they are still interested. Then one day you realise that they never think of the garden, that they have lost interest in flowers; they have moved on. You have worked all those years and produced nothing, nothing that you can share."

Rebecca walked on in silence aware that she was listening not to a spontaneous outpouring of regret, but to a much rehearsed, private, painful, testimony. For all the outward poise of her mother over the past nine months; for all the bustle and bravado, her mother was hurt, deeply hurt, hurt in her very soul. She regretted that she had ever called her silly. But Marion quickly hid again.

"Fiona is different. Sometimes it works, sometimes it doesn't; that's my conclusion and it's not much of a conclusion, is it? Best not to try and sort it out. It is too tangled. Better just start again."

She tried to sound philosophical but she sounded weary, and Rebecca searched her young mind for the right words of comfort, but her slight experience had not yet crafted them, so she said what she could.

"Could you not start again with dad?" she said.

Her mother smiled sadly at her and shook her head. You would have thought after all of this Rebecca would have relented, would have cancelled the holiday, would have understood. But she persisted because her understanding was too deep for argument and too accurate for reason.

"It's just one week, mum, just one week. We needn't see dad if you don't want. Please, go for me. I'm going anyway."

Then Marion, tired of argument and tired of refusing her daughter, relented. Almost immediately she regretted it. Many times, during the intervening weeks she considered telling Rebecca to call off, but she never did. Openness and honesty are poor virtues at times like these.

Helen had a much easier task and accomplished it much more easily. She has considerable experience and had leverage on her subject: she did his washing. She had brought it down, freshly ironed, and had Louise with her to blunt any outburst she might provoke. But before she could begin her approach John launched into his own campaign. He made her a cup of tea and offered her one of her own scones. What should she expect? Something about the house. No, the house belonged to her but John would like to live in it. She couldn't use it yet; it was too small, not a family house, so could he, John, lease it from her? For, say, five years, or if that was too long, two, or even a year at a time? But how much rent? It didn't seem right to charge him for living in his own father's home. John insisted. Cockburn Heath would set the rent at a commercial level. Helen agreed, but would talk it over with Alex; five years would be all right. John would tie it up with Cockburn Heath. Oh, and he would be allowed to sub-let it if he had to move away for a new job. No, there was no new job at the moment, but there would be.

In the afterglow of that agreement Helen broke the news about Marion and Rebecca coming to stay at JP's cottage for a week in August. She presented it as a fait accompli and John shrugged his shoulders. What he felt she didn't know and he didn't understand. Was he pleased? Was he annoyed? Was he excited? All three. He would have liked to ask Helen for advice, but could not bring himself to do so.

"If that's what Rebecca wants." was all he would admit to. But Louise (who had been playing with the companion set and apparently not paying any attention) reported afterwards that Uncle John took another scone when he already had one on his plate.

Before the deal on the house could be done, Helen's right to it had to be established. John was sure that Margaret's challenge would fail at law and he thought that he knew his sister well enough to believe she would not pursue it to the end. She might be pushy and a snob, but not mean-minded. Roddam would be the stickler. He saw the house, John believed correctly, not as a house but as a property advert:

"In an outstanding location in an attractive seaside village, with sea views and established garden, this rare stone-built house represents a unique opportunity for a discerning buyer to acquire a perfect retirement or holiday home."

(Yes, my pedantic computer, I know it is a convoluted sentence but that is the way these people talk.)

What irritated Roddam most was that the house had been left to someone who clearly undervalued it. Helen saw it only as a place to live.

On Thursday at the solicitors, Roddam, decked out in fighting plumage of yellow waistcoat and spotted bow tie, showed his agitation by strutting like a bantam cock about the reception room and constantly looking at his watch. Margaret, on the other hand, sat slumped in a chair looking unusually disconsolate. Then, as the town clock chimed two (the appointed time), Roddam rushed out of his corner and ignoring Mrs Somerville's protestations barged into the solicitor's room. Margaret and John trooped after him. They found Cockburn hunched over a model yacht gluing a green starboard light into position.

"Come in," he said, genially but unnecessarily. "It's Mr Craig, isn't it; come about the late William Swansen's will."

He put out a hand, which Roddam grabbed rather than grasped, only to find himself unable to let go as he stuck to Cockburn with the super glue the solicitor had been using. Cockburn laughed and apologised. Even Margaret saw the funny side of it and smiled a little as she helped her husband to extricate himself from the fingers of justice. This gaiety increased Roddam's irritation and he immediately demanded that they should get on with the meeting; not everyone had time to play around with boats. Cockburn acceded to this request by ushering all to the table, clearing a space for each of them and asking Mrs Somerville to bring in the necessary documents. Whilst she was away, Roddam grandly announced to John and the solicitor that he had done what he had threatened; he had taken counsel; he had sought advice from Rennie Murray, from Derek Geddes, Senior Partner, no less. When he said this Margaret glanced at him nervously. But she need not have worried; Roddam knew what he was doing; he was posturing in his corner. He had no intention of fighting; at least, not on the basis of what Sir Derek had had to say.

Mrs Somerville returned with a previous copy of the will, dated seven years earlier than the new will, shortly after Jane, John's mother had died. Most of it lay unaltered but the clause about the house had been changed. Cockburn read out the original. Formerly it read, "I leave my house, Braeshiel, Birsett, in the County of Berwickshire, to Margaret Jane Craig, of, Flat 3/14, Leith Hill, Edinburgh EH3 4DG". The stated address plainly discomforted both the named party and her husband.

"That was a temporary arrangement before we moved to Morningside," she rushed to explain. But she didn't need to explain it for the rest of the party knew the real story; all, that is, except Cockburn and he had known but had forgotten. At the time of the original will, twelve years ago, Roddam had left the Property Agents in which he worked as office manager under circumstances that he and Margaret would prefer to forget. Goaded by his wife who had formed the opinion that he did all the work in the office he had presented his firm with an ultimatum, namely, that they make him a director, or he would resign. They refused to make him a director and were relaxed about his resignation. Out on the street he bumped along the bottom of the labour market in various low paid clerical jobs for three years. The family could no longer afford the mortgage on the house they were buying in Colinton and had had to sell up and take the furnished flat in Leith Hill. Hence their embarrassment now, and Willie's generosity then. But give Roddam credit, he had worked himself out of the hole by finding a billet in Patterson & Partners, and working his way up until he added his own name to the partnership. Within five years they had recovered middle-class security in Morningside.

"You will note," said Mrs Somerville, "that the name, address and relationship of Margaret has been stroked out and that of "Helen Paulin, my niece, of 21 Upper Birsett, Birsett, Hecklescar" has been written, if that is the description, underneath". She glowered at Cockburn who recognised his own scribble and winced.

"You will see particularly that, "my daughter" has been stroked out, and, "my niece" has been written in. The fault lies with the typist, whoever she was." (Another glower, another wince).

Everyone looked at Roddam who played for time by poring over the document. He knew that they had no case. Sir Derek had told him that; had told him that all he could expect if he pursued it was a hefty legal bill. He needed a way of retreat.

"I'd like to refer this to……."

John saw his opportunity and cut in.

"Roddam, there is a simple way out of this. I will take over the house on a lease from Helen and will pay her a rent determined by Mr Heath here. You may use the house whenever I have no use for it. The property will be put to good use. Helen gets the rent, the family gets the use of the house, and I get a home."

Roddam made pretence of considering the proposal, then beamed suddenly and took John by the hand.

"It's a deal," he said in his best Estate Agent voice. Then he shook hands with Cockburn and with his wife, but he drew the line at Mrs Somerville.

The rent was fixed at £300 per month, John to be responsible for maintenance, insurance, council tax and repairs.

John, surprised at the ease with which it had been settled, put it down to the advice Roddam had received from Sir Derek. He was only partly right. The Morningside pair were distracted by less learned but more penetrating counsel. Margaret had noticed a lump on her left breast and had attended the Western General for tests the day before the meeting with the lawyer: results would take a few days. John did not know this, but he did notice that on the way back to their car Roddam and Margaret held hands. He had not seen them do that before.

CHAPTER TWENTY-TWO

John had not reckoned that his offer of free board and lodgings would be taken up quite so quickly, but within a week Margaret rang to say Abigail wanted to come down to Braeshiel for a few days. Alone? No, not alone. You're coming too, you and Roddam? No, not me and Roddam: Jude. Not him again!

But before he arrived a phone call from Belinda Boyd presented John with an even more painful prospect. Loyalty wanted their car back. Jim Arkwright had been complaining about having to drive in and out of the factory in a Rover 75; his position demanded a BMW at least. Loyalty balked at buying a BMW for someone who, in their intention, was a stopgap. Then Ms Waltham, whose duty it is to care for employees, earned her performance pay by awarding John's Mercedes to Arkwright. Loyalty had every right to the car; they had been generous; they had allowed John to keep it for almost two months longer than commercial decency demanded. On Monday a driver would arrive at Braeshiel to collect the car. With him would be a security man in case their former Managing Director cut up rough.

John, you had better settle with this lot before they put

a tank on your lawn!

Giving up the Mercedes hit John hard. He should have given it up when he left Loyalty; should have told them where to stuff it. But he had held on to it believing that he had enough control to choose where and when he would hand it over. He must now strip off that vestigial dignity:

'Give up your toy, our discarded M.D.; we have let you play with it long enough; Jim Arkwright wants a turn.' Jim Arkwright!

There was more to it than indignity. It is not just a car; it is a Mercedes CLK. John is not a snob, but, as we have seen, he thought of himself as a success. He had worked his way up from a little village school to the head of a large and important enterprise. He had bought his family a swish house in one of the best parts of York; he had sent his children to good schools and dressed his wife in designer clothes. He attended, by special invitation, civic lunches, prestigious occasions and important conferences. He wore Saville Row suits and New Bond Street shirts. He had his own named parking space and business cards with his rank in embossed italics.

Apart from the clothes, these symbols of position and influence had been ripped from him one by one. Each one had taken away a strip of his confidence. When he thought of how far he had fallen he felt wretched. There remained only the Mercedes CLK. Every time he saw it, sat in it or drove it, it reminded him of what he had achieved and perhaps what he could achieve again. Now the Merc is going and, when it had gone, no symbols remained. Would his self-belief survive such a shock? For a wild moment John considered asking Loyalty if he could keep it, even if he had to buy it, but no sooner did the thought enter his mind than he saw it as a mirage. The car had to be a company car, a prestigious company car, a company Mercedes. John felt physically sick at the thought of losing it, sick and mind-weary. When Alex called with a couple of cod fillets, John poured out his despair to him.

Alex could not see why a car should cause such grief. He had always bought his own car, always second hand, from Hecklescar Motors, run by David Burns, who gave you a good deal on the old one. And there was always the Aurora's van in an emergency. His car provided a mechanism for getting from one place to another; he could not see what the fuss was about.

(Think Alex; think what the Silver Cord means to you; that's what the Mercedes means to John. 'A car! Like the Silver Cord? You're joking. How many lobsters can you catch with a Mercedes? It's a toy! He doesn't need it.')

He said to John,

"David will find you a good car."

That did not make John feel any better. Nevertheless, he went to David and David found him a nice clean 2-year-old Peugeot 406, low mileage. Every time he saw it, sat in it or drove it, it mocked him.

After the loss of the car, John's job search became more frantic. He widened his net and blurred his focus, cold-calling smaller companies and applying for lower level positions – Operations Director, Works Director, even Chief Engineer and General Manager. He was, without admitting it, accepting Zack's way of thinking and lowering his sights, moderating his demands, chasing lower bucks. To make him look more affordable, he took out of his CV those facts that had previously given him most pride: his substantial salary, his benefits package, the car. From most of his applications he received no more than an acknowledgement followed by weeks of silence before an enquiring phone call informed him that the position had been filled, or he wasn't on the short list, or he wouldn't be called for interview. Once or twice his hopes flared when a sympathetic director rang to ask a few kindly questions, but always at the end, the dread words, "nothing at the moment, but we'll bear you in mind if..." The word, "*abandon*" crept its way down the results column of his Executive Search Control Sheet.

Zack's counsel, though it sounded corny when he first heard it, now comforted John - *"the chances of landing your dream job increase in proportion to the number of applications you send".* But every one he posted ate into his self-confidence; every CV depleted his self-respect, every accompanying letter sickened him. He tried not to recall the occasions when he had received them at Pinkerton and had scribbled "No" across them and sent them back to Sarah. The thought began to torment him that all Chief Executives of all decent UK companies now knew about his despairing attempts to find a job. He even contemplated ringing Zack again. He hadn't informed Zack that he no longer wanted his services but it made little difference for Zack had abandoned John; he had candidates on his books much easier to place.

John rang for an appointment to see Dr Stacey; he had to find something for these persistent headaches. He had to wait three days. At Pinkerton when he needed a doctor, he asked the factory MO to call in. He came to office; not quite a personal physician, but very like it.

Now it was different, John found himself sitting in the waiting room at Hecklescar Health Centre amongst Monday morning's collection of pale-faced children, geriatrics, malingerers, hangovers and hypochondriacs. He felt out of place. He could tell that some of them recognised him and knew his story. They smiled and whispered to their neighbours. Ella somebody or other came in and addressed an unseen receptionist through the hatch. John could hear only one side of the conversation.

"It's me. You didn't ring."

"You said you'd ring."

"But you promised."

"Blood test results."

"If they're here, why didn't you ring? You promised to ring."

"Is it down?"

"My diabetes. Is it down?"

"What?"

"Within acceptable limits! What does that mean?"

"So, it's down?"

"I thought it would be down. I've been sticking to the diet; I thought it would be down."

"I've to make an appointment with Dr Elliot."

"Him, not her."

"Twelve o'clock on Friday."

"This Friday?"

"Twelve o'clock's no use. That's me man's dinner time."

"Eleven o'clock on Monday? Next Monday?"

"That's next week. Can ye no' mak it this week?"

"Friday, twelve o'clock? Is that all, that's the only one you've got?"

"Alright, put me down. But me man's no' gonna be pleased."

"You're sure me diabetes isn't down? I've been sticking to the diet."

The whole waiting room is party to this sketch and they are all entertained - except John. The paltriness irritates him. But it isn't paltry to Ella, John. She is old, she lives on a miserable state pittance, she has diabetes, she often feels ill, and she has an awkward husband to keep, and they didn't ring her as they promised. But she keeps at it and draws income from a cleaning job two mornings a week and strength from two nights in the fellowship of the Bingo: her hope lies in a lottery ticket on Saturday night. Listen and learn, John. Of such is the kingdom.

There is nothing entertaining about John's interaction with the National Health Service. Dr Stacey heard what he had to say, checked his blood pressure, sounded him and arranged for a blood test. The diagnosis? Stress. The remedy? Ease off; learn to relax. Did he have a holiday planned? He did. Where? At home with the family. Then take full advantage of it, and take paracetamol for the headaches. No need to come back, unless it gets worse.

Later that day his beloved Mercedes was driven out of his life and Abigail and Jude arrived in its place. St Andrews University had gone down and Abigail had a long free summer to pursue her interests. Her interest in Birsett had been stimulated when she was last down by the motto of the Hecklescar Fishermen's Association, "Of boats and men", and she had convinced Jude that a few days toying creatively with the phrase in oils would amuse them both. It would, incidentally, also go towards the portfolio she had to submit in the autumn. They arrived at Braeshiel with the intention of staying until the Friday or Saturday. In the end that is not the way it turned out.

On their arrival, the problem of sleeping arrangements immediately presented itself. If the pair had reckoned that John would change the house rules to accommodate them, they had reckoned wrongly. John was in no mood for accommodation and threatened Jude with immediate expulsion for suggesting that John was jealous because he "wasn't getting any". John continued his stay in the back bedroom, Abigail took her grandfather's old room and Jude would sleep on a folding bed in the living room. When Mr Scott discovered this arrangement, he offered Jude a room in his house but Jude, for reasons that can be guessed and will become obvious, declined.

Thankfully, for the first two days the weather stayed fine and Abigail and Jude spent most of their time out of doors, coming home in the evening to dine at the Basking Shark in Hecklescar before returning to Braeshiel. If you think that the painting project was a mere device for a free holiday you must take yourself in hand; you are becoming cynical. Between them they produced four pictures each attempting to capture the spirit of this tranquil part of the country and its toiling workers. If you like panoramic scenes then a couple of Jude's seascapes would look nice, one over the other, above your mantelpiece or in your hall. You can buy limited-edition prints in brushed brass frames at Margaret's shop in Morningside for £80 a pair – but you know that already. I wouldn't recommend Abigail's productions unless you like black skies, yellow waves, purple boats and stick fishermen with crimson faces.

Having survived a night and a breakfast with the artistic pair, John took his report to Gainslaw Globes and was given a warm welcome by Kate. She said she had good news; Colin had gone to Glasgow to sign up the order with Caledesign Solutions for the Scottish Foodflair range. But good news rarely comes unalloyed in small businesses. They would have to buy the tools themselves (normally they are supplied by the customer). That would cost £20,000; £20,000 they didn't have.

"Once the deal is signed, we'll go to see our friendly bank manager," she smiled.

John took advantage of the brighter mood to ask if JP could have a look at the business. Kate demurred.

"We can't afford it; he's a merchant banker, isn't he?"

"It's free," replied John, "and who knows what he might be prepared to do for you?"

Kate relaxed and said she would persuade Colin to accept the offer. John could take it as agreed unless he heard from her. He didn't hear.

John came away from his visit feeling better about himself and better about Gainslaw Globes. But if Kate had been strictly honest and told him her fears, he would not have been so sanguine.

CHAPTER TWENTY-THREE

I will not bore you with the details of Jude and Abigail's stay at Birsett. However, something took place on Wednesday so uncommon that we must take full advantage of it. It comprises a clash of minds no sociologist could have inveigled into the same room.

On that day in the evening Mr Scott had called on John whilst John was having a snack in the kitchen of Braeshiel. He had not been long settled when Jude arrived looking for Abigail who had apparently gone off without telling him. Jude, at a loose end and in a prickly mood, was looking for someone to bait and Mr Scott seemed as good a prey as any. Without invitation he helped himself to coffee and settled for the affray. But before he could let off his ranging shots, Helen arrived looking for David who had gone missing with the family car. He had passed his test, but he had not told Helen where he was going. The fact that Abigail had also disappeared persuaded Helen that she should wait for her return suspecting that she might be able throw some light on David's whereabouts.

Jude could not believe his luck for now he had three prime paid-up members of old blinkered society in his sights. He started on the old minister.

"You've never married," he said.

"No, I have not had that blessing."

"You think it would have been a blessing?"

"Yes, I think so."

"Even to someone like yourself."

John gasped and Helen narrowed her eyes. Mr Scott looked intently at Jude.

"By which you mean?" he mumbled.

"Forgive me", said Jude, "I am naturally suspicious. Considering that ministers, at least in your days, could have the pick of the female crop in the parish, I get to wondering why one hasn't married."

"Well, I didn't," replied the old minister, trying not to read Jude's meaning.

"Oh, come on," said Jude, "You can be open with me. Some of my best friends are gay and I've been there myself more than once."

Helen and John cried out at once.

"That's sick," muttered Helen.

"That's enough, Jude" snapped John, standing up.

Mr Scott put his hand on John's arm and pulled him back into his seat. John looked at his old friend expecting to see anger or discomfort. Certainly, he saw discomfort yet the old bachelor held Jude's gaze.

"What you think is your own affair," he said quietly, "But let me say this to you. (Excuse me, Helen.) Sexual pleasure is not all. Some of us have managed very well without it."

"Oh, come on," cried Jude enjoying the reaction he had provoked, "You're all afraid of it; you're homophobic!"

"What?" asked Helen.

"Homophobic!"

"What's that?" asked Helen

"It is the fear of homosexuality," said John

"I'm not frightened of it," said Helen; "I just think it's weird."

"Ah!" cried Jude, turning to Mr Scott and John, "See what I mean."

John opened his mouth to defend Helen but before he could speak Jude launched into a sermon on the beauty and excitement of sex lavishly illustrated with scenes from his own experience. His message was not designed to convert his congregation but to embarrass them. This it did: long before he had finished, they no longer looked at him. They studied the walls and the floor and waited anxiously for the benediction.

"You see, there is no need to be afraid of it; enjoy it, celebrate it, but most of all" (and surely, he had rehearsed this) "embrace it." He laughed at his own wit and exulted in the discomfort of his congregation. But one of them was not interested in debate.

"You need to grow up," said Helen.

Jude, nettled, retaliated with an attack on small town attitudes and buttoned up females. He put up Aunt Sallies and knocked them down: older people needed to wise up. (He thought of himself as young). Their time is past: their attitudes obsolete: the holy restraint game lost.

"People will have sex; you can't order them not to; that genie is out of the bottle; you can't put it back; you have to accept that things are the way they are, not as you think they should be".

"It's a noxious tide…." started Mr Scott

"A noxious tide!" mocked Jude and renewed his attack.

He was enjoying this. Mr Scott fell silent. If he could have said what he wanted to say this is what he would have said: (and here I must admit I have tidied it up and organised it. If I reported it as it careered through the old minister's mind you would not be able to follow it.)

"A noxious tide," he would have said, "has flooded into and polluted the very soul of our society. It floods across our screens and into our literature, and even into our news; it has made voyeurs of us all. In every area of human intercourse, all the quiet pastel shades of human affection, all subtle kindnesses and gentle innocence, all humour and entertainment, all decent care and friendly love are now overrun by it. It rampages through our society like an aroused bull - and we are all bullied into silence. Do not try to tame the beast! Do not seek to bridle it! Do not cry for help! It is the spirit of the age! We can do nothing about it; it is the way we are made!"

Jude paused in his lecture. Mr Scott again attempted to pull something out of the tumult in his mind.

"Do you not think it has blighted our regard for each other?"

The question was meant to be rhetorical but Jude was in no mood for any rhetoric but his own.

"On the contrary," he boomed, "it is life-enhancing". He launched forth again linking the development of sexual freedom with the explosion in creative expression; in literature, art, music, dance. But we have heard it so often. Let us listen instead to the hidden voice of the old man:

"It has blighted our regard for each other. We treat each other as sexual objects, toys. We see sexual motives everywhere. A man may no longer treasure the friendship of another man, or a woman, a woman's. We dare not speak to a strange child for fear of accusation, or give them a carry when they are tired; teachers may no longer dress a wound or put their arm round a distraught child. Vulnerable adolescents are pushed into the path of predatory adults and given condoms and advice on hygiene instead of standards and good examples. All those kind and friendly acts between men and women are regarded as foreplay and sniggered at. Physical consummation is all. Love, in all its loveliness, warmth and tenderness has been reduced to a compulsive animal act."

Jude streamed on full flow: "Sex has always dominated the mind of man (and women for that matter); just nowadays we are more open and honest about it. All that's changed is that the old hypocrisy's gone. Nowadays, even vicars are admitting they're gay."

He won't leave it alone, will he? Mr Scott ignored his assault.

"The old hypocrisy," said the old minister, as if weighing the word. "Hypocrisy, yes. How would you define it?"

"Pretending none of us has dirty knickers," clipped Jude. Mr Scott ignored the crudity but picked up the meaning.

"Yes, true. But are there no hypocrites now?"

"There are still some around," said Jude.

"But not you?"

"No, we believe in being completely open. We try, at least, to be honest."

"A noble creed," said Mr Scott, "But that doesn't exclude hypocrisy. Our hypocrisy, the old hypocrisy, what was it?

'But where ye feel your honour grip, let that aye be your border'.

"That's Rabbie Burns......."

Jude broke in and outlined a lecture he is working up on the influence of Burns' morality on Scottish art in the early nineteenth century. If you would like to hear it, he is presenting it at a summer school next summer. Details from *www.artontheedge.com*. For now, we will listen to a voice not often heard:

"Like Burns" Mr Scott thought but did not say, "We don't always 'reck the rede', keep the counsel, but we feel the grip; we have an idea of honour; of what man should be; what he could be. Modern hypocrisy is different. There is no vision of what man is or what he is for; he is a just the plaything of his instincts and opportunities. We have learned to silence our conscience with explanations and justifications. Having lost our honour and our confidence in goodness, we try to make a virtue out of letting everyone do what they like. Even though our behaviour is destroying us and the society around us, we pretend it is acceptable, that it is causing no harm, that it is derived from some higher principle, some nobler purpose, to which we put a name but never quite explain."

Jude had stopped.

"Personal freedom, that's the problem," said Mr Scott confronted with silence.

"But you can't be against personal freedom, surely," snorted Jude. This was new; Jude had never met anyone who had dared challenge such an obvious good as personal freedom.

"I think I am," replied Mr Scott, "Isn't it just another name for self-indulgence?"

"Oh, God," sighed Jude, and patiently explained how only by freeing the mind from external authority, and mutually cancelling commitments can people rise above their environment and cultural typecasting.

While he did so Mr Scott roamed free in the rich jungle of his own thinking:

"Freedom," he could have told Jude, "is a great cause for the weak and oppressed, but for the strong and already free it is a claim to be rid of the weak. This brand of freedom causes mayhem: it shatters families as one partner or the other asserts their rights: it blights the lives of young people with drugs and drink and over-indulgence. Worse, it turns them into inconsequential butterflies, flitting from sensation to sensation, relationship to relationship; discovering nothing, learning nothing; looking for depth in the shallows; seeking a harvest without labour. How many end up in cardboard boxes on the streets? Or alone and dislocated in dismal flats and bed-sits? Or on a social worker's list? And is that list not full? Are they scratching around for work, the social workers? Is the Welfare bill, the bill for human misery, lower now? Is Alcoholics Anonymous disbanding? Are drug clinics closing down? Are we paying off policemen because we can't find work for them in our happy and peaceful community? Do old people not die terrified and alone in bleak tenements? Are bairns not left in filthy holes while their deserted mother sells herself on the streets? Do we not rake unborn children out of the warm womb? And whence all these blessings? The gospel of personal freedom! I think I am against personal freedom."

He came back to the conversation when a new voice interrupted the lecturer's ode to freedom.

"Provided someone else looks after the bairns," he heard Helen announce, "and the old folk. I mean, who looks after your bairns?" Both John and Mr Scott stared at Helen. Jude's bairns? He doesn't have children, does he? Oh yes, he does; well, not children, child. How did Helen know? She had made it her business to find out; she had asked Abigail.

"That's beside the question," sniffed Jude, "My family affairs are for me to sort out."

Helen ignored him. She had caught sight of a rabbit and determined to chase it.

"But where are they? With their mother, I bet. She'll have to feed them and get them up and wipe their bottoms. You've chickened out, so she'll have to work to keep them."

"There is only one," snapped Jude, "and she's well cared

for. I do what I can."

Oh, how lame that sounded after all the grand talk. John and Mr Scott smirked at each other.

"And who looks after your little daughter......what's her name?"

"Aphrodite."

"Aphrodite! Poor bairn, saddled wi' a name like that. Anyway, who looks after Aphrodite when her mother's at work? No, let me guess; it'll be her granny, or her auntie! And what about your parents? Is your mother still alive? Who looks after her?"

"They don't need anyone to look after them; they are both fit and well."

"How do you know? When did you last see them?"

Jude refused to be interrogated further. He had not seen his parents for two years. Mind you, for the first of those they had been on a world cruise. Mr Scott rescued him by switching the discussion back to generalities.

"This new age of yours, does it have any virtues apart from self-indulgence?"

"Of course! I've given you two already, honesty and freedom. Another is tolerance. Yes, there you are: honesty, freedom and tolerance. If you want virtues that should be enough."

He fell silent and now Mr Scott has the floor and we do not have time to rearrange his words. So, like the old parishioners of Birsett, I'm afraid you must 'redd it oot for yersels.'

"Oh, we must have virtues. Cement of society. Not values, note, virtues. We talk about values, but it's virtues we need. The Victorians understood that. Aggregate! Not cement. Have you ever laid a footpath?"

He didn't wait for an answer; he assumed (correctly)

that Jude had not stooped to such a task.

"Aggregate! I once laid a footpath, but it broke up, crumbled. The builder: 'not enough aggregate.' Not the theory, the studies, the debates, the laws. One hand for the ship and one for yourself. We have let go of the ship. The task of society is not to make people happier but to raise them higher; the beast is always just behind us. Two hundred years ago an old man swept the horse muck off the turnpike at Dunbar; I was reading about it in Somerville. He could quote Plato; knew about the stars, astronomy. Nowadays graduates can't do that! They take the Daily Record, go to rock concerts and bet on the National Lottery. Choirs sang in harmony. I have a tape of a broadcast at Hecklescar; a service in 1960; butchers, grocers, fish cadgers, shop assistants. Little Eck sang Gerontius: he was a fisherman: Gerontius! Civil society needs aggregate: virtuous people living decent lives, salt of the earth, or society breaks up."

"But I've given you virtues: three! How many do you want?

"No! They're not virtues. Gentleness, kindness, faithfulness, humility, patience, self-control – they're virtues: Galatians five, Fruits of the Spirit. Yeast hidden in the dough. But laughed at by the cognoscenti; despised by politicians and sportsmen; shouted down by your virtues which are not virtues at all. Stuck up on the balcony, your virtues - for observers and cynics; not in the street; the old virtues were virtues of the street. Many people in the street are gentle, faithful, kind – young people are often kind. Morag, Helen, is kind."

"Who, our Morag?" said Helen in surprise.

"Yes. She brought me a lovely bunch of daffodils at Easter."

He switched back to Jude.

"What you have given, these three, are not virtues, no,

no. They are vices masquerading as virtues. No that's too strong, though they might be vices. Accommodations - that's what they are: accommodations. Honesty! Not true! Cheat if you can win by it - that's Okay. But that's not what you mean. Your honesty is admitting to dishonesty I think; that's dishonest. That's all; very feeble. Freedom accommodates - to Rott; Rott is free; you should meet Rott – see what freedom is."

"But not in a dark alley," mumbled John.

Mr Scott continued.

"And tolerance! The moral coward's last bolthole. Not understanding - that's a virtue. Not discretion. Think of it! We have lost the will to improve human nature. *'Ma per seguir virtute e canoscenza'* - we have forgotten 'not made to live as brutes'. Oscar Wilde, The Picture of Dorian Grey: what is happening in the attic while we are tolerating? But do not judge or condemn. Examine it! Come to conclusions! This great experiment of gorging our appetites hasn't worked. It was Freud; discredited now - he fiddled his results; but accepted still; too seductive to reject. We are deceived. A slide into barbarity, that's all it is. But give it a virtuous name: call it tolerance."

Mr Scott had rattled excitedly through this speech almost without pause, but now he stopped suddenly and gasped for air. His face was flushed and his hands trembled. John put his hand round his shoulder and looked into his eyes.

"Blood pressure", said the old man, trying to smile, "I have a pill for it." He fished in his pocket for his pillbox, took out a tablet and sucked it.

"My apologies," he said, "I feel strongly about this; I hate to see what has happened. Not only you, Jude; our generation. We let things go. We sold our birth right for what? Eh, John?"

John nodded and Jude, to his credit, took no advantage of the confession.

Mr Scott, however, had something more to say. He was

no longer interested in society and trying to reform it. It was from his heart that he now appealed to Jude.

"Jude, do not waste your life collecting sensations; it will bring frustration, not happiness."

Jude was taken aback by both the warmth and lucidity. He smiled uncomfortably.

"What else is there?" he said flippantly. "All you need is love."

"Love," cut in Helen, "What do you know about love? I'll tell you what love is. No, I'll show you. Cecil and Dorothy, that's love."

Jude looked blank. John vaguely recalled Cecil, Cecil from Surrey, in the bungalow on the A1.

"Cecil knows what love is. He's eighty and he looks after his wife; she's eighty-six. She no' keeps weel; can't do anything for hersel' so he does it a'; he gets the messages, does the cookin', and the cleanin'; takes her round the garden in her chair; reads the paper to her; she's nearly blind. Cleans her up when she has an accident. And he's done it for over eight years, every day for eight years, he's doin' it the day, now, that's love!"

Jude ignored this outburst. Helen didn't understand the rules: don't drop into particulars; keep it general. Besides he had never met and didn't know anyone like Cecil and Dorothy. Again, Mr Scott came to his rescue. He picked up on Jude's last question.

"We need love," said the old man, "Certainly, but more. I've thought about it. It comes to this: trust God, do what good you can and make an attempt at the truth. If we keep at those, we might gain satisfaction, and with good fortune, perhaps happiness."

"Has it made you happy?" asked Jude locking again onto his first target.

The question was never answered for as Jude spoke the door opened and in came Abigail and, just behind her, David. Attention, particularly Helen's, diverted to more immediate and particular matters of virtue.

Helen took David home, John walked Mr Scott to his house and Jude went to bed, at first to his own; then, by invitation, to Abigail's. Later Helen also went to bed with Alex. If you expect me to spy on either couple you've picked up the wrong book. But this I will tell you: that although what they did was roughly the same, what they accomplished was altogether different.

CHAPTER TWENTY-FOUR

When John discovered that Jude had spent the night with Abigail in his father's bed, he sent both of them packing, and told sister Margaret he didn't want them back. She didn't complain; she had other things on her mind.

She reported in some panic that tomorrow she had to attend the Western General Hospital for investigative surgery on the lump on her breast. Afterwards could she and Roddam spend a weekend at Birsett. John expressed concern and agreement. They would be welcome.

John thought he had better visit Mr Scott to check what harm the encounter with Jude might have caused. The old man hadn't slept much and was tired, but in reasonable spirits and said he hoped that John hadn't sent them away on his account. He had quite enjoyed the encounter, but wasn't sure that he had said what he wanted to say. He felt that he may have been too hard on the present generation, too condemnatory. We may be sure Jude felt no such qualms about his contribution.

Coming out of Mr Scott's John ran into JP toiling up the brae.

"This hill gets steeper every time we come back," he puffed to John. "I like the exercise, but I am beginning to think it is too much of a good thing. I was on my way to you to see if we could arrange the visit to Gainslaw Globes you promised me."

John arranged it and, on Friday, JP shook hands with Kate and Colin and began gently to interrogate them about their business. First, he toured the building, asking questions, examining paperwork, talking to operators, making notes, all the time under an unremitting barrage of explanation, justification and obfuscation from Colin. Then he moved into the office to examine the systems and accounts. His discipline impressed John. He seemed to be working from some sort of mental checklist and left nothing to doubt. Every answer Kate or Colin gave he wrote down. If they quoted a figure off the top of their heads, he asked them to confirm it and waited until Kate found it in the files. He worked through their balance sheet and profit and loss statement and picked line by line through the most recent monthly financial reports. He probed the value of the physical assets and identified sources of finance and associated costs. At the end he asked to see a cash flow prediction (how cash would flow into and out of the business in the next year) and harried Colin when he tried to bluff his way through the answer.

"This order from Caledesign Solutions for Scotia Home-Flair," he asked, "Is it firm?"

"Yes," said Colin, though Kate looked dubious.

"Could you let me see it?" asked JP.

"I don't have it in writing yet."

John thought JP would show impatience. He didn't.

"You can let me have the quotation?"

"Yes." Colin remained seated.

"Now?" requested JP politely. Kate fetched it for him.

"When do you expect it to be confirmed?"

"Shortly."

"This week, next?"

"Next week."

Colin had been anticipating the sort of conversation he frequently had with Kate: vague, blustering arguments he invariably won - largely because he was boss and became tetchy when pushed too hard.

JP wasn't interested in arguments.

"When you get it would you let me have a copy? If I don't receive it by, say, next Friday, I'll assume you won't be getting it. Is that fair enough?"

"Yes," said Colin, doubtfully. JP's precision unsettled him. He liked hustling. Precision took the excitement out of sales.

JP suspected he wouldn't receive it. He therefore calculated the forward chances of the business with the order, then without it.

It didn't matter much either way, he told John when they talked it over a couple of days later. In an attempt to land the order, Colin had quoted low. The company had also to buy the tools. This combination made the profit margin very tight. Colin had also agreed to a penalty clause; if the first delivery of the product were delayed the company would lose an agreed amount for every day late.

"It is crazy to agree a penalty clause when you have no experience of the product or the tool; there are bound to be delays. The order simply isn't lucrative enough to justify the risk. If it comes off, they will make a tiny profit; if they hit a problem they are sunk. The business is living from hand to mouth as it is. Kate is keeping it alive by chasing cash in and postponing cash out. Any run on cash would tip it into insolvency; they simply don't have enough behind them."

"I was right then," concluded John. "It doesn't have much of a future."

"Looks like it…. unless…"

"Unless what?"

"Well, something Flambert Pinkerton said the last time I saw him. He's been playing around with tracking devices. They have a plastic body and various other plastic components. He could be looking for somewhere in this country to make prototypes. It's the kind of work Gainslaw Globes should be chasing – low volume, high value, with a foot in the door for high volumes if the product takes off. But they need to be different to what they are now. They would need a toolmaker, and if they did go into high volumes, they would need more machines. They're not in a position to take it on."

"But could they set themselves up to do it?"

"Two problems with that. One: they don't have the money; two: Colin. He is what I call a busy fool. He works the clock round, has his fingers in all the pies, doesn't plan ahead, makes snap decisions, and is happier chasing than catching. The company would be better run by Kate."

"Do you mean that?"

"Yes," laughed JP, "for a start she's a pessimist; and I prefer businesses run by pessimists. As well as that she looks ahead, she's organised, she lets everyone do their own job and she knows what's happening. She'd be a good manager, if he would let her."

"He wouldn't, would he?"

"Not a chance."

"And the money? Where would they get that?" John was fishing; JP could lay his hands on it if he wanted.

"Where indeed?" replied the banker reading John's mind. "Investing in that business couldn't be justified: debts too high; returns too small, risks too great. No-body but a sentimental fool would look at it."

"Do I tell them the bad news now?"

For a moment JP made no reply.

"No, not yet. Let me think about it for a couple of weeks."

"Why?"

"I like Kate," he smiled, and no matter how hard John pressed him, he would say no more.

Margaret and Roddam arrived for their recuperative weekend much chastened but with good news. The lump had proved benign; there was no sign of cancer; Margaret would have it removed at Murrayfield Private Clinic at any time convenient to her.

Her brush with mortality brought out a kindlier side of her nature and she brought a bunch of exotic flowers from "Morningside's top florist" for Helen by way of a peace offering. Helen received them graciously but confided to Alex that she preferred Margaret antagonistic. Her wish would be granted for within a month Margaret had abandoned the role of wounded swan and went back to scavenging seagull.

The effect on Roddam was subtler and longer-lasting. While Margaret rested, he accompanied John on his daily walk and used the opportunity to confide in him.

"It has been quite a shock, all this with Margaret," he said, "I thought I might lose her." His voice almost broke as he said it. "She means a lot to me, Margaret." He kept repeating her name as if to call her back from the edge of life.

"It must have shaken you both," said John, "I know it hit dad hard when he lost Mum. In a way he never recovered."

This didn't cheer up Roddam at all. He looked at John with something close to panic in his eyes.

"It makes you realise what is important. All this material pursuit, chasing the almighty dollar, pushing paper around in airless offices, rushing about in crowded streets, buying and selling in Vanity Fair. You've made the right choice, John; pack it in while you're still young enough to enjoy life. You have enough, and you've settled for it; we should do the same. Good to hear that you and Marion are getting back together, by the way."

John interrupted him to tell him he had not packed it in, had not settled for anything, and that his sojourn in Birsett was temporary. The fact that he had leased the house for five years simply gave him a base and Helen an income from her inheritance. But strangely he did not deny that he and Marion were attempting reconciliation. This was not an oversight; he thought about denying it, but didn't want to; he did not want to confirm it either. Could it be that he did not know what he wanted, or rather, knew, but did not want to admit it?

"Once the summer is over, I'll be taking up a position elsewhere," he said, as if it were planned.

Yet there were no plans, and John knew it. Roddam, however, had noticed what John had not: that, like a man rowing a boat, he faced in one direction but headed in the opposite. In his mind he might be still planning to retrieve his executive life, but his decisions and actions made it clear that he had all but abandoned it. He had drifted too far, part repelled, part attracted, to go back now. It would take something quite convulsive to stop that drift.... But we are getting ahead of ourselves. Roddam isn't listening; he is advertising his dreams.

"I've picked out a nice little property in Wester Ross; an old croft, refurbished to a high standard, lounge/dining room, open fire, kitchen, two bedrooms, bathroom with shower, on mains sewage (I don't want to be bothered with a septic tank), peat-fired central heating, a little garden, in a crofting township, not far from the sea. Ideal for Margaret and me. Margaret can paint her pictures; I can go fishing, a good book, and nights by the open fire."

"Sounds nice," said John, repelled by the vision but trying to sound supportive.

Roddam rabbited on about his flight, their flight, his and Margaret's, to sanity and serenity. They were walking inland up towards the old lonnen, away from the haar that rolls up the brae when the weather is warm and the wind is in the east. They walked in warm sunshine along lanes lush with summer green, thick with briars, bramble, raspberry canes, emblazoned here and there with the first flush of pink-purple willowherb, decorated and scented with exuberant clouds of meadowsweet and stippled and streaked with blue and yellow vetch. Grasses, some green, some straw, many now bronzed, some golden, danced in the breeze and flashed in the sunshine. Behind the flourishing hedges of hawthorn, apple and blackthorn, a sea of ripe barley rippled and surged in feathery waves across the fields up towards Whitfield. The breeze rustled in the trees, crackled in the grass and hissed through the standing field; adult birds, free of their broods, piped and whistled from hidden perches; parties of excited young birds exploded from the undergrowth in a cacophony of squawks and screams. But Roddam, absorbed in his escape to tranquillity, noticed none of it. Give John credit, he did notice the bindweed rampaging over the hedge, and he smelt the honeysuckle and occasionally looked up to see if he could see what bird was singing. The country had started to draw him in.

As they walked, they caught up with a couple of old ladies they had seen picking their way along the rutted path, their arms linked; alongside them a little dog struggled through the long grass. As they closed on them John saw that one of them was blind. Then he recognised her friend. He had seen her before but could not recall where or when. She, however recognised him immediately. but could not could not recall her name but she recognised him immediately.

"Hello, you're Willie Swansen's son, aren't you?" said Mrs Dryden,

"Yes," said John,

"I was sorry to hear about your father," she said, "I didn't hear about it until it was all over. I would like to have been to the funeral. I saw him often in the early days."

It dawned on John who she was. Earlier in the year, when out walking with his father not far from this very spot, they had met her with her dog. Willie had introduced her as Mrs Dryden, and then, John recalled, had added that they shared in the fellowship of cancer.

"I'm sorry, Mrs Dryden," said John, "He would have liked you to have been there,"

"This is my friend, Emily," she said. John found the hand of Emily and shook it.

"This is my brother-in-law, Roddam Craig."

"Do you like the countryside too, Mr Craig?" asked Mrs Dryden.

"Love it," clipped Roddam, "but tied to the city, I'm afraid. For now, anyway."

"I've brought Emily along here to hear the reed warbler; it has a nest in that thicket over there. But we haven't heard it yet."

On cue the bird launched into its song, a flickering song interspersed with a whirring chuckle or two.

"There, do you hear it, Emily, do you hear?"

"Yes, I hear it," said Emily excitedly.

"Did you hear it?"

The men said they did, and after a suitable interval, walked on. They had important things to discuss. Only later did John realise that he had not enquired about Mrs Dryden's health. He hadn't forgotten she was ill; it just had not seemed important, somehow, alongside the reed warbler singing its way into Emily's darkness.

In case you are impressed by Roddam's conversion to country pursuits I should like you to know that although his disturbance lasted longer than Margaret's, it was not profound. A request from Mark (Mad Man) Bedlam, the rock star, to find him a luxury flat in the New Town re-routed Roddam's interest and relegated the croft in Wester Ross to the back burner, then off the stove altogether. The episode, however, did have some lasting effect. He changed his diet to avoid known carcinogens and every second Friday brought Margaret a bunch of flowers to show he loved her.

CHAPTER TWENTY-FIVE

Life would be less confusing for humanity and more convenient for writers if Fate were more consistent. Her blessings and banes come in dollops as if she, having fallen asleep on the job, she wakes up to a full in-tray and, panicking, dumps the whole lot on some unfortunate head. This time Helen and Alex bore the brunt of her indiscipline.

Helen saw the first blow coming when Morag, closely followed by Louise, ran into the house and scuttled up to their bedroom without speaking. Shortly afterwards Helen opened the door to a pair of policepersons (one male, one female) enquiring if a girl called Morag Paulin lived here and if she did, they would like to see her. Morag was sent for and came down the stairs courageously accompanied by her sister. Helen listened in astonishment to the story that emerged. Or rather the two stories that emerged. You must accept whichever you take to be true.

One came from the police persons who heard it via the mobile phone of a concerned citizen of Hecklescar who happened to be driving past Birsett School when he saw a small body wriggling out of a window with a plastic bag in its hand, obviously with loot in it. Another body, even smaller, took the plastic bag from the wriggling body. Both bodies ran away when he stopped the car. Enquiries had been made. The wriggling body was Morag Paulin, her accomplice her sister, Louise.

The police had now arrived to hear the other story: Morag's version of events. Workmen working at the school had left a window open. Louise had reported to Morag that a sparrow had found its way through the window and was flying about in the classroom. The workmen had gone home for the day. Morag had decided to rescue the bird and had climbed in the window with a plastic bag to catch it. She had failed and was climbing back out of the window when she was spotted. The empty plastic bag was produced as evidence; Louise backed up her sister's story. The police persons wrote down this version of events and said a report would be prepared for the procurator fiscal once they had checked with the school to find out what was missing. As far as the authorities were concerned punishment would be deferred awaiting a social report; as far as her mother was concerned Morag got a skelp as soon as the police left. But when the story spread through the village Helen stood up for her child and shared her dishonour.

"There's many a wor bairn than Morag," she protested.

"She never knows where those bairns are," opined the gossips. But then, no-one in Birsett ever did.

The wheels of justice ground slowly and not until October did the family learn that a warning would suffice as punishment. Not, mark you, a warning to Bovey, the contractors, for leaving the window open, but to Morag, the ten-year-old child, and to her mother and father. 'Don't get into a legal wrangle with the big boys; they have legal departments; pick on somebody small - a child, a mother and a fisherman; we can deal with them; frighten the children; dangle a court case over the parents for a few weeks; make them sweat. We'll make decent citizens of them yet - and while we're at it, why don't we slap a supervision order on the mother for assaulting her child.'

The sparrow, by the way, found its own way out.

Morag's brush with the law was not, however, the worst of Helen and Alex's misfortune that summer. For the whole of the school holidays David had been awkward. Before this year his holidays had been filled with happy activity. He often went off to the fishing with his father and could handle most of the work on the boat. He also indulged in sport, football mainly, and in expeditions along the coast and up the country. He invested in a bit of amateur crab fishing with a few craves amongst the rocks with some of the Birsett boys. For leisure he took the bus down to Hecklescar for fish and chips, a can of coke and whilst there, for interest, chatted up the girls from his class at the high school. Apart from mealtimes, Helen scarcely saw him. But this year he lay in his bed half the morning and drifted around the house most of the day listening to pop music or playing gruesome games on his computer. He still went occasionally to Hecklescar in the evening, but now his visits troubled Helen. She knew about underage drinking and had heard of drugs and feared for her boy. She never smelt anything on him, but he often came in later than he should and went straight to bed without supper.

Worst of all, he had stopped talking. Of course, Helen tried to talk to him, but her attempts ended in a monologue interrupted by occasional grunts, or in a walk out. Alex's advice was to leave the boy alone; he would come out of it; it would sort itself out. But that constituted Alex's advice in any crisis. He did try to persuade David to come off with him in the boat, but David sneered at the suggestion. He also sneered at George's invitations to take up golf; George knew where he could borrow a driver, a 5 iron and a putter. He didn't want to play golf, or football; he wanted to do his own thing, which seemed to be practically nothing at all. Helen blamed Abigail.

It came as a big relief when David asked if he could go on Delightful's bus outing to the Hibernian-Rangers match in Edinburgh. Delightful, for his sins, is a Hibs supporter and makes a point of attending his team's first home match of the season, in the hope that they will demonstrate an ability he had not seen the season before. Year after year he has done this, and year after year he is disappointed, but he keeps following. Is it loyalty or the leisurely journey home that attracts him; a journey with many stops for refreshments? The bus driver always stays sober and brings them home in time for bed. David had been on the trip last year, but his parents had not expected him to volunteer this time and willingly paid his fare and ticket. Perhaps, they thought, in this lay the beginning of David's journey back to them.

The bus, one of Nicholson's twenty-three seaters, leaves Birsett Inn at 10 o'clock with twenty souls aboard, including Robin (Batman) of Alex's crew and two male members of his tribe from Hecklescar, Jimmy Possum, Willie's old friend, Eck Spiers and Andrew Douglas, both postmen (Andrew you remember won the silver medal with his pigeon). Much to the disgust of the older men and to the wives of the younger men of the party, three women of maturer years have also taken their seats in the bus, the back seats. These are a widow, Lizzie Mitchell, whose husband had no sooner sold his boat and licence to a Dutchman for £400,000 when he died, Agnes Pallin, unmarried sister of the man that makes the scones, and Marlene Mitchison, ex-wife of one of the brothers of Batman who is also on the trip. Before the divorce, she had always accompanied her husband on the outing and saw no need to draw out because of her changed circumstances. These ladies are intent on having a good time and, in spite of local prejudices, are genuinely interested in the fate of Hibernian football team. To prove it they are decked from head to toe in the green and white of their team. They look ridiculous.

But there are two other ladies on the bus who have no

interest in football. These two are Dot and Spot whom we last saw behind the Poo stall at the gala. They will be let off in the vicinity of Princes Street and will spend the afternoon shopping while the rest are at the match. Dot, you will remember, is the wife of Del and as the wife of the organiser of the trip takes responsibility for the six underage youths that go to the match but not to the watering places afterwards. Amongst these youths is Ian, Del and Dot's own son, a lad of fifteen, and, of course, David.

In charge of this varied and convivial party there is, of course, Delightful himself aided by Kit, his second in command. They have hired the bus, arranged the meals, bought the game tickets, and determined the charge; they will make a modest profit. But in fairness we should record that they will convert some of those profits into liquid assets on the way home for the benefit of the seatholders. There is another member of the party we should draw attention to, though to be honest, he hardly needs it for he draws attention to himself. It is the other member of Delightful's crew, Marvin.

Marvin, you may remember, is a Rangers supporter, and we do not have time here to explain why so many Scotsmen who would have difficulty finding Glasgow on a map, nevertheless support that city's famous football club. Some think it has to do with religion, others blame the Freemasons; the Scottish Executive blames bigotry and is passing a law to ban it. Whatever it is, Rangers is Marvin's team and he sits in the bus clothed in his Rangers jersey, a little blue island in a sea of green. Marvin's allegiance constitutes a problem for two reasons. First, he will not be allowed into the Hibs end of the ground dressed like that and will have to watch the match alone among thousands of people he does not know in the Rangers seats. Secondly, it is almost certain that Rangers will win and he will want to celebrate the victory whilst the others will want to drown their sorrows. Nevertheless, he has paid his whack and sits in sullen isolation in the second back seat, gazing resentfully out of the window and singing sectarian songs quietly to himself.

Everything went as anticipated, even to the result: Rangers won 3-1. But for a blind linesman and a lucky bounce it might have been a draw. The Hibs party found their bus and climbed aboard in reasonable spirits. There was enough controversy to keep the party lively and enough doubt to keep hope alive. Marvin joined them and remained sensible enough to admit it had been much closer than the score suggested.

Not until they picked up Dot and Spot in George Street, did they notice that one of the party was missing: David. This surprised everyone but Ian, Del's son.

"He told me he wasn't coming back, I thought you all knew."

Dot looked at her husband and he looked at her.

"When did he tell you that?" she asked her son.

"On the way up; he said he was going to stay with his cousin in Edinburgh; he had a holdall with him; he went off after the match."

Dot turned to Del.

"Helen said nothing to me about it; did Alex say anything to you?"

He hadn't. No one else knew anything about the arrangement. Concerned, Dot said they should go straight back to Birsett. The bus disagreed; an important part of the trip lay ahead. Why trail back early to Birsett just to hear that Helen knew all about it but had forgotten to tell anybody?

"That's not like Helen," insisted Dot; Spot backed her up.

The bus rationalised: the lad had told Ian; it wasn't a secret; he's old enough to know what he's doing; he's not a bairn.

The driver had double-parked in George Street, and was

protesting that he must move on. Dot agreed he should find a safer place to stop. From there Del would use his mobile phone to contact Helen. The phone rang out at Helen's number. Dot was outvoted and overruled (Del abstained); the trip would go ahead; head for North Berwick. Another call from there again produced no answer; on to Dunbar. By now Dot was in no mood for compromise; David had gone missing; his mother Helen would have told her; something must be wrong. She ordered the driver to drive straight on; no votes against. At eight o'clock Dot and Del were at Helen and Alex's door. They were surprised to see them.

"You're back early. Where's David?"

CHAPTER TWENTY-SIX

Helen immediately went upstairs and returned shortly to confirm that David had taken some of his clothes, the boxer shorts he slept in and his toilet bag. He had also taken his mobile phone and his bank book, but that was no big deal; there was only a few pounds in it. She regretted that she had not taken the number of David's mobile when he had offered it.

Helen wanted to charge off to Edinburgh but Alex restrained her. Dot and Del supported him; the bairns needed her at home. Someone must go. Alex would go, and Del would go with him. But where? Edinburgh's a big place. Helen was in no doubt.

"Find Abigail," she said, "and you'll find David."

Where was Abigail? At her parents' home in Morningside. Where in Morningside?

'I have the address somewhere; we only write at Christmas. Where's the address book? Never mind with that; ring John, he'll know.'

John welcomed the ring of the phone; it interrupted his first nervous contact with Marion and Rebecca. They had ar-

On Such a Tide

rived in Birsett earlier in the day, had settled into JP's holiday house at Partan Row and had walked up the brae to Braeshiel at John's invitation. Better to get it over with as soon as possible, John had thought. Once they had been to Braeshiel, he'd feel better about it. He had offered them tea and had served them some of Helen's scones, but he felt awkward; serving his wife. It surprised Marion that he was capable of serving anyone; but he had not forgotten she took sugar in her tea. She formed the impression that he was making a big effort to be attentive, and she thought well of it. They avoided talking about what was uppermost in their minds and made do with the weather, scenery, and the journey north (by car, Marion driving; no traffic up here compared with York and the A1. Rebecca and Marion also revealed that they needed to go home on Thursday for that was the day Rebecca received the results of her A-Levels.

"You'll come back, for Friday and Saturday, though," John said realising that now they were here he did not want them to go away. "It's not far; we could all go," he added, "we could make it a day out."

That was agreed. Then the phone rang out.

John left the room to take the call in the hall. When he returned, he told his family what had happened and that he had volunteered to go with Alex to Edinburgh; he could do no other. He knew where Margaret lived, and Abigail was his niece; he felt responsible. He suggested to Marion that she and Rebecca should visit Helen. Marion understood but, perhaps, Helen might not thank them for turning up at her house tonight. They would just take a walk and go back to Partan Row. This lent an unsatisfactory conclusion to the evening, but it could not be helped. They would have to start all over again.

Now that John had volunteered, there was no need for Del to accompany Alex. Alex and John drove to Edinburgh in John's car. On their way they rang Margaret but received no reply and they did not leave a message on the answering machine. Not long after ten, they arrived at Merchiston Heights, and rang the bell. No-one came to the door. John walked into the front garden and peered through the window not realising he was under surveillance by Neighbourhood Watch. A door opened across the road and a man emerged. A shadow hovered close behind him.

"Can I help?" he shouted nervously.

"I'm looking for Mr & Mrs Craig, I'm Mrs Craig's brother." said John going down the drive towards the neighbour. The neighbour relaxed but kept his distance.

"They went out about seven o'clock. To a concert, I think, at the Festival."

"They're not on holiday."

"No."

"We'll wait then."

In Birsett this would have elicited an invitation to come in, but the neighbour retreated behind his door and left the curtains open in the lounge to show the strangers who claimed to be relatives that they were still under observation. This is the advice given in the booklet for Neighbourhood Watch.

John and Alex did not have long to wait. After ten minutes John recognised Roddam's BMW moving along the street. It turned into the drive of No.14 and Margaret and Roddam alighted. They were surprised to see their two cousins from Birsett and even more surprised to hear why they had come. They had not seen David and what is more they had not seen Abigail. That wasn't surprising for Abigail had a place of her own, found and paid for by her father. It lay in one of the new developments off the waterfront at Leith. Margaret tried to assure the two men that David would be safe if he was with Abigail, but if she believed it Alex and John did not. They set off for Leith. Roddam offered to accompany them but they turned down his help.

"Be careful," he said, "It can be quite...." (John thought he was going to say "rough", but Roddam glanced at Margaret and said "lively").

They drove to Leith and into the throbbing nightlife that takes over the re-developed dock area on a Saturday night. As Roddam had promised, it was lively; John and Alex felt it might also be risky. They found Abigail's apartment in a smart new block in a quiet but brightly-lit street off the main thoroughfare. From a door across the landing came the dull rumble and reverberating beat of rock music backed by the muffled shouts, cries and laughter of people at leisure. They rang Abigail's doorbell; there was no answer. They rang again, then knocked without success. They tried the handle: the handle would not turn. They rang again. Abigail was out - perhaps at the party across the landing. John rang the bell on the noisy door. When no-one came, he knocked. A flushed-faced young woman in a purple strapped dress opened the door. A bulky male in pink shirt and black trousers hovered behind her with a glass in his hand.

"I'm looking for Abigail from across the landing; I thought she might be here."

"No, Abigail's not here."

"We need to see her; do you know where she is?"

The flush-faced woman shouted back into the hubbub.

"Anyone know where Abigail is; there's a couple of hunks looking for her."

The crowd (at least the ones that heard) ooed. But someone spoke. The purple dress conveyed the message to John.

"She's at a hen party."

"Where?" said John.

"Where?" shouted his mouthpiece; someone bawled an answer

"It's a pub crawl, ending at The Gilded Galleon. Some of us are going over later; about midnight."

"Where is The Gilded Galleon?"

"On The Shore, the waterfront, far end."

"Thanks."

The door closed. John looked at his watch. It was a quarter to eleven. They left the car in Abigail's street and set out to find The Gilded Galleon. They made their way onto the waterfront and stepped into a swirling, singing, laughing, screaming, shouting stream of young people all decked out for partying. Some were walking, some staggering, some dancing, some sitting on benches, bollards, walls, window sills, the ground. Couples drifted along; some hand-locked, some embracing, some seemingly intent on eating each other. Others were in groups, mainly single-sex groups, whirling, turning, running, hurrying, strolling, chattering, screaming, ducking, diving, carrying on. The place throbbed with life, a cauldron of energy and excitement, of something barely contained, primed to explode. A phalanx of strutting youths headed towards John and Alex. The two men avoided eye contact and stepped aside. They felt out of place; they were old, improperly dressed and not intent on enjoyment; they felt menaced. As they passed a group of girls, one of them, no doubt incited by the others, hauled up her top to flash her bare breasts at the two men; the group squealed and wheeled away.

"Would you like your lassie loose here?" Alex asked John.

"No," said John, "but Abigail is not a lassie."

"No," said Alex, "but David is a laddie."

John tried to reassure him – and himself.

"A different generation, and they're not all bad; most are just out for a good time."

They found The Gilded Galleon: dark, packed, noisy, thumping with rock music and incredibly hot and stuffy. They pushed their way to the bar and ordered a half-pint of lager for John and an export for Alex. John, because he was the driver, thought of ordering a glass of orange or lemonade, but decided not to call any further attention to himself and Alex. All the seats were taken so they wormed their way to the wall to wait until they could find one. After quarter of an hour a party moved on and they wedged themselves into a space on a padded bench between a grossly fat young man with tattooed arms and a waif of an Asian girl who was crying on the shoulder of her companion, a girl of her own age but twice her height with vivid orange hair. The two men sat, stewed, and tried to be inconspicuous.

At a quarter to twelve to a battery of squeals and shouts and drunken laughter, Abigail and her companions barged past the bouncer at the door into the darkened bar. Alex shot out of his seat and grabbed Abigail by the arm and shouted,

"Where's David?"

His movement was so decisive and his shout so intense that the hubbub in the bar ceased abruptly. Only the rock music thudded on. Everyone turned to where Alex held Abigail. The bruiser from the door moved towards them.

"Who the hell are you?" she cried.

"I'm David's father," he shouted, "Where is he?"

John came to the side of his friend. This seemed to jog Abigail's memory. She steadied herself and smiled.

"Alex! It's Alex, it's alright, it's alright," she giggled, "Don't get upset, he's alright."

"Where is he?" demanded Alex.

"He's alright, Alex," Abigail repeated, "He's with Jude. I had a hen party. He couldn't come to a hen party. Cecilia's getting married. Cecilia, this is Alex! Cecilia? Where's Cecilia? Oh God, we've lost Cecilia and it's her party!"

She found this funny and started to laugh. Alex raised his hand to slap her face. The bouncer moved forward. John restrained Alex.

"Abigail," said John, "Come outside."

As they left the rest of the bar relaxed, the hubbub returned, the music thundered on.

Outside, without her audience, Abigail became more coherent; she had palmed David off onto Jude so she could go to her hen party; Jude had taken David to his place. Where? She didn't know. She had never been there; he always came to Leith. Up The Bridges somewhere, she thought, or the top of Leith Walk, or the Canongate. But it would be no use going there anyway, he wouldn't be in.

"It's Festival Time," she said, stating the obvious, "He'll be at a show somewhere."

She didn't know which show from the hundreds of shows in Edinburgh that night. She had his mobile phone number, in her bag, in the pub. She retreated to retrieve it. John wrote it down.

"Where's David?" demanded Alex again when she came out.

"David'll be with him. Don't worry, Jude'll take care of him. He's a big softie really."

That was all they could drag out of her. They let her reel back into The Gilded Galleon.

John and Alex ran the gauntlet of merrymakers back to the car, John relieved that it was not the Mercedes). From the car he rang Jude's number; the phone had been switched off.

Alex did not want to leave his son in the grip of the roistering city but John persuaded him that they could do no more that night. They knew where David was, or at least whom he was with. Alex, not knowing Jude as John knew him, accepted John's assurances that David would safe. John was not so sure, but he had no option but to put his faith in the freewheeling artist. Besides he was not sure what Alex might do if he and Jude came face to face this night, or even what he might do to David if he found him. There are some things better done by daylight. They would take stock in the morning and decide what they must do next. Jude's phone would be back on then. But John kept Jude's number to himself; he wanted to stay in control; he had seen Alex's reaction to Abigail.

They drove home along the deserted roads of East Lothian and Berwickshire. At half-past one in the morning they stepped out at Birsett into a cool clear night with the quiet and beautiful stars arching over them like a benediction. But no other blessing reassured the Paulin family that night. Helen and Alex went to bed and gave each other what comfort they could, but they did not sleep much.

John went home to no wife, yet his wife slept only a few hundred yards away, and his daughter. Tonight, he felt it; he felt lonely; they were so close that he felt lonely. For the first time since their separation nine months ago he wanted something to hold onto, *someone* to hold onto. He wanted Marion in bed with him.

CHAPTER TWENTY-SEVEN

Any plan of campaign that troubled Alex and Helen during the night was thrown into confusion in the morning when Helen answered the phone and heard David on the other end of it. She battered him with a dozen questions before he nervously told her that he was all right. Abigail had told him to ring.

"You're with Abigail?"

"No, I'm at Jude's place"

"Where is that? Your dad will come and get you."

"I don't want him to come and get me. I'm alright."

"You must tell me where you are."

"I can't."

"Why not? I'm your mother. I have a right to know."

"I'm alright."

"When are you coming home?"

"I don't know."

"I'll give you till to-morrow. I expect you home to-morrow."

"I don't know when I'll be home. Jude says I can stay as long as I like."

"My God, David…" Frustration struck his mother dumb. Alex took over.

"David, listen, son, you have to come home. Your mother is upset."

"I'm not coming, dad, I'm not a bairn. I can make my own choices."

"Those aren't David's words," thought Alex.

"Is there anybody with you there?"

"Jude's here."

"Put him on."

Jude said, "Hi."

"Jude, David's got to come home. Give me your address and I'll come and collect him."

"Look, I don't want involved in a family squabble. I'm not giving you my address; nobody gets my address."

"Then tell David he has to come home. I'll pick him up anywhere he likes."

Jude's reply staggered Alex.

"You're not listening to what your son says, are you? I'm not keeping him here against his will. He's free to go any time he wants. But he says he doesn't want to come home, and I respect his wishes, so should you. He's having a good time here; it's the Festival; it's where every young person should be at this time of the year."

"I'll have to report this to the police."

"Feel free, but what they'll tell you is what I'm telling you. He's over sixteen, he can go where he likes and do what he likes. He doesn't need his parents' permission. You know that."

Alex did know that, but what other leverage did he have?

"You're upsetting his mother."

"Not me. I'm sorry she's upset. I've even talked to David about it; I persuaded him to ring you; I'm beginning to wish I hadn't. You need to face it; David isn't a bairn." He pronounced "bairn" carefully; mimicking their language.

Alex fell silent. Then he asked Jude to put David on again. He spoke to his son quietly.

"David, your mother is upset. I'm asking you to come home."

"I'm not coming, dad, not yet."

Helen tried to grab the phone from Alex's hand. She would tell her son that if he wasn't home by to-morrow, he needn't come back at all. Alex would not let the phone go. For a while he stood silent mastering his thoughts.

"David, are you still there?"

"Yes."

"You have your mobile phone?"

"Yes"

"Well then, son," he said, gently, "When you want to come home, give us a ring. Give us a ring any time, any time."

He put the phone down and faced the wrath of his wife; then her tears. Then he went down to Braeshiel to tell John about the phone call. The report filled John with apprehension. Jude had reassured Alex, but John was not reassured; he remembered Jude's encounter with Mr Scott too clearly for that. Where, he wondered, would Jude lead David - and to what?

Although it was Sunday Alex and Helen didn't go to

church that morning. John and Marion did, with Rebecca. Louise, Morag and Calum came bustling into Braeshiel to go with them. Helen had tried to explain why their Auntie Marion had shown up again and they had been warned not to say anything and not to ask questions. Nevertheless, Louise insisted on sitting between John and Marion and finding the hymn numbers, first for one, then for the other. Mr Mordun, the minister, for reasons of his own, explained in his sermon why Moses could not enter the Promised Land but Joshua could. In his prayers he prayed for the Queen, both Parliaments and the Christian Church in Pakistan, but did not trouble God with the anguish crushing two of his parishioners up the brae, nor with the confusion in the life of the family in the third pew from him on the right.

On Monday morning, Helen and Alex set about life without David, but their legs had been cawed from under them. Alex rose at five but had little to eat before he walked down the brae to the Silver Cord. A cross-dive churned the sea at the harbour mouth, wind and wave disputing direction, spray exploding from the rocks; the sort of day that would make work uncomfortable. But he went anyway and with Batman and Dod he pulled and shot two hundred and fifty craves in Goswick Bay. But there was no ripping for mackerel, no chat, no banter; the radio lay silent most of the time. He did the work he needed to do and spoke only when necessary. They came in at three-thirty with forty-three lobsters and three boxes of crabs - not a bad day. The Aurora came in just after the Silver Cord, but Alex didn't wait for Delightful. Batman went with Marvin in the van to take the catch to Hecklescar.

On the same morning Helen, much to their surprise, let the bairns lie in their beds until after nine then fed them and chased them out of doors. George and Calum stayed out the whole day apart from mealtimes, but Louise kept returning to her mother. When Alex came home, he found her asleep on her mother's knee. Not even the gay Morag could lift her mother's spirits. After he had had his evening meal Alex lit the fire, but the house still felt cold.

The pain for Alex and Helen increased on Tuesday morning when an A4 envelope enclosing David's Highers results landed on the mat of his home. Alex was at sea, so Helen picked it up and put it behind the clock. This simple action troubled Helen for she realised that, had David not gone away, she would have opened it without waiting for her son; she now understood she would have been wrong to do so. Now it must wait until he came home. He would come home shortly, wouldn't he? He must decide what he wanted to do with his life. Then Helen went mechanically through the day, pretending to the rapacious gossips of the place that David's stay in Edinburgh was a late holiday for the lad before he started school again. None of them believed her. There had been too many witnesses on the Hibs bus trip for that.

Marion visited Helen every morning during the waiting days, and Helen welcomed her visits. She could be open with Marion; she didn't belong to the place, wouldn't gossip and didn't blame; she didn't even give advice. Helen poured out her fears and frustrations. She blamed David for being headstrong: she blamed Alex for being too soft with him: she blamed herself for being too hard on him. She asked Marion where she had gone wrong; first Morag in trouble with the police, now David. Marion couldn't tell her. She asked Marion what she should do next; Marion told her to wait - David will come to his senses; it's an adventure, that's all. She told Helen that she had done all she could and she must hope, pray, that they had done enough. Helen felt reassured – until the next morning when she had to be reassured all over again.

"It's not much of a holiday for you, having me greetin' to you every day," she said.

But Marion said it suited them well; John was busy in

the morning anyway.

"What does he do?" asked Helen

"I thought you might know," smiled Marion, "I think he's job-hunting, though I think he calls it Executive Search."

Marion was correct. John, although he had abandoned any real hope of securing the sort of job he wanted, had to work. And what other work was there but to slog away at his CVs, his cold calls, his inventive letters of enquiry, his Executive Search Control Sheet, his daily trawl though the executive opportunities pages? He had even taken to badgering Zack again but Zack proved elusive.

The opportunity John is seeking, however, will not arrive through any of these; it will burst on him from an unexpected quarter. We have, however, no way of telling him that he is wasting his time. Even if we had, he would not listen to us. He needs to work; what else would he do with his time? If he didn't have executive work, the commonplace of Birsett would swallow him up. He must distance himself from that.

What was there to interest him? The launch at Hecklescar of the Serenade, a new 10-metre boat, or the ridiculous outfit the skipper's wife wore to the reception? Or old Jim Porteous taking his wife of forty-three years to the hospital, then coming home and not able to make himself a cup of tea because he didn't know where she kept the tea bags? Or that The White Rose and The Purple Heather, pair trawlers of Hecklescar were looking for three crewmen between them? There had been a fall-out and Eddie the Eagle and the two Anderson brothers had walked off the boat. Or the latest on little Johnny Armstrong that went missing amongst the rocks in May? He would have been ten on Saturday and Susan, his mother, had bought a birthday cake from Wilson's just in case he turned up. But the long day passed without him coming home, so at nightfall she threw the cake out to the gulls. Did John see anything of consequence in any of this? Not much, he had more important matters on his mind: he must find a way back to the busy world of pushing paper and people around, making things, making money, making things happen.

The coffee reception for Marion and Rebecca postponed from Saturday took place on Sunday evening after a day helping Helen and Alex through their crisis. By now the family had something common to talk about, so the evening passed without too much tension. They decided what they would do with their week together. They decided that each one would choose what to do, turn about. Marion wanted to see Mellerstain again so on Monday they toured the beautiful mansion and walked down to the lake in the sunshine. On Tuesday John took them to Chillingham across the border to see the wild herd of white cattle, direct descendants of the cattle that roamed the woods and marshes of Britain after the Ice Age. These were clever choices for it kept the minds of the participants on external matters, and allowed for proximity without intimacy. Had a stranger listened to their conversation during those two days, he might have assumed they had just met on a bus trip. Rebecca, however, much more wisely, chose by instinct. She wanted to pick raspberries; she recalled doing it with her grandfather when they came on holiday. But her memories lay not in the place, or with the raspberries. she remembered the laughter, the friendly competition and the easy fellowship of those occasions. On Wednesday they would go to Blackhouse farm to pick raspberries.

If you have not been to Blackhouse in August you must go, even if you pick no berries. I'm sure Mr Swan, the farmer, will let you stand in the field. You are on ground rising from the distant rivers Tweed and Whiteadder towards Bunkle Edge. Spread before you like a rich tapestry is the fertile Merse with its pattern of fields; some gold, some green, some dotted with bales, others lined with rows of vegetables, some speckled with cattle and sheep. You will see trees, singly or in coverts and plantations, all stitched together with dark hedges. The houses, farms, hamlets and villages (there are no towns in view) settle into the landscape as into comfortable armchairs. The flowing, bending, bowing land stretches away over the invisible border to the distant hills of Northumberland, to Humbledon, Kyloe and on the far horizon, Cheviot: a land much fought over, now at peace. Above it all white galleons of clouds sailing in the widest, highest and bluest sky you have ever seen.

Look down and here, in front of you, row upon row of burgeoning raspberry canes heavy with berries. Surely you want to pick a pound or two for the freezer, to make the best of jams, or to eat today with a little cream? Just £1.25 a pound Pick-Your-Own: go to the fruit shed and pick up a basket: weigh them when you're finished and take your money to the second house up the lane. Of course, you have time. An hour and a half here in the embrace of the sun, soothed by the breeze and listening to the swallows will restore your faith in life, if not in God - and you will have five pounds of raspberries as a bonus. What productivity, John.

Morag and Louise have come with the Swansens, taken out of their mother's way for their own safety. But they are more intent on fun than berry-picking: Morag spends her time creeping along a row out of sight until she is opposite Rebecca, or Marion, or if she's brave, Uncle John. Then she jumps up to surprise them. We will not report her for mistaking a stranger for one of the party; the woman she startled took it in good part. These high spirits add to the occasion and call John back when his mind strays from this blessed place to offices, law courts, letters and interview rooms.

What happens next is not planned, it has not been thought out; there is no strategy, no tactics, no foreplay. Working down his row John finds himself opposite and close to Marion in her row, the line of canes between them. She is intent on her picking, her head bowed, the sun on her hair, the familiar faint smile on her lips.

"This is nice," John heard himself saying to her.

"Yes, it is," she said, looking up and, for the first time for a year, their eyes met.

"I'm sorry, Marion," he said.

"So am I," she replied.

That was all. For however much circumstances and events had prepared John for this conjunction John had not prepared for it at all. Marion too was surprised. They could think of nothing else to say; there was a fence of raspberry canes between them. They looked away and went back to picking raspberries.

But something had changed: a door long closed had slipped off its latch and a light had flashed across Marion's threshold. The light reflected the scattered spectrum of a complete life that existed before it was split by ambition and self-importance. The light had little warmth yet, but it was a light and it had been seen.

CHAPTER TWENTY-EIGHT

It is unlikely that Marion's nausea on Thursday morning arose from her encounter with John in the raspberry canes; she is not a squeamish person. Nor do we think it was a contrivance to give John and Rebecca time alone together. The heat in the raspberry fields may have had something to do with it or raspberries she had eaten afterwards. Perhaps she didn't wash them thoroughly, though that is not like her. Whatever the cause, she did she not feel up to a long drive to York to pick up Rebecca's A level results; she thought she needed to be within easy distance of a loo. But she insisted that John and Rebecca should go. Rebecca offered to postpone it but her mother persuaded her to go; she knew her daughter was anxious to collect her results; she herself would be all right in Helen's care. John and Rebecca left at nine on a fine August day to make the three and a half-hour drive south. They would be back that night at, say, eight o'clock.

They had not been gone long when Rachel, JP's wife, knocked at the back door. Although the two women had exchanged pleasantries during the week, until now Rachel had not shown any inclination to set foot over Marion's door. However, there had been more substantial contact between the parties. Rebecca and Ben, JP's simple son had got to know each other.

JP had been thoughtful enough to provide a paved terrace along the front of his holiday houses. Facing south-east, it provided an ideal place to sit in the sun in the mornings. There is no road at the front of the houses; the road serving the houses runs along the back doors until a few yards beyond the last house, JP's; it ends abruptly at the cliff face. At the front, beyond the terrace there is a shingle bank and beyond that the rocks and the sea. So close are they to the sea that in a south-east breeze the residents of Partan Row keep their front doors closed; in a gale they shut the storm doors and shutter the windows.

Marion, if you remember, spent most of the mornings with Helen, so Rebecca resorted to the terrace with a book and a bottle of something cool. Rachel and her son were in the habit of doing something similar and on the first morning Rebecca was surprised, almost alarmed, to see Ben grinning at her across the little low wall that fenced off JP's house from the rest of the row. His mother called him back and apologised to Rebecca, but in that generous spirit that Mr Scott noticed among young people Rebecca had made friends with Ben. It consisted of very little; Ben would scramble down the shingle bank and bring up various rocks and shells for Rebecca to admire; he could name some of them. Or he would set up an old beer can on the shingle and they would see who could knock it down first; his co-ordination was quite good; Rebecca did not need to go easy to let him win. He would also show Rebecca his books and demonstrate how he could read them. He delighted particularly in handing a cup of coffee to Rebecca when his mother made it.

Rachel appreciated the attention Rebecca gave Ben and set restrictions on her son so he did not become a nuisance. He was not allowed to cross the wall and after a while she would ask him to let Rebecca get on with her book. But Marion and Rachel had not made any progress towards friendship until the Wednesday evening, the day they had picked raspberries at Blackhouse.

When Marion returned that evening, she had taken Rachel a basket of berries, and now, the morning after, Rachel came to her door. Rachel had brought two glasses containing raspberry cranachan for Marion and her daughter. Raspberry cranachan was not precisely what Marion relished on this morning but she invited her neighbour in and explained that Rebecca had gone with her father to York.

"Then we are both work widows to-day," said Rachel, smiling, "You would think at sixty-two Jacob would have had enough of big cities but to-day is one of his London days; he will be back to-morrow evening – and he will have raspberry pavlova for dessert."

She smiled pleasantly and spoke softly; Marion warmed to her instantly.

Marion explained that it wasn't work that took John away, but Rebecca's 'A' level results.

"I hope she does well, she has been very kind to Ben. Most people are half-afraid of him, but he is as gentle as a lamb and very affectionate."

"Rebecca tells me he can read," said Marion before realising she might sound patronising. But she need not fear; Rachel was much too wise to equivocate about her son. She wanted to talk about him; wanted to explain to Marion that she should have no fear for Rebecca. She had seen so many mothers draw their children back from friendship with her son.

"He has done very well," she said. "Considering his ability, he is a high achiever." She smiled again. "We sent him to a special school; they did wonders."

"And you worked with him at home, no doubt," put in Marion

"Of course," replied Rachel, "He can read, he can print, he can do simple arithmetic and can make simple objects. That is what the course promised and that is what he can do. We are very grateful. As I say, he has a gentle nature and is really quite contented. Oh, and he can operate a computer – which is more than I can do."

"You sound quite proud of him," said Marion.

"We are," said Rachel. "He has done very, very well."

"Do you have any other children?" asked Marion. But wished she had not asked when she saw the look in Rachel's eyes.

"No, I'm afraid not," she said, "we left it too long; Ben was born when I was forty-two. Until then we were…" (here Rachel paused as she riffled through all the excuses, she had made over the years to people she had called friends, then decided she might tell the truth to a stranger). "Too busy I suppose, or, too selfish."

Marion guessed she wanted to talk about it, to explain it, if even only to herself.

"I'm sure that's not true," she said

"No, I think it is. Jacob's work took us all over the world: Frankfurt, Singapore, Hong Kong, Geneva, New York, Johannesburg, even Tokyo for a few months."

"Sounds a great life."

"It was; many people envied us. When I look back, I wonder that it really happened; it was so very, very, good. Nothing seemed to disturb it; it just went on and on. We were healthy, well off, in need of nothing money could buy, blessed with good friends; we had nice houses wherever we went, and a permanent home in Kent if we wanted to come home. We had a farmhouse in the south of France for holidays (I believe people have started calling them gites). We went where we wanted and did what we liked. Jacob was the ideal husband; still is. But the years went on - we didn't, marry until I was thirty-one. We had always intended to have children; always imagined ourselves with them. When we stopped long enough to do something about it, I found myself over forty. Even then we thought we could turn it on like a tap, or order it up like buying from Fortnum and Masons." She smiled sadly at this attempt at humour. "But it didn't happen, not for a few years – then I was pregnant and along came Ben. We were delighted. Jacob settled in the London Office and we moved into a beautiful house in St. John's Wood with its own nursery suite; we interviewed nannies. This seemed to crown our lives. He was six months old before we realised there was something wrong."

Rachel had related her story in a soft voice at a gentle, almost dispassionate pace. Emotion lay there but it was restrained, controlled, subdued. Now she suddenly stopped.

"You don't want to hear all this," she said, "Tell me about your family. I know about Rebecca, but I seem to remember Jacob talking about a boy. He must be quite grown up now?"

Marion told her about Robert and his university course, and what he would like to do afterwards and about Rebecca and her hopes of attending university too. But as she talked about her ambition for her son and daughter she felt as if she were inflicting blow after blow upon this mother in front of her. Questions disconcerted her as she struggled not to contrast her own maturing children with Rachel's child, for he was, and would remain, a child. What were her dreams? Had she any left? What did she look for? What did she face? What did she dread? She could not look after Ben forever. What then? What had this mother chosen? How could she rise in the morning to face another day?

Marion finished her story with Rebecca's trip to York.

"It all depends on her results today; we will need to see."

"It must be a worrying time for you all," said Rachel, and Marion felt tears of pity rise to her eyes. Worry? Us? What have we to worry about?

"How do you find Birsett?" Marion asked, abruptly.

Rachel found it very well, away from everyone at the foot of the brae, living their own life, doing their own thing. Jacob had his boat, Ben liked the boat, had enjoyed the sail to Shetland this summer. She liked Partan Row particularly in the winter when the doors were shut; with the sea running and the wind rattling at the doors and windows. They had a coal fire and after Ben was in bed, she and JP sat and read their books and listened to music, classical music, and felt safe.

"Sounds a bit like Daphne DuMaurier," said Marion trying still to lighten the conversation.

Rachel laughed and her whole face lit up.

Not Daphne DuMaurier; Jacob says it's Jane Austen."

"Why is that?"

"Well, I have my embroidery and my music. We don't visit or go to parties or have people here. We scarcely watch television. Jacob has his computer; that's how he keeps in touch with the city. Ben has his computer, and his play station, whatever that is; and we have a wireless. I bake and cook."

There was something quietly defiant about the way she said this, as if she were putting down an unheard antagonist; so much so Marion thought she sounded like a teenager demanding to do her own thing. It reminded her of the arguments she had with Rebecca about giving up ballet for disco-dancing. But this was in reverse; Rachel had turned her back on a lifestyle most women would envy, and had chosen instead life in a backwater village looking after what many would regard as a simple son.

"What kind of music do you like?" she asked Rachel.

"At the moment," she said, "I am working my way through the Beethoven sonatas."

"You work through them," queried Marion, "You have a set – on CD?"

Rachel laughed.

"Oh no, we do have a set, but I am trying to play them. Have you not heard?"

"Yes, we heard a piano, but we thought it was a record."

"Well, it might have been. We do play CDs and I do try to play quietly. At the moment I am tackling No 23; do you know it? In F minor."

"No, I'm afraid I'm not particularly musical. But I like music. I'll listen more carefully in future."

Then she asked the question that had intrigued her since she first met Rachel.

"Are you happy here?"

This is not what she meant. She meant how can you possibly be happy looking after, bound to, hemmed in by Ben. but she dares not ask that question. Nevertheless, that was the question Rachel answered.

"We no longer ask ourselves that question," she said quite openly. "Happiness is what we had before we had Ben. What we have now is our child, and our life with him."

Marion made to speak, to apologise for the question she had not asked but wanted answered. But Rachel continued.

"It is not so bad, you know. Ben goes three days a week to Gainslaw; they have a centre there, and for a fortnight every four months to his old school for his holidays. When we can no longer look after him, he is well provided for. We are content; we have made ourselves content. You will lose your children, they will grow up and leave you, we will always have our child."

She said this last with a smile. Marion understood what she meant and smiled back. Rachel stood up to leave.

"You must come in some evening," she said suddenly and brightly, "and perhaps your…." (she was going to say "husband", but corrected herself) "…. John, might come; if that would be all right. Shall we say Friday?"

"I'm sure that will be fine, and will we hear you play?" said Marion, playfully.

"Oh, no," said Rachel laughing, "That would be too much like Jane Austen – even for me."

CHAPTER TWENTY-NINE

On the way to York John longed for his lost Mercedes, but they made good time in the Peugeot. If John were honest, he enjoyed having his daughter in the car with him; recently he had travelled too often on his own. *Soften* But he didn't want to be honest in case he gave Rebecca more hope than she ought to expect. When she pressed him, however, he admitted to finding the holiday enjoyable, and that pleased her. She chattered away quite happily until they were south of Thirsk, only a few miles short of York. Then she fell silent and John realised that she had been talking for him; now her thoughts had turned towards herself and the purpose of the journey.

"You're not worried about the results, are you?" he said.

"No," she said; "Well, yes; I found the Maths hard, and Economics."

"You took Economics?"

"Yes, I thought I told you."

"You probably did, but I wouldn't be listening," said John with a frankness that surprised and pleased her.

"And what course are you wanting to do?"

"I told you that too," smiled Rebecca.

"You did, that's right," said John as he recalled a distorted snatch of a distant conversation. He didn't want to disappoint her again. "You want to do a nursing degree. I remember."

"No, not now," said Rebecca with a sigh, "that was a long time ago. I've applied for Sociology with Economics at York University."

"Sociology with Economics! What on earth for?" exclaimed John, in an attempt at humour. Rebecca cut in.

"I thought I might go in for Human Resource Management. But they don't do a course in that at York. They do one at Strathclyde University in Glasgow. Mum says I should go for it, but I want to stay at York. They say I'll get some exemptions from the Institute's exams if I take this course at York."

This sounds like a simple statement of fact, but, even to someone as insensitive as John, it ought to have conveyed something more significant. Poor girl, she is too young to be taking all this on herself. She wants to go into management because her father is in management: 'maybe me going in for it will somehow put right what has gone wrong and help me and him to stay together; I don't want to lose him'. She doesn't want to leave her mother alone in York: 'Mum needs me, I can't go away. But York doesn't do Human Resource Management, so I'll go for the nearest I can get, Sociology with Economics'.

God help her, she ends up on a Sociology and Economics course, three precious years of her young life, to accommodate her parents, but she can't tell them what she has done. They think they only want her happiness, as if it can be dished out like jam and is not bound up with their own fractured lives. How much of this John guessed I do not know for he fell silent but in light of what happens he must have guessed most of it.

Before she commits herself to Sociology with Economics, she has to gain the required 'A' levels, she needs at least three Bs, and she doesn't think she has done well enough. All her elaborate planning, all her manoeuvrings depends on what is in that envelope behind the door at Poppleton.

"You'll be fine," said her father as they drove up the drive, "You always did look on the gloomy side."

Rebecca opened the door and collected the pile of mail from behind it. There, among postcards from friends, discounted car insurance offers, Christmas Catalogues and the latest bargains from Tesco's was the big envelope, addressed to her in her own hand.

She opened the envelope and took out the paper. Before she read it, she looked to her father and grabbed his hand. He felt it tremble and he gripped it to steady it.

"Go on, softie," he chaffed, "You'll have done it."

She read it slowly to herself. Then she turned to face her father.

"A B, two Cs and a D for Maths."

"Good enough?" asked her father, fearing the answer.

"No," she said, "Nothing like good enough. I've failed. Oh, dad!"

She turned to her father, put her arms round his neck and wept. John seized her and pulled him into his embrace - and cried.

All his sorrows, all his disappointments, his known injustices and felt injuries are now gathered up by his daughter's failure into one monstrous wave that has crashed down and overwhelmed him. He clutched his daughter desperately and cried. He did not cry when he broke with his wife; he did not cry when he could not save his factory; he did not cry when he lost his job; he did not cry when he heard about little Johnny

Armstrong; he did not cry when his father died; but now he clung to his daughter and wept without control. She, by her love and her failure, had found a way into his heart; had found a way in and cracked it open.

For ten minutes they said nothing. Then John muttered in his daughter's ear, "This will have to be sorted." He used the old Birsett word in a sense he had not used it for years, that is, to put right, to make whole. However you may judge his subsequent acts, that is what he meant at this time.

"It's all right, Dad," mumbled Rebecca, breaking from her father's embrace, "I can take them again. I'm sorry."

"I'm sorry too, Rebecca," he said.

But the work-worm still eats away at John. They have not long dried their tears and drunk their consoling cup of coffee before he puts into action an idea he has been toying with ever since he knew about this trip to York. He will take a poke at Zack Mallinger, the ever-unavailable Search Consultant to the Blue Chips. It is too good an opportunity to miss; they are in York; he is in Leeds, not thirty miles away; he could be in Zack's office in forty minutes. Now you would have thought that his daughter's distress and his own guilt would have driven all thoughts of executive search from his mind. If you do then you have not yet understood our man. Rebecca is still filed in the cabinet of his mind under "Domestic and Personal" and whilst we have been watching he has closed that file and put it in the pending tray. He has picked up another from the central section: "Executive Search"; it must be dealt with. He is genuinely sorry for what he has done to Rebecca, and sincere about his determination to make things better for her, but there are pressing matters to be settled. Zack is within range; he needs to be taught a lesson. Managerial success is a matter of taking your opportunities when they pop up in front of you.

He rang Zack's office. Michelle, the blonde receptionist

answered.

"Who is it?"

"Mr Swansen, oh yes, just a moment, I'll see if Mr Mallinger is in".

Thirty seconds of Led Zeppelin.

"Hello, Mr Swansen, I'm sorry but Mr Mallinger is out of the office to-day; but I have left a message for him; he will call you when he gets back."

John put the phone down. 'Thank you! Thank you! Better than I thought – not in a meeting, or unavailable, but out of the office! Do you think I am an idiot? Have I not pulled the same stunt a hundred times? You know he is in; you work in the same square yards; he cannot enter or leave his office without passing you; you know he is not out; you have just spoken to him. Right, here I come; see if is he out when I arrive! Oh, Rebecca, are you still here?'

"Rebecca," said her father, "Would it be possible for me to run over to Leeds before we go back to Birsett; I have a bit of business in Leeds? Do you mind?"

"No, dad, that's all right," ('The last thing I want is to have time on my hands to-day; I want to run away; I want to go home to mum; please don't ask me to sit in the car on my own to-day.')

"You can just stay in the car; I won't be long."

"That'll be all right, dad."

The meeting with Zack delivered all that John wanted: a rout. John marched into reception, demanded to see Zack and followed Michelle into his office. Zack was interviewing a client.

"Excuse us," said John pleasantly to the candidate, "Mr Mallinger and I have business that cannot wait." The man looked at Zack; Zack nodded. The man left with Michelle.

"Now then," said John, "Tell me where you are; your secretary seems to think you are out of the office."

That day Zack closed the Swansen file, wrote off the fee, and vowed he would never take on another fifty-year old that had been fired; no more Scotsmen either. But the encounter did John no end of good. He felt exhilarated; he had exercised power again, had demonstrated his executive skills, felt in control. He had forgotten his tears.

John and Rebecca drove straight back to Birsett. John wanted to stop for the slap-up meal he had promised Rebecca but, at her request, they bought sandwiches and a bottle of water and ate in the car. They rang Marion on their way home, but Rebecca didn't tell her mother the results. Marion, however, knew her daughter had failed for, if she had succeeded, she would have shouted the news down the phone immediately she opened the envelope. Marion prepared a meal for them, for consolation and for herself.

But before her daughter arrived other events took precedence. Alex had had a phone call from David. He wanted to come home.

CHAPTER THIRTY

Abigail meant David no harm. All she wanted was amusement, and David was no amusement to her with the festival city full of artistes a long way from home. She set her sights first on a stand-up comedian from Atlantic City appearing at Venue sixty-seven at midnight four nights a week, but there came a night when there were only two in the audience and she discovered the other woman was his wife. Now she pursued a wealthy undergraduate from Cambridge appearing twice nightly in an obscure play about chickens, but she also assisted an all-ladies group that gave comfort to the Jazz Brass Ensemble from Kiev. These activities left little time for David, or, for that matter, Jude. She tried to persuade her mother to take David off her hands, but Margaret preferred not to know David's whereabouts in case Helen asked. Jude, therefore, took custody of David.

Nor did Jude mean David harm. To him David represented a trophy; he had won the game; he had proved his point; young people had to break free from their parents in order to realise their emotional potential. He also relished, as aging revolutionaries do, the discipleship of youth. The fact that David had come to Edinburgh seeking Abigail rather than enlightenment did not trouble him. But Jude meant no harm. He is not a wicked man so we must assume he thought he was doing good – 'good' as he defined it. But Edinburgh at Festival time is no time for a middle-aged free spirit to be shackled by goodness; life is short. Jude chaffed at his responsibility.

For the first two or three days, David enjoyed trailing around behind Jude, taking in the shows, eating in the cafes, dancing in the streets and drinking in the pubs - and very occasionally bumping into Abigail. Why should he not enjoy himself? To be young (or even not so young) in Edinburgh at Festival time is very heaven, with the city full of creativity, vitality, ingenuity, eccentricity, excitement and good company. Ultimately, however, these strokes were not enough for Jude. With the desperation of fading youth, he sought stronger sensations; strong enough to feed his sensual hunger. Such a drive easily overcame his sense of responsibility and he found it convenient to leave David to his own devices. Besides, we must not forget that Jude is a philosopher, if only of art, and modern philosophers have this weakness: they find it difficult to distinguish between instincts and principles. When the instincts of ordinary, decent, non-philosophical citizens lead them into trouble (though usually not before), their principles ride to the rescue and, with a bit of luck, set them back on the straight and ordinary with no harm done. But Jude does not think of himself as ordinary; he is a thinker, a modern thinker, a new man, a moral revolutionary. When it comes to the pinch, his instincts are his principles. At the crux, he has nothing to hold him back; he will walk off the edge before he sees the cliff.

In this instance, however, it is not Jude who is in danger, but David. As Jude's responsibility wanes David becomes fearful of the places he is visiting, the company he is keeping and the opportunities opening up before him. He is accustomed to his mother and father keeping him right and who has he now but Jude? Yes, I know his parents have been too protective. They and Hecklescar High School are to blame for not conditioning him to the world as it is, with all its diversity, wickedness and unscrupulous manipulators. But such innocence is common in Birsett and elsewhere in Scotland, apart, that is, from sink estates, the seamier parts of inner cities and the sad novels of Irvine Welsh. David's inadequate upbringing is no match for those who inhabit the world into which Jude now leads him. He is loose amongst sexual predators who are not as highly principled as their friend Jude. They see in David not a young disciple of liberty, but an unspoiled object of desire. All he has for protection is his revulsion at what is proposed, a mobile phone and his father's assurance he can ring him at any time. And ring he does, in blind panic, from a locked toilet cubicle in The Rampant Thistle in Rose Street at half-past eight on Thursday night.

Alex did not wait to change out of his working clothes. Helen wanted to go but Alex would not hear of it. He called John, but John was not at home; away to York with Rebecca. He called Delightful and Delightful agreed to accompany him. He diverted Marvin in the Aurora's van to Alex's house and the three of them set out immediately. At ten minutes to ten they barged into The Rampant Thistle and silenced the bar.

David had obeyed his father and remained locked in the cubicle. Eventually the landlord, Aubrey, had drawn Jude's attention to the fact that his young friend was blocking one of his facilities. Jude had half-guessed what had happened and when the three fishermen arrived, he was standing with the landlord outside the cubicle door trying to persuade David to open the door and deliver himself into his protection. Alex pulled him aside and spoke to his son. The door opened and David, ashen faced, emerged into the embrace of his father. Without stopping Alex led him through the crowd of spectators to the Aurora's van parked on double yellow lines outside the pub. Alex put his son into the back of the van and locked the door.

"You can come if you want," he said to Del and Marvin. They went with him back into the bar. Once inside Alex made a beeline for Jude and his party who had retreated to a dimly-lit corner. There were six of them and they were laughing. The landlord guessed Alex's intention and ran round the counter to head him off.

"No fighting, no fighting," he shouted.

Alex, backed by Del and Marvin, came face to face with Jude.

The bar fell silent. Jude's friends backed away. Jude opened his mouth to expound his version of events.

"No fighting," piped Aubrey, attempting to insert himself between Alex and Jude. Alex pushed him aside into the arms of Marvin.

"Where's his claes?" demanded Alex.

Jude relaxed and started to give his address to Alex. He got no further than the number. Alex's fist travelled less than a foot. Jude staggered back, tripped over a chair, crashed across a table full of glasses, hit a wall and collapsed in a heap with blood streaming from his mouth and nose. When the audience turned back to the fishermen, they were gone. They looked out to see the red lights of the Aurora's van speeding along the road. Aubrey rang the police.

In consequence, once again the establishment, in the shape of the law, loomed over Alex and Helen. But Jude saved them for, true to his principles, he didn't like the police and refused to press charges. Besides he did not know who hit him and to his friends all the fishermen looked alike. Alex didn't tell Helen about the assault but Marvin noised it about Birsett. Most of the villagers agreed that Jude deserved all he got. Alex's reputation in his home village rose in the same proportion as Jude's sank amongst his set.

A sort of justice was done. Which is just as well, for the establishment that keeps threatening this caring couple sits on its hands and refuses to rule on that other couple that have caused so much distress - on the grounds that actions nowadays are not right and wrong, only alternative.

    We are creating a tolerant society. Predatory, too.

.

CHAPTER THIRTY-ONE

Helen wanted to hug her son and she wanted to hammer him. She did neither. Although it was after eleven, she fed him and handed him the envelope she had kept for him. He was surprised to see it had not been opened. The results were good; sufficient for the Engineering HND at Napier College he had promised his father he would take. But Napier is in Edinburgh, and Edinburgh had paled in all their minds. Leave it for a few days; nothing needs to be decided now. Helen and Alex slept easily on Thursday night.

Rebecca, too, slept well knowing that although she had failed her exams something had been accomplished that day. Not so, Marion; like John she blamed herself for her daughter's failure, but unlike her husband she had not promised to "sort" it. She could see no way forward that was not a step back and backward she would not go; she could not surrender ground so painfully won. She made sensible plans with Rebecca for the new term and for taking the exams again at Christmas or next year. She achieved some sort of stability by the time they went to bed. But she lay awake listening to the sea soughing among the rocks and sullen rumble of the waves on the beach, feeling bleak and lonely and wondering what lay ahead. Then she remembered her commitment to visit Rachel and JP next door. She could see no way out of that either.

Considering the circumstances, the visit next door passed off pleasantly. John came and Rebecca made no great fuss over her results, giving her hosts the impression that she had achieved more or less what she had wanted. Rachel, however, was sensitive enough to realise that Rebecca could not be bothered overlong with Ben, so after a while she despatched him to his room. Rachel had prepared what she called a cold collation of quiche, sausage rolls, vol-au-vents, canapés, various savoury biscuits with various pates, and a selection of fruit and cheeses, all accompanied by very good, and, Marion suspected, very expensive, wine. Rachel explained that Jacob had intended a barbecue with him as master chef, but she had banned it on the grounds first, that with the wind in the east it was too cold an evening, and secondly, that no one liked cindered sausages or burnt burgers. JP laughed easily at this put-down and enjoyed sitting with his guests at the table in the conservatory, looking out over the darkening sea and sky. He made a good host and kept everyone in the conversation.

JP, however, kept clear of the question that turned in everyone's mind: had the holiday brought a reconciliation closer? He came nearest when he asked Marion how she had enjoyed her stay. She had; had seen much of interest; had revived old memories; had had a good rest. And Rebecca? She had enjoyed her stay at Birsett: there was so much to see; she liked the house; she had enjoyed lazing about on the terrace. She could have said that best of all, it was good to be part of a family again, but she didn't. JP did not ask a similar question of John until they were alone. The party split when JP invited John to step outside onto the terrace and take in the sea air while the ladies did the washing up. (Do I need to explain that the men did volunteer to help? JP actually had a tea towel in his hand at one stage and John was hovering with intent. But they were shooed away.)

"Well, John, have you enjoyed having Marion and Rebecca here?"

John had not expected the question but welcomed it. He did not answer it directly.

"I've learned a lot this week," he said, and fell silent. JP did not ask him what he meant. Being a questioner by profession, he knew when to keep quiet. John would tell him when he was ready. He did.

"I see now how badly I have let down Rebecca. I'm sure she would have gained the results she needed if Marion and I had not split up."

If he sought reassurance, he did not win it.

"You are probably correct," said JP, "I'm sure you and Marion thought it wise when you decided to separate, but Rebecca had no reason for breaking up the family; there were no compensations; it proved a complete loss for her."

John had not expected such candour.

"Yes," he said. JP obviously had something more to say. He was not sure he wanted to hear it, so he added,

"It's nice out here; you can just see the white water on the Carr Rocks; it's what? Half-tide?"

"Three hours to full," said JP, then added a code they both understood.

"There's that damn factory cat again."

John looked at JP and they both laughed.

"It's as obvious as that, is it?" said John.

"I'm afraid it is," said his friend.

'The factory cat' is a happy memory from their time at Pinkerton's in York. When chasing an idea, Flambert Pinkerton hated anyone contradicting him. He wouldn't answer the contradiction; he would simply change the subject. The case in mind came when JP turned down Flambert's proposal to squander a million or two. Flambert suddenly strode to the window and announced that the factory cat was climbing over the directors' cars. They had all laughed, including Flambert, and the story passed into company folklore.

"When are you going to put your family back together again?" persisted JP gently.

"I am not sure it can be done," said John almost welcoming the opportunity to say what was in his mind.

"Why not?"

"I'm not sure that is what Marion wants."

"Have you asked her?"

"No."

"Why not?"

"Because I'm not sure what she'll say."

"But she came here this week; that must count for something."

"No, I don't think so; she came because Rebecca badgered her."

"To me she doesn't seem to be a woman to be badgered against her will. If she had not wanted to come, I don't think Rebecca could have persuaded her."

"We both keep doing things for Rebecca because we feel guilty. She dragged us along to an outing to Castle Howard at Easter."

"And did you enjoy it?"

"Yes, as a matter of fact, I did; a bit like old times."

"You enjoyed being with them then; you have enjoyed being with them now. It strikes me you are both in a standoff; each waiting for the other to make a move. You need to ask yourself what you want, John, and go for it."

John fell silent as the picture of Marion in the raspberry field leapt into his mind. But a more vivid image chased it in and replaced it: Marion in a summer dress with Malcolm at the door.

"I think Marion has someone else in the frame. She introduced me when I was down there last month."

"Ah," said JP and changed the subject.

"About Gainslaw Globes," he said, "I think I have persuaded Flambert to give them a shot at the bodies and clips of two of his devices. If they'll give me security on the assets, I'll put in a hundred thousand."

"What!" exclaimed John; "I thought you said it wasn't viable?"

"It probably isn't."

"Then why?"

"I'm an old softie," he smiled. "But there's one condition; Kate has to be in charge; Colin has to be taken out of management. It's a long shot anyway but with him as MD it stands no chance at all; he has to go."

"Go – you mean out of the company."

"No, there's no need for that. Just somewhere where he can't mess things up."

"How will you manage that?"

"I'm not going to try; I thought you might do it."

"Me?"

"Yes. You're the manager. Let me know when we can talk to them."

John agreed but could not explore matters arising before Rachel, Rebecca and Marion joined them on the terrace. JP, with a smiling glance at John, pointed out to them the white water breaking in the darkness over the Carr Rocks.

At the end of the visit John escorted Marion and Rebecca the few yards to their own door, but seemed reluctant to leave. Marion invited him in but he refused. Then he walked up the brae in the darkness to the blank windows of Braeshiel. He did not notice the sky bright with stars above him, or the wind chasing around him, or even the crash of the waves on the beach. Tomorrow, Rebecca, his daughter and Marion, his wife would go home without him.

The holiday was over; the week which had seemed so long in prospect had fled past and tomorrow there would be no afternoon outing, no evening together. So easily had he slipped into the routine that it had become almost normal, so normal that it needed no effort. Now the new routine would re-assert itself and with it the new normality, the new normality of empty days and pointless tasks.

John did not sleep well that night. A nagging doubt he had subdued all week played back into his mind. No, not a doubt – alarm – and distress; he saw again Marion dressed in her best to welcome Malcolm. During the week they had spent together, he had ignored the memory and played down its significance but it had not lost any of its sting. He must deal with it. Now! Otherwise it might be too late.

Too late for what? Hopes, plans even, that he had not acknowledged had formed secretly in his mind. Now he must admit to them or they would dissolve; he must grasp them now or give them up. He must see Marion before she went away: first thing to-morrow.

Often ideas bright in the darkness pale in the light of the sun. At nine, John found himself walking down to the house at Partan Row much less sure of his intention than he had been during the night.

Marion, for her part, was not entirely surprised to see him. Since they had recognised each other over the raspberry canes she had been expecting John to make a move; had considered making a move herself; had been (if she were honest) disappointed when no approach came. It must be decided; this half-life was no way to live; it should be all or nothing. And what were the terms for 'all'?

She answered the door and accepted John's invitation to walk with him along the shore. Then she went back into the house to put on her jacket and tell Rebecca of their plan. You do not need me to describe the delight of Rebecca.

Together the separated couple walked along the road that winds round the foot of the cliffs past the old fishermen's houses.

As they walked John discovered that although he had something to say, he could not find the words to express it. For so long had he locked them away in a dark corner of his mind that he could not find them. The phrases that came to him were not formed by the powerful feelings of the night before. They were of the sort that had regulated his relationship with his wife for the past few years; phrases assembled not for their meaning but for their effect; not to communicate or interact, but to defend, repel; to impersonate concern but to commit to nothing.

"I feel bad about Rebecca," he mumbled.

"Yes," said Marion

"I feel that the separation has mucked her up. We were too hasty; we probably didn't think enough about the implications."

"No, probably not."

"Do you think there is anything we could do to help her?"

"I do what I can. We have talked about it."

"What does she say?"

"Do you not think you should ask her for yourself?"

John silenced the words that came into his mouth. Did he hear exasperation (exasperation already!) in Marion's reply? This conversation is going the same way as all the others – a descent into petty pricks and parrying.

"Yes, I should," he said, finding a different answer. Then added, "I promised I would sort it."

"And what did you mean by that?"

"I don't know, I just know it is unsatisfactory....' (Could he leave it there? Dare he leave it there? No) '.... for Rebecca."

Marion had had enough of this verbal fencing.

"And what about you, John? Is it unsatisfactory for you?"

John stumbled over the answer.

"Yes, yes, of course."

"Then what do you want, John?"

They had reached the place where there are no houses. On a full tide the unsettled sea slapped waves onto the rocks beside the road, sending intermittent showers of spray sparkling across it. Above them the fresh sun glowed through the clearing mists of morning, out of the sea a soft breeze rustled the tall grasses and scrub willow on the brae; gulls glided like silken wraiths out over the rocks and waves then soared up the cliff before swooping down to the sea again: close by a blackbird acclaimed the new day. Nature had set the scene; a new, refreshed life beckoned. Marion had fed him the line. If John had stopped and poured out his fears and hopes, embraced and kissed her perhaps, it is likely that our story would have ended right here with violins playing, the whole cast dancing and "happy ever after" somewhere in the closing paragraph. But no! He stuck to tired words.

The question, remember, is: "what do you want, John?"

"I think we should think about getting back together for

Rebecca's sake."

A wave of disappointment, frustration and anger swept over Marion.

"Do you?" she said tersely, afraid to let her anger rip.

"Yes," said John, "I think we owe it to her."

(God! Man! Why the excuses? Why blame Rebecca? Why does he not say what he really wants? Why does he not admit that he needs Marion?)

Marion swallowed the words that leapt into her mind - "to hell with Rebecca, what about you and me, John; what about us?".

"And on what terms are you asking me back?" came out of the turbulence in her mind.

This struck John as mercenary. He had anticipated encouragement. Marion would agree; they would say sorry to each other (again) and to Rebecca (again) and he would pack up in Birsett, move back into the family house and resume his job-hunting from there. They could keep Braeshiel for holidays and weekends. But what was this: "what terms?"?

"What do you mean?"

"I mean, John, there is no way back. You must offer me..." She stopped. The selfishness of what she was about to demand appalled her.

"Oh, John, John! Let's stop this right now. There is no point!"

"I don't understand, surely you want the best for Rebecca."

"Of course, have I ever wanted anything else? But next year, or the year after that, or sometime, Rebecca will leave home and what then, John? What then, John, for you and me?"

John had been asking himself this question, or rather

had been composing then avoiding it, for weeks. Disturbed by the image of Malcolm, unsure of Marion's response, he did not know how to ask it, nor how to answer it. Now he heard it in the mouth of Marion. He had hoped she might know the answer, but apparently not. He recalled JP's words about stand-off and realised with a thump that no words, no discussion, no talking it over, were going to solve this impasse for it was not of the mind, nor of the heart, but in the life. He threw out a last despairing line. Fortunately, it was his best.

"I'm all wrong, Marion, I need to sort myself out. When I do, can I get in touch to see what we can work out?"

The suddenly arrived desperation melted Marion. She smiled.

"Please do," she said and kissed him on the cheek. Then they turned back.

When Rebecca asked her what had happened, Marion simply said, "Your father and I will be seeing each other again."

"Soon?" asked Rebecca.

"I hope so," replied Marion.

Before she left that morning, Marion paid one last visit to Helen. David was with his mother; Rebecca with Marion. Rebecca smiled at David with the smile she had inherited from her mother. David was charmed; charmed and excited. But in half-an-hour she was gone and David regretted that he had been in Edinburgh while Rebecca holidayed at Partan Row.

CHAPTER THIRTY-TWO

After a restless week, life settled to normality for the people we have been shadowing. For most of them life had changed, if only slightly. But Del will tell you that even a point off course over a distance will land you somewhere different. For one the change was dramatic; the week had proved decisive, his life essentially altered.

Abigail and Jude continued in their various ways to enjoy the Edinburgh Festival and were present in Princes Street gardens (Jude with temporary fillings in his two upper front teeth) for the fireworks display that brought the glorious three weeks to a close. But neither of them mentioned David nor spoke so much about their mission to free up the young people they met. Margaret and Roddam were glad that the Festival was over and were thereby no longer obliged to attend plays they could not follow, music they could not fathom and art they could not comprehend.

Mr Scott received an appointment to see an orthopaedic consultant in February, this date easily beating the Scottish Executive's target for no more than six month's suffering before you see someone to talk to. No doubt he will be provided with his new knees within the targeted two years so will only be eighty-seven when the operation is carried out - if he lives that long. If he doesn't, then the waiting list will go down by one and some other eighty-year-old will have the benefit of bearing their pain for only two years. In the meantime, Mr Scott will make his life among his books, papers and the good and not so good folk of Birsett.

Delightful and his crew along with the other crabbers and their crews left Birsett harbour on the days when water and weather allowed them, and returned later with their catches and their complaints. Alex carried on with his fishing during the week and sea-anglers at weekends. Helen returned to providing for her family, visiting her old folk, setting the hair of her customers, and living down the disgrace of her son and daughter. The schools opened again after the long summer holiday. Morag, now too old for Birsett Primary School, joined Calum and George in the school bus that took them each morning the two miles to Hecklescar High School. She came back on the first Friday asking for a trumpet so she could join the school band. Louise now went alone to Birsett School and on the first day reported to her mother that there were only two in the beginner's class so the school would have to shut. Helen knew this last wasn't true; at least, not for now. She also knew that one of the beginners was Julie, the little sister of Johnny Armstrong who is still lost among the rocks, and that her mother Susan 'grat' all the way down the brae after leaving her. She knew this because Wanda told her. Wanda had walked home with Susan and stayed with her until she had settled herself. The other beginner was Wanda's own, Torquil, who now joined his brother Quentin in the playground.

Two days a week JP took the train down to London; three days a week Ben bussed to the Gainslaw Centre and every day Rachel baked, cooked, embroidered and, for at least an hour, worked with Beethoven on his sonata. She also went with Helen to the opening meeting of the WRI and was almost elected President.

Marion and Rebecca went on from Birsett to spend a few days with Marion's folks at Clydebank; then they returned to York. But Rebecca met no one she liked better than David. At York Marion took up her job again and her charity work and her church work, and week by week continued to meet Fiona, Mack's wife. Fiona kept her up to date with the end story of Pinkerton and of Mack's new job in consultancy. Marion told Fiona about the holiday and about John, but not about John's promise to call. This she looked for rather than expected. Rebecca, once August was past, went back to school to tackle her Maths and Economics again and to brag about her handsome cousin in Scotland. She, too, thought about her father, and her mother, and about the future. It looked brighter, she believed.

During the remaining weeks of August, John developed a plan for putting his life in order. There wasn't much to it, but it cleared his mind and settled him. Under Personal and Domestic, (these are my categories, not his) he set the aim as claiming back Marion from Malcolm, to be a father again to Rebecca, to recreate a family life. Under Position and Career, his objectives were to teach Loyalty a lesson and find himself a position that matched his abilities and aspirations. He ranked these last first; he could not settle down without them; he could not, in the modern phrase, move on.

On Monday, he resolved to ring Belinda Boyd to arrange a meeting to review progress. He wanted a date for the hearing. He feared, if he could have admitted it, that his anger had cooled in the quiet life of Birsett. That his dispute had become an old, unhappy, far-off thing, a battle long ago. Any thoughts of amelioration, however, were put to flight by an announcement he read over breakfast in the Financial Times: Sir Frank Wantley had been appointed Deputy Chairman of the Loyalty Board. He rang Belinda, rehearsing his tirade. 'Belinda is not here; she is on holiday; she keeps her own diary; ring next week.'

Wait, oh no, it can't wait, won't wait. He rang The Sunday News newsdesk and poured out his story to a seemingly sympathetic reporter. Yes, he would be prepared to give an interview, and yes, he would be in London by the end of the month. I should have done this weeks ago, he told himself, and drank freely of his refreshed indignation.

But this is not the essential change we spoke of earlier for John trundles down the same old track. It is not John that alters course; it is David.

Ever since Alex had discovered that David had a decent headpiece on him, he had determined that he should take up something better than the fishing. He had in mind Engineering. David, following the predestined path chosen by his father had, as we have seen, done well enough in his Highers to take up an HND course at Napier College in Edinburgh. He had a provisional place; all he had to do was to prove his results and turn up for enrolment. But he kept putting it off. Helen put this down to his fear of leaving home, Alex to his fear of failure; both to the fright sponsored by Jude. But when they finally coaxed him to tell them what he really felt he startled them by saying that he wanted to go to the fishing. He'd been inquiring; there was a berth on the Purple Heather at Hecklescar.

After a brief attempt at reason, Alex lost the head. He accused his son of causing them grief (again) and deliberately trying to frustrate their hopes for him. He ranted at his son about wasted lives and lost opportunities; how he would live to regret it; that the fishing was hard work, insecure, failing. You made no money in it now and God knows how little in the future.

"Look at the fishermen of Birsett." he said, "How could you envy any of them? Who? Delightful? Dod? Batman? Marvin? Marvin! What do you want to be, when you're fifty, son? A crabber, going out in all weathers, scraping a living, trying to keep a boat in the water? Or, someone with a bit clout, with your own house, a nice car outside and a bit of money in the bank? Look at your Uncle John; he started as an engineer, now he's a Managing Director – look how well he's done for himself. Set your sights higher, son, don't be like ...."

Who? Helen knew who; so did David.

"You've done all right, dad," he said

"All right! All right! Is that what you want to do all your life – all right!? There's no future in fishing, not the sort done in Hecklescar, piddlin' about in little boats catching a puckle haddock and whiting wi' the EU changin' the rules a' the time, the fishery cruiser breathin' down yer neck and a satellite spyin' over yer shoulder. They've admitted they're trying to make fishing unprofitable – lose your livelihood, lose your boat, lose yer sanity – preserve the fish. In a few years there'll only be the big boats left, like the Orcades Viking up in Orkney, or the Lunar Bow in Peterhead - that's the future, factory fishing. A boat like that catches more fish in a single trip than the whole Hecklescar fleet in a fortnight, and Hecklescar harbour's too small for boats that size. Ye ken, there's a crab boat in Scrabster that catches 20 ton of crabs in four days, working day and night. We're sprats caught between two whales - the bureaucrats in Brussels and the big boys up north; if one doesn't kill us off, the other will."

As he spoke Alex turned in his chair and hauled The Fishing News out of the magazine rack. He found a page, and pushed it into David's hand and stood over him.

"See, read for yersel. There's a Hecklescar boat: 'Vessels for Sale: MFV New Hope LH142, built of wood, MacDonald Boatbuilders, Arbroath, 1987, Overall Length 21.3 metres, Engine Cat 3412 565bhp, Reintjes Gearbox, Jennison Winch, 2 x 10-ton Net Drum, Atlas Crane, Pullmaster Cod End Winch'. Good boat, good gear, but too small. And there's her pair trawler 'MFV Mary Jane LH232 with or without PSL & Track

Record'. They're too small, there's few fish, and the big boats are scooping up what there is. They're giving up: sell the licence to the Dutch, retire to Spain I expect. They see no future in fishin' at Hecklescar, son; and they're fishermen."

"But you do all right at the poos and lobsters, Ye've got yer ain boat."

"Aye, I've got ma ain boat. But did ye ken what it cost to get it?" (He glanced at Helen) "and where's the next yin coming from? It'll have to be bigger. There're too many boats inshore. We'll need to go out fifteen, twenty miles, carry more craves, so it needs to be bigger. Where am I going to get the wherewithal for a bigger boat? Ye ken the Scrabster boat that's clearing the Pentland Firth of crabs: how much did it cost? I'll tell you. Two million pound! There's no money here, with little people doing little things; the money's with the big boys. Be a scientist or a bureaucrat, son, and get paid for telling the fisherman what they can't catch. Look at your Uncle John, he left Birsett a laddie like yersel', went in for engineering and look at him now."

"Uncle John doesn't do anything," David said, "I'd rather be on the sea, doing something. Auld Willie said when the sea's in yer blood, ye canna fight it."

"And Auld Willie was a romancer; he gave it up as soon as he could. The sea's not a notion, and it's no in yer blood; it's lumps of water, and cauld, and careless. It gives ye nothing ye don't rive from it. Ye'll be sick of it in a week."

Alex wouldn't budge; David would not be persuaded. Helen proposed a compromise: don't turn down the place at Napier; the course doesn't start for a few weeks yet: take the berth on trial, if Big Dod'll let you; then in a couple of weeks we'll decide; once you've had a taste of it. It satisfied neither party but suited both.

Big Dod, skipper of the Purple Heather, graciously, would give the lad a chance. Big deal! He couldn't get anyone else! On Sunday night Helen packed a food box and a holdall for David and Alex took him to the boat for a four-day trip, pair trawling with the White Rose.

"Good luck, son," said his father, "Take care!"

David was sick for twelve hours, but stuck it out. He came back on Thursday, pale and tired, but went the week after and the week after that. By the end of a month he had become a fisherman. Alex grieved for six months, and was only consoled when George said he'd never go to the fishing; he fancied a job like Uncle John's or the man that came with Auntie Margaret in the big car. Morag wants to play football for Brazil.

Changes were also afoot at Gainslaw Globes, though not the changes JP and John had plotted. John walked slap into them when he called at the factory without notice in the first week of September. He found Kate and Colin slinging insults at each other. He had never seen Kate out of temper before; she was blazing. He calmed her down and teased out the cause of the dispute. It lay with the order from Caledesign Solutions for Scotia Homeflair; Colin had landed it at last.

"That's good news, isn't it?" said John.

The pair answered together but differently.

"Yes," said Colin, trying to sound calm.

"No", snapped Kate.

"You first, Colin," said John holding up his hand to quieten Kate.

Colin used the audience of John to list his grievances against Kate. He had been chasing this order for months, working all the hours God sends, up and down to Glasgow like a yo-yo; must get it; no option but to get it; to plug a hole in the order book; or the machines would be idle; he'd have to lay off a couple of people; the company would go belly up if he didn't get the order; now he'd got it, after all his effort, he'd landed it, in the lap, signed on the dotted line but some people weren't pleased. Some people are never pleased. Colin rattled through this again and again in wild despair. In the end John had to intervene.

"Now, Kate, what's the problem?"

"It will bankrupt us," she said, quietly but firmly, "we have had to buy the tools – with money we don't have. The delivery date is too tight – a week on Monday for the first delivery; we've never run a new job right first time, if we don't this time, we have to pay a thousand pounds for every day we're late..."

"They wanted two thousand," cut in Colin. John silenced him. Kate ignored his achievement.

"That's seven thousand pounds a week. In four weeks, it wipes out any profit we might have made on a year's sales. Even if it runs (which it won't) the profit is 12% gross; that's nowhere near enough to cover overheads; he's cut the price to get the job. This order will ruin us."

It could have been JP speaking and John's heart went out to Kate. He saw in her defiance her last stand, her last futile stand. Her beautiful eyes filled with tears, she shook her head gently, then stood up and walked out of the office. He doesn't deserve her, thought John.

"She'll get over it," said Colin.

"She might," said John, "But I don't think the company will."

Colin stood up, defiant in his weariness.

"Who dares wins," he announced. John had heard the phrase before; it was a favourite of George at Pinkerton. To George it was a joke; Colin was serious.

"Not always," John said, "and not this time."

"Watch me," said Colin, pulling himself up straight.

John will, and we will. Circle the date: Monday 16th

September. It has to be on a lorry heading north on the sixteenth of September, a week on Monday. He hasn't even proved the tool yet.

CHAPTER THIRTY-THREE

"D'ye think you could gie's a hand at the craves?" Del asked John at the door of Braeshiel.

"Me?" exclaimed John. "At the craves?"

"Aye," said Delightful, "ye've been out wi' Alex a couple of times, and he tells me ye've had a shot o' the wheel."

This was true. John had been with Alex a couple of times; once to the craves and once with sea anglers, but just as a spectator. He didn't take the boat; he held the wheel; that was all; he did nothing.

"No, no, I can't do that," protested John.

"I have a problem," said Delightful, trying to speak in a language he hoped John might understand. "I'm a man short. Kit has sprained his wrist; he can't handle the craves; he can empty them and bait them, so I have to haul them; stack them and shoot them; but we need somebody to keep the boat going ahead. Ma fither-in-law has been standin' in but he's awa' the morn at the Borders General wi' his varicose veins. Ye'd manage it; there's naethin' tae it."

"You're a man short!" said John. "Marvin? Where's Marvin?"

"Marvin's gone?"

"Gone?"

"I had to get rid of him."

Del explained that Marvin had pushed his luck once too often, or, rather twice too often. He had not turned up for work on the Monday and when Del phoned in from the sea to find out where he was, Dot told him that Wanda had put him out of the house.

Seemingly, on the Sunday Wanda had made a special effort to make a nice family dinner for Marvin: roast beef, Yorkshire pudding, potatoes, carrots and broccoli, with a rice timbale and peaches to follow. She had not tackled anything on such a scale before, but had made the effort for two reasons. One was that Marvin's reputation had risen in Birsett by association with Alex (he had been there when Alex sorted out the poncey painter from Edinburgh). He had not been drunk since the incident and had not once missed the sailing time of the Aurora. Wanda felt she was at last making progress in her campaign to make Marvin respectable. Perhaps they could now scrape together enough money to get married. The other reason can be found in an article she had read at the hairdressers (she couldn't afford to go every week, but scrimped enough for a monthly shampoo and set at The Restless Wave in Hecklescar). Here, we must put in a plea to women's magazine writers: please be more modest in your claims. "Beef Up Your Partner" Wanda had read. It argued that good food made for good relationships; and although the modern man can cook for himself, it does wonders for mutual bliss if the woman occasionally turns it on.

Now Wanda is only a moderate cook; or, perhaps moderate is an exaggeration. She can open tins and heat up packets and has learned to operate a microwave, but her efforts at anything beyond this are, well, only adequate - if that is not overstating it. To be honest, the highlight of Marvin's week is a fish supper from McMaggie's on a Friday night. In truth, Wanda looked forward to it herself. Marvin knew about Wanda's cooking and accepted it as part of the bargain by which they rubbed along together; he had learned neither to praise nor condemn; he just ate what Wanda put in front of him. But on the Sunday before the absent Monday he had been lured into something more, and for Wanda it was one humiliation too many. She had borne many, but this, coming dressed in so much expectation, proved too much.

Dermot, Marvin's cousin manufactured it. He had, as blind fortune will have it, won a couple of thousand pounds on the lottery. He could have used the money to pay back some of the debt owed to his cousin, but this is Dermott, by-name Rott, we're talking about. He wanted to celebrate with friends but did not have many, and what few he had did not care to be around when he had drunk too much. He picked on his cousin to share his luck and drink his happiness in The Restless Sole. Marvin had gone but promised he would be back in time for the special lunch at half-past twelve.

He came back late; Rott came with him. When they entered, they found the table set, with a white cloth, matching cutlery and what passed for Wanda's best china; in the centre a little bowl of flowers from the garden. By each place a wine-glass (4 for 99p from Hecklescar Discounts) and by Marvin's place, for him to pour, a bottle of red wine (she had asked Susan and she thought it was red wine with beef). She had washed and polished Torquil and Quentin, dressed them in their best clothes and confined them to the house until their father should arrive.

Wanda's heart sank at the sight of Rott coming in behind Marvin. This was not what she had planned. Then Rott assaulted her with a beery kiss and hands groping her buttocks. She felt she like vomiting. Time was when she had been flattered by his attentions; now she loathed the man. Nature, like the lottery, gives her gifts without discretion, and Rott had been given an unequal share; he was tall, handsome, intelligent, and strong, Marvin smaller, fatter, duller. Rott's parents had indulged him and now he indulged himself. He had spent his assets on his appetites, circulating from the pub to bookies to the bed of any woman who would have him. Anyone who got in his way he trampled. He had preyed on his parents until they despaired of him; now he preyed on Marvin and Wanda. But for some time now Wanda had resisted him and it rankled. He could not understand how any woman could prefer Marvin to himself. But Marvin had a warmth Rott had never had, a gentleness too. He was generous and when sober, decent; Wanda preferred that.

Now a half-drunk Marvin demanded that his cousin should share their meal. Wanda, fighting back her tears, agreed and asked them to sit in. Rott took Marvin's place at the head of the table; Marvin squeezed in beside Quentin. Rott grabbed the wine bottle, opened it and poured himself a glass. Marvin then helped himself. Wanda served fruit juice in little glasses to her family and their guest. Rott drank it in one gulp and sat pulling the flowers out of the little bowl while he waited to be fed; the children attempted to join in; Wanda stopped them. Marvin drank his juice. Rott helped himself to more wine.

Wanda served the main course, created with her own hands; carefully created, taking hours, everything according to the book, all in the proper pans and trays, properly brought together at the right time, properly arranged on the plates, properly presented. Still something might be salvaged; Marvin might still enjoy it, might be impressed, might taste the devotion with which it was prepared. Wanda watched him cut into the roast beef. It was tough; he sawed away for a while, then noticed Rott picking his meat off his plate with his fingers.

"Fucking leather," Rott howled, "It's like fucking leather; nail it on yer boots."

He pushed his chair back and yanked his foot onto the table. Then he slapped the meat onto the sole of his boot. He guffawed. The bairns stared at him. Marvin grinned nervously and glanced at Wanda. As Rott dragged his foot from the table he toppled the wine bottle splattering a red flood over the white cloth.

"And these," Rott seized the Yorkshire Puddings, "Bloody soggy footballs." He roared at his own wit. Then he took one and flung it at Quentin. "Catch." The bairn caught it and laughed. Rott threw another one to Torquil. Quentin threw his back, then, Torquil, shouting, joined in and finally, finally, Marvin. In the middle of the mayhem, Rott stood up.

"Come on, our kid," he shouted to Marvin, "Let's go and get some decent fucking food."

Marvin stood up. He looked at the table, then at his rioting children, then at Wanda. Wanda looked at him and caught his eyes. For a moment he hesitated, held her gaze, then he turned away, laughed, threw another Yorkshire pudding at the bairns and went out with Rott.

After they left, Wanda mopped up the wine and tearfully served the sweet, the rice timbale with peaches, to herself and her boys. The boys wouldn't eat it.

When Marvin staggered home blind drunk at one o'clock in the morning, he found a locked door. After banging, kicking and cursing for half-an-hour the police arrived. He spent the night in a cell at Hecklescar: breach of the peace and threatening behaviour. Wanda had made her choice: she would try no longer; see how he would fare with his cousin.

What Marvin did not realise was that he owed his berth on the Aurora to Wanda. Every time Delightful had threatened to fire him, Wanda had pleaded with Dot and Dot pleaded with Del. Now he had no-one to plead his case. Marvin lost his job and he lost his home; but Wanda lost more: she lost her dream.

John didn't have to go with Delightful after all. Jimmy Possum stood in and made a better job of managing the boat than the Managing Director would have done.

It proved the last chance the Aurora, or any other boat, managed to the craves for four days. Fishermen know to expect a gale around each equinox as the earth rampages into spring or collapses into winter, but this year the autumn gale arrived early. The storm blew in from the south-east; worst of all airths for Birsett harbour. For days the breakers fumed and foamed over the rocks and crashed against the outer breakwater, sending spray and spindrift scudding up the brae, drenching the rock, scorching the trees and splattering with salt the walls and windows of the houses, even those at the very top. In the harbour, the boats rocked and jostled and strained at their confinement. Each morning around daybreak, as if in obeisance to the storm, the crews would assemble, debate what they had already decided then disperse to their enforced leisure. The storm doors and window shutters along Partan Row were bolted against the rage of wind and water. John from Braeshiel looked out on a white broken sea.

After four days the storm abated and the sea settled back within its bounds. After the storm Ben, exploring along the shore, came across a child's broken body. Rachel rang John; John rang the police then rang Helen. Helen told Wanda who went down the brae to tell Susan. She should know first. Better be told by a kent face than by a uniform. It took a week to confirm the body as that of little Johnny but the whole village knew immediately.

Susan needed no confirmation. The gnawing uncertainty was over. He hadn't run away, or been taken, except by the sea. At least he had come back; she knew where he was; she could pay her last tribute of love and bring him in from the cold wide world into the compass of a small safe plot of earth.

The Rev Mr Mordun had to attend a committee meeting in Edinburgh on Rural Deprivation and was not inclined to cancel it for someone who never came to church. Mr Scott stood in and stumbled through the service, his broken words giving a comfort no formal liturgy would have matched.

CHAPTER THIRTY-FOUR

JP had long learnt that London streets are paved with concrete. (Find out by whom, and buy shares.) but John hopes they are still paved with opportunity. They thrust back at his step, unlike the paths of Birsett that accept and absorb it. The city exudes activity, power, prosperity and success; John breathed it in but did not sense the excitement it used to elicit. It smelt stale. The air at Birsett tasted much fresher.

As he walked down Regent Street to the offices of Booth, Blair and Brown he tried to recapture his former impressions – and his appetite for justice.

"I've been asleep" he muttered, as he recalled Sir Frank's deceit – and subsequent promotion. He had an appointment with the reporter on the Sunday News at three; that gave him an hour and a half to put some beef into Belinda Boyd.

Ms Boyd, however, won't be bullied. She has bought a dog since his last visit, a Jack Russell. It ran at John when he entered her office.

"Don't worry," she said, "It doesn't bite." It nipped his ankles; John winced.

"He means no harm," corrected Belinda, "Hattersley,

sit!" Give the dog credit, it sat, then lay, then stretched out with its nose on John's shoe. At any movement of his foot it growled. John should have told Ms Boyd to shift it, but he didn't.

Their last meeting had been three months ago but Ms Boyd had not been inactive. She had sounded out the other party again, and secured a date for the hearing: November 15th; but she was still waiting for instructions.

"I told you to proceed," John stated, trying to sound decisive.

"And I told you to settle out of court. Here's the deal: we asked for £200,000 and an early retirement pension of £35,000 a year: they offer, £180,000 and £30,000. That is £20,000 and £5,000 below our figures and they were exaggerated. It's generous; you should accept it."

"Legal expenses?"

"They pay if it doesn't go to court."

"Any conditions?"

"Just one; neither party speaks to the press, or anyone else. You can talk about your departure being amicable, that's all."

"Hah, I thought so!"

"What did you expect? They want something for their money."

"That says it all; they're as guilty as sin."

"Maybe, but we couldn't prove it."

"They're not on!" said John, firmly; "I want it tried. See this!" He slid the cutting from the FT across her desk.

She read the announcement of Sir Frank's elevation then turned it over to see if there was something more relevant on the other side.

"So?"

"He's getting away with it. No! Benefiting from it!"

"Benefiting from what?" She snapped irritably.

"Corporate corruption!" said John grandly. "The transfer of manufacturing from York to Bainan was bent; it stinks!"

Belinda sighed.

"Mr Swansen, the facts are these: Loyalty took a strategic decision to transfer manufacturing from York to Bainan. Many companies are doing the same. You fought it and lost; they sacked you: Sir Frank Wantley supported them and won; they made him vice-chairman. All grist to the great commercial mill; nothing in the least illegal; I doubt if it is even doubtful."

"But I want to see Loyalty, Walter Radleigh and particularly, Sir Frank answer for their actions. Surely that is not too much to ask, even nowadays. There must be a remedy. The fact that I can't prove it chapter and verse is beside the point; they must speak for themselves, explain themselves, or expose themselves; that is what I want; I don't want money, I don't even want a verdict, I want...."

"Revenge!" Ms Boyd cut in. "You want revenge."

"No, no."

"Yes! And you want us to go to trial to get it. We don't stand a cat's chance in hell of winning but you want us to present a case."

Her words rattled like machine gun bursts.

"We could have it dismissed as frivolous. We'd be laughed out of court; our reputations damaged. You want me and some unfortunate barrister to risk that, just to make your former boss squirm in public."

John attempted to speak, but the solicitor put up her

hand to stop him. She closed the file and for a moment John thought she was going to ask him to leave: case closed. But she put the file aside and pulled a notepad into its place.

"This is not my job," she said, "but somebody has to do it. The rate is five hundred pounds an hour. Now then, forget about unfair dismissal, loss of office, breach of contract or any other legal device. Tell me why you're angry. I take it you have no other appointments?"

"I am seeing a Sunday News reporter at three," said John,

"Not enough time," snapped Belinda, flicking her pad closed. Hattersley stood up, ready for ankle duty. "Him or me? It is a him?"

"Yes," said John.

"Well?" said the lawyer.

"Okay," said John, "Can I call him?"

"No," said Belinda.

The Jack Russell resettled on John's foot.

We do not need to listen to all that went on; we were there when it happened and we've heard it all before. Ms Boyd is very patient; teases out each strand of John's resentment; conjures up the faces that tormented him – Radleigh, Mortimer, Arkwright, Ms Waltham, Sir Frank; delves into every conceived injustice, slots in every detail, analyses every claim, tests every argument, probes every motive. It takes two hours (that's a thousand pounds worth; it's cheaper on the National Health but not so therapeutic). In the end she gives her opinion.

"What makes you angry is not corruption, or deceit, or even your dismissal. What makes you angry is the fact that you were outplayed."

She had hit the target. He denied it. Belinda pressed on.

"Let me guess," she said, "If Loyalty had offered you a slice of the action, a seat on the board, international travel and a generous expense account, you would have taken it."

"Not at all," exploded John

"And you would have found ways to explain it to yourself."

"No!"

"And fitted it into your morality."

"No!" repeated John.

"Not only that but you've loaded your guilt onto Sir Frank. 'He's got away with it; I didn't; let him take the blame'. Is that it?"

"Not true," protested John.

"Don't play the saint," said the lawyer, "I haven't met a strictly honest businessman yet, or, for that matter, a strictly honest anyone."

"Not even a lawyer," snapped John.

"No, they're worse than most, but we know our limits; you don't. You had limits once; clear fences, but they've fallen down, and you haven't noticed. If you had been where Radleigh was, you would have done the same."

John conceded this by ignoring it. He changed track.

"I would not have done what Sir Frank did. I am convinced he bribed the Bainan government ministers and officials, and almost certainly pocketed a backhander himself."

He expected another wave of opinion, but Belinda relented.

"Probably not, but you would not have blocked him. You might have questioned it, but if you had been in and not out you would have gone along with it; you would have said 'it happens' and accepted it."

"No," said John. Ms Boyd ignored him and ploughed on.

"Now we know the cause let us find a remedy. Loyalty won't let you play with their train set. Go and buy one of your own. Take the money and the pension and move on. That is my opinion."

She stopped and looked at John. John stared back in frustration, but could think of nothing to say.

"Look," she added almost kindly, "I think I know how you feel, but it's not the end of the world. 'Vengeance is mine', saith the Lord, 'I will repay'. Life is short. When does your salary stop?"

The question took John by surprise; he didn't know the date.

"Six months," he said.

"The operative date was April seventeenth. It is now September; that's five months gone; you have one month left, and then what?"

John had considered the question. Marion had drawn his attention to it in the lounge at Poppleton weeks ago. But he had done little about it. When money has flowed into your bank account for so many years you can easily forget that someone else has their hand on the tap.

"You had better settle," insisted Belinda.

"No," said John, but even in John's own mind the rebuff lacked its former conviction.

"I'll give you a fortnight," said Belinda, standing up. John did the same. Hattersley nipped his ankles. Like dog, like owner, he thought.

Later that day, he rang the Sunday News to postpone the interview; he would contact them again soon. They did not seem surprised or disappointed. They smelt a deal; not for the first time, a disgruntled chief executive had been bought off.

John was not yet prepared to abandon his campaign against Sir Frank - and his complaint had narrowed to Sir Frank; he had not enough resentment left to spread further. He needed time to think, but, as we shall see later, before he reaches a conclusion, an unexpected encounter will resolve the issue for him.

John had reckoned on spending the night in London, half-imagining that he would be wined and dined and cosseted by the newspaper. He had booked himself on a train the following day to travel to York to wind up the contract on the flat. The year's lease finished in November anyway but for the last two months he had asked the agent to sub-let it. Now he wanted rid of it altogether for it reeked of a way of life turned sour by regret.

When he stepped out of Booth, Blair and Brown he found the streets of London had lost the the little appeal they had had. Ms Boyd had spoiled his mood; had made him feel like a sulky schoolboy. He recognised the accuracy of her analysis and the soundness of her advice but it sickened him to think that his treatment at the hands of Loyalty (how he loathed the sound of the word) was not unique; and not particularly unfair; just a straightforward rout, a routine management skirmish; the sort of thing he had shrugged off when he had heard of it happening to others. He nursed his conviction that Sir Frank had crossed the line, that his behaviour had been particularly nasty, but no longer did it add up to what he wanted. The streets had grown cold and bleak so he decided to travel to York that night, stay in the flat, then keep his appointment at ten the following day with the agent. He felt glad to be on the train, first class, travelling north, away from the metropolis.

When he arrived at the flat, he found it occupied. Self-absorbed, he opened the door and entered the hall before he heard the shouts of children. They tumbled out of the lounge:

two Asian girls dressed in shalwar suits. Behind them came their mother and behind her their father.

For a moment they froze into a tableau of surprise. John apologised profusely, explained he was the leaseholder, had been away, was unaware the flat had been sublet and would find somewhere else to spend the night. To his relief they all laughed and he retreated to the safety of the street.

At first, he did not plan to spend the night with Marion. He did try a couple of hotels without success before the idea occurred to him, and he tried two more before he called a taxi and set off for Poppleton.

CHAPTER THIRTY-FIVE

John had rehearsed his opening lines carefully.

"I'm a refugee," he said on the doorstep, "looking for asylum."

Marion let him in; Rebecca leapt at him and kissed him. He explained how he came to be stranded in York. Rebecca believed him without question; Marion gave him the benefit of the doubt.

While he explained himself and took his supper, the thoughts of all three drifted (as, no doubt, have yours, my suspicious reader) to the question of where John will spend the night. There is no real problem. There is the spare room, the room he had occupied for two years before he left over ten months ago. The bed is still there, and the chest of drawers, and the wardrobe, and, still inside them, some of his unclaimed clothes; pyjamas, for instance; still there, where he had always kept them, in the bottom drawer, beside the bottles of shower gel, packs of talc and the anti-stress foot roller Rebecca had once bought him. Marion had not cleared the room because at first, she had expected John back soon, then she had not known what to expect, so left it, awaiting decision, but whose decision? Why, when John's room was available, did it occur to all three that he might spend the night in the master bedroom, in the double bed where Marion still slept, in their old marriage bed, with Marion?

Rebecca went to her room and John took the opportunity to.... well, to tell Marion what had happened in London with Belinda Boyd and of his continuing contempt for Sir Frank. When Marion tentatively agreed with Belinda and suggested he should put it behind him and move on, she detected less of the resentment she had suffered over the past few years. John did not show any sign of agreeing with what she said, but he did not rubbish it, or fend it off.

Marion, however, had asked the question for her own reasons. She wanted to know whether he was still wrapped up in business, still courting power, still wedded to the car, suite, secretary and the title on the door. His answers gave some slight reassurance. She took further comfort in his reports of Gainslaw Globes and JP and Rachel and their life split between London, Birsett and the sea. They talked about Rebecca, her prospects and her studies, but beyond common courtesy, John asked Marion very little about her life. Although his fears called out to him to enquire about Malcolm, he dared not venture into that territory.

. At midnight they went to bed, without fuss, to separate beds; deliberately to separate beds, Marion to the front room with its double bed, John to the room squashed alongside Rebecca's at the back of the house. No one suggested any other arrangement, although I believe that nowadays an introduction is scarcely needed; mutual attraction authorises all. No one suggested they share a bed even though on their own old-fashioned terms, they had a certificate that gave them permission and many years of precedent. They went to their separate rooms and there they lay, these two and their daughter, not asleep, but awake, thinking, feeling, fretting.

To Rebecca it represents progress; they are in the same

house again; the room and the bed would come later.

Once he closed his mind's file on cases and opportunities John was surprised by the intensity of his feelings for Marion. He had felt something like it recently when he lay in Braeshiel and Marion in Partan Row, in the same village; now he was in the same house, just over the landing. What he felt was not desire in the sense that Jude or Abigail would understand it or, rather, feel it. There is no risk of a driven man crashing into Marion's room rampant with passion. It had never been like that. At the beginning it had been intriguing, sensational, delicious; in the end mechanical, vapid, a matter of mutual obligation. But for many years in between John and Marion had shared a physical and emotional harmony that impregnated all they did, gathered it all up, made it whole, strung all the separate and shared events into a single coherent experience. Although treasured it was not precious; it was practical rather than sentimental, crafted from the stuff of life rather than manufactured from any philosophy of relationships. It was not by any means untroubled, but the troubles were reckoned in it and accepted as part of the whole; it made for a good life. Whatever the happy or evil day had thrown in their path, at night they went to bed together, slept within touch and woke in each other's close presence; sometimes they made love. Sometimes when the day had divided them, they used their inevitable proximity to close the gap with an encircling arm or a reconciling kiss.

John's redemption had progressed so far that he now longed for this embrace of love. But insensitive as he may be, he did not expect it to be recovered by some single compulsive act, so he crept to his narrow bed and eventually fell asleep.

Marion did not know how John felt and felt her bed empty and cold that night. Bleak memories gathered like ghosts: lying waiting for John to come up; conversations cut short by indifference; cold kisses; unclasped hands; waking to his absence; excuses, rationalisations, rows; the treacherous decision to abandon the common bed. They paraded in the darkness through her tired mind. But what depressed her most was her own helplessness. She felt the boat so patiently crafted being swept away, she struggled to hold it in place, to hold onto it, to touch it at all, to pull it back, but could not turn the tide; it flowed irresistibly against her; too strong; overpowering, tumbled over by it. Now she did not know how to recreate what they had had; could not remember how it had been done, but knew it had more to do with what they did together in life than what they did in bed. She had resolved that she would accept nothing less than what they had once shared. She wept before she slept. Why put yourself to so much pain, Marion? Your ambitions are too idealistic for these days. Tune into the spirit of the times, Marion; opt for the fleeting sensation; compromise. Settle for less, Marion, or you may have to settle for nothing at all.

They breakfasted together, made vague promises to see each other soon. ("Come and pick blackberries," John said, remembering the raspberry field.) Then Marion went off to work, Rebecca to school and John to wind up the lease on the flat. Marion wondered what significance she should read into this act but came to no fixed conclusion.

CHAPTER THIRTY-SIX

After his meeting with the agent, John travelled up to Birsett. By habit he made a cup of coffee and then checked his mail. It contained nothing much; mailshots mainly; one from the Harvard Business Review did him no good: '*Leader, Strategist, Mentor, Architect, Builder, Co-ordinator, Counsellor*'; magnificent titles; what chief executive does not believe he is them all, is master of all? What have I lost? '*When your colleagues talk about your organisation, they're really talking about you and your ability to lead: that's why you should be reading Harvard Business Review*'. What organisation? Ability, yes, but no-one to lead. Does anyone remember John Swansen now?

Then he checked his e-mails; amongst the junk, a gem.

John,

Something has come up. In Eastern Europe. Contact me soonest.

Jacqui.

Jacqui! Jacqui Boutelle!

He rang the offices of Sumner and Frieburg. Jacqui was away for a long weekend, away to Geneva, with her partner.

She'll be back on Monday. No, there is no number you can ring; she shields her privacy.

"Damn!" said John, and ripped up the offer for 12 issues of the HBR for the professional rate £109, and thereby cut himself off from: *'Breakthrough Ideas: Fifteen Articles that Define Business Practice Today': free.*

A long frustrating weekend faced John, but he tried to make the best of it. On Friday he called into JP's to bring him up to date on the court case.

"Take the deal; you need to move on," said JP then asked him what progress he had made on removing Colin from the management of Gainslaw Globes. John told him about the new order, Colin's recklessness and Kate's despair.

"Could be terminal," said JP, "if you don't act quickly. Flambert is chaffing at the bit."

John promised he would pick it up on Monday, as planned, of course, as planned.

Rachel asked about Marion and Rebecca and welcomed his news about his overnight stay, but did not ask for details. She was pleased that they might come in early October to pick blackberries. It had to be arranged. Where would they stay? She asked. John recognised the question, smiled and said that he wasn't sure, not yet.

On Saturday, more to keep his mind off Jacqui Boutelle than interest, he agreed to help Alex with a party of sea anglers from Newcastle. Alex's crew had deserted him; Dod had been commandeered to go shopping with his wife and Batman had tickets for a pop concert in Glasgow and thought he might persuade Lizzie Mitchell to go with him. (Lizzie Mitchell, you recall, is the rich widow we met on the football bus). Lizzie is a little old for pop concerts and a lot older than Batman, but he sees no other route to early retirement and a bungalow on Millerfield, the new executive estate at Hecklescar.

There were nine sea anglers from a club on Longshields Council Housing Estate in Newcastle whose sole activity seemed to be a Saturday outing to Birsett or Hecklescar once a month from April to October. They were led by The Chairman (the others called him by nothing else and Alex couldn't recall his first name; John sneered at the title).

On a pleasant autumn day, the Silver Cord butted into a long low swell that rolled in from the north-east; it would make fishing uncomfortable. The Chairman told Alex where to stop and instructed his little shoal of fishers what bait or lure to use. Most of them took no notice but this didn't seem to bother him. He looked like a snowman on stilts. His body didn't seem to belong to the same set as his legs. It looked as if it were attached by a bracket and could be detached and bolted onto the right pair of legs whenever they came along. He had allocated a place for himself alongside the wheelhouse on the starboard side, facing the land. He was dressed like a gamekeeper in tweed jacket, waistcoat and trousers, checked shirt and woollen tie; on his head a deer stalker hat; on his feet green wellies.

John sat down not far from him.

"Not a fisherman then," he said to John.

"No"

"What then?"

"In business."

"What kind of business?"

"Manufacturing."

"Here?"

"No, not here."

"Redundant?"

"No."

"Lucky. Me eight years ago; never had a proper job since. Security now; sit in a hut on a site. Me! Made a micrometer in my journeyman year. Now watching breeze blocks."

"I'm sorry."

"What trade?"

"Engineering."

"Snap! Light or heavy?"

"Electronics."

"Lucky. Me, heavy; Clarke Chapman's, man and boy. Thirty-eight years."

Silence for a few minutes. John fished out his diary and consulted it. There was nothing in it he wanted to see; he just wanted to shake off The Chairman.

The Chairman was not be put off.

"See them."

John saw he was pointing to the land. He looked to see what had caught The Chairman's attention. The rocks, cliffs, fields, hills, sky were as quietly inactive as always.

"See them on the road; the A1; the Great North Road." John could make out car dots and lorry smudges moving along the road. The Chairman waved his hand north.

"Them up there going down there." He swept his hand south.

"Them down there." He waved again. "Going up there." He swung his arm north. John nodded.

"Running away. Don't want to be there." Arm to the south. "Don't want to be there." Arm to the north.

John sought to ignore him without being impolite. He glanced up, smiled, and went on studying his diary

"Once there, they'll come back. Keep travelling. Running away. Holidays? D'ye like holidays?"

"Yes."

"Not me. Running away - holidays. Running away; used to; not now; stopped running; take it now, life, now, here on the sea, here, now."

John wondered what The Chairman could have been running away from, but didn't want to start a conversation. He smiled. The Chairman's rod came to John's rescue; it bent suddenly and the line ran out singing. The Chairman let it run then slowly and carefully reeled in the fish. As he brought it to the boat, he poked a net towards John. John took the net, leaned over the side of the boat and after a few clumsy attempts scooped a large thrashing fish out of the water. The Chairman slopped the fish onto the deck, coshed it, wrenched out the hook, and slapped the fish into a fish box lying beside him. The club turned and cheered.

"Codling," he announced, "lugworm."

He re-baited his hook and cast the line arcing into the sea fifty yards away. The boat rocked in the swell, the waves slapped and clucked along its sides. One of the fishers bent over the side and vomited. The others ignored him. John settled to his notes and hoped the codling had silenced The Chairman. No chance!

"Wife?" he shouted to John.

"Yes," said John

"Lucky. Not me; died five year ago; mugged for drug money; never recovered; devastated."

He surveyed the shoreline and gulped once or twice.

"Children?"

"Yes."

"Lucky. How many?"

"Two."

"Girls?"

"Boy and a girl."

"Lucky. Not me: lost the only one; stillborn; wife knackered for more."

Another fish, another codling, another cheer. Two to the Chairman: none to anyone else.

A shouted consultation. "D'ye want to move?" *Coordinator*.

A chorus of "Yes".

"We'll stay here for a bit. Good fishin' wi' the right bait; lugworm." *Strategist*.

Grumbles John didn't pick up.

"Well, ye should've brought some. You was telt." No offer to share. *Mentor*.

The line sang through the air and punctured a grey-green wave. The Chairman hauled his bag from under his chair, opened it, pulled out a vacuum flask and poured himself a cup of something hot.

"Cocoa," he said to John, "Better than coffee, or tea; holds the heat to your lungs."

"No thank you," said John, then realised it was an announcement not an offer.

"Like some?" *Conciliator*.

"No"

"Pension?"

"Yes, when I want it."

"Lucky. Mine's frozen. Worth nothing when I get it. And Tony's squeezing OAPs. Work till you're seventy. Christ! Never enough!" (Tony is Tony Blair, Prime Minister)

A shout from the port side. Gub's caught a saithe.

"Not worth keeping. Throw it back. We'll move. Right, skipper, a mile south - off the bothy." *Leader*.

The rods were pulled in and Alex motored to the spot. En route, flasks came out, sandwiches and soft drinks.

"No alcohol on board ship," The Chairman informed John, "Club rule, since we lost Les."

The rods were put back out; except the sick one; he lay in the bows covered with his coat. He would not recover until he ate cold baked beans straight from the tin at half-past twelve. This, The Chairman explained was a pattern; he always did it; it was his way of enjoying himself.

John took the chance of the break to rid himself of The Chairman. He joined Alex in the wheelhouse. Alex had nothing to say; he sat with his nose in The Daily Record. When he had read it, he read The Fishing News although he had already read it twice. The day drifted on; the boat motored in snatches at The Chairman's command, a mile or two south, out a bit, in a bit, south again until they lay half a mile off Magdalene Fields at Gainslaw. John sat in the wheelhouse, or walked the deck, or sat in the stern, and kept clear of The Chairman. At three Alex, without reference to The Chairman, turned for home into a breeze mending from the north. The sun had deserted the day leaving it grey and cold.

The tide was not yet full enough to allow them back into the harbour, so Alex brought the boat head to wind and lay off. John stood in the lee of the wheelhouse and watched the swell surging and scattering among the rocks and breaking over the breakwater. The Chairman joined him.

"D'ye live here?"

"Yes,"

"Lucky. Me, tower block, fourteenth floor, maisonette!"

On Such a Tide

He smiled. "Sea view - 10 miles away; past Blyth power station. But when I retire, I'll buy one of those; live by the sea." He pointed to Partan Row. John didn't tell him that he couldn't afford one, but he did tell himself that The Chairman was a loser.

Although the man was a victim, like himself, of circumstance, John credited The Chairman's case to his genes; his own lay in human treachery and temporary misfortune.

They stared at the shore for a while in silence. Then the Chairman nudged John and pointed to the dark grey green water rolling and heaving beneath them.

"A mystery - the sea. From there" (he waved his hand to the land) "just a dirty grey carpet. From here see it, alive, profound; a country below the waves, teeming; we're floating in the sky. There, nature in chains: roads, concrete and Asda: here, unfettered, wild, dangerous, will feed you, will devour you. The tide – untamed power, free, sea city on the move, twice a day. D'ye feel it? Moves me. Twice the man out here."

John studied the sea; it looked like lumps of water; felt like lumps of water. The Chairman saw it in his eyes.

"You're what? Fifty?"

"Fifty-one"

"Same plus ten. Birthday?"

"30th May."

"Near enough; 28th! Alter Ego ten years on." The Chairman's familiarity disturbed John; he had nothing in common with this man.

Or did he? And was that not the reason for his disquiet? That this man, clinging to his little brief authority, embodied what John had begun to recognise in his own futile attempts to recover power and position?

The tide half-filled the harbour. The Silver Cord rode the

swell in behind the breakwater. John helped the fishermen up the ladder to the quay. The Chairman, last to leave, handed up to John the bag containing his heavy catch.

"Nice to meet you. You're a lucky man. Not as lucky as Alex, but lucky." he said. He walked a couple of paces then turned and came back. He held up his catch bag.

"Like a fish for your tea?"

"No, thank you," said John.

"A wasted day then," he said, smiling softly. *Counsellor - of the deaf.*

By going fishing with The Chairman, John missed the Brae Trolley Dash that is held annually to raise funds for the Village Hall. (In Willie's time it was a pram race, but modernisers have recently substituted supermarket trolleys, provided by Safeway). Teams of four push a trolley up the brae with a fifth sitting in it. Shortest time wins. Hecklescar Coastguards won in a time of four minutes, forty-one seconds. Second were Birsett Bikers. The Mitchison Family team were third and the PTA fourth. Birsett Fishermen were last in a time of six minutes, twenty-two; a creditable performance considering they had Delightful in the team. Although he is forty-five and takes no exercise, he considers himself fit and insisted on taking part. He collapsed at the kirk, scarcely a third of the way up; no harm done, just whacked.

Wanda served in the PTA team and made it all the way to the top. At the tea in the hall afterwards Marvin came up to Wanda and said he was sorry for what he had done; he had been drunk. Wanda told him that was no excuse; he had humiliated her once too often; she wouldn't take him back – ever. He went down to The Basking Shark in Hecklescar and got drunk. Then sat outside on a bench and cried. Then smashed up the bench and got arrested. Everyone in Birsett told Wanda she was well rid of him. But Wanda missed Marvin. When he was sober and not with his cousin, he was a decent sort of man. The boys missed him too.

CHAPTER THIRTY-SEVEN

On Sunday morning John caught sight of a spider's web shining in the autumn sun. A fly had been caught and the spider was slowly binding the struggling insect. The image tracked through his mind gathering accretions: the codling in The Chairman's net, The Chairman, the struggling fishermen of Birsett, JP and Rachel saddled with Ben, Cecil from Surrey with his invalid wife, Kate with Colin, Colin with Gainslaw Globes. Me! The mood stayed with him all day. He resisted any attempt by Helen, Morag and Louise to feed, jolly or cajole him into a better frame of mind.

When he opened the door to Mr Scott on Sunday evening, his vexation had reached screaming pitch. He didn't want spend time with the old man; didn't want to play Scrabble; didn't want to listen to Your 100 Best Tunes; didn't want to be his own father. He needed time to brood on his misfortunes, time to think about not settling with Loyalty, time to worry about his salary stopping, time to speculate about Jacqui Boutelle's East Europe "something".

The summer was waning, the summer that had been his excuse and solace, the summer he was taking off before...... before what? He felt that he had fallen into a ditch and was being tumbled along it by events beyond his control. They had brought him to this: sitting in the dreary room of his father's house, on a dreary Sunday, playing Scrabble with a dreary old man while the dreary year ran down to winter. So strong did this current surge through his mind, so powerfully did he feel he had washed up on some desolate beach, so tense had he become, that the slightest jolt would trigger an explosion. There is no doubt that if he had drawn a "Q" without a "U" from the Scrabble bag, or five "I" s, he would have thrown over the board, insulted his father's old friend and regretted his action for the rest of his life. But just as the noxious game started, the phone rang. He picked it up and heard Kate's voice; she sounded distressed.

"John," she said, "could you come to the factory? It's Colin."

"What?" snapped John, "Yes, I'm coming in the morning; I'll be there about…"

"No," said Kate, "Could you come now?"

"Now?"

"Yes, I'm sorry. It's Colin; will you come? He'll listen to you. Please!"

"Alright, I'll come."

A single security lamp above the door of Gainslaw Globes glared coldly on the empty car park and cast stark shadows along the building. Kate opened the door before John reached it. She had been crying and, John noticed, had dressed more for a party than for work. She put her finger to her lips to silence him and led him into the office. From somewhere inside the building there came the deep throb, gasp and staccato slap of a moulding machine. The office lay in darkness, but light from the dimly-lit workshop seeped through a window and allowed John to see someone sitting at Colin's desk. At first, he thought it was Colin, but then saw it was Charlie, garbed in his usual boiler suit. He nodded to John but did not speak.

John turned to Kate, but before she could say anything, John became aware of a low syncopated sound, a long articulated howl. At first, he thought it was mechanical; hydraulics, perhaps, but as it increased, he heard in it a voice; a voice chanting; a voice chanting a litany; a hollow, sepulchral voice repeating, enunciating, syllable by syllable, a single word. It grew louder. Kate pointed. At the back of the shop, behind the 150-tonne machine, John saw Colin. Lit only by the arc lamp above him, he was performing a grotesque ballet, his shadow mimicking the dance on the wall behind him. He was in dressed in a lounge suit, white shirt and tie; his jacket was open, his tie pulled away from his neck and the top buttons of his shirt undone. In rhythm with the thrust of the machine he bent forward like a mechanical doll, his gloved right hand jerking into the machine, groping for the finished part, left arm grotesquely above his head holding a heavy steel test jig. Then he snapped up straight, slapped the part from his right hand into the jig his left, then pulled it out in a grandiose gesture and flung it across the shop towards a skip twenty yards away. Then repeat: hand into a box beside him, the stiff bow into the machine, right hand jerking in, left hand flourishing high, over and over again - and as he flung the part a banshee wail:

"UN-AC-CEP-TA-BLE. UN-AC-CEP-TA-BLE. UN-AC-CEP-TA-BLE."

John became aware of a nearer descant. Beside him Kate sobbed softly,

"Colin... Colin... Colin... oh ...Colin.

Dirge for a dead company, John thought. Surely this would finish it. He turned to Charlie.

"What's happened?"

"He's been working all week on the HomeFlair bracket. It won't run. It has a steel insert. You have to locate it on pins in the tool; when the tool closes it encases the insert in plastic. But the plastic is flashing over the metal; causing the part to jam in the mould and you have to lever it out by hand. We have to eliminate the flash; it's a critical setting. But he wouldn't let me near it. 'I'm too slow', he said. He's worked every night for a week. Wouldn't let me touch it. He came in this morning, worked all day until Kate came and took him away. She asked me to come in to keep the job going, but he didn't want me. Kate dressed him up and took him out for a meal. In the middle of the meal, he rang me up and asked if it was running. I said no. He slammed the phone down and the next thing I know he stormed through the door and pushed me out of the way. Kate came behind him, begging him to come away, but he told her to bugger off, then he slapped her and threw her away. I tried to go back in, but he said he would hit me with jig if I did. He won't let anyone near. I said we should call the police. But Kate rang you."

John went back to Kate. Litany and descant droned on. He stood for a second or two watching Colin trying to decide what to do. He approached the door of the shop.

"Be careful," sobbed Kate.

"That jig could brain you," whispered Charlie. Then as John put his hand on the handle:

"He's over-ridden the safety gate; if the tool closes on his hand, he'll lose it. Don't distract him when his hand is in the machine."

John hesitated.

"We'll switch off the power to the machine. Where's the switch?"

"On the machine," replied Charlie.

"No, the Mains switch."

"It's behind him. With a red handle. It puts out the machine lamp as well. But you can't reach it without him seeing you."

John nodded, opened the door and stepped into the shop. Gulping sobs now punctuated Colin's eerie recitation but the hissing slap of the tool into the mould maintained its insistent sinister rhythm. In imagination John saw Colin's hand dicing with the machine cycle: piston back; hand in; push in the insert; piston slams shut - 150 tonne of thrust; the hiss of release; hand gropes for the part... then the hand in too quick, into the snarling tool! Don't distract him!

John's heart thumped and his legs trembled as he crept through the shop towards Colin. Each time the machine clattered in its cycle he took a stride. Pace by pace he made his way across the shop floor, ducking behind machines, racks, stillages. In the half-light, a few yards short of Colin's machine, John tripped over a box and sent it clattering over the floor.

"Stay way, Kate," yelled Colin, brandishing the jig, but he continued to feed the machine, his hand trembling in the straining tool.

"Colin, it's me, John. I've come to help."

"Ha, John! John! Come to gloat, come to gloat; clever Dick, clever bloody John ...you're right, Charlie's right, Kate's right, John's right. It won't run. Colin's wrong. UN-AC-CEP-TA-BLE."

"Colin, stop the machine!"

"Can't stop now. It's a week late. A thousand pound a day. All gone. Can't stop. Have to make them. They'll take five thousand to-morrow. Five thousand! Should do that! Send the lorry. Keep trying, keep trying. UN-AC-CEP-TA-BLE. We can do it if we try. Stay away!"

John had spotted the red main switch, on the wall behind Colin, to his left about four feet away. If he could reach it within the cycle time of the machine, Colin's hand would be clear. He counted the cycle: seven seconds. He edged closer to the switch. He would have to time it just right.

"Stay away", Colin yelled at him and threatened the throw the jig. Still his right hand diced with the machine. "UN-AC-CEP-TA-BLE." He threw a discarded bracket at John. John dived for the switch; Colin flung the jig. Darkness engulfed them. John heard Colin yell then fall.

The main lights in the workshop flickered on; Charlie at the switches. John looked round and saw Kate running towards him. Colin had collapsed and cowered against the wall in a tight ball. Both his hands were inside his jacket hugging his chest. Then, just as Kate reached him, John saw blood spreading across his white shirt. Kate shrieked, knelt beside her husband and reached inside his jacket for his hands. She drew them out clasped in her own; they were entire; blood flowed from a wound on Colin's wrist. Kate put her arms round her husband and curled up beside him on the floor and wept. Above them a motivational poster proclaimed:

As Individuals we may be Strong but as a Team we are Invincible

"Colin, it's alright, it's alright. John's here, John's here, it's alright, Colin, Colin," Kate sobbed. John stood over them numbed, saying nothing.

After a few moments she turned to John and said flatly,

"This is the end, isn't it?"

John looked at her but still did not, could not, say anything. He turned away to speak to Charlie.

"You tidy up here; I'll take them home and come back."

When he returned Charlie was working at the 150-tonne machine.

"I think we should go home," said John

"Given time, I think I can get this to run," Charlie replied with a nervous intensity. "It's a process of elimination, adjust the temperature, check it; if there's no improvement, put it back. Then adjust the cycle time, check it; if it's not right, put it back; then check the stroke. But always put it back if it doesn't improve. Colin" (he paused as if speaking of the dead) "Colin, when he panics, just dibs about, changes everything, keeps on changing everything till it works. That works sometimes, but when the settings are critical like this, you have to check them one at a time. It's slow, but it's methodical. I might be able to crack it. He wouldn't let me near it."

He stood over the humming machine eager for John's permission to proceed, anxious for John's belief in him...... and the company.

"If you think it's worth it?" he added, "Kate said it was the end."

"Try it," said John, trying to sound decisive. "But not tonight; let's go home."

They switched off the lights, locked the door, and let the factory sleep.

CHAPTER THIRTY-EIGHT

John felt honour bound to turn up at Gainslaw Globes first thing on Monday morning, but it grated that he would have to postpone his call to Jacqui Boutelle. John knew that in a crisis the best way to steady the ship is to maintain the routine as far as possible. By the time John arrived, Charlie had opened the factory and shortly afterwards Kate came in. Colin was still asleep; his mother watching over him; Kate would return at lunchtime to take over. Together Charlie and Kate put the workforce to work then Charlie locked horns with the NB 150 to see what he might accomplish.

Kate wanted to discuss the future of the factory but John played for time by insisting that they carry on as if everything were normal; he wanted to talk it over with JP. He thought that something might be saved. For the moment they must sort out the bracket mess. John told Kate to sweetheart Caledesign; blame the delay on Colin's illness if need be; tell them they were close to curing the teething problems, anything to reassure them: be strong. They must stem the losses. They were a week late and Charlie had just started to see what he could do. They must concentrate on that. By the time John left the factory at midday a semblance of normality had returned and Kate had settled her faith on John. She could see no way forward, but convinced herself that John would find it. John, we know, is good at giving that impression. By four on Tuesday Charlie had the bracket job running, producing acceptable parts. If they worked nightshift all week, they could deliver five thousand by Friday. That would be only twelve thousand pounds in penalty payments. *Only* twelve thousand pounds!

"Colin had ironed out most of the wrinkles," Charlie said to Kate to give her comfort. He was lying – and Kate knew it.

When John phoned Jacqui Boutelle she had gone out for lunch, but came back within an hour and returned John's call. The call was worth waiting for; the sort of call he had longed for all summer. Sumner and Frieburg, Jacqui's company, had been retained by an American corporation to search for a location in East Europe to manufacture components for their range of domestic appliances. They had identified a suitable site near Grodwice, the financial package had been agreed and the building well advanced. Now they were looking for a management team. An American would be Chief Executive but they wanted a European to head up manufacturing and eventually take over the top job; they had asked Sumner and Frieburg for names. Jacqui had remembered John. Was he interested?

Was he interested?

Of course, he was interested! What did he have to do? Can I come to find out more?

No need for that just yet.

Could she send more details?

Yes.

What's the name of the company?

Can't say at this stage.

But you know me, Jacqui, I'm not a stranger, you know I can keep a secret, who is it?

Are you seriously interested?

Of course!

Alright then, it's GANY, Global Appliances (New York). GANY! **The** *GANY! The very same.*

Send me all you can.

'Don't get too high, John, it's early days; we have other candidates and no doubt they have. I'll send the stuff. But John, what about your spat with Loyalty. Is that settled? It could get in the way. You know what the Americans are like.'

"No, that's all over. We've done a deal: amicable all round. It's in the past. I have to move on. Life's too short."

"That's good", she said, "Because GANY's looking for three referees: one would need to be from Loyalty. Walter Radleigh's the man, if only because he sounds historical, the Americans like that sort of thing and will never notice the "d". You will need someone to swear to your moral worth. The Americans are jittery about sleaze at the moment; you've no skeletons in any of your cupboards, have you?"

"No!'

As soon as he put the phone down the frightening thought hit John that he may have told Belinda Boyd to talk to Jacqui Boutelle about Sir Frank. It would be disastrous if she did so. GANY wouldn't touch him with a barge pole if they thought him prickly about Loyalty's dealings in Bainan. No doubt GANY had just done some such deal with officials at Grodwice; what sweeteners did that involve? He knew that he had intended to ask Belinda to contact Jacqui, but had he done so? He could not remember clearly what he had said when he spoke to her; the conversation had not gone quite the way he had planned.

We readers can look back a few pages and confirm he made no such request, but he can't. He rang Belinda and told her to accept Loyalty's offer. He was calling off the dogs. Unconditionally. Yes, he'd sign a gagging clause. But they must play ball too; he needed a good reference from Radleigh; that has to be part of the deal; and, Belinda, don't speak to Jacqui Boutelle - especially don't speak to Jacqui Boutelle! Bring it to an end quietly. That's what you advise, isn't it? Well, do it. Now!

Ms Boyd gladly concurred with Mr Swansen and sent off an acceptance letter to Loyalty's legal advisers. By way of celebration she gave half of her teatime Kit-Kat to Hattersley.

"All these businessmen are mercenaries," she said as she dropped the biscuit into the dog's mouth. The dog did not contradict her; he was a mercenary too.

The sun that warmed the fields and gardens of Birsett now warmed John as he stepped out to walk down the brae to tell JP about Gainslaw Globes. The gentle waves chuckled among the sleeping rocks as John walked along the beach to Partan Row. He had a proposition to put to JP. But first he must tell him what had happened last night at the factory. It was only last night, wasn't it?

JP listened quietly to the story and saw where John was headed long before he reached the proposal. But he let him put it anyway.

"This gives us the chance we are looking for," said John. "Colin will be out of action for months. Kate can run the factory and Charlie can handle the technical bit. But it needs financing. The penalty clause is costing them an arm and a leg."

"You want me to rescue it?" said JP, smiling.

"Yes," said John with a confidence coming from Grodwice but not admitted.

"I agree," said JP, "but your proposal needs amendments. Charlie does the technical bit. OK. Kate runs the factory. OK. But you run the business. OK? Be chairman if you like."

"I can't do that," protested John

"Why not? You're not doing anything else are you?"

This forced John to tell JP about Jacqui Boutelle and Grodwice.

"It'll come to nothing," he said brutally, "they're all at it, these consultants; they see Eastern Europe as the new Eldorado. But don't believe them; there's money to be made there, but not for a while. The way the world economy is at the moment no one is investing in anything. Be careful, John. Anyway, that doesn't stop you taking care of Gainslaw Globes for now. We'll go tomorrow and sort things out."

The contrast between heading up a GANY plant abroad and being stuck at Gainslaw Globes appalled John.

"I don't want to become too involved here; I might have to re-locate."

"You might not. We'll go tomorrow."

"But...."

"John, can you not see that people need you?" said JP gently, "Think of Kate's smile; she needs to smile again. When? Two o'clock tomorrow; you arrange it."

Before he left, Rachel asked him about Marion and Rebecca; when were they coming to pick blackberries. John felt better about Marion coming now that he had the Grodwice job in prospect. He thought it part of his plan; things were falling into place: first the job, then the family. But psychology played a bigger part than strategy; he felt better about himself. He rang Marion when he got back to Braeshiel. She was out; he kept forgetting she would be at work during the day. That evening he rang back and eventually shot down enough of her excuses to secure her promise to come for a couple of days during Rebecca's holidays in the third week of October, that is, Thursday and Friday, 17th and 18th October. (Put them in your diary; they are important dates in our story.) Marion, however, refused the invitation to stay at Braeshiel; she would see if Rachel could accommodate them in Partan Row. Rachel would, of course.

John arranged the meeting at Gainslaw Globes, settling in his own mind that he could give it two months, say, before moving on. No, he wasn't jumping the gun, wasn't assuming that the GANY job was already his; he is merely doing what we all do when our ambitions are triggered: dreaming, and he didn't want Gainslaw Globes to spoil the dream. He wished Gainslaw Globes and Kate, especially Kate, well but not well enough to commit a year or two of his life to them. He wanted to make a contribution, not a sacrifice.

When Kate showed John and JP into the meeting room, they were surprised to see Colin sitting at the table. He looked ill. He had been dressed in what he called his business suit no doubt because he realised the importance of the meeting.

"I'm sorry about the other night," he said as he shook hands with John, "I was way out of order." His hand trembled as John grasped it. Colin sat down beside Kate. Kate gripped his hand under the table.

"You shouldn't be here," said JP softly to Colin, "but I'll be as brief as possible - and let me assure you; I'm here to help. It may not look like it at the start, but that is what I am here for."

He laid his laptop on the table where they could all see the screen and made a short presentation setting out his understanding of the position of the company before the inclusion of the Caledesign Solutions order. Most of the figures on the screen were red.

"If you had to pay your creditors you would not be able

to so without liquidating some of your assets, even if you were paid all that is owed you. You would have to sell something."

"Now let us factor the Design Solutions order into the Profit and Loss statement," he said. More figures on the screen turned red.

"Now the penalty payments you have already incurred." All the figures turned red. John was impressed by JP's icy logic.

"Here is the cash flow projection."

"And the balance sheet."

Kate did not need the presentation; she lived with the reality every day.

"We are technically insolvent."

"Yes."

Colin did not react. He sat with his head bowed over the table, playing with a pen.

"What I propose is this. You put the company into administration; that will clear your debts. One of my companies will buy the assets. We will then re-finance it and invest in new equipment and systems. A colleague of mine that John knows has work he can place here. I believe we can rescue it."

Kate smiled but it was not Kate's smile but the cold smile of acceptance. Colin raised his head and looked at JP with eyes full of suspicion.

"But in the end, who owns the company? Us or you?" he said.

"Me," said JP, bluntly, "I will own the company. Kate and John will run it with Charlie's help. You must take a long break – on full pay."

"That's unacceptable," said Colin, angrily.

"If you say so," said JP, gathering up his papers.

"No, wait," said Kate; "can we have a few minutes alone?"

Kate led Colin out of the room. After ten minutes she came back alone.

"We accept the offer. Colin has gone home. Thank you," she said, but did not smile.

"I'd be grateful if you would contact your solicitors as soon as possible," replied JP. "If there is any help I can give, please don't hesitate to ask. Now could we have a cup of coffee?"

"That was rather brutal," said John to JP in the car on the way back to Birsett. He had not seen this side of JP before.

"Not as brutal as the reality," said JP, "I have discovered that reality does not listen to rationalisations and cannot be swayed by argument; you cannot make peace with it; you must engage it on its own terms or be overwhelmed."

"But I didn't realise you were going to take over the company," said John.

"No? What did you expect?"

"I thought you might give them a loan, or buy a stake in the company."

"What good would that have done? The money would have gone to paying off the debts, leaving nothing for investment. No doubt they have been given money in the past, but Colin has run through it. He would do it again. Small businessmen specialise in survival; they become experts at it. I have no interest in that. If something is unprofitable kill it or it will kill you. You can't afford to be sentimental. You saw what it did to Colin and you see what it is doing to Kate. Somebody has to be the big bad wolf; this time it's me. This is the best way, believe me."

Thus, Colin and Kate gave up their ailing child. Kate watched over it while it died on November twenty-ninth at two o'clock in the afternoon at the offices of Mortice Recovery Ltd, Blackett Street, Newcastle upon Tyne. JP went with her and made sure he paid enough to keep the couple's house out of the hands of the banks. By the time the banks have taken \their slice there will be nothing left for the creditors - and nothing for Kate and Colin. Nothing for the years they have watched over it, cared for it, worked for it, screamed and cried over it. Nothing for the sacrifice of their young lives; nothing at all; nothing belongs to them anymore; not even the pen they used to sign the body into the hands of Marwick Enterprises Ltd.

The name remained, that's all: Gainslaw Globes. Kate became Managing Director; John, Chairman and Charlie, Technical Manager. Colin, job-less and title-less descended into the pit of depression; he would not clamber out of it for many weeks. During that time, Kate tended him when not tending JP's company. Her life consisted of work, sleep, worry, pain and gnawing regret. She didn't smile much.

John, you can't desert her now, can you? No matter what GANY may offer, you couldn't possibly leave her on her own to cope with all that. Can you, John?

CHAPTER THIRTY-NINE

John's exhilaration ebbed a little when the information promised by Jacqui did not arrive. But He made himself busy. He found GANY's website on the Internet, and browsed for news items on those of major European and US broadsheet newspapers. It confirmed what he already knew. GANY was a huge corporation whose operations sprawled across the world. Although its share price had suffered like most American corporations in the downturn it was still worth $100bn and its management still held the confidence of market analysts and major investors. It would be well placed for growth when the upswing came. The President of GANY, he read, was Irvin Saltzer, by all accounts an upstanding man, well above the sleaze and greed that had sucked down other company bosses recently. He served on a congressional committee on corporate ethics. Not another Sir Frank, then, eh?

The corporation consisted of five product groups of which Domestic Appliances was largest. It operated through three geographical divisions, including one for Europe. The head of the European division was a Vice President by the name of Jochen Muller - a German, no doubt. It would be Muller, John thought, who would make the Grodwice appointment. John could find no mention of Grodwice in GANY sources, but the American Business Review did note GANY's interest in Eastern Europe. It all fitted and looked inviting.

Then he found Grodwice on the World Wide Web: an

industrial city with 115,036 citizens of whom 65,342 were women: 9.09 children were born live per 1,000 of the population; home to 3,123 trading companies, of which 2,818 had limited liability, 175 were stock companies, and 4 state enterprises; 9,230 people were self-employed.

Then a surprise - on the industrial development page: "enter here to see an artist's impression of the new plant being built at the Krokla Industrial Complex for the GANY corporation".

It slid onto the screen as a sleek low glass fronted building nestling amongst an architect's symmetrical trees. Slightly offset at the front of the building, flanked by flagpoles flying the stars and stripes and the national flag, a short flight of broad steps ran up to a gleaming glass door. Behind the door could be glimpsed a glittering reception area complete with shadowy receptionists and indistinct executives; owners, no doubt, of the swish limousines parked in the flower-decked car park. As the graphic spread across his laptop screen it seemed to flow on into John. He felt a thrill shiver through his body. He saw himself striding up those steps, nodding to the receptionist and proceeding to his office on the first floor. The image overwhelmed him. When he came back to Birsett, he came with a jolt. Where was the stuff from Jacqui? What the timetable for the appointment? And where was Marion so he could tell her, show her the picture, talk about the job, hear her encouragement?

After four days the information pack had still not arrived so John rang Sumner and Frieberg. It was in the post. Whether it was or whether it wasn't it arrived a week after Jacqui's first phone call and contained little he did not already know. All documents from consultants are fat and, so fat was this one, that the letterbox at Braeshiel would not accept it. John was roused at a quarter to seven to collect it at the door. But no Victorian lover ever received a communication with more excitement. He made his breakfast then sat down to feast on what bountiful Fate had brought him.

Page after page of what he already knew: blurb on GANY: blurb on its products; blurb on its structures and divisions; map of world-wide locations; praises for its world-embracing principles and values; praises for its world-wide sales and profits; profiles of its management (with photographs (smiling, confident, sincere)); profiles of its buildings (assorted countries, but all the same – like the one in Grodwice). And information on Grodwice supplied by the Grodwice Development Corporation: ideal for business; ideal for residence; ideal for holidays, climate, position, food, cultural history, ideal for life; at the centre of emerging East European markets. Then, at last, the pieces of paper he was looking for. First, an outline of the operation at Grodwice, then the route map to achievement: the job description.

The Grodwice plant would manufacture domestic appliances: specifically, washing machines, dishwashers and tumble dryers. Most of the components would be brought in from other plants in Europe and the US; some would be sourced locally; not a lot, but enough (plus more promised) to settle local fears. At Grodwice they would fabricate the bodies and drums and assemble finished product. The processes were flowline, automated where feasible, ergonomically designed where not (Mack would be impressed). John understood not only the logic but also the motivation. Fabrication and assembly plants like this are labour intensive: labour costs in this part of Eastern Europe are $1.40 an hour; in the UK they are $15.

The job description was impressive - six pages long, high-flown phrases, multi-syllable words. John skimmed through it, conflating the sentences, picking up the sense, delighting in the possibilities:

Title: Head of Operations (not MD but Americans are different; it'll do for now)

Reports to: CEO (Chief Executive Officer) (the top man on site; Head of Ops'll be deputy)

Responsibilities: Everything but Finance and Product Development (substantive this, authentic; none of the Mickey Mouse trash Zack sent)

Employees: 350 rising to 500 in five years (*big!*). Key staff from GANY'S plants in Germany and Co. Durham, UK, would set up the plant then recruit and train nationals to take over all but the most senior of positions. (*No cultural hang-ups: can stamp own values on new operations*)

Annual turnover: $20,000,000 in second year after set up. (*Steep learning curve. Can do!*)

Profitability: 35% gross by year three; 15% net by year five. (*Can do! What bonus?*)

Compensation: Generous salary (What? £150,000? £200,000? What's that in dollars? $250k - $300k. Free of tax!) Usual international package (Should be good. Car? Mercedes? Lexus? Housing, Expense account, Pension, Health Care, whatever you ask for, eh?)

Language: English used; Top managers expected to learn conversational local language or German. (*I can get along in German now.*)

Relocation: House provided (*Ah, thought so*); all relocation expenses; schooling; trips home (*Home? Would Marion come with me?*)

He missed nothing out of the picture he painted for himself. But he did miss this - that managers in Germany and in Gateshead, Co Durham were assuring their workers that GANY had a continuing commitment to their site. At the same time, they were drawing up redundancy lists. Just as he had done at York. He accepted it now - it's the global economy; no point in crying about it; make what you can of it; go with the tide.

Now he had to wait. He sent off, as requested, his CV, revised to give it a global slant (*I understand the issues; my last company had to make similar painful decisions*). He also emphasised his willingness to go anywhere in the world; he had no commitments. He put into practice what he had despised in Zack: '*the point of a CV is not to get a job but to get an interview; don't lie, tell the truth, but tell only the truth you want them to know*'.

While he waited, he did what he did every week, for although John insisted that his sojourn at Birsett was transitory, he had, in practice, adopted routines similar in many ways to the settled life of his father.

On Sunday he went to church with Helen and Alex and sat beside Louise; then he went to Helen's for lunch; afterwards a walk if it was fine, or a read by the fire if it wasn't. On Sunday evening, as we have seen, Mr Scott came and they played Scrabble, listened to 'Your Hundred Best Tunes' and set the world to rights. Jimmy Possum still brought the Fishing News on Friday and still expected a cup of coffee; he brought John all the news of Hecklescar; John was not always uninterested. On Wednesday he entertained Louise, or rather Louise entertained him. She told him her stories, made him play roll-the-penny and bagatelle; sometimes she sang the songs she had learned at school. When Helen came for Louise, she drank her cup of tea and ate one of her own scones, for John could not bring himself to learn how to make his own. If he showed any interest in the gossip, he had heard over Sunday lunch she brought him up to date. Duncan Johnstone and Sandy Donaldson no longer came to Braeshiel on Wednesday evenings to play dominoes, but Sandy did call to collect Willie's proxy stake in the weekly lottery ticket. Since Willie's death they had twice won ten pounds. They did not mention it to John but between themselves they speculated that Willie was now in a better position to influence the draw. On Monday, though not always in the afternoon, John called in to see old Bessie Raeburn, his mother's ninety-five-year-old cousin. He had to do this because he had not cancelled The Berwickshire News that Mussent Grumble still delivered on Thursdays. Grumble thought he had hinted that John could well collect it from his shop in Hecklescar, but the hint went unnoticed amongst the drizzle of his other complaints.

As well as continuing his father's routines John had developed some of his own. In the morning after breakfast he worked either at home or at Gainslaw Globes; after lunch he read the Financial Times for half-an-hour then on Mondays, Tuesdays and Fridays, if he had no visits to make, he went for long walks along the cliffs or up into the country. Do not think of this as enjoyment or nature study; he did it to keep in trim; he had not tracked down a gym worth attending near Birsett (men and women in their fifties should raise their heartbeat for twenty minutes at least three times a week). On Wednesdays before Louise came and after she and Helen had gone, he tidied up the garden and replenished the bird feeders but, unlike his father, he couldn't name all the birds that came to it. On Thursday afternoon, he generally drove to Hecklescar to do his weekly shopping. In the evenings, he read, watched a little TV, usually did some work and occasionally visited JP. At night, he made himself a milky drink, watched the News at Ten, then went to bed with the FT crossword; most nights he finished it before going to sleep. If sleep eluded him, he rose and either read or did some work. Whilst you may question this work that John manufactured for himself, you must admit that the long hours he has spent on his '*Setting up a Company from Scratch*' treatise might well pay off in the interviews for Grodwice. Certainly, he thought they might. They may also inform his work at Gainslaw Globes.

John also interacted with the local intranet. News, events and stories cyber-travelled through Mr Scott, Possum, Duncan, Sandy, Helen, Alex (who looked in two or three times a week), the bairns, Grumble and many other regular or occasional contacts. These included Bessie Raeburn who although she was house-bound managed to stay hooked up to the buzz of the place. He heard about who is friendly with whom, who is getting married, who is splitting up, who is brilliant and off to university, who is too big for their boots, who is dying, who is being neglected by the doctors, who is dead. (Look in Grumble's side window for the funeral notice when you are next down in Hecklescar: 'Who is it? Who does she belong to?' 'Oh, that's who she is. I thought she left us a while ago.' 'No that was her sister; this is Maggie, married to the Glasgow man; he came with the BB.') 'Did you hear that Dorothy is in hospital again and Cecil from Surrey is trying to visit her every day?' 'That's silly, he should take the chance of a rest when she's away; he looks worn out.'

'What's the council up to now? Car parking charges, that's what! Two pounds a day charge on the Smiddy Brae Car Park. So, everybody parks on the pier and you can't get moved, but the Car Park is empty.' 'And did you hear about the bright boys in the Sailing Club? Spent weeks building a dinghy in one of the fisherman's old stores in Doddie's Yard but had forgotten the door wasn't wide enough to get it out? They had to knock down a wall.' 'Then there was a funny-looking man doon the brae last Saturday taking pictures of bairns; he must be a paedophile, but the police haven't tracked him down yet; if they'd get out of their cars and walk, they'd see what's going on.' 'And the school, what's going to happen to the school? The roll goes down to just eighteen next year; that's not enough for two teachers. Mr Hirsell, the headteacher, says he's not staying if it goes down to one teacher; he says that's not what he came for.'

Much of this current passed John by, but sometimes an item dragged him into the stream: the fright at the news of the sudden death of Arthur – a classmate of his, same age; the delight of Steven Cook when he held up his new baby daughter, ('what's her name? Rebecca!'): the success of Douglas Pallin, in gaining a place at Cambridge - a fisherman's son moving up; the promotion of Bessie Raeburn's grandson to Deputy Chief Actuary at Scottish Mutual Life. These all dipped him in the tide that washed up and down on this particular beach.

In subtler ways, too, John was drawn to Birsett. Occasionally the sea caught him out sloshing into his consciousness, and sometimes at night the stars surprised him. The trees and fields and hills occasionally found ways of embracing him as he walked. He felt it along the heart. Of course, he belonged to the place, had been born there, had grown up there, so everywhere he went had a past as well as a present. He remembered some of it, like days spent among the rocks and in pools, mucking about in punts in the harbour, and diving off the breakwater, higher and higher, scared out your mind, other times falling in. The time the dolphin pushed Malky along with its nose just outside the harbour mouth. John's knowledge lay detailed and particular; he knew the names of the rocks: Black Scar, The Dumpling, King Pinnacle, The Treasure Stone, The Golden Shore, and the pools: Murphy's Gully; Horses' Hole; The Rip; Poddlies; Tangle Pool - names found on no maps. He knew where on the brae to collect the best rose hips to make itching powder and remembered how he made it. *Put the hairy seeds out of the hips into a match box; shake the box vigorously one hundred and one times (one hundred times is not enough); remove the seeds and leave the hairs; the hairs left in the box are the itching powder.*

If he were not otherwise absorbed when he reached Breeches Brae on the cliff path up to Hawk's Ness, he shuddered at the sight of Betty Brison falling over the edge on that summer day forty years ago. She survived but it left her paralysed from the waist down. (He knew too that over the forty years, her mother cared for her then and cares for her still in an adapted house down the brae) Betty has taken a degree in Maths and is now something of an expert in relational databases. He also remembered the excitement of robbing fulmars' nests and the stench of the jet of vomit when the gull caught them at it. One day he diverted from the old lonnen into the Micknowe Plantation and conjured up Gloria Pate, top doll in his class at Hecklescar High, walking with him here and not pulling her hand away when he took it. He felt the afterthrill even now. He also felt again the turmoil of seeing her moon-dancing at the school dance with Hips (John couldn't recall his real name; he was a Stevenson). She eventually married Hips and went with him to Australia.

Some of his other classmates both at Birsett Primary and Hecklescar High he began to recognise in the faces of middle-aged people he met around the village and at Hecklescar. Back in the spring, they had passed without speaking, thinking he was passing through but now they tried to engage him in conversation, fishing for reasons for his reappearance. Fishing for answers: What had happened to the big car? The big job? His wife? She's isn't from here, is she? Others he had known acknowledged him now they believed he would not intimidate them with his success. They waved to him out of their cars and gave him an "Ay," when they met him in the street or on the brae (strangers hear "Good morning" or "Nice day"). When he called in a tradesman: a builder, plumber or an electrician he knew them or knew their family. One of the painters at present weatherproofing the outside of Braeshiel against the winter had been a classmate of his; the other an ex-boyfriend of his sister.

Before Jacqui's phone call and the promise of Grodwice, John had all but accepted that his life lay amongst these places and people. His initial revulsion to the place had cooled to a depressing acceptance. The folk of Birsett had never placed him on the pedestal he had fallen off. They knew who he was and where he came from. He was Wullie's son; he's a manager or something down south somewhere. Over the past few months they had let him back into the fold; a wanderer returned, convinced now, like them, that there are 'a lot worse places to bide than Birsett'. Their determined acceptance of him had softened his fall, and, although he would strenuously deny that he had settled for the quiet life, he nevertheless had concluded that there was nowhere else that he wanted to be.

Jacqui's call had changed all that. Grodwice called, postion and power called. He was on his way again. Goodbye Birsett.

And what a difference it would be this time when Marion and Rebecca came! He could relax; he would not have the anxiety of job-hunting hanging over him. He could even spend more time with them.

In such sentiments we see that John is unaware that a top job in Eastern Europe conflicted with his future happiness. Oblivious of any change in his aspirations, John thought that Grodwice lay on the course he had set since he left York, but we know that other destinations have beckoned, and he has veered towards them. Along with increasing settlement into the life of Birsett, he had found growing satisfaction in the company of JP and Kate. Even stronger than these he now longed for a return to family living; to Marion and Rebecca.

He would find none of these in Grodwice.

CHAPTER FORTY

Ten days passed before John heard from Jacqui Boutelle again, a long frustrating delay made bearable only by his frequent visits to Gainslaw Globes. John was surprised how rapidly the company improved. Kate took down all the inspirational posters and repainted the office a pastel shade of lime. Colin's machine in the workshop and his desk in the office were tamed and brought into line with the general tidiness of the place. George organised the workshop the way he had always wanted. Now that Colin no longer unsettled the troops and charged at problems, real or imagined, work flowed through the shop in orderly succession. Paperwork that Colin used as a rough script for his own theatricals now informed the production process and allowed operators to know what was to be made and how it was proceeding. Kate left George to manage the shop. They met first thing every morning to review what they did yesterday, to plan what they would do this week and next, and to enquire what might be needed to keep things flowing smoothly. Kate also set up a computer programme to make sure that prices quoted were profitable. Another system made sure that production met times and volumes and costs. It became orderly, ordinary and effective.

Between them, John, Kate and JP found a way out of the crazy contract with Caledesign Solutions. John bullied them, Kate sweet-hearted them and JP paid them five thousand pounds out of court and gave them the tools. They thus cleared the decks for Flambert's hand-held communicator which, as you might expect, was running late. No matter, it would allow them to streamline production flow, computerise management systems and rationalise storage and warehousing. And who better to advise them on streamlining than Mack, Ian, John's friend and Engineering Director at Pinkerton?

"We'll pay him," said JP, "But not fancy consultant's fees. When you find him, offer him two-fifty a day; tell him it's a small company."

John had not spoken to Mack since he left Pinkerton, a fact that now embarrassed him. But, he rationalised, he had refrained from contact in Mack's own interests. Loyalty knew that John had brought Mack to Pinkerton and, John pretended, he might undermine Mack's position if he contacted him. He need not have worried. If he had kept in touch with his friend, he would have known that Mack had left Loyalty in August and now worked for a consultancy. John now heard it from Marion who had been told by Fiona many weeks ago. They were returning to the West of Scotland. Ian would be covering Europe, but he had done a deal; he'd be working out of Glasgow. Fiona was going home. What pain did that give Marion?

What is the name of the consultancy? A familiar one - Sumner and Frieburg. Jacqui had not been alone in thinking of John for the GANY project; Mack had remembered his friend.

Jacqui rang John before John rang Mack. In the pleasantries before the substance John mentioned the co-incidence.

"No co-incidence," she said, "Once we knew he was free we went for him; we liked what we saw at Pinkerton." Then she turned to matters in hand.

"About GANY," she said, "They want to see you, next Thursday. Will that suit?"

"Yes," said John, impressively decisively, "That's fine."

But we know it is not fine and it doesn't suit. Next Thursday is the 17th of October; that's the first day of Marion and Rebecca's two-day blackberry holiday. If he'd put it in his business diary, he would have noticed it, but the page, in tune with his ambition, bore no record when he looked; Marion and Rebecca are in a separate section of his interest.

It was two days later before he realised that he had made a mistake, and would not have done so even then had he not called on JP to review progress at Gainslaw Globes. When he was leaving Rachel suggested that when Marion and Rebecca came, they should get together for a bite of supper.

"Thursday night would be best, I think," she said.

The word Thursday smacked into John's mind. Which Thursday? Not this……? Yes, this Thursday. Now he connected. Rachel wondered why he delayed answering her.

"Would that be alright?" she said.

"There's a problem", he mumbled, and told them of his conflict of interest.

"You'll have to tell GANY you can't come that day," said Rachel, who considered it a simple problem.

"No, I can't do that," said John, "I've agreed to go."

"But they will understand; it's an easy mistake to make,"

John bridled at the word "mistake" so his answer was sharper than he would have wanted.

"That wouldn't make a very good start would it? A mistake at the first hurdle."

"They'll agree to postpone it if you explain; say it has just come up. Bury your granny again if necessary," put in JP.

"I can't do that," said John, "They'd take that as reluctance. I never liked people calling off appointments. It showed a lack of commitment."

"Or a lack of self-worth" said JP, softly, "You mustn't let them believe you are theirs for the asking. Postpone it. You can't go when Marion and Rebecca are coming. If GANY want you they will wait for a couple of days."

"I daren't risk that," said John, "It is too important. I'll explain it to Marion; she'll understand."

"I'm not sure she will," said Rachel.

"That would not be a good idea," said JP, "Explain it to Jacqui Boutelle rather. Try her,"

"It makes me look disorganised," snapped John

"Precisely," thought JP but said nothing.

It would not have mattered. John had determined to speak to Marion; she must make way for GANY – but not, he told himself, in importance - only for the day. They'd have Friday and Saturday morning together. They could pick the blackberries on Friday; have a nice meal out somewhere on Friday evening to make it up to them. He might even be back early enough on Thursday to accept Rachel's invitation for the evening. Anyway, visiting Rachel would give Marion and Rebecca something to do while he was away. He regretted that it had turned out this way; of course, he regretted it, but he saw no alternative. He mustn't miss this opportunity of a lifetime for the sake of a few hours. Marion would see that.

He would not have been so sanguine if he could have read Marion's thoughts in the days leading up to the holiday. She (no doubt like many readers) is becoming more and more frustrated by the roller coaster ride of her contacts with John. Just when she has settled herself for a life without him, he turns up looking for a wife to share his troubles. No sooner has she decided to move on and leave him in the past than he barges into her present and wakes up what she had put to sleep. It could not go on like this; this trip in October must decide it one way or the other. At least he had taken the initiative, had invited her; perhaps at last he understood where the best of life lay, and would abandon his love affair with success. She would give him this one last chance. She would even initiate the conversation; list her demands (yes, *demands*, she had been patient too long); ask him what he really wanted, *really* wanted. She must bring the matter to a conclusion – and put it to this test: did he care enough to put his marriage and his family first?

Oh dear!

John phoned Marion that evening; Rebecca answered; her mother had gone out to something at the church. John chickened out.

"Just checking that you were still coming next Wednesday evening."

"Of course, we're looking forward to it."

"So am I."

"Thanks, dad," said Rebecca, "Thanks for inviting us. Shall I get Mum to ring you when she comes in?"

"No need," said John hurriedly.

Rebecca's enthusiasm put a doubt in John's mind. His confidence in his ability to explain and Marion's to understand had waned. He now suspected that if he told her before she came, she might not come. He could sell it easier face to face, couldn't he? But his deceit, although he described it to himself as innocuous, sat in his mind like half-cooked stodge sits in the stomach.

When the joining instructions for the interview arrived, he could have reconsidered and rearranged, but he didn't. For all his emotional indigestion he could not stomach postponing the interview. Actually, it wasn't announced as an 'interview', but a 'Selection Exordium', but John put the fancy wording down to the consultants; he guessed it would be a selection panel. They asked him to confirm by e-mail his intention of coming. He told them he'd be there.

In many respects, Wanda is in the same position as Marion; both care more than is sensible for the men who are tormenting them. But Wanda has one advantage over her wealthier sister; she has fewer choices. She has no income of her own; her predicament is not only romantic, it is economic; she needs Marvin's wage. Of course, Gordon Brown, the Chancellor of the Exchequer has offered to provide for her children and to lift them out of poverty but he also insists that she find a job. But she likes the job she has – keeping a home for her children, and Marvin - if he would behave himself. After a month on her own she begins to plant enough clues in enough ears to make sure that Marvin picks up the tang of a friendlier wind. Wanda's mother also tastes the wind and tells her daughter she's a fool to even think of taking him back. But Janet (that's her name) is biased against men. She was expecting Wanda when she married Wanda's father and regretted it the day after and every other day until he went back home to Aberdeen to look for a job and never came back. You could say she didn't want her daughter to end up in the same mess. But Wanda still thought she could sort out Marvin if she could keep him away from the bottle and his cousin.

"You'll make nothing of him," she counselled her daughter, "I tried, it's impossible. Quit while you're ahead."

Wanda didn't feel she was ahead; she felt she had gone backwards since Marvin left. And Marvin certainly felt he was no further forward. The day after the police escorted him from his own front door, he collected his belongings from the same front step and moved in with Rott. He had done this before; it was not the first time he had been evicted. Rott lived in a single person's flat in Hecklescar supplied by a benevolent state to help him escape from any pressure to behave himself. Marvin slept on a shaky bed in Rott's lounge awaiting the expected call from Wanda to return to the fold. But as the days stretched into weeks, he realised that this time it was different. As we have seen he even asked to come back, something he had never tried before. After a few nights touring the pubs in Hecklescar with Rott, his money ran out and his cousin turned nasty. After a week Rott put him out. Social Security housed him in a holiday flat, but insisted that he found himself a job. He did not need much persuading. He did not like where he was headed; he wanted Wanda, his two boys and a home. A job would be a good start.

You can always find a job at Holy Smoke, the salmon factory at Langton, fifteen miles up country from Birsett. There they take salmon from all over Scotland and fillet it, slice it, smoke it, freeze it, bend it and shape it, add to it and mix it up, spice it and sauce it, then vacuum pack it for supermarkets and gourmets the world over. It employs well over two hundred people in a sparsely populated area; they are always looking for staff. Marvin who, as a fisherman, could use a filleting knife proved an asset. He went to work on early shift in four degrees centigrade wearing two shirts, two sweaters and two pairs of trousers under his padded boiler suit. He started work at six and hated every minute of it. He hated the speed; seven seconds a fish: he hated the regimentation; standing at a bench in a row: he hated the regularity; start at six, break at eight for breakfast (twelve mins), at twelve for lunch (twenty-eight minutes), stop at two (put your knives down then, when the buzzer goes, not before). He hated the cleanliness, the stainless steel and particularly the hat with the hairnet: he hated being indoors; he wanted the breeze and the sea and the boat. But he stuck at it. He had not learned to blame social deprivation for his troubles so he tackled them himself. He had no principles to guide him, no experience to teach him, no family or friend to back him up. He would do it because he had to; he would do it for Wanda and a seat at the table with a plate of Wanda's latest effort in front of him and the bairns fighting over chicken nuggets.

How long he would have kept at it without support we need not speculate. After three weeks he picked up Wanda's signals and arrived on the doorstep washed, brushed and generally smartened up. Wanda accepted his contrition and put him on a short leash. Two rules to be kept: stay off the drink and keep clear of Rott. Wanda could not yet persuade Dot to persuade Delightful to take him back to the Aurora. His berth had gone to a Gainslaw landlubber; not as strong but he turned up every morning without fail and without hangover. Marvin slogged it out at Holy Smoke for the time being. Torquil and Quentin were glad to see him back.

But Rott had not yet done with Marvin, or with Wanda.

CHAPTER FORTY-ONE

As John drove to Gainslaw station to pick up his wife and daughter, his prospective trip to London griped. He tried to hide it but Marion picked up his discomfort long before they reached Birsett. She had something difficult to say, awkward questions to ask; perhaps John had questions too? To be tackled sooner rather than later. She said they would settle themselves into Partan Row then she would come up to Braeshiel alone while Rebecca had a shower. Their daughter would join them later for the meal John had promised. John welcomed the opportunity to come clean with Marion alone; welcomed it reluctantly.

Although their meal lay only an hour away Marion accepted the cup of coffee John offered her. While she waited for the coffee, she collected her thoughts; while he made it, John collected his. With so many thoughts collected some were bound to collide.

"I have a confession," said John, when he had settled himself behind the coffee table, "I have to be away to-morrow." There! It was out. Marion knew.

Marion sipped her coffee, and when she lowered the cup, she stared into it. She said nothing.

"I have to go to London, for an interview. It has just come up. I didn't have time to tell you. I couldn't get them to postpone it."

As he heaped lie on lie, he felt sick; sick at his own duplicity. Marion sat at the other side of the coffee table; her small neat body leaning forward, her head bowed. John noticed that her hair was streaked with grey; had it been like that before? She raised her eyes to meet his; those eyes, that, smiling, had first excited him now disturbed him. He looked away, his heart racing. He knew that she saw what he was hiding and that she heard what he was keeping quiet. He rattled on hoping heaped words would counterbalance his deceit. He explained how the job came out of the blue; he wasn't looking for it; just a phone call, there it was waiting for him on the answer machine. He explained that it provided too good an opportunity to pass up; worth investigating at least. He described GANY's scope and ambitions, and what a compliment that they should come looking for him; the job fitted his experience and aspirations. He told her about Grodwice and explained that it would not be forever; a three- or five-year contract, at the most, it would see him through to retirement (not, note, through to the top job; better not tell her that!). In it lay his last big chance. He expounded the opportunities: green field site: recruit his own team: stamp his own values on it. He extolled its virtues: developing country: poor people looking for decent work and, Ian, yes, Fiona's Ian, was pushing him to take it. Eventually he shut up.

"You invited us here," said Marion, quietly, "I didn't want to come, but I came, I put off what I had planned. I came for Rebecca's sake. Could you not stay for Rebecca's sake?"

"No, it's impossible, it's the only possible day for them; I tried to get them to change it, I explained I needed to be here, but it is tomorrow or nothing. They are only here on Thursday." Echoes of old and practised lies.

"Then you could have said you were not available. What is the phrase, "family commitments"?

"But I would have lost the chance."

"And that is worse than losing your family, is it?"

"Well, of course not."

"Is it, John? Is it worse than losing your family?"

The sound of his name in Marion's mouth stung him; his treachery kicked in his mind. He lashed out.

"I seem to remember it wasn't me that broke up the family. I was quite happy the way things were. We would have still been together if it hadn't been for that damned Parent's Night."

"Oh, no, John," said Marion, leashing in her leaping anger, "Do not confuse occasion with cause. It had been coming for a long while; Parent's Night was the last straw. For months, years, you had no time for your family, no time for me, no time for your son, or daughter; no time for Rebecca. And here we are, a year later and you are still on the same track. 'Rebecca will have to wait; father is chasing moonbeams.'"!

"Not moonbeams! No! It is important. You seem to forget I am unemployed. You seem to forget I was sacked, pushed out, that I don't have a job. I thought you of all people would understand that. I do care about Rebecca and about you but first I must get a job; that's essential. You must see that. Once I am settled then...."

"Oh, I see it! I see it very clearly!" cut in Marion, "I see that I have been far too indulgent. That I let you believe that your executive games were all important. But they weren't that important, were they? *You* see it! They were so important that they could do without you! For all I hear Jim Arkwright made as good a job of it as you did. No, John, it wasn't important in the great scheme of things. It wasn't important even in Loyalty's scheme of things. It was important only to you - and it still is. You don't need a job. Any time you like you can pick up a big pension and a lump sum bigger than most people earn in a lifetime. You don't need a job. What you need is status. Being a human being isn't enough, being a husband isn't enough, being a father isn't enough. What you need is propping up. What you want is a pretend world where you are a boss and everyone else pretends to be impressed. Well, John, if that's what you want, take it. But don't suck Rebecca into it – or me. We'll go home tomorrow."

This onslaught bowled John over. He stood up and stamped to the window, arguments and counter arguments wrangling in his mind. He had answers to all these accusations. He could refute them all. She didn't understand. But John knew that she did understand; that she understood precisely. And he dare not venture onto such open ground.

"Please don't go," he said, "We'll have Friday, and Saturday morning. I might even be back early enough tomorrow to come with you to Rachel and Jacob's."

Marion looked up in enquiry. John answered her look.

"They've invited us for supper tomorrow night, all of us."

"And you are going to disappoint them as well?"

"I've apologised to them."

"And to me, and that makes it alright? Well, here's your daughter, you can apologise to her."

Rebecca entered. John apologised. Rebecca said she understood. The meal was cold and unappetising. John was glad when David turned up to walk Rebecca down the brae. John and Marion walked behind, each with wrangling thoughts but no words. Until they were at the door.

"Please stay, Marion. I'm sorry, but I have to go."

"We have come to see you, John; you invited us to come. If you go tomorrow, we will not be here when you get back."

She walked into the house. John knew he had been here before. He turned into the night to walk home. As he started up the brae, rain started to fall. Then he remembered his tears at Rebecca's results and his promise to his daughter. He was wet, cold and miserable when he reached Braeshiel. But the following morning he drove to Gainslaw and caught the train for London.

En route, First Class he prepared himself for his interview. A mature executive knows how to manage problems, no matter how serious: keep your nerve; back your own judgement; deal with them one at a time; concentrate and don't be deflected; dedicate time slots to each one: Thursday for job, Friday for family, a wise and equitable distribution. One is no more important than the other; there is time for them all. But what if the family isn't there on Friday? The mature executive knows how to evaluate risks.

John imagined the script of the interview and worked his way through it. His CV would stand up to scrutiny with a record of steady progress and solid achievement. He could present: an engineer who understood the processes to be managed; an experienced manager with the management qualities they were looking for: leadership: planning: discipline: constructive interaction: decision making: judgement: goal-setting and monitoring others. He had track record in them all and could quote instances, either listed or unlisted (someone would be checking them off at the interview). To them all he would bring a maturity younger managers could not offer; he knew what these management qualities demanded in the long campaign. Then he carefully prepared answers to the questions he feared: Why are you unemployed? Why had did you leave Loyalty? Do you have problems with offshore manufacture?

The location of the Selection Exordium surprised John. He had imagined a room with two or three men behind a table and him in front of it. He found himself in a suite at the London Hilton. It opened off a reception area where the candidates were assembling. He noticed that there were no chairs in the room and only two tables: a long one spread with a white cloth for serving the coffee, and another bearing a projector aimed at a screen behind it. He looked round the room half expecting to see Jacqui Boutelle; she wasn't there. A smart sweet slick receptionist from Sumner and Frieburg greeted John as he arrived and gave him a name necklace to wear, coloured blue; she had others that were orange. She led him to the coffee table. He was, she told him, the second of five to arrive, but John noticed that apart from himself and the receptionist there were five men and a woman in the room. The receptionist gave John a cup of coffee and offered him a shortbread biscuit. He turned down the biscuit anticipating correctly there would be nowhere to put it while he drank his coffee; he must avoid awkwardness at all costs. If only two of the people in the room were candidates the rest must be either on the interviewing panel or were GANY plants; he checked the necklaces, most of them were orange; orange must mean GANY; he was already under surveillance.

Have you not been where John found himself now, launched into a large quiet room with small groups of people you do not know talking in low voices at the end furthest from you? Have you not tied up at the end of the slipway or run aground in the shallows half way down the room, sipping coffee, studying the ceiling, or walls or carpet and hanging onto your cup as if it were a life belt? But John is not like you; he knows better than to be stranded. He strode up the room to the group of three containing the woman and introduced himself.

"John Swansen, from Scotland; I'm a candidate."

"Me too," said the man with a blue necklace, "Peter Metier, from Rhiems." He held out his hand to John. He was younger than John - about forty; handsome too, and affable, John thought. His handshake was firm and friendly. The plump pleasant woman introduced herself next.

"Hi, I'm Martinne, a foot soldier from GANY, or Project Leader if you want to stand on ceremony. Grodwice is my baby." John took it she was American.

"I am Gordon McAllister," said another American voice, "from Scotland originally, I guess, but now from London. I head up Manufacturing in Europe."

He took John's hand, smiled and looked directly into John's eyes; it wasn't so much eye contact as visual assault. John knew he must hold his gaze; he did. McAllister was younger too, John thought, in his mid-forties perhaps.

"This is a bad start," said Peter Metier, laughing, "I am already at a disadvantage for not being Scotch."

"I wouldn't worry," smiled McAllister, "the Scotch spend all the time fighting each other, eh, John?"

"Only when the English aren't around," quipped John, and everyone laughed. John felt he had made a good start. John used his memory training to remember the names; Martinne he shaped as a martini glass in his memory; he put McAllister in a tin can wearing a Gordon tartan kilt; "McCanister" was near enough.

It is important, of course, that when businesspersons meet like this they do not talk about business and no one attempted to. Martinne and McAllister were assessing social skills, John and Peter anxious to demonstrate them.

John counted in the other candidates. One, a spare bookish young man, took his coffee and went into a corner on his own. Martinne peeled off to join him. When she left, another GANY plant joined the group; he introduced himself as Dwight Graf, Human Resources, Europe. John logged him in his memory as a walking "white" statistical chart. After a while McAllister took Peter away to join another group and in a few minutes Graf and John were joined by a small, wiry man, thinning hair, wearing rimless spectacles and a dark suit that seemed too big for him. As he introduced himself, he seemed to inflate.

"Good morning," he said, "I am Jochen Muller, Vice President, Europe. It is good of you to come." His necklace was orange; a deeper shade of orange.

This was the man; the rest could huff and puff, test and assess; this man would decide. Dwight Graf glowed and mumbled.

Muller looked at John with unflinching clear blue eyes but made no attempt to shake hands; instead he gave a slight bow that John returned. John would need no mnemonic: Muller was Muller. John thought he was about the same age as himself, or perhaps, younger.

"Is your wife with you?" he asked politely. The question startled John. This is the man whose opinion counts and he asks a question like this. John hesitated before answering. Had Muller noticed the hesitation?

"No, I'm afraid not, we have a daughter still at school." said John seeking to explain. Seeking to explain what?

"Can't be helped. We're having a small reception at six, just a buffet, nothing formal, but she would have been welcome. I should have included the invitation with the joining instructions. Unreasonable, springing it on you, would you say?"

"Not at all," said John,

"Ah, but yes," said Muller. "We must have our family lives too, eh?"

Did this constitute part of the selection? Was he digging

for something? Did he know about Marion? Had he ever told Jacqui about Marion? Is that how he knew? How could he know? Nobody knew. Perhaps he is just being polite? John answered none of his own questions.

"But you will come?" asked Muller,

It was a question and John could have said no. He could have said that he had half-promised to get back to his wife and daughter which, whilst true, may also have been right. But he agreed to come; he saw that European Human Resources wrote down his name.

Then Muller excused himself to enquire after the other candidate's wives and eating engagements. Another GANY executive came to make up the group.

"Hi! Rupert, Community Relations, Europe" (John filed him as a red-nosed reindeer).

John recognised the scheme: everybody circulating; every GANY body must talk to every candidate. Then Graf led John away and left him with Mike, Corporate Strategy (a microphone with a face). Eventually John had met all GANY personnel, but only one of the candidates. Jacqui Boutelle hadn't showed up; she mustn't be coming.

Then Human Resources, Europe banged the table and called for attention. He welcomed them all to the Exordium and outlined the 'skedule'. It was not what John had expected. He had thought that the selection panel would assemble in one room, the candidates in another then in turn they would be wheeled in for a grilling. That wasn't the 'skedule'; it wasn't even part of the skedule. But how could his expectations be accurate when he had never been to an exordium before? He had not even bothered to look it up in the dictionary.

Rupert, Community Relations, asked them to gather round the projector table. There he announced a video that would 'introdooce' them to GANY. It covered the same ground as the website and John made a point of referring to the website in the question he felt obliged to ask at the end of the presentation. (He asked about logistics; not something we need to explore; John is seeking approbation not answers). Martinne then showed a video on Grodwice followed by a knock-about piece about the potential and perils of offshore investment; warmly applauded. Next a few words from the man himself, Jochen Muller, stressing GANY's commitment to Europe, painting the big economic picture, envisioning the great vision. Then the meat.

CHAPTER FORTY-TWO

If you had arrived at the Exordium expecting something unusual then you do not understand how consultants work. They offer simple remedies under exotic names; managers prefer it that way. You might have easily mistaken it for a meeting. The five candidates sat round three sides of a large table; between each of them a GANY executive, ten people in all. On the fourth side sat two empty chairs. When the ten were in position the door opened and in walked the Vice President Europe followed by a woman John recognised instantly - Jacqui Boutelle. She looked as attractive, articulate and confident as John remembered her; the men in the room melted; Martinne, the camp follower, slumped.

"This part of the exordium is divided into two phases," Jacqui announced, "in the first we will propose two business scenarios, the sort of scenarios that may confront the successful candidate at Grodwice. Each one will be explored by the GANY people at the table until they arrive at a consensus, or an hour has elapsed, whichever is the shorter. The candidates may at any time intervene with questions, comments, or, (and this is crucial) criticisms of the way the GANY group are going about their work. In the second phase, this afternoon, the roles are reversed, with each candidate being given a scenario that might confront them at Grodwice. Their fellow candidates will support them in tackling that dilemma; GANY staff will question, comment and criticise. The Vice President and I will observe but not contribute. In case you are wondering: yes, the GANY staff round the table do have an input into the selection process - and we may as well come clean by using the in-company name; we will call them Gannets" (laughter all round).

"Is that clear? Any questions?"

Crystal clear! Put them in a pressure cooker! (If you want to read up the method there is a book: *'Pressure Selection: getting at the truth'; Torke and Berry; Modern Business Press; 1999*). John worked it out: if he were too easy on the GANY staff he would be marked down as malleable; if too hard, they would roast him when it was his turn. Now he saw the point of the buffet before they left: to soothe tempers and heal breaches. Everything would depend on the scenarios, particularly the one he had to present in the afternoon.

I am sure you do not want to know the details of the exordium but by lunchtime the bookish young man got his wish and ate alone and in silence. The other four, including John and Peter, the Frenchman, felt they had performed well. John deliberately sought out McAllister (Manufacturing, Europe) to knit up a stitch or two he thought he might have dropped. McAllister proved affable and cheerful, supportive almost. John also took time to speak to Jacqui. She seemed pleasant enough but a little distant, John thought. Nevertheless, John took his seat at the table after lunch feeling confident. They drew lots to see who would go when; he would go last. He gave support to his four fellow victims without causing any offence to the Gannets.

Then Jacqui lobbed John's assignment at him and retreated.

"The company has a contract with a local sub-contractor to supply plastic plugs. European Materials Resourcing has now discovered a much cheaper source in the Far East. The Grodwice contractor cannot survive the withdrawal of the order and is part-owned by the mayor."

John dealt with it brutally. He knew what to say. This was selection not problem-solving; they were interested in him not the answer. He said GANY's interests must come first; he'd switch the contract (*put him down as decisive*). Isn't that tough on the Grodwice company; it'll go bust? Yes, but he'd give them time to adjust (*negotiator - but on how, not whether*). How long? Three months (*tough target-setter*). Isn't that unscrupulous? Yes (*fights his corner*). What about corporate responsibility? John's memory brought up Irvin Saltzer, GANY's President, on the committee for Corporate Ethics. Talk it over with the government; explain and entertain; ameliorate but don't abdicate (*judicious*). What about the mayor? Give him a job (*sense of humour*). Muller must be impressed; said so at the buffet. But what about the promise to Marion and Rebecca to return to Birsett as soon as possible? Can't be helped (*fool*).

Not all the trains from London to Edinburgh stop at Gainslaw. John caught the last one that did – the seven-fifty. Until Grantham he bathed in the euphoria of the day. It had been successful. He felt he had impressed Muller. He convinced himself that he must be one of the front runners – another could be Peter Metier. One thought about Metier niggled; Jacqui had made of lot of him, not exactly flirting but something close. Of course, they were both French speakers. That's what they had in common: French. Nevertheless, what he felt was close to jealousy.

Such niggles couldn't spoil the day's benison. He felt bigger, cleaner, integrated. Just to be in a suit amongst other suits had been reassuring. He had talked to business people about business, discussed familiar topics in familiar words, had felt the power, tracked intriguing decision paths, made the journey, had driven through. If this all sounds mechanical then your ears are attuned correctly, for the clean complete image in his mind is not of a living thing, a magnificent animal or a superb flower; it is of a humming machine, built for purpose, shining, oiled, running sweetly, steely. The model is as unsullied with emotion as his day has been. Life is simpler that way. Business life is simpler that way. Metal can be cut, plastic moulded, product assembled, files opened, bills passed, books signed off, and money made more easily if you do not consider what you are doing to people. Or what they think of you. Close the place, he had said. It had proved a good answer, had earned him exordium points. But then the shades of George and Sarah and Marina at Pinkerton and the others began to haunt him. At Doncaster, Colin and Kate boarded his mind and by York the low discordant rumble of Marion, Rebecca and life at Birsett disturbed the steady business rhythm and he wished he were not going back to their convoluted lives and cloying concerns.

The train reached Gainslaw at a quarter to twelve and John reached Braeshiel just after midnight. Before he went to bed he looked up 'exordium' in the dictionary: "introduction" it said, or, "opening phase". He had a long way to go yet before he reached Grodwice.

He intended to brazen it out with Marion; to arrive at Partan Row ready for blackberry picking immediately after breakfast; to be attentive and enthusiastic; to overcome any ill temper with insistent patience and abounding kindness, a willingness to do anything, go anywhere; at their beck and call for the day.

But he had overlooked the weather. Weather is of no concern to people attending an exordium in an overheated London hotel, but it matters if you intend to stand in a ditch below a hedge on an open road. The rain that lashed the windows of Braeshiel caught John by surprise that morning. But it had not surprised Marion and Rebecca; they had seen the forecast and picked their berries the day before accompanied by

Rachel and Ben.

John learned this from Rebecca when she arrived at his door before he had finished his breakfast. He could not have learnt it from Marion. She had gone home to York the evening before.

"I tried to persuade her to stay," his daughter said, "but she wouldn't."

"Did she say why? Did she have to get back for something?"

"No," said Rebecca, "she was angry."

"Ah," said John.

"It isn't good enough, dad," Rebecca said, sadly, "We came especially. Mum didn't want to come. She had other things to do, but she put them off. But you wouldn't postpone your trip to London. It spoiled everything."

It is much easier to argue with your determined wife than your disappointed daughter. John tried to explain why he had to go and why he could not postpone it, but he did not convince Rebecca and could not quite convince himself. Before the event he had seen it as all-important; it had not been an exordium then, it beckoned as the opportunity of a lifetime; not an event, an adventure. Now he saw it as just a meeting, just a preliminary meeting, almost like… yes, like an indulgence. Contrasted with the simple expectation of his daughter – that they should be together for the day, it presented as a gross indulgence. He had to recover control.

"Look, I'm sorry, Rebecca. It won't, I promise, it won't ever happen again."

"There won't be an again, dad. Mum said."

"Don't be so pessimistic," John said with a confidence he did not feel, "and I'm glad you stayed. Let's make up for lost time. We'll have a good day. What'll we do? Anything you like."

"Thanks, dad," she said, "but I must go home. Mum and me fell out. There's a train at five past ten."

John's outing is a run in the rain to Gainslaw to take Rebecca to the train. As he waits in the queue in the ticket office (to upgrade her ticket to first class) he catches sight of his daughter standing in the concourse. He sees gaiety saddened. Rebecca is not tall, and not particularly pretty, but she is all of a piece, compact, finished, and there is a warm openness about her that is disarming. She is dressed this morning in her favourite outfit: a long black coat trimmed on the lapels with black nylon fur. It reaches almost to her ankles, where it reveals flared denim jeans that overlap white trainers. Around her neck is wrapped and knotted a striped scarf of many colours, bright colours: pink, tangerine, lime, lilac, turquoise; a brooch holds it in place, a red enamelled teddy bear with bright black eyes. Her head is bare, her black hair severely parted in the middle and frizzed at the ends; on her hands multi-coloured gloves, each finger a different colour, a bright colour matching the scarf. Her very presence, young, bright, innocent, expectant, disconsolate, censures him. That and the fact that she had stayed to see him.

"Look, Rebecca," he burst out, as he helped her onto the train. "What should I do? What can I do?"

"Tell her how you feel," she said without conviction and then stopped.

"No," she went on, "It's no use, dad, there's nothing you can do; you're too late."

Nothing! The words hit him like a fist in the stomach. Too late! The door slammed; the train moved off. Too late! This wasn't in the plan; there was no deadline in the plan. The plan unwrapped itself before him: first the job, but not any job; he had to recover his self-respect. He couldn't crawl back to Poppleton without the job, the title, the status, the salary, the car; he couldn't go back to Marion like that. But once he had landed the Grodwice job, he could invite Marion back into his life; no, not invite her, seek her out, bring her back in, court her, woo her, if necessary. Marion had heard the plan. She must come back. It couldn't be too late! John felt the strength of these feelings but could not comprehend them. Like a rescuer at an earthquake he could hear his own voice calling from somewhere deep down in the rubble, but could not make out the message.

He slept badly that night and for many afterwards and walked towards his new opportunity with a more hesitant step.

CHAPTER FORTY-THREE

Most Birsett folk have not yet learnt to accommodate fellow citizens who act despicably so John was castigated for deserting Marion and Rebecca. Most criticism rumbled behind his back but Helen held him to account face to face. JP and Rachel, too, made it clear that they thought he had strayed out of line. Even sympathetic Mr Scott made no attempt at sympathy when John complained to him. There were two people, however, who thought Marion was over reacting. They lived, not in Birsett, but in the capital and have, perhaps, absorbed the non-judgemental culture advocated by the Scottish cognoscenti. They were Margaret, John's sister, and her husband Roddam. With immaculate timing they rang John on Friday morning to invite themselves to Braeshiel for the weekend.

Roddam told John that he thought he had acted reasonably and argued that if he found himself in similar circumstances Margaret would not be as awkward as Marion had been. Mark you, he waited until Margaret was absent before he put this forward, but that should not make us suspect his sincerity. Margaret told John that the incident made clear what had caused the rift in the first place: he had been too accommodating. Marion, she opined, should get a life, buy a shop or something; they could then establish a less dependent relationship. She offered to explain this to Marion either in a letter or over the phone (she couldn't spare the time to talk to her in person). John declined her help and found no comfort in their support. If anything, it confirmed his misgivings. Instinctively he valued Helen's antagonism above his sister's sympathy.

He suspected that Margaret and Roddam were not at Birsett on a purely social visit and on Saturday evening they confirmed it. They had spent all day buttering up their persecuted relative before broaching the subject in mind. They had taken John out for a meal at the new Tandoori Restaurant in Hecklescar. Over their Chicken Tikka and Tandoori King Prawns they homed in on their target: the house, Braeshiel. If John were moving to Eastern Europe then he wouldn't need the house; the house could not accommodate Helen's family, so she would want to sell it. It would save her a lot of bother and fees if she could sell it privately. They were prepared to give her a decent price that included (or more accurately, excluded) a discount seeing as they were family. Their interference irritated John.

"I'm not sure Helen would look very kindly at that," he snapped.

"At what?" asked Margaret.

"You taking over the house."

"Why ever not? It would keep it in the family."

Were they really as insensitive as this? Did he have to explain it? Yes.

"I think she holds you responsible for what happened to David."

"That had nothing to do with us," Margaret blustered, "or Abigail for that matter. If it was anybody's fault but his own, it was Jude. We were disgusted to hear about it. I nearly wrote to Helen, but thought it was best not to. We no longer have anything to do with Jude."

"That's good to hear. You have stopped buying his pictures?"

Margaret and Roddam spoke at once but not together.

"Yes," said Roddam, giving the right answer.

"No," said Margaret, giving the correct answer. They looked at each other. Roddam's Chicken Tikka fell from his fork. He put it down and slurped his wine.

"I mean," gushed Margaret, "socially. We don't see Jude, socially. I buy his pictures sometimes, but I give him less than I used to. We were very angry with him. We told him. Didn't we, dear?"

This time Roddam did not trust himself to speak. He nodded and chewed his chicken.

"Anyway," said John, "the job is far from mine. I would like a base in this country so I'll hang onto Braeshiel for the time being. If Helen doesn't throw me out for associating with schemers."

He laughed, but they didn't.

"How is Abigail?" asked John to change the subject.

"She's changing her course," said Roddam, "She's switched to Media Studies. She thinks the head of department is more……."

Here Roddam scrabbled for the word. He looked at Margaret. She couldn't find the correct word either. The sentence hung unfinished, but they all knew what it meant.

The rain that expounded John's disgrace on Friday led to a week of storms. For four days the Aurora, Silver Cord, Boy Peter and the smaller boats bucked and tossed at their moorings in Birsett harbour. On Wednesday, a watery sun and a lull in the wind provided a lure to the skippers to haul their creels. Although modern industrial parlour creels can survive a storm, the bait in them rots after a day or two. Like us, lobsters and crabs prefer their fish fresh so the bait has to be changed regularly; the men, therefore were anxious to lift and re-shoot their craves. When fishermen are anxious, they take risks. This coast is haunted by the ghosts of the fishing disaster of 1881 when men anxious to fish after a barren week, took a risk and went to sea with the pier head glass howling danger. A third of the fleet was destroyed and one hundred and twenty-nine men lost their lives; of those twenty-four were from Birsett in the Excellent, Transcendent, Guiding Star and other smaller boats. That was in October too.

This day dawned less deceitful than that day, with a light wind. However, a growling swell rolled in from the north, crashing savagely over the breakwater and flaunting its barbaric beauty in a wide creamy flounce along the shoreline. The wind would mend in the afternoon, from the south-east; this would create cross dive when water driven by the local wind thrusts across the swell rolling in from way out. Hauling and setting craves would be arduous and they would not have gone had they been out the day before or the day before that. The Gainslaw man on Delightful's crew did not want to go; he had fished on poor days but not on one as poor as this. Del said he could stay ashore if he wished but the man's pride would not let them sail short-handed.

At four-thirty on a dark morning, the boats left the harbour and heaved into the swell. The Boy Peter's craves lay in Goswick Bay, south of Gainslaw, but Alex and Delightful had discovered a fishing ground twenty mile east of St Abb's Head. If you want to know how far that is, stand on the breakwater at Birsett (or anywhere else) and fix your eyes on the horizon; that is two and half miles; multiply it by eight: it's a long way out in a forty-foot boat on a sea like this. Thank God there is another boat going with you. It would take them three hours to arrive on the ground, two hours to haul the craves, three hours back; safe home before the wind mended.

The Silver Cord and the Aurora did not work alongside each other, the Aurora being three or four miles southeast of the Silver Cord, each boat lost to sight in its own surging seascape of crests and troughs. Kit, hauling, performed miracles: ride the wave, clutch in the winch, haul away, hold it until the wave passes, drive again, now brace against the gunwale, grab the crave as it bursts out of the water, hoist it aboard, dump it on the bench in front of Del. Delightful tore open the crave, ripped out the sealife wriggling in it, stripped out the old bait, thrust in the new and slapped the creel shut again, all the while dodging and dancing to keep his feet. The Gainslaw man staggered and stumbled, peched and panted, tripped and fell as he wrestled to stack the craves on a bucking deck awash with seawater and the wriggling, swirling, glutinous detritus from the craves. As they shot the second fleet, Kit stopped and looked towards the engine hatch.

"What is it?" asked Del.

"A knock, can you hear a knock?"

Del listened. He could hear a knock but not much of a knock.

"Nothing serious?" It was half question and half conclusion. Kit nodded.

"We'll haul another fleet," he said.

As they hauled the third fleet the knock grew louder. Kit fretted until all the creels were aboard. If the engine failed in the middle of a fleet the creels in the sea would pull the boat broadside into the swell and swamp it. Once the last one was aboard, Del decided to call it a day. They would shoot the fleet then head for home; the rest would have to wait; the light was fading, the wind rising. They must get back.

Del called up Alex and told him that he would shoot the third fleet then head in. Alex agreed. Once he'd shot his third fleet, they would make for Birsett too. Del powered up; the boat surged forward for a hundred yards. Then the engine screamed and stopped. For a few hundred yards the Aurora sailed on forlornly then gave itself up to the motion of the sea. The sound a fisherman hates most is the sound of silence. It is worse than a screaming gale. As long as its great heart beats the boat lives. It dies when the engine dies. The skipper loses control, the boat becomes flotsam, driven by wind and wave. Kit cleared the creels from the engine hatch and heaved it open. A hot acrid mist rose from the space. This lay beyond a running repair, perhaps beyond repair at all. Kit closed the hatch. The boat wallowed and bucked in the swell.

Delightful called up Alex first; Alex was on his way; he'd be there in half-an hour. Then Del called for the lifeboat.

In Hecklescar a rocket cracked overhead, then another. The folk of the town; in the streets, in the shops, in the pubs, in the offices, in the boat yard and the fish yards, in the medical centre and the day hospital, at the school, in their houses and their gardens, on the pier and on the Bantry, looked up and said in a single distributed chorus:

"That's the lifeboat; what'll it be?"

Women with men at sea sang a lower song:

"I hope it isn't my man's boat."

Dot and Spot in the Co-op at Hecklescar heard the rockets and hurried down to the harbour. There they met Mark who works for the Harbour Trust.

"Any word?"

"Not yet, but what a day to be out. Del isn't out, is he?"

"Yes."

"It'll be skin divers; it's always skin divers. There's Jimmy, he'll ken, he's a coastguard. Jimmy, have you heard?"

"Aye, it's no' a Hecklescar boat."

"Thank goodness."

"There's the lifeboat away! We'll take a run round to the lifeboat station; they'll tell us who it is. Get in."

A group of men sit hunched in the control room, the radio crackles in the background spraying staccato phrases into the room. Jacky ("Commodore") leans over the radio.

"Commodore," Mark says, "What is it? Is it a stranger?"

"No, it's a Birsett boat."

"Which one?"

"The Aurora."

"The Aurora! What's wrong?"

"Engine failure and it's no day to be stuck out there without power."

"This is Dot, ye ken, Laurence's wife."

"Laurence?"

"Delightful," said Dot.

"Oh, sorry. They'll be all right! They'll be all right!"

"And this is ...."

"Spot, Kit's wife."

"Don't worry, they know what to do and the lifeboat's away."

"Where are they?"

"Twenty mile off."

"Twenty miles! How long will that take the lifeboat?"

"With a sea like this, two hours."

"A' that?"

"Aye, the lifeboat will be stotting as it is, and the wind's mending."

"Oh God!" muttered Dot.

"The Silver Cord isn't far off and will stand by."

"The Silver Cord! Alex! Thank God."

The Silver Cord would there for the Aurora but much would be against her. The Aurora has a low freeboard and a low gunwale. She ships water in all but the flattest of seas. A couple of years ago Del and Kit had had a steel chaser fitted that lifted the bow a couple of feet to keep the water out of the boat when the boat was driving forward but it offers no protection today with the boat wallowing in the swell. The waves broke at will over the gunwale and surged over the deck. Like a monstrous pendulum, the heavy unshot craves on her deck pulled the boat down in the water and swung it violently from side to side. Frequently the gunwale went under as the boat yawed into the swell. Del flung out a sea anchor astern in an attempt to keep the boat's head to the waves. The men braced themselves in the cramped wheelhouse knowing for sure that the water sweeping across the deck was squeezing its way into the bilges below deck. There it grew into a heaving lump of water that would slop back and forward in the swell, back and forward, a wave loose inside the boat, back and forward, gathering momentum, back and forward until . . . .

Don't believe anyone who tells you that the seventh wave is bigger than the rest; the sea cannot count. It might be the third or the tenth or the hundredth. Two may roll in together, one chasing after the other: the boat oscillates violently, port gunwale under, then starboard, the mast clutching at the sky in a drunken arc, the deck a surging torrent, waves untamed on board, rampaging. Then the boat fails to come up, staggers, founders, capsizes. There is no telling where those waves are. But they are out there somewhere, making, mending, gathering, greedy.

"We'll have to dump the craves," said Del. Kit rose to follow him.

"I can't," mumbled the Gainslaw man, his face grey with fear. Del longed for Marvin.

"Better on deck than in the wheelhouse if she goes under," spat Kit. They leave the Gainslaw man to his nausea and tumble out. Each crave is lifted, lugged across the greasy, heaving deck and thrown over the side; each crave trails a rope coiled for tripping behind it. Off the gunwale the sea rises ten feet above them, then sinks ten feet below. Each crave weighs fifteen kilos; there are fifty of them; Del and Kit will shift three quarters of a tonne between them in the next ten minutes. It is deadly dangerous work; to go overboard from a disabled boat in a sea like this is to drown.

Do not blame the Gainslaw man for turning down such a career opportunity. Next week he will stand on an unheaving floor behind a static bench packing dead sausage rolls for freezing. In the dry canteen at lunchtime he will try to scare the girls with his tales of the sea.

As Kit threw in the dhan to mark the dumped craves, the Silver Cord heaved over the swell off the starboard bow like a providential angel. A towline soared across the waves. Kit attached it to the helpless boat. Moving slowly ahead the Silver Cord gave the Aurora surrogate life and steerage. That is how the lifeboat found them, fifteen miles out in a freshening south-east breeze. The lifeboat towed the Aurora the rest of the way. The Silver Cord sailed behind to take the stern rope when they came to dock in Hecklescar. Night had fallen by the time they reached the harbour. Dot was there and Spot and Helen, and, taking the mooring rope, Marvin.

The engine proved beyond repair. A new one would cost six thousand pounds. They bought an old tractor engine from a scrap yard for five hundred; Kit and a marine mechanic adapted it for marine use; it took them three weeks; total cost: twelve hundred and fifty pounds - and near divorce for Kit.

When the Aurora sailed again, Marvin was on board.

The morning following the rescue, the Advisory Committee on Fishery Management recommended a complete ban on fishing for cod; any cod, even cod caught in shoal of haddock or whiting or in a prawn trawl. For how long?! For five years, ten, twelve; for as long as it takes to save the cod. To hell with the fishermen and their families! Alex showed the article to David, but didn't say 'I told you so'.

CHAPTER FORTY-FOUR

The week in Birsett, however, provided some relief from gloom. Thursday brought Halloween and in the last few years, the bairns of Birsett have revived the old custom of guizing. If you had been in the village on that magical night you would have seen little groups of guizarts going from door to door. You might meet a half-coven of witches or a wizard or two, skeletons, white sheeted ghosts, walking black bin bags topped with gruesome masks, perhaps a mummy, bound head to foot in bandages, or a couple of vampires with long teeth drooling blood.

Not every household turns away from Coronation Street or Sky Football to entertain the bairns. Some switch off their lights to pretend they are not at home, some won't answer the bell, others shut the door in the bairns' faces. But Helen is busy all night with apples and sweets and twenty pence pieces; so are Dot, old Bessie Raeburn and Mr Scott. Three red-horned devils brave One Partan Row. This is an act of grace, for JP is away and Rachel is feeling low; they are made welcome. John is disturbed only once - by Louise and Morag and two other black cats with tails and whiskers. He sits at his laptop and listens to their songs. He has no apples or sweeties but gives them a pound each out of his pocket; that pleases them enough to say they will return at Christmas to sing him carols.

Did the mention of Christmas make the house feel empty after they had gone? Possibly, but it had felt like that increasingly since Marion and Rebecca had deserted him. He wondered where he'd be at Christmas, *what* he would be at Christmas. The morning after brought a clue. Jacqui rang to say that he had "cleared" the Exordium and would now "graduate" to the next stage – a formal interview with the European Vice President, Muller, Gordon McAllister, Head of Manufacturing for Europe and Dwight Graf, Human Resources. Success in the interview, said Jacqui, would bring him a "field trip" to Grodwice in the company of McAllister: only two candidates would progress to this final stage. The appointment would be made mid-, late-, December, just before Christmas. So long, thought John, seven or eight weeks!

This information arrived just after he had been assaulted by another piece of news - in the Financial Times, under People and Appointments:

'Sir Frank Wantley, Deputy Chairman of Loyalty plc has joined the board of SEA Corporation. Sir Frank, previously a junior minister at the Department of Trade and Industry with Special Responsibility for South East Asia brings his valued experience to the board at a time when SEAC are seeking fresh opportunities in the emerging economies of the area.'

Until Jacqui's call arrived this many-pronged sentence had nettled him; once he had heard from Jacqui, he absorbed it with only slight irritation. Opportunities out East were opening up for him too.

As he waited impatiently for the summons, he had plenty to occupy him. Mack arrived to look over the production flow at Gainslaw Globes. With Kate and Charlie, Mack talked about machines and flow lines, conveyors and automation, feeder systems and computerisation, storage and warehousing. Mack promised a plan within a fortnight. When John had approached him about the fee, Mack had parried him. Now John tackled him again.

"You need to tell me," pressed John

"It's free," said Mack.

"No, you can't not charge."

"A hundred pounds, then."

"Ian, come off it. Sumner & Frieburg will never agree to that."

"It's not Sumner & Frieberg that are doing it; it's me."

"Do they allow that?"

"If I say so, yes. It's my time, so I will charge what I like. A hundred when the project is complete and accepted. OK?"

This was the Mack that John knew well. John was certain that Sumner & Frieberg would never agree to Mack taking on personal projects; no doubt they had spelt it out in his contract; no doubt Mack had read it. But Mack had always played to his own rules; John had suffered from this independence but had learnt to value the man. Mack refused to join the executive game. The game required you to play for position, to strive for advancement, chase higher pay, pay homage to the hierarchy: or, if not, to be afraid to gamble your job, your position, your salary. But Mack didn't play the game. He respected his own judgement more than he respected rank; he had a touching belief that expertise, not stripes, should decide outcomes. Bosses must take him as he is. They could not intimidate him for he had no ambition but to enjoy his work and take care of his family. If he did not enjoy what they gave him he would find something that did. John could have learnt a lot from Mack but would not accept that life could be so simple. He had always admired his friend; now he envied him.

They enjoyed their time together but didn't talk much

about their shared past at York; it was too recent and too raw. They talked not at all about Marion, although she hovered in the minds of both during the visit. Mack proved true to his word: he came up with a costed programme of work within ten days. JP funded it, John implemented it, and it was ready for Flambert's new product the week before Christmas.

Mack's visit heralded the second coming of Flambert Pinkerton. He greeted John from inside One Partan Row after JP had called John down to meet his old friend. He had grown older, fatter; battered by life but still wearing his hallmark checked shirt and casual slacks. They had last met ten years ago, but Flambert spoke as if he had just stepped out of the office for a few minutes. He spent no time in reminiscences. He dived into his pilot bag and pulled out a mock-up of the tracker ("call it Flamtrac" he said,) then drawings of the body and the components he wanted Gainslaw Globes to make.

"The tools will be sent before Christmas."

"Where? To you."

"No, to you."

"Have you proved them?"

"No. God, John, you'll do that."

"Of course," said John and thought of the last time Gainslaw Globes tried to prove a tool. JP smiled.

As they travelled to the factory together, John caught something of the harmony they had shared at York, twelve years ago. Sometimes such harmony develops in a company: a conjunction of personalities, shared interests, mutual affection. Do not believe you can buy it from a consultant, or learn it at a team-building course; it is a gift from God. If you stumble on it treasure it; if you find a way of bottling it, your fortune is made.

Flambert, in his wide brimmed trilby and long flowing olive greatcoat, marched into Gainslaw Globes, greeted Kate effusively and took over the office. He spread the drawings on the table, pointed out the critical features, answered questions, praised the product, praised the factory and called Kate "my dear" in every sentence. When she told him Charlie would prove the tools, he strode onto the shop floor and introduced himself to the man. When Charlie grumbled about likely problems, he talked at him and over him until he fell silent. Kate promised him quotations for the body and components within a week.

"I'm sure they will be acceptable, my dear," he said.

On the way to the station at the end of the appearing, Flambert enquired after Marion. John tried to explain the position. Flambert listened carefully.

"Another woman?" he asked bluntly when John had finished.

"No."

"Sure?"

"There is no other woman."

"She's got another man?"

John disliked Flambert's line; he made it sound tawdry. He wouldn't tell him about Malcolm.

"I don't know; maybe she has."

"You're a fool, John, a fool. She's a good woman, exceptional, I would say. They're in short supply; I have had three since York, lookers all of them; gave them what they wanted but where am I? They took it and left; I'm on my own. If you don't want Marion give me her address."

John laughed but Flambert didn't join in. He wasn't serious, was he?

"Get her back, John, as soon as you can; if she'll have you. Court her, woo her, send her flowers, take her to Paris. If you don't, someone will. You're letting it drift, John. Do something!"

It sounded like an order. John said nothing - and said nothing about Grodwice either. He knew Flambert: he worked on the assumption that everyone is as committed as he is to whatever he is committed to at the moment; loyalty is all.

Kate's quotes were accepted within a week. The parts would be profitable – if the tools would run. They dribbled in over the next couple of months (they weren't all there until the third week in January).

John also accepted his settlement with Loyalty that week. He received a cheque for a hundred and eighty thousand pounds and notice that a pension of two thousand, five hundred pounds less tax would be paid into his account by Scottish Widows on the fourth of each month, starting December; it would be increased every year and would last as long as he lived. If anyone else in Birsett (apart from JP and Lady Flemington) had received such news they would have broken out the champagne and booked a world cruise, but John winced. He had been used to three times that. The document laid out another clause: his widow would be paid half the pension after his death.

He did not intend dying, and he didn't intend living on a pension. GANY's liberal salary would so add to this paltry sum that in the end he would be better off, far better off than he had been. That's what's important: better off than with Loyalty, *far* better off. In the meantime, for pension purposes, he had to confirm that he was married: *please send wedding certificate and wife's birth certificate*. He had neither; they were at York; how could he ask for them?

On the fifth of November he attended, at Louise's insistence, the bonfire and fireworks Mr Hirsell the head teacher had organised on the beach. The night came clear and crisp and if he had been there in mind as well as in warm clothes, he may have enjoyed it. Louise enjoyed all of it but the burnt onions on the hot dogs Delightful sold from his barbecue stand (profits split fifty/fifty with the school). Morag enjoyed it, particularly the bangs and the leaping sparks, and Ben and Rachel enjoyed it; many others too, for most of the village turned out.

As John climbed the brae after the display, Mr Scott called him in and led him to his front room. It lay in darkness. The sash window had been pulled down from the top and before the window stood a tripod and, strapped to the tripod, binoculars; behind the tripod an upright kitchen chair.

Like Braeshiel higher up the brae, Mr Scott's house faced almost due east so on a night like this Mr Scott looked out on stars. John had not noticed the stars but now Mr Scott's enthusiasm led him on. The old minister pointed out Pleiades, the Seven Sisters, below them Hyades, the horns of Taurus, with the orange giant, Aldebaran, at the tip. Above rode the constellation of Perseus, with first magnitude star Algol for an eye. Chasing Perseus, Auriga, the Charioteer, with star Capella driving. Away to the south, a string of stars Mr Scott called Cetus. With the excitement of a schoolboy, he called John to sit on the chair and look through the binoculars. They were directed at the faint bright shadow running through Auriga and Perseus. John sat down and put his eye to the Milky Way. From long memory he knew what he was expected to see, but it still surprised him: the sky stippled with specks of light, crowding into the lens, swathe upon swathe of stars, some massed in fields of light, some in bright clusters, others in glittering streams; dazzling diamonds some of them, set in frayed collars of lesser gems. Once his eyes became accustomed, he could see the colours: white, blue, yellow, orange.

"Look at Pleiades," urged Mr Scott, rocking on his arthritic limbs, "now down, see the star to the left of Aldebaran is a double, and the one to the right. Magnificent, isn't it?"

It was, John admitted, magnificent. He let the old man sit down and look through binoculars.

"I don't see well, but did you see the double stars?"

"Yes," said John.

"Then come outside, I will show you a stupendous sight."

Mr Scott unhooked the binoculars, pulled on his coat and hustled John outside to where the clothesline crossed a little patch of grass.

"See," he said pointing directly overhead, "see the bent W; that's Cassiopeia, but you know that. Do you know the Square of Pegasus? There it is. Now take the binoculars and run a diagonal from the bottom star there to the one top left and keep going up towards Cassiopeia; there's a line of stars running up towards it; now can you see a faint glow, as if a torch were shining through a blanket, just a smudge of light? Lean on the line to steady yourself."

John ranged among the stars but couldn't find it.

"Keep looking," cried the old man.

John made to hand him the binoculars.

"No, I can't see it now, but it's there; keep looking.

It suddenly leapt into John's vision - a bright blur.

"I've got it."

The old man cheered.

"The Andromeda spiral", he pronounced, "A spinning cloud of stars, hundreds of thousands of suns, so far away we see it as a smudge. We're looking beyond our system, beyond our galaxy, out across oceans of space to another island like our own, two million light years away, yet we see it. If we look, we can see it. It is real. It is there; on this night it is there; we can see it; it is a wonder."

His words did not flow, they stuttered along as he groped for an understanding he knew lay beyond him. He hoped the words might open up the stars to John; to help him *feel* the universe. As always, on such nights he caught but a passing presence. This night John caught the shadow of it, too.

John handed the binoculars back to the old man, but Mr Scott wasn't paying attention. He stood gazing at the night sky, stilled by the immensity, lost in awe.

"We are spectators, John, excluded by our own arrogance; outsiders. We are of no significance ...." he murmured, but John knew the sentence wasn't finished. As they went indoors, Mr Scott gripped John by the arm and looked him in the face.

"...except to each other, John, except to each other. The stars cannot love."

The intimacy embarrassed John; the message disturbed him. What had he bought with the love he had traded in?

"You have a fine dark garden for studying the stars," he said, "No street lights!"

"There is one street light," said the old man, "that shines straight into the window, but they put a shade on it when I asked them." He gave a short laugh.

"That was very good of the council," said John.

"Not the council," said Mr Scott, "Delightful and Marvin. Twenty pounds; worth every penny!"

CHAPTER FORTY-FIVE

The following morning, in the post, a letter inviting John for interview. *Date: Tuesday, 12th November, Time: 2 o'clock.* Same place: London Hilton; not an interview, a 'Colloquy'.

Any serious study into methods of recruitment has found that the interview is a poor method of selection. It persists because it plays to the conceit that managers can recognise talent when they see it squirming on a chair in front of them.

John once again reviewed his answers to the awkward questions he expected. This time he could flesh them out because he knew the people he would meet. First Awkward Question: why are you presently unemployed? Or, if someone were nasty enough (and Americans could be nasty): if you are as good as you say why has no one snapped you up? Second AQ: why did you leave your last company? Or, if someone were penetrating enough: you were fired from your last company, weren't you? Why? Third AQ: you have no experience of working abroad; how would you handle a foreign workforce? Or, if someone were perceptive enough: you seem to have a problem with moving work offshore? I believe you fought it in your last company. Mr Swansen, you're a hypocrite, aren't you? Can we trust you?

John's interview would be the second of four. Paul Metier would be last, tomorrow afternoon. John would have preferred that position, for the impact of the last candidate tends to erase or jumble the memory of the others. John need not have worried; the Colloquy would be videoed and reviewed later.

Gordon McAllister (Head of Manufacturing, Europe) and Jochen Muller (Vice-President, Europe) greeted him as if he were an old friend, Dwight Graf (Human Resources), more formally. John entered the room, but again found no table with three chairs behind and his in front. Here were wooden framed easy chairs with a coffee table in front and a tray with coffee jug and cups on it.

"Please don't regard this as a formal interview," purred Graf, pouring the coffee, "we really just want to get to know you; find out where you have been, what you have done, explore your achievements." Which is as good a definition of an interview as you'll get - but we'll take the man's word for it: it isn't an interview, it's a colloquy.

We do not need to follow the interview to discover what we already know about John, but it will be worth our while to see these three at work. It may help when you next apply for a job. Do not be deceived by Graf's claim of informality. These are professionals; they know what they are doing and have prepared carefully. Graf will explore John's training and experience and probe his motivation and emotional stability. MacAllister has been charged with finding out what John knows (and doesn't know) about managing a factory. Muller will check out John's suitability for work in GANY and his understanding of the politics of managing a factory in a foreign land. John is prepared for Graf and McAllister but not for Muller. He will be caught by surprise.

The inter..., colloquy starts with chat. Graf leads. 'A pleasant journey? Where is it again you come from? York, isn't it? No, of course not, Birsett. Where is that? What kind of place is it? What do the people there do to make a living?' Muller is scribbling down the answers? Why? You'll find out.

Then Graf starts. In his mind he has a pendulum; on his pad he has a replica; it hangs limply downwards, indicating nothing. He will now dig for evidence of motivation, self-motivation. If he finds it, he will push the pendulum to the left through a scale than ranges from average to well above average (coloured coded pale to full green, for GO). If he finds no evidence, he will let it hang, if he finds no inclination to take risks, he will shift it right (average to well below average (shades of red). (If you want to find more about the method, see the work of Munro Fraser, Aston University, Birmingham, UK). But where will Graf gather evidence on John's motivation?

He asks John about his father. What did he do? How did he earn his living? And tell me about your mother? Did you have brothers or sisters? What has this got to do with motivation? This: Graf is laying a marker. He assumes that a son who becomes a manager in the firm his father owns is much less motivated than the son of a labourer who rises to become, say, a bookmaker. John is a fisherman's son who has made it to Managing Director; pendulum moves left positive. But not so good on career moves; these have been prompted largely by other people: a recruitment agency had thrown him into the path of Flambert who had virtually shanghaied him into the production manager's job, then promoted him to General Manager: in the right place at the right time: pendulum hardly moves.

Graf picks his way patiently through JP's chairmanship of Pinkerton and the take-over by Loyalty and at last understands that John is Managing Director by default: in the wrong place at the right time; leave the pendulum where it is. But how does John now find himself out of a job? We know John is ready for this: disagreement with the board over strategy: he believed in investment, could see a route to prosperity, but the board lacked nerve; he stood his ground, couldn't support the lack of vision. Graf likes the self-belief: pendulum pushes into "above average" (for losing the game!). All the while, McAllister and Muller are making notes.

Graf shifts to *'Emotional Adjustment'*. How on earth will he rate John on that? We have watched John for a year now and are still not sure how he ticks; Marion has lived with him for twenty-eight and is still waiting for him to adjust emotionally. Yet Graf thinks he can work it out in an hour and a half. What does "emotional adjustment" mean, anyway? Not much actually. Graf wants to know how John handles pressure. The Human Resources Head has a pendulum for this too. To the left he places people like the Prime Minister, Tracy Edwards off Antarctica in a single-handed yacht and Jochen Muller, his own Vice President; on the right, alcoholics, drop outs and deserters. But where to place John? Not a dropout certainly – he has been fighting it for months now. Graf decides that if other people in the past have given this man responsibility, he must be reasonably tough; and he has stood the pressure of being top man at Pinkerton for ten years with no sign of a nervous breakdown, or time off for stress: push the pendulum left. John has done well, both pendulums in the green zone - above average.

McAllister then leads with questions about what John did at Pinkerton, probing his management ability and experience. First, he fishes for John's mindset. He is expecting UK traditional batch and queue (heap up product at each stage of the process until you have a big pile then process the big pile and shift it to the next station in order to gain *economies of scale*). But he is surprised that John has discovered Lean Production and believes in pulling each item straight through the whole process, dropping it in at the front and whipping it through to the end without delay. Surprised and pleased for GANY has learnt Lean Production from its Japanese subsidiary but has found it difficult to convert batch and queue managers in Europe; pendulum pushes left. Not only does John understand process flow and talks the language, he has done it, and would have done more (no need to credit Mack with the thinking); pendulum pushes to above average. McAllister uncovers some technical gaps mainly in metal forming, assembly and computerised control, but that is to be expected. Cost and budgetary control both understood and practised; man management first class (John talked up his team, mentioned his affection for them, then apologised). Finally, had he given any thought to what he would do if he were starting a factory from scratch. Had he thought? He has written a thesis on it. (A thesis? We've never heard of a thesis. Oh, the book he had been working on. It's a thesis now, is it?). "Thesis" went into the notes of McAllister, Graf and Muller. McAllister's pendulum pulled up on the border of WBA, Well Above Average, full green, GO.

The waiter brought more coffee; Graf closed his file and questioned the biscuits. "Ginger", confirmed McAllister. The tension slackened; four executive colleagues relaxing. Make him think it's all over; colloquy as chat.

"This Birsett place sounds very attractive," said Muller.

"Yes," said John, "It is; but then I'm biased; I was brought up there."

"I got the feeling you thought it less prosperous than it used to be."

"Yes, there isn't much apart from the fishing and that is failing."

"So, what do the young people do? Is there anything else?"

"No, not really, some knitwear units but they are mainly for women and they don't usually last long. There is the plastics factory I mentioned but it's small scale, I doubt whether it can survive for long."

"So, there is no work for young people?"

"Not in the place."

To illustrate he cited David and bent his story to make it appear that David had no option but to be a fisherman in a declining industry.

"That is a shame; it sounds quite depressing."

"It is."

"For you or the place?" Muller laughed.

"Both," smiled John

"So, you'll be glad to be clear of it?" A hint, thought John. No, it is a question and a lure.

"I must admit I will," said John taking the bait, "I'm looking forward to being in the saddle again."

"You are not thinking of calling it a day and settling down back home? Loyalty are paying you a pension; I think you said."

John thought the question was about his age. He moved to assure Muller.

"No, no," said John, hastily, "Much too young for that; I have a lot to give."

"You have, I'm sure, but could you not give it to the people of...Birsett."

"No, no," smiled John, "they can manage without me."

"Can they? "pressed Muller, "I thought you said there wasn't much future for the young people?"

John woke up. This is not a chat; it's cat and mouse with

the Vice President chasing; but what?

"There's not much I can do." John mumbled.

"Could you not develop this small plastics company? Grow it, perhaps."

"That would need intensive attention and finance and even then……..," said John, trying to escape. Muller glimpsed at his notes and cut in.

"Mr Marwick, the Investment Banker, seems to think it has potential. He thinks you have pulled it round. What will happen if you desert them?"

Where on earth had this come from? From JP's reference, of course. John had given JP's name for a reference (no restriction; contact him any time).

"I'm a big company man," said John, trying to free himself in a single bound. He jumped into the fire.

"Once someone else has made the company big," laughed Muller. Graf and McAllister laughed too, if only because this time they were not the mice. John caught the cold light in Muller's eyes and didn't laugh. For a moment the job hung in the balance.

"Touché," smiled John, and thereby saved his bacon. Had he protested he would have been fried. Fried and finished. But Muller had not finished.

"You see Mr Swansen, if we do not care for our own people, how can we care for foreigners?"

Care? Is he serious?

"Nowadays," continued Muller, "It is not enough to invest in factories, to serve customers and churn out profits. We must be good corporate citizens. We must care about the communities in which we locate."

Then John recalled that Irvin Saltzer, GANY's President and his seat on the Committee for Corporate Ethics. How could he have forgotten?!

Muller pressed on.

"Your answer at the discussion, er, exordium," he smiled at Graf, "your answer worried me a little. I thought you were a little severe on the local supplier, though relieved you might give the mayor a job."

He smiled to take the edge of his comment but kept up the pressure.

"Tell me what you think about globalisation."

John heard the request with relief. He was glad to be clear of Birsett and its particular needs. He had not given them much thought; certainly, he had never regarded them as his problem. Globalisation was different; it could be studied at a desk, and he had studied it. He demonstrated to the Vice President his grasp of the issues: large multinationals moving into poorer countries changing old methods, forcing local companies to the wall as they brought in new, more productive methods of work, cheaper products and lower costs through efficiencies of scale. Then he gave the answers he thought Muller sought: globalisation is a good thing for although it caused change and painful change at that, it spread wealth and know-how to poorer countries.

"Sounds an undiluted blessing," said Muller, blandly, "so why do so many people oppose it?"

John wanted to say, "unreconstructed socialism", but he thought he had better steer clear of politics.

"Nostalgia," he said.

"For what?"

"For a simpler way of life."

"Ah! Would you explain that?"

"Yes, these people have a rosy view of the past where communities were self-sufficient and everything was decided locally. It's a myth. Communities like that always struggled to survive. They were desperately poor."

"And we are rich, eh?"

"Comparatively"

"And taking the gospel to Grodwice, is that it?"

"Yes,"

"Are you a good preacher?"

"I hope so," said John to whom the thought of being a preacher had never occurred. But clearly the Vice President viewed the job at Grodwice as more than just running a factory.

"The preacher must behave himself, yes?"

"Of course," said John who should have realised by now that Muller had not given up the chase, that he had picked up a scent and would hunt it down. His next question slammed into John's mind.

"You are a happily married man," he said. John realised he must not hesitate.

"Yes,"

"Good," said Muller, "Forgive me, I am not prying into private matters. But we have discovered to our cost that lonely men in strange places are open to temptation. It has caused local difficulties for us, difficulties we would rather not have. We take a very conservative stance. We try only to recruit happily married men."

He smiled. John had difficulty smiling back.

"If you are appointed, we would prefer that your wife comes with you. Would that present any problems?"

"I don't think so," said John, hoping they could not read his thoughts. "My wife has a job in this country but, of course, we will talk it over."

"That is all we can expect at this stage," said Muller graciously, and fortunately, left it at that.

All this took place on Tuesday. On Friday he received two letters. One had been sent by Dwight Graf, Head of Human Resources, Europe, saying he had been selected to go through to the final stage – a visit to Grodwice. They would very much like Mrs Swansen to accompany him, as a guest of GANY.

The other letter came from Marion - asking for a divorce.

CHAPTER FORTY-SIX

As John read the two letters, the ramshackle life plan he had cobbled together crashed around him. The resulting cognition could not have been less forcibly forged. It came not as a mental revelation, a switch flicking on in the mind and flooding the subject with a pure light. This carried a far more valuable sort of knowledge – facts in the face: that his life had splintered; that, if he did not take action to repair it, it would remain shattered. This sudden insight exploded the castle of self-deceit he had carefully constructed over the past few months. Now it would stand up no longer. It demanded attention.

For over an hour he sat stunned the by the alarming proposition that he could not 'have it all'. Eventually, not knowing what to do with either letter, he read them again.

He then laid aside the GANY letter and sat down to write to his wife. His first reading of Marion's letter had been lit by the light of Graf's letter. This had blurred its contrast and obscured its contents. Only the word 'divorce' had been sharp enough to penetrate his understanding. Now that he read the letter with a calmer eye, he realised that Marion was not, in fact, proposing divorce, but putting it forward as the only way out of the impasse in which they were entrapped.

He spent the rest of the morning trying to compose a

letter to Marion. He had lost any skill he may have had in such writing and all his phrases now seemed phoney or contrived. This incompetence increased his unease but he stuck at it and by lunchtime the following script glowered back at him from his laptop screen:

My dear Marion

I scarcely know how to reply to your letter but I think I can understand the feelings that give rise to it. You have been very patient whilst I have tried to sort out myself out, and I can't blame you now for wanting an end to the uncertainty.

I now know that my action in attending the interview rather than honouring my promise to holiday with you was insensitive, but to be honest I could not see then, nor can I see now, how it could have been avoided. I suppose the honest thing would have been to advise you of the engagement before you came and give you the choice of coming or not, because in spite of what I said at the time, I did have notice enough to have told you beforehand. To be honest I was afraid to do so in case you decided not to come.

I think we need to meet to talk through the problem. I do not want a divorce because it has always been my fondest wish that we should get together again and I truly believe that that is what Rebecca wants more than anything else. When we meet, I will do all in my power to persuade you to give our relationship another chance. I thought that when you were here in August, we had established some basis of an understanding. I did not follow it up at the time because I believed that I should not involve you in the uncertainty of my attempts to secure employment. I thought it important to get that out of the way first. I am now well on the way to resolving that issue and feel that we should now meet to talk about the opportunities it affords for our future.

Once I know you have received this letter, I will give you a ring to try and arrange a time and place for meeting.

I would like immediately to add a disclaimer: I do not think this is much of a letter and would not recommend you copying it to anyone you care about.

I believe he didn't think much of it either for he now employed an old office trick: if you can't write what you mean don't keep dibbing away at it; put it aside; take a break; go back to it later. John took his lunch, then called up the letter for inspection. He could not think of a way of improving it, so he printed it out and produced an envelope. He prepared to fold the letter when an image hit him in the face. He saw Rebecca again, at the station, saying, "Tell her how you feel." He re-read the letter and realised he had not done that; that he couldn't do that; at least, he couldn't type it; couldn't make a permanent record of it. But he could write it. He scribbled at the bottom of the regimented text words in his own hand:

Please give me another chance to prove that I love you and want to live with you.

Love,

John

As he wrote the words his pen trembled in his hands; a strange warm sensation ran through his whole body as if some dead nerve path had fired up again; it felt disconcerting and exhilarating at the same time. He folded and sealed the letter and went out and posted it before he could change his mind.

Oh, Rebecca! We hope your mother does not give you it to read. It will strike you as cold. If she does, ignore the type, read the scribble. Keep believing!

John had promised to take Mr Scott to the Border General Hospital that afternoon. It was a distraction, but also an opportunity to think about how he might reply to the GANY letter.

Mr Scott had, as he put it, a problem with his waste disposal system: blood in the stools. The doctor had made reassuring noises, taken samples and arranged for tests. Now the old minister would learn his fate; he had an appointment with the consultant at four o'clock.

Alex normally took Mr Scott but today he had to attend a meeting of fishermen in Hecklescar at which a European Union Official would explain how fishermen would benefit from giving up fishing for cod, haddock and whiting in the North Sea. John had stepped in.

After days of rain and gloom, a mellow sun blessed this day and they drove through a countryside bedding down for winter under the warm-coloured blanket of autumn. Mr Scott drank it in and tried not to think of the indignities awaiting him.

John drove largely absorbed in his own thoughts; only occasionally did a flaming maple or golden beech startle him from the insistent replay of the seemingly irreconcilable futures that lay before him. He wanted life with Marion; he wanted to be a father again to his daughter and his son. He wanted the job at Grodwice!

Whichever way he guessed the future, these desires excluded each other. Rationally, he could plan ahead. He saw life in Grodwice with Marion; GANY would settle them in a superior house; they would have enough income to do whatever they liked. Maybe even Rebecca would come too; they would all be together again. He would limit his workload, spend more time with Marion; explore the old cities and landscapes of Central Europe, but keep the house at Birsett for regular trips home. It would be a new start with all unpleasant memories of the last year washed away.

This vision enticed him but, even as he conjured it up, it dissolved. He did not have the job and might not get it; he did not have Marion and her proposal was for separation. Yet he could not let go of the image.

If Marion agreed to meet him and talk, would he tell her what Muller had said about managers and marriage? No! This screamed danger. She would immediately suspect his intentions Yet, he believed, he was not fitting her in, not using her to land the job, no, not that. Dare he ask Marion to come with him on the trip to Grodwice? To make up for the mess he made of the blackberry holiday? And would it not also help him gain employment; she would understand that.

In such reasoning we see the rationalisation of an addict. For there lay a territory into which he did not venture: that he should give up all thought of Grodwice and put himself before Marion as a repentant prodigal home at last from the far country.

He came to with the sun hanging low over the Eildon Hills and Mr Scott reciting the Ettrick Shepherd:

> 'Scowled the broad sun o'er the links of green
> Liddesdale
> Red as the beacon light tipped he the wold
> Many a bold martial eye
> Mirrored that morning sky
> Never more ope'd on his orbit of gold.'

John realised that the old man had concerns too. He was afraid of what he might be told. He had watched Willie walk along a similar path and did not think he had as much courage as his friend. John told him it would be all right and Mr Scott tried to believe him.

John had completed one corner only of the FT crossword before Mr Scott hirpled back into reception. The consultant had been pleased with him; internal haemorrhoids, he had concluded. Clearly the subject disgusted the old man.

"I never thought I would be pleased to hear I had piles," said Mr Scott, sourly, and gave no further report.

The sun had despaired of the day by time they set out on their journey back to Birsett. These dark narrow roads make for uncomfortable driving for anyone unfamiliar with them, so John's attention locked onto quixotic white lines, squirming verges and looming trees for most of the journey. But after Langton, on more familiar territory, he shared what he had been thinking with Mr Scott. He felt he could talk to the old minister and he needed someone to listen to him; now more than ever. After he had listened, Mr Scott recognised clearly the danger John faced.

"If I were you," he said, quite bluntly, "I wouldn't even mention it. Go to Grodwice by yourself. Don't involve Marion, (no he didn't say 'Marion', he said 'your wife') at all."

"But it may be just the chance we need."

"I don't think so. Keep it simple. Don't risk it. You want her back more than you want the job, don't you?

The old minister asked the question but knew John could not give a truthful answer. John himself did not know where the truth lay. He still could not choose between his desires. He wanted both.

As John helped him out of the car, Mr Scott made a final attempt to help his friend.

"If we strive to do better than well, we do confound ourselves with craftiness," he quoted.

John, recoiled from this attempt to tell him what he already knew. None of us like to be reminded of what we have hidden in our emotional cupboard.

They had scarcely started their tea when Jimmy Possum arrived to update them on the week's news - and to learn the latest details of Mr Scott's disease for onward communication.

'The Sure Guide coming out of Hecklescar harbour on Tuesday,' Jimmy reported, 'hit the navigation light stanchion and bent it but went to sea anyway without reporting it. They reckon that Calamity Joe, the skipper, wouldn't have reported it at all had Jimmy on the pier not said he'd seen the boat run into it. Joe reckoned something mysterious had gone wrong with the steering, but the word is that Joe was speaking to the bookie on his mobile at the time.'

'The Birsett Inn is changing hands again; an Edinburgh couple this time; he's a merchant seaman. They say the last lot, they were English, left debts everywhere; they say that Peter Herriot is owed two thousand pounds for butcher meat. He was daft to let them run up a bill like that, but he was taken in; they talked posh.'

'The pigeon postie, Andrew Douglas, says he'll be out of a job if the Royal Mail cut the second delivery. They'll do Birsett and Hecklescar from Gainslaw he reckons. He's thinking about the oilrigs, but he'll have to leave his pigeons. There'll soon be nae jobs at a' for the young folk.

'Ye missed yersells the day! Ye ken Delightful bought a new van with the insurance money he got for his engine that blew up. Well today he buried his auld van at sea. He towed it off the beach and dumped it at the back of the rocks.

(If this disturbs you ecologically, let me assure you that what Del did is environmentally friendly. The decaying van will provide a haven for small fish, protecting them from the predations of rapacious trawlers. If the Department of the Environment had wanted an artificial reef, they would have commissioned research, sent it to scientific committees, discussed it for three years and spent half-a-million pounds. Delightful did it in two hours for nothing. Give the man an MBE!)

CHAPTER FORTY-SEVEN

What did John decide to do the trip to Grodwice? He decided not to decide, not yet. He would talk to Marion first. What would he say to Marion? He would leave that until he saw her. If she consented to see him, that is.

How did John reply to Graf's letter? He left it for a few days, explained he had been away (which qualifies as neither the truth nor a lie), expressed his appreciation and pleasure at being selected and said he looked forward to seeing Grodwice. He ignored the suggestion that he should bring his wife; said nothing about it at all - as if he had not read it, or had forgotten to deal with it. How does he account for this dithering? Easily, every good manager knows it is best to delay a decision until you *have* to make it; who knows what new facts may emerge? He rang Marion - in the evening. At last he had remembered that she worked during the day.

Marion had been dithering too. If John had signed his letter after the typed paragraphs, she would have known precisely how to reply to it: 'no, no, no point in meeting'. She would be fighting on depressingly familiar ground, negotiating a painful but inevitable retreat. But the scribble at the end surprised her, and found a hearing in her heart. She loved John. She wanted him back. She did not know what she would say when John rang; she would make up her mind as he spoke. She didn't show John's letter to Rebecca because she had not told her about her own.

****

"Hello, Marion, this is John, did you get my letter?"

"Yes,"

"What do you think?"

"About what?"

"About meeting."

"I don't know."

"Please Marion, I could come down to York."

"That's not a good idea; Rebecca knows nothing about my letter, or yours."

There was a pause; John being tempted to talk about Rebecca: refused.

"Okay then, somewhere in between. Say, Durham, yes, Durham."

"I don't know John; we've been through it all so many times." She sounded as weary as she felt.

"Please, Marion, I promise not to put any pressure on you. Just this once. Say Durham, we can meet at Durham, at the Cathedral." (Where did that come from?)

"No, John, I've decided. It's no use. We'll just go over the same old ground. Let's just leave it."

Then John gathered all his courage and knelt before his wife.

"Marion, I love you, please give me a chance, please

meet me."

Silence.

"Marion, are you still there?"

"Yes, I'm still here." Weariness still, but now mixed with confusion, frustration, anger, protesting to her God, 'This is not fair!'

"Please, Marion."

Silence.

"Marion, on Saturday at eleven I'll be at the North Door of Durham Cathedral. Say you'll be there."

"I don't know, John."

Silence. Then the dial tone.

On Saturday John will make the trip to Durham not knowing whether she will be there or not. To the cathedral on a pilgrimage of faith. And love?

When Marion put down the phone she sat for a while, then rang Malcolm to say she would not be at the Christmas Sale at the church on Saturday. When Rebecca asked who had rung, she told her of the meeting but could not share the resultant joy. Why did she allow herself to be talked into meetings? Why did she keep trying? Hope, was it? Love? Rebecca concluded it must be love. Nothing else suffers that long; in that lay her hope.

This happened on Tuesday. On Friday, John, waiting for a frozen Quiche Lorraine to defrost, heard the doorbell. He opened it on a familiar welcome face: George, his production manager at Pinkerton.

"Hiya, boss," said George in his rich remembered Yorkshire growl, "Tracked thee down."

"George," exclaimed John, "Good to see you. Come in, come in. What on earth are you doing here?"

"Y' should know there's no escape from a Yorkshire man tha' owes money to."

"I deny it," laughed John

"I'll get Joan,"

Joan, his wife, came in, opposite in every way to George: tall, slim, retiring, quiet-spoken. They were on their way to a Salvation Army Band weekend in Edinburgh and George had insisted on tracking down John. Joan sat and drank tea whilst George recounted the history of the last days of Pinkerton.

"I wasn't in at the death," he said, "I got offered a job back end of August and jumped. Jim didn't want to let me go. Things were getting a bit hairy. He threatened to cancel my early retirement package if I didn't serve my notice. Serve my notice! Three months' notice! There were only four weeks left. He dug his heels in so I appealed to thon woman, what d'the call her; Wallace...."

"Waltham," John corrected.

"Aye, Waltham, and she said I could go – but Jim docked my payment in lieu of notice. They carried him out, tha knows, in the end; carried him out."

"Carried him out? Dead?!"

"No, dead drunk! On the last day, stoned out of his mind. So, I was told."

"An old weakness," said John, "but you said you had a job."

"Yes, manager for HomeBuild Superstore on the Ousebank Industrial Estate. D-I-Y supplies. The money's not so hot, but with the pension, I'm not that much worse off.

George than ran down a list of names, giving John a running commentary on where they had gone and what had happened to them. John was alarmed to discover that some of the people, people who had spent their days with him and for him, had almost faded from his memory, names only now, stripped of faces, stripped of meaning and sentiment. But one name, acutely remembered, he had not mentioned.

What about Rita, my secretary, did she get something?" John asked

"Bad news there, with Rita. She had to leave in July, stress or something, nervous breakdown, I think. I haven't heard since. They bumped her to the office, y'know to make way for Arkwright's bit of stuff. It hit her hard. Did you not know?"

"No, I thought it better not to be in touch."

John felt sick, sick at what had happened, sick for not knowing, sick for not finding out, sick of his excuse. That this woman who had devoted her days, months and years to him, who had anticipated his needs, shared his confidences, protected him from intruders, defended him against critics; that this woman, Rita, had slipped off the road and fallen into a ditch and he did not even know.

John, after a few moments of embarrassed silence, changed track and enquired about George's family. They had all flown the coop; his son Paul was working for UNICEF in Pakistan. One of his daughters was married in Halifax and had blessed them with two grandchildren, both boys. He had a photo. The other daughter was doing a doctorate at Cambridge: Social Economics, he thought.

"But don't blame me," said George, "I wanted her to do something useful but her mother wanted her educated."

Joan laughed at her husband's wit and demonstrated the comfortable affection between them. George hesitated to ask after John's family. He didn't know how he should go about it. He put out a feeler.

"How is it with yours?"

"Robert's still at Leeds, Rebecca's still in sixth form at

York; she didn't do as well as she hoped in her A levels."

There was a slight pause as George, not usually stuck for words, struggled to find some that would do. John read his thoughts.

"Marion keeps well, she's still at York. But we're talking."

"That's good," said George, "I liked Marion."

"So do I," said John then surprised George and himself by adding, "But not enough. I am trying to put that right."

"That's good," repeated George embarrassed by his old boss's frankness, "and is there anything on the job front?"

John told him about Grodwice.

"Sounds great," said George, "if tha needs a rough shirt for the shop floor you know where to come." He turned to Joan.

"You'd like it in Eastern Europe, wouldn't you?"

"Oh yes!" she said, meaning 'Oh no!'.

They stayed for two hours and when they had gone John felt as if a light had died in a dimly lit room or as if a book half open and unfinished had been closed for ever. Although he had left the factory for the last time over six months ago, although he knew it had been closed for two months, it had, until this moment, lived on in his mind and there still throbbed and bustled about its business. George's visit shut it down; it fell silent; the space where it stood now occupied by an untouchable memory, a static memorial, nothing more. That impression left behind it another: everyone had dispersed; they were loose in the world; seeking a place to settle; some had already done so. It also shot round a familiar and destructive circuit in John's mind: he was loose too; he no longer rated as the former Managing Director of Loyalty Pinkerton, York; he had become John Swansen, unemployed, holed up for the time being in Birsett.

Was it George's happy familiarity with his wife, the pride he had in his children and his delight in being a grandfather that made John sure that settling should include Marion; must include Marion? What value lay in a big seat behind a large desk in a grand office in Grodwice without her?

At the door, George had paused.

"We all thought a lot of you," he said, "standing up to Loyalty. It took guts. 'No man has greater love than this, that he lays down his career for his friends.'" He smiled.

The undeserved tribute walloped into John's stomach. He wanted to admit his duplicity. He scrambled for words to tell George the truth but could not find any. The time for truth had gone; he must live with the lie and be persecuted by it.

"No, no," he said, "It wasn't like that."

George took this for the humility of a martyr.

CHAPTER FORTY-EIGHT

'*Towering over the town in truly awesome fashion, Durham Cathedral and Castle symbolise together the spiritual and secular powers of the Bishops Palatine in a manner which, once seen, will never be forgotten*'.

Perhaps such an impression suggested it to John as a meeting place. He and Marion had been there before, many years ago with the children.

It had been a long drive from Birsett to Durham; for John long and fearful. What had he to go on? Marion had not promised to come. She had put down the phone without giving an answer. That was all - she hadn't refused. This slender hope was all he had.

If she did come, he had made up his mind: he would not mention the trip to Grodwice. He would take his chances with Graf. Would make an excuse - wife tied up with Christmas and all that. That would have to do. He wanted Marion back, not for a day trip to Eastern Europe, not to meet a job specification, but in his life, in his heart.

The decision gave him a little comfort; but he felt tired; tired and defeated. What would he do if she did not come?

'One the most striking features of the North Door of Durham Cathedral is the bronze, lion-like Sanctuary Knocker. Throughout the Middle Ages, Durham Cathedral became a place of sanctuary. A fugitive fleeing from the law wishing to claim protection used the knocker to attract the attention of the two watchmen in a chamber over the North Door. He was then admitted and given sanctuary for thirty-seven days during which time he had to choose between trial and voluntary exile. If he chose the latter, he was escorted to a port wearing a badge in the shape of the cross of St Cuthbert stitched to his shoulder and carrying a rough wooden cross tied together with rope. Once at the port he was required to embark on the next ship that was due to sail regardless of destination.' Grodwice, perhaps.

John arrived at the North Door at ten to eleven on the twenty third day of November looking for sanctuary, certainly, but not caring about at all about thirty-seven days. Only one day mattered: today. He understood with crystal clarity that if she did not come today, she would not come at all. Rebecca's words chanted a persistent litany in his mind. 'It's no use, dad, it's too late.'

There were few other people there, so he felt obvious and rather foolish as he waited. On a cold clear day, the breeze chilled his chosen sunless rendezvous. When Marion came, if Marion came, she would emerge from the South Gate onto Palace Green in full view. John fixed his eyes on the gate and longed to see her slight figure stepping into the pale morning sunlight. He must have looked at his watch ten times before the great cathedral clock struck eleven, pausing between each stroke as if giving Marion every chance to arrive on time. But it ran its course and no figure stepped from the gate. Other figures came and went but not hers. The digits on John's watch flicked over to 11.05. Reflecting John's apprehension, a cloud crossed the sun and darkened the Green. Then, in the shadow, a figure stepped out of the gate and walked round the green towards him. Marion had come.

"The train was late," she said in a rather flat voice, "I didn't mean to keep you waiting."

John struggled with his first words.

"How's Rebecca?" he said.

"She's fine; she's Christmas shopping this morning."

"Let's go inside," said John, "Its cold out here."

The choice of the cathedral as a place to talk proved an inspired, though unconsidered, choice. We might safely speculate that had the great building not quietened them the dialogue would quickly have descended into strident recriminations of the old sort. For, truth to tell, neither had come prepared. Marion was in no mood to be conciliatory. She had come looking for a way out of the pain of uncertainty: the more severe the cure, the better. John, for his part, had an unfamiliar role. He came as suppliant, and men who think they are Chief Executive material do not take comfortably to supplication.

For a while they walked in silence. Then John dived in. The early exchanges were stilted clichés. Neither wanted them, but they were the only phrases that came to mind.

"I don't like the idea of divorce."

"It seems to me the only answer. We can't go on like this."

"There is no need, we could go back to what we had."

"There's no going back, John, not after all this time."

"Well, forward then, we could start again."

This was going nowhere. They had reached the Transept and turned into the Crossing. A gothic notice invited them to sit in the Nave and pray.

"Let's sit down," said John.

"We'll keep walking," said Marion, afraid of intimacy.

They went on through the screen into the Choir.

"Look, Marion," said John, trying to break through to her, "I know where I went wrong, and I'm sorry."

"Do you?" asked Marion, "Are you?" She sounded angry – no, not angry - frustrated, fragile.

"I put my work first; that was wrong."

"A man must work."

"Not this one; not now. I'm a pensioner."

"You accepted the deal? You said you would fight them."

"I'm tired of fighting."

They had reached the Bishop's Throne.

"What will you do now?"

"That's not important. What is important is that we should be together again. I miss you, Marion."

Marion turned, looked at John and caught his eye. In it she thought she glimpsed sincerity, but she did not smile. John almost winced at her look. He pushed Grodwice deeper in his mind. She must not see it. For although he had loosened his grasp on it, he had not let go of it; for all his present sincerity it still lured him.

"You are giving up work."

"If that's what it takes."

They stopped before the tomb of St Cuthbert and involuntarily read the label:

"Borne by his faithful friends from his loved home of Lindisfarne, here, after long wanderings, rests the body of St Cuthbert. Throughout the Middle Ages it was a shrine for pilgrims and a place of miracles."

They walked on; Marion picked up the conversation.

"You said 'if that's what it takes'. What it takes for

what?"

"For us to be together again."

"Let's get this clear, John. You are saying you will give up work for good, if I come back to you. Is that it?"

"Yes, but…"

"And you think that I would want that."

Her voice had risen. A guide close by frowned at her.

"Well, I thought…"

"John, you still don't understand, do you? I don't want bargains. If you do this, I'll do that. That is not the way it was. We were not a commercial arrangement or contracting parties, we were one. We didn't always agree, and we fought our corners, but we were one and always made it up to the whole again. Until you were seduced by your job. No, not your job, the whole executive thing. You cut me off; it wasn't a separation; it was betrayal; not of me only but of Rebecca and Robert too. You still don't understand what you destroyed and at what cost. It can't be put right by a bargain; it can't be negotiated; we are not a trade union."

Marion had said this sort of thing before; the argument old, familiar and ugly. Her heart sank as she heard herself repeating it. Yet this time it felt different. Before Marion started, John did not comprehend what he had done, at the end he did. Or, at least, he caught the sense, for this time he had listened. The old pattern fractured. Marion expected counter arguments, denials, protestations. In their old formations they came marching into John's mind with banners flying, ready for action. This time John dismissed them.

The winter's sun filtered through the Millennium Window and diffused in the South Aisle, casting shadows, creating mists, confusing the eye with streaks of light. Not for ten years had John spoken to his wife the way he did now.

"You are right, Marion" he said, "I don't understand. I see what we had as through a glass darkly. I can't get it in focus, Marion. It is all a blur; I know it is still there in me somewhere. I felt it when we met in the raspberry field and when I went with Rebecca to collect her results. Did she tell you about that?"

"Yes, she did."

Marion said this quietly and quickly. She did not want John to stop speaking; this was new, different. She felt the tears in her eyes and her heart melting. Could it be? Could it be?

"I don't know what to do," John continued, "the thought of being out of work terrifies me, of never again having power and influence, of being stuck there in Birsett for the rest of my life amongst its trivialities and gossip. It depresses me."

"Does it depress the people in Birsett, Alex, for instance?"

"No, but they were born to it."

"Where were you born, John?"

"I know what you mean; it's not the place, it's me. I've grown quite fond of Birsett. It has worked its way into me, but life must be more than piddling about in that little stream, being pushed about by bureaucrats, hemmed in by regulations, fobbed off with the dregs, having no power over your own life, scraping a living, quietly rusting away. I feel I can do better than that. I must do better than that. I am beginning to feel a failure and it frightens me. The only way to break out is to get a job. I was in London a couple of weeks ago and immediately felt better. In amongst businessmen I felt stimulated, alive, part of the action."

John walked on in silence for a moment or two. Marion said nothing, knowing he had more to say.

"Yet I found it scary," he continued, "because there amongst all those suits, I did not feel me, as if it were some manifestation, as if some other life force had taken me over. Had I just forgotten what it was like? I don't know."

For the first time Marion smiled.

"You make it sound like science fiction," she said, and they both felt a connection click into place and hold; a connection of the old sort. John grasped Marion's hand. She did not withdraw it. They walked on across the South Transept, down the South Aisle, past the Miner's Memorial and case of Father's Smith's Organ. As they walked John talked of mistakes, of repentance, of confusing dreams and ambitions, Marion of regrets and lost years. But of hope, although she felt it stirring in her heart, she said nothing. Instinctively they made for the North Door as if they knew something had been accomplished, as if the great cathedral had brought them the beginnings of a benediction.

'I unhesitatingly give Durham my vote for being the best cathedral on planet earth' (Bill Bryson, Notes from a Small Island)

They came down from the mount to Emilio's on Elvet Bridge for tagliatelle and vegetarian risotto. Afterwards they went to the station and parted with a commitment to meet again in a fortnight and decide then about spending a family Christmas at Braeshiel. Marion would talk it over with Rebecca and Robert. John kissed Marion when they separated; only on the cheek, but it was a kiss.

John had not mentioned Grodwice, not in the cathedral, nor in the restaurant, not even when Marion gave him the chance over coffee. In the new spirit of the day she raised herself above her resentment and asked how he had fared at his interview.

"Ok, I suppose, it's ongoing," is what he said; nothing about the trip to Grodwice with a wife as an advantageous extra.

    Marion, for her part, did not mention Malcolm although over the wine John did wonder whether to enquire about him. Marion did not need to explain Malcolm, for there is nothing to explain: he is her church elder and a happily married man with three grown-up children. His wife was sitting in the car that day John called at Poppleton. If John had been in a healthier state of mind, he would have noticed her. If we had been less concerned with drama so would we.

CHAPTER FORTY-NINE

For all his unreconcilable prospects John found the dark days of the next week more pleasant that he had known for a while. This provided slight relief from the depressing news that had fallen on Birsett, and not only on Birsett, but on every fishing community in the country. Cod, haddock and whiting quotas to be cut by fifty-five percent. Newspapers wailed over the loss of thousands of jobs.

Thousands of jobs! How we love big numbers, but it is the small ones that do the damage: six men in the boat out of work; seven out of this fish yard, eight out of another; four in the family without an income; three weeks away from home every month in a distant hated job; two old folks facing empty days when the young folk move away; one frightened child in a strange class in a strange place; three boats left rusting in the neglected harbour when all the rest have gone; too many men and women pushed to the brink by depression; too many walking the cliffs, wondering; too many pushed over the edge.

The statistic that most concerned Alex and Helen was David. The fishing had won him; he liked everything about it: the boat, crew and camaraderie; the competition and uncertainty; the sea, sky, wind: shooting the net in darkness before dawn, hauling it, hoisting it, ripping it open, spilling the catch; the bucking streaming deck, the clatter of the gear, the hiss of cascading water, the sting of salt water on the hands and face; the smell of fish and sea, even of diesel. Best of all, riding the swell into the canyon at Hecklescar harbour after a four-day trip with fish in the hold and the prospective feel of a wad of notes in the back pocket. He envied neither princes nor pop stars.

Coddled men, however, secure in centrally heated offices who never fight the wind or feel the spray, are calculating to snuff out David's dream. Remote politicians whose floor does not buck and roll under them have a mind to agree with them. They are annoyed at the fishermen, annoyed that the solutions of the past twenty years, all their bright ideas, have not worked: license the boats, tie them up, subsidise them, decommission them, break them up; tighten the meshes, make them diamond, make them square, open up the cod-end; limit the catches - quotas for cod, quotas for haddock, quotas for whiting; change the quotas; limit the fishing days, limit the fishing grounds. Spy on the fishermen, call out the frigate, watch them from the sky, trap them when they land, confiscate the catch, fine the fishermen. We're fed up with fishermen; nothing we do works because the fishermen insist on catching fish. Stop them; that's the answer: the final solution.

Why don't you listen to the fishermen; give them their own fishing grounds to protect and conserve; trust them? We can't do that! There is a grand principle at stake: common access to a common resource; everyone must be allowed to plunder the North Sea. Besides, we'd lose our power to interfere and every politician agrees that interference from the centre, from Edinburgh, London and Brussels is good for us all. We can't have the fishermen deciding about fish. We're not hard-hearted: we'll let you catch less than half of what you caught last year and pay yourselves accordingly. Now let us hear you say thank-you. Good boys!

Alex spelled all this out for David but his son didn't want to hear. Alex told him that his chosen career led into a cul-de-sac but David wouldn't change track. As long as he could jump aboard a boat on Sunday night, he would keep going; after that he would take his chance. He had access to advice his father, the Fishery Minister, the Scientific Committee and the whole European Commission did not have. Rebecca, he revealed, thought he should go for it. Then Alex understood why the phone bill had been so high since the blackberry holiday - and why it was no use arguing with his son.

Mussent Grumble too, when he brought The Berwickshire News brought John gloomy news. Gabriel Orkney, the undertaker had handed him a funeral intimation to put in his window. Mrs Dryden, of Willie's cancer fellowship had died, quite suddenly, apparently. She had been in Grumble's shop only last week looking for a Christmas Card to send to a nephew in Canada; she wanted an iridescent card with 'Greetings from Hecklescar' on it. He had explained that the one she bought last year had been left over from the year before because people didn't buy them. He had also been left with a dozen Hecklescar Millennium Cards that he couldn't sell again, so what's the point of ordering things when people won't buy them. Mrs Dryden had accepted this exposition of retail economics and taken a *'Greetings from the Old Country'* instead. Now that he thought about it, she didn't look well. Now her intimation appeared in the window:

'Cremation at Warriston Crematorium, Edinburgh, on Monday 2nd December at 10.30. No flowers please. Donations to Cancer Research.

Signed: Jessie Collin: Relation to the Deceased: Neighbour.'

John had decided he could not go but Helen decided he must. He should go for his father's sake; people would think it strange if he didn't go; Willie seemed to be her one of Mrs Dryden's few friends and those she did have might not take the journey to Edinburgh for the service. Mr Scott said he would go with him. He had never met Mrs Dryden but had heard of her through Willie and Willie would have gone if he had been here. By proxy Willie kept faith with the fellowship.

Before John could do his dark duty, he had something to cheer him. On Friday, Dwight Graf rang to arrange the trip to Grodwice. It would take three days: fly out on the sixteenth, visit Grodwice on the seventeenth, return to the UK on the eighteenth; stay two nights in the TransContinental Praha (Prague).

At the end Graf asked whether he should make arrangements for John's wife to accompany him.

"That's what we are planning," said John, "but it might be difficult; this is a busy time for her at work." He thought Graf would identify with workload pressure.

"I'll let you know by Monday first," he said crisply, "Is that soon enough? We'll talk it over at the weekend, see if it can be done." John hoped Graf would think this was considerate; considerate, yet decisive.

The follow morning Ian (Mack) rang. Jacqui had told him that John had been selected to go to Grodwice. Congratulations, good luck! The other candidate, by the way, was Peter Metier and "on the QT, John, he's the front runner: age, mainly". This did not concern John greatly. He had already discounted it. Peter Metier had the disadvantage of not being married.

On his afternoon walk, John tried to work out what he should do about Marion and Grodwice. The easiest course would be to say nothing; excuse her from the trip; go alone and hope for the best. But this gave the advantage to Metier. The boldest (and most honest) would be to tell Marion and ask her to go, but this was so dangerous that John heard himself saying 'No' to the hedge along the back field. The cleverest course would be to invite Marion to Grodwice; tell her it constituted part of the selection process, (she would need to know that and, anyway, she knew about the job) but don't tell her about GANY's preferences for a married man; certainly, not that. But, for all his rumination, he walked up the path of Braeshiel no nearer a decision than when he left and failed to notice that the jasmine by the window, winter's promise, had dressed itself for him in sweet yellow flowers.

He needed someone to talk to, someone like Marion, attentive but straight. He could not speak to Helen or Alex because they regarded it as a simple problem with a simple answer: be straight with Marion, she's your wife. Mr Scott had been tried already and had given the same wrong answer. He decided to talk to JP; he would understand the complications.

JP readily agreed to talk but had a job in hand. He had left his boat in Birsett harbour longer than he had intended and had chosen that day to take it round to Hecklescar for the winter. However, if John would sail with him, they could talk on the way.

The day dawned bright, with a cold onshore breeze force three; a decent sailing day. Ben went too and once they were clear of the Carr Rocks and the sails set, he took control of the wheel and was told to hold course for St Abb's Head. John and JP settled themselves in the open cockpit with a mug of hot orange.

John explained the problem and sketched out the options. As he listened, JP, rolling gently to the motion of the boat, fixed his eyes on the surf-fall on the rocks at the base of the cliffs. Now and again he would glance up at the sail and mutter a quiet command to Ben. When John finished his analysis, he asked JP what he thought. JP went on watching the sea for a few minutes. At first John thought he had not been paying attention, and he appeared to confirm it by asking a question that seemed unconnected.

"What do you know about investment, John?"

"Not as much as you do," said John, a little irritated.

'A point to the west, son,' JP instructed Ben

"What do we know?" laughed JP, "We make guesses, we look at the history, then we make guesses about the future. That is all you can do."

This commercial folk wisdom grated on John; he wanted answers. He asked his question again.

"You think this Grodwice job is worth taking?"

"Yes, if that is how you want to invest your life. But what is the return? In five years, ten years what will you have that you do not have already?"

"I'll not get another chance; if I don't go for this, what do I go for?"

"Hold her steady, Ben."

"Why not settle here? You have your pension; bring Marion here, and Rebecca. Rachel tells me she's friendly with Helen's boy. If you must work, work up Gainslaw Globes. I could also put a little investment analysis work your way too."

"I'm too young to retire...."

"A poor excuse," cut in JP. "That's like throwing your money at a no-go just because you have it. But, unlike money, once you have spent your years you can't borrow more. What do you know about balance sheets?"

"Enough: what you own balanced against what you owe."

"That'll do. Think of what you own, John, think of what you have here." He swept his hand round the great circle of sea, sky, and land. "Do you really prefer four walls to this? Listen, John, can you hear the wind and the water? Would you rather listen to traffic, phones and machinery? Breathe the free air.

Would you rather breathe it recycled from the air-conditioning? Would you rather be pushing papers round a desk or arguing with pretentious prats than be engaged with the elements here? Wake up John, you have much to lose by signing yourself up to GANY."

"Let her off a bit, son."

John did not answer JP. He studied the surf and said nothing. His friend was pushing at a door already half-open, but John still wanted it closed. He felt frustrated. This was not the conversation he wanted. He wanted a simple answer, not a lecture on country pursuits. He must go to Grodwice. He needed no help with that; it lay beyond discussion. The question in mind was whether he should tell Marion or not. Should he invite her to Grodwice? How much should he tell her, if anything? Why wouldn't the man answer the question?

"John, I'm sorry", continued the banker, "forgive an old cynic who has seen too much. I am jealous, that's all. I'd give everything to be your age with as many years in the bank as you have. I would do things differently."

"Watch your leech, Ben; a touch to the wind."

"Don't listen to me," JP continued, "We can't all give it up and live like peasants or fishermen. We're all bound to the Great Mother Cow, the market. We are serfs, John, well-paid serfs, but serfs nevertheless. We feed the Cow and it feeds us; we can't leave it or it starves and if it starves, we starve. Some poor sods must keep feeding it, sods like you and me. I can feed it with cash, you seem determined to nourish it with your days and years. Are you prepared to get up every morning and feed it?"

"It has not fed you well recently by all accounts. I thought you had all been hammered," put in John by way of gentle retaliation.

"Not as bad as some," JP laughed, "I didn't buy into

the dotcom bubble, so I've fared better than most. I am now worth forty percent less than last year at this time, but sixty percent of what I had is more than sufficient. I'm not complaining. Have we learned our lesson? I doubt it. I often think that we have forgotten the intrinsic value of things and are just shovelling paper from one pile to another. We don't make anything that lasts anymore. You know that old drag dredger they've put up on stilts at the harbour end down in Hecklescar? Part of the maritime museum the QC from London is setting up."

"Yes, it's one of Brunel's isn't it?"

"Yes, Isambard Kingdom Brunel; built it in 1860, and it still works apparently. And us? What have we to show for all our stress? Where is Pinkerton? Most of the other companies I have backed have gone bust, or been taken over, or ripped off by their bosses, or turned into investment vehicles - manufactories for money and nothing else. I have grown tired of it, John. Lately, (and I'll deny I ever said this), lately I wonder if we are not simply engaged in one gigantic confidence trick, a pyramid with everybody buying everybody else's stock."

"We'll go in now, son. Turn her head towards the Hurkur Rocks, let the sheet out."

"But one of these days, John, investors will stop buying paper and look for value. Then the whole thing will implode and the edifice will come crashing down, perhaps it is already. When I first started, making money seemed the point of it all. Now I like to think I can do some good with it." He smiled. "Does that sound corny? Maybe it is; but nowadays I only back companies that make something, something I can hold in my hand, something I can see being used."

"Is that wise?"

"Probably not, but it makes sense to me. Because I can see it being made and I can see it being delivered and I can see it being used. It has a human face, John, and in the end that is the only thing that counts – somebody making a wage, somebody making something that makes life easier for somebody else; someone made a little happier. Now you know why I back our friend Flambert and why I have bought Gainslaw Globes."

"I thought you bought it because you liked Kate!" quipped John.

"I rest my case," he smiled

"Bring her head to wind, Ben, we'll take down the sails."

"But there's something else," he added "it's part of what I owe"

"What you owe?" asked John when the sails were stowed, the engine started and the boat under way once more.

"The other side of the balance sheet: what we owe."

He smiled at John but said no more as he swung the boat between the rocks at the entrance to Hecklescar bay. John thought he knew what he meant, and didn't want to risk another lecture by seeking further enlightenment. JP, he suspected, was filibustering to avoid answering his question.

"But what do I do about Marion and Grodwice?" he repeated.

'What was her reaction when you mentioned it at Durham?'

'It didn't come up,' John replied, then added hurriedly, 'but she said she didn't want me to give up work.'

"Well,' said JP slowly, 'If you are determined to go to Grodwice, ask her to go with you."

"But isn't that risky?" exclaimed John.

"Extremely," said JP as he steered the yacht into the canyon at Hecklescar harbour.

On Saturday around teatime, when he was sure she

would be in, John, in spite of his resolution on the way to Durham, rang Marion and invited Marion to come with him to Grodwice, a fortnight on Monday.

CHAPTER FIFTY

Marion had returned from Durham in a less equable frame of mind than had John. He had achieved what he had anticipated; she had acquired what she did not expect. She no sooner sat down in the train, than the euphoria of the meeting waned and by the time she reached Poppleton she had returned to discomfort. Over the year she had become reconciled to a life alone and had equipped herself to deal with it. This had left her unprepared for what had happened at Durham. Was she happy? Of course. Was she dismayed? Of course. What would she do? She didn't know. By good fortune she had gone to bed by the time Rebecca returned in the evening and mastered a goodnight bright enough to keep her daughter in the dark.

She lay awake most of the night wrestling with the conflicting claims of decayed trust, corroding resentment and reviving affection. She revisited the cathedral but two other memories haunted her. One was the encounter in the raspberry field, the other, the locked door of Braeshiel on the morning of the blackberries. The memories triggered strong and contrary currents that surged through her mind. She rose with the conflict unresolved. Should she venture or should she hold back? Could she afford, could she bear, another hurt? In the morning with Rebecca she blamed her indisposition on a touch of flu and kept the conversation on Rebecca's doings of the day before. Then she went to church. Perhaps God knows about these things.

When she came out, she had all but resolved to take John on trust. Not that the sermon or the prayers had dealt with the subject for they were concerned with religion not life. But they had given her the opportunity to think in the daylight and daylight evens up the odds of will against emotion. Her decision to gamble on goodness was an act of will for her reason gave her no counsel. It would not recognise it as a good plan, and she did not feel like it; she did not dare feel anything. She would go for it and see what happened. An act of will – and faith.

To prevent second thoughts, she told Rebecca over lunch what had happened at Durham. Rebecca, surprised and delighted, rang brother Robert immediately to persuade him to abandon his girlfriend at Christmas - they were all going to Birsett to spend it with dad. 'Yes, mum too.' 'I want to speak to mum.' 'Yes, Robert, it's true,' she said. But it did not ring true in her own mind.

John had rung Marion on the Saturday like every attentive separated husband should, to make sure she had reached home safely. He rang her again twice during the ensuing week. As they talked, they relaxed and as they relaxed the conversations became longer and friendlier, and as they became friendlier Marion's fears melted. They dealt with ordinary things: the wedding certificate for Scottish Widows and her birth certificate; her rights in the pension; the mortgage on Poppleton; thanks for the flowers; 'will you not have to reduce the monthly payment to Rebecca and me?' 'No, no need for that just yet; we'll see how things go.'

'Yes, we'll all come for Christmas, but I'm working till lunchtime on Christmas Eve.'

Then this phone call about Grodwice, this gigantic leap.

'John, why do you ask me this now? How can I answer you? I want to venture, to find again what we once had - when the children were young. Well, not only then, later too, before the job seduced you. And what kind of job is this you have in your sights, John? It seems a big, absorbing job too. In a strange country. What would I do? Away from everything I have come to depend on? Have you thought of that? No, you have not thought of that! Here is the old selfishness, John, rearing its head again. No, no, don't think like that, Marion. Remember what he said in the cathedral; he understands now that we can't go back to that; that I won't go back to that. Oh, Marion, Marion, it is you that is being selfish. He needs a job. He looked so small, so worn down, so defeated. Would I want him like that? Why is he asking me this now? Why could it not wait until I know what is happening to me, to us? Why now? But now is the time, or rather, tomorrow night; it can't wait; he is ringing back to-morrow night for an answer. If I say yes, I may find myself back where I started, worse, farther back. If I say no, it could be the end for us. Oh, John, why now? I had begun to believe we were getting somewhere.'

"No, Rebecca, I am not anxious about anything, just a return of the flu. I think I'll have a bath and an early night."

The time of waiting lasted long. The time for the call came quickly.

"Hello, Marion, have you thought about this trip to Prague? I hope it hasn't upset you. I feel bad about it now. Maybe I should have left it alone. But I thought you might enjoy the trip."

"John, I really don't know what to say. Whichever way I look at it, it seems a bad idea. It's too big a step too soon."

"I can see that, Marion, but if you could think of it just as a short holiday, that's all. Forget about the job and what might happen. I'm not the preferred candidate anyway. Just think of it as a chance to see Prague at Christmas time; as a treat."

"I don't know, John."

"Look, Marion, I understand. I really shouldn't have said anything. It was just a spur of the moment thing. Forget about it. Just leave it. I'm sorry. Look I'll see you a week on Saturday somewhere and we'll arrange for your visit to Braeshiel at Christmas. I'm looking forward to that. Just forget about Grodwice. It'll be alright."

"No, John, I'll come."

As you can imagine, Marion's decision delighted John. The delight furnished a week and a half with plans and dreams and castles in the air. In the castle, Marion, and sallying forth, King John of Grodwice, restored to power again. Do not believe him when he says it is just a holiday, he has in mind a new life; it spreads out before him like a golden road and every day takes him further along it.

Even his gloomy trip to Warriston Crematorium to honour his father's friend did not retard his progress. John was glad he attended the cremation for the farewell party was small - seven in all including a minister pulled from the duty list by a fee. Mr and Mrs Collin, her good neighbours, were there, Emily, her blind friend, and Mrs Dryden's home help, Biddy, another of the great Mitchison clan, and John and Mr Scott: a little party for such a long life, a poor endorsement of such a brave one. The minister read out a tribute from her nephew in Canada. Her husband had been notified by Mrs Collin but, due to ill health, could not make the journey.

Christmas like a bonfire on a dark cold night threw forward its light and warmth into the winter village. It touched the council houses first. A Christmas tree appeared in the window of No.10 Upper Birsett then lights in the upstairs window of 15; then the bare rowan at 21 sprouted glowing red fruit. Like a gathering frost the light spread sparkling through village; more trees in more windows, in others light arches with mechanical flickering candlelight; frantically flashing trees appeared outside front doors and, tied to the knockers, wreaths of holly, fir, and synthetic fibre with plastic cones and artificial fruits. Windows normally blind with lined curtains were left open allowing the sight of cosy firesides and decorated rooms to warm nosy neighbour and curious stranger alike.

The Great Spirit of the season crept along the Hecklescar road to the bungalows and villas. At Dam Brezi it transformed a grotesque hedge into a reindeer with a red nose. Down the brae it ran (the spirit, not the reindeer), past Mr Scott's, Coastguard's Row and the kirk, to the harbour cottages, then along the road at the foot of the cliff, to Fisher's Row, touching each house, stopping only when it had blessed them all. Number One Partan Row received it last and placed in the window a silver tree bearing golden fruit; on the front patio, for Ben's sake, an eight-foot tree flashed bright defiance to a sullen winter's sea.

Up the brae, Dot and Spot icicled the eaves of the village hall with dripping light and Melinda the artist decked three of the six lampposts with five-foot hangings of the Kings, the Shepherds and the Holy Family in gold, red and flaming orange. At the school, snowmen, robins, and Christmas trees of all shapes and sizes cluttered windows peppered with cotton wool snow. At Birsett Inn a board outside proclaimed

'Festive Lunches

*Smoked Salmon
Turkey and all the Trimmings
Christmas Pudding/Sherry trifle
Mince Pies: £8.95
Coffee & mints: £1.50
Free bottle of wine with every meal for 4.'*

The new owners hung an illuminated sign on the gable: *'Be safe this Christmas'*; the word is they got it free from the brewery as their contribution to this year's anti-drink campaign.

These sights, however, were nothing compared to Batman's house. Carloads detoured from the Hecklescar road to take it in and others from the Great North Road would have done so had they known it was there. Uninhibited by any artistic ability and unrestrained by any woman, every Christmas Batman transforms his house into a winter palace of light. This year's theme is Harry Potter. A hardboard sheet panelled in purple and blood red and studded with bulbs for nails has transformed the council front door into the gothic entrance of Hogwarts School for Wizards; eerie stalagmites hang from the eaves; bats with red eyes hover from the clothes poles: an owl in dazzling yellow sits on an upstairs window sill and hoots when you clap your hands; a swollen green toad glows on the front step. All the windows are framed with lights flashing and twinkling and, if you listen carefully, playing Christmas pop songs. Glowing reindeer labelled *"Hagrid's Magical Creatures"* gallop over the walls and light streamers squirm across the lawn masquerading as snakes wriggling round cauldrons and broomsticks.

What does it matter if Hermione resembles last year's Snowwhite in a black frock and Harry and Ron Weasley two of the Dwarfs in pointed hats? They are flamboyant, floodlit, and friendly; no one leaves without a smile and a donation to The Royal National Society for Deep Sea Fishermen.

Christmas touched the hearts of the people too, sparking excitement in the children, determination in the women and blind panic in the men, as Santa letters were posted, secret presents were purchased and savings poured out of leaking bank accounts. Folk fretted about Christmas cards, the young hesitating over Mr and Mrs in case their friends had separated during the year, and the old cautious about sending one at all in case theirs had died. Along the night streets and up and down the dark brae crept phantom postmen, stalking up paths, pushing those same cards through letter boxes and scuttling away to escape detection: cut out the Post Office, save the stamps, do-it-yourself, but don't get caught!

In Braeshiel, Christmas was welcomed with open arms. John looked ahead to a fortnight of warm satisfaction. First there rose the trip to Grodwice (with the tingling prospect of a self-restoring job at the end of it) followed by the blessing of a Christmas with his restored family. His star had suddenly risen; glad tidings of great joy!

Advent indeed. But Advent is also the time of reckoning - for our sins, not only of commission, but of omission too, things left undone, truths not told; can we get away with those; can he? He thought so. He bought a wreath and put it on the door, Morag brought him some holly; he ordered a Christmas Tree from Delightful. (Do not enquire where he gets them.) When Mr Scott arrived on Sunday evening, he entered into the season by asking for the Christmas mugs seeing as it was now the first day of Advent. He described them: Victorian street scenes, tall snowy houses, a snowy church and snowy trees and wrapped up Victorians trudging through snow beneath a starry snowy sky.

"Your father always took out them out for Advent and we used them until the Twelfth Day. Silly old men."

John could not recall having seen them but Mr Scott knew where there were kept - in the kitchen cupboard. At John's invitation he hauled himself through to fetch them, but returned empty handed.

"I can't find them," he said.

"Margaret!" exclaimed John and the following morning rang up his sister at her shop.

"You haven't seen two Christmas mugs dad had, have you? Mr Scott said there were in the kitchen cupboard. Victorian snow scenes."

Had she seen them! She was looking at them as he

talked; in the display cabinet labelled *'Bygone Christmases, price: £10.99 or £20 the pair'.*

"No, I can't say I have, but I'll look in the box Roddam brought from Braeshiel. We haven't had time to unpack all the stuff. If I find them do you want them back?"

"Yes," said John, "they seem to mean something to Mr Scott."

"You weren't thinking of giving them to him?" She sounded mildly alarmed.

"No," said John, "they'll stay at Braeshiel. If you find them send them on."

"No need for that," said Margaret, "We'll bring them when we bring the presents, if you can wait. By the way, John, what are you doing for Christmas? You could come here if you like. There'll just be me and Roddam and Roddam's aunt. Abigail has been invited to the South of France, by the head of...... by a friend. What do you say?"

"No thank you," said John with some satisfaction, "I'm spending Christmas with my family."

It sounded delicious; Margaret's ensuing silence more so; John sensed a coup de grace.

"With who?"

"With Marion, Rebecca and Robert."

"What? You are going to York?"

"No, they are coming here," said John as the fatal thrust.

"Oh, how nice....... That's good....... I tell you what...... we might take a run down ourselves, to see them...... say Boxing Day."

Serves you right, John for being smug. How are you going to get out of that?

'No, I'm sorry, madam, they're sold.'

Advent also brought salvation to Colin of Gainslaw Globes. It happened in this wise. On a cold clear frosty morning, Flambert drove up to the factory in a Lexus SC430 Cabriolet with the hood down, dressed like Dr Zhivago in a Cossack hat and a fur coat. He needed a part for a prototype he had to demonstrate in New York. He had to have it before Christmas: the screen aperture frame for the top-of-range. Charlie had tried everything he knew but it was still flashing. The tool, he had said and said again, and had said every day for the past week to Flambert, needed modification. Now Flambert had arrived to see him say it again - and to tell Charlie again to fix it.

"It needs a toolmaker and I'm not a tool maker."

"Well, get me one," demanded Flambert.

"There's none round here," said Charlie.

"Yes, there is," put in Kate, "There's Colin."

"Colin?" said John, looking at Kate.

"Colin?" exclaimed Flambert, "Who is Colin?"

"Kate's husband," said John, "He ran the company before......before JP took over."

"Is he any good?" Flambert asked Kate.

"He's a very good toolmaker."

"He is," confirmed Charlie.

"Then why isn't he here?" demanded Flambert

"Because he's been ill," said John.

"What with - broken leg, two broken arms?"

"No," said John, and looked again at Kate.

"He's had a nervous breakdown," she said flatly,

"Nonsense," said Flambert, "That's no excuse. Where is he?"

"He's at home," said Kate.

"Well, fetch him," ordered Flambert

"He won't come for me," said Kate, "I've tried." This came as news to John.

"Then I'll fetch him," said Flambert, "Where do you live?"

Kate gave him the address. John went with him to show him the way.

"You wait in the car; we don't want to overpower him," said Flambert who had no other intention in mind.

John stayed in the car and after half an hour Flambert came out with his arm round Colin's shoulder. Colin looked ill and apprehensive. All the way back Flambert effused screen aperture frames, the tool, flashing and modification. At the factory he marched Colin through the office and into the workshop. There he stood over Colin whilst he removed the tool from the machine, then hauled him off to the tool room. He stayed with him for six hours, until nine at night. By then the tool had been modified, the part was running and Colin had come home. The Lord has visited his people.

Where Flambert spent the night, John did not know. One minute he sat in the office, the next he had gone like a horseman in the night.

John and Marion met on Saturday in York and I am pleased to say that nothing significant happened. It resembled the old intimate, ordinary days, except perhaps that John was more attentive and Marion more considerate. They admired the street decorations, looked round the shops, had lunch, and made arrangements for the Christmas visit: John would provide the Christmas Lunch, something Marion would never have allowed had they been on better terms.

They talked little about the trip to Prague, John anxious

not to disturb the arrangement, Marion disturbed by it. Before John went for the train, they stepped out of the frantic streets into the quiet church of St Martins le Grand, in Coney Street, thanking God for reawakening love and praying for tranquillity to let it flower again. Marion told John that she would be in this church on the Sunday evening before Christmas singing in her choir. Her choir? Marion in a choir? He then remembered that in the distant days, at Clydebank when they first met, she was in a choir, the Clydebank Lyric. He had forgotten that she liked to sing. He told her that on same evening he would be listening to the Messiah in The Queens Hall in Edinburgh. Nothing so grand for us, she laughed, just Christmas carols and inspirational songs; Fiona sang in the choir too. Then before they left, in the seats there, they kissed. Is that allowed in a church? Surely.

CHAPTER FIFTY-ONE

The arrangements for lunch on Christmas Day were revised two days later when Marion spoke to Rachel on the phone. Rachel would provide the meal; they would be glad of the company. John was relieved. So were Marion and Rebecca.

On Tuesday, John went in good spirits to the School Christmas concert at the Village Hall. I would like to invite you to the next one for, if ever an event captures the spirit of Christmas, this is it, and we must all drink in the spirit of Christmas when we can for what else will sustain us through the winter? I would like to invite you to the next one but there may not be a next one. The school roll is falling and those entrusted with the welfare of our children are planning their deportation. After Christmas they are taking away the infants' mistress, Mrs Douglas, veteran of thirty Christmas concerts. Who will produce next year's concert?

'No whining you lot! What do villagers know about demographics, universal standards, lifelong learning, resource allocation? Do you understand budgets? No, I thought not! They think that education is just a matter of teaching the bairns to write, read and count and putting on concerts at Christmas.'

You had better make sure that you take it all in this year.

Come to the long wooden hut next to the school. You will find yourself among friends. Here you will meet Helen and Alex, Delightful, Kit and Dod. Cecil from Surrey is here but not his wife; she's in a care home now. There is Batman still making way with Lizzie Mitchell by the look of it; Jimmy Possum's just come in, and behind him Duncan and Sandy, Willie's old dominoes companions and behind them Bessie Raeburn with her niece. Dave Pallin, of the Boy Peter, has run into Dot; I think she's telling him he's late with his two dozen mince pies. Gloria is here to see her bairns perform and this year will do it without tears. Sitting next to her is Avril who has left her husband to live with her accountant boyfriend in Hecklescar: deserted and deserter together. Avril's daughter Jessica lives with her granny now to allow her to continue to come to Birsett School with her friends. Jessica plays the innkeeper's wife. That's Rachel arriving now with Ben. Mr Scott has gone in beside her so she will not think herself a stranger. David is standing at the back with the other young fishermen, some of them young fathers. They won't sit down and will pretend the kid's stuff on the stage does not much touch them. Morag and Calum are about somewhere. And there is Wanda peeking out from the kitchen door with Susan, little Johnny's mother; they'll be on tea duty later.

The concert this year, well, every year, is the Christmas story. We have had space men and animals tell it but this year it is the old story told from the point of view of "The Hoity-Toity Angel": an angel with attitude. She believes she is the "most stupendous angel in all the starry universe" and takes exception to singing for shepherds and babies in cattle troughs; she prefers the three kings and Herod. In the end she gets her come-uppance (or rather come-downance) in the stable among dumb beasts and common folk. Mr Scott disapproves of this dumbing-down of the Christmas story, preferring the mystery of the old tale told in awe, but he is prepared to thole it if his ambitious executive friend picks up the message of treasure hidden in the ordinary and mundane.

The lights have gone down and the children march down the aisle and squat at the front of the stage until it is their turn to take part. Mrs Douglas nods her head to Mrs Little on the piano. Mrs Little (musical director, peripatetic music teacher, wife of the gasman, pianist) sounds a note; the children stand and sing, "O little town of Bethlehem". In stilted actions and carefully learned speech, they lead us through the story, take us to Bethlehem, introduce us to Gabriel, Joseph, Mary, Shepherds, three Wise Men, a nasty Herod and his henchmen, a galaxy of little stars and a host of Angels. We can see that Torquil and Quentin are shepherds; Louise, our own heroine, is the eponymous Hoity-Toity Angel having given up the star role of Mary, the Mother of Jesus, to Julie, Johnny's sister, even though she is just a beginner. If we are willing, we can let the children lead us to see what they see with perfect clarity - the mystery of God come through all eternity to this night and across all the universe to the village hall in Birsett. It would be ungrateful to resist them for they have practised for months to bring us the saving message and we are all in need of it. They have worked hard for your entertainment; do not deny them your pleasure. Closing song: full chorus and all principals: "Good Christian Men rejoice"; women too; then switch the urn on for the tea.

Morag, although no longer a pupil, has volunteered as curtain drawer, which partly explains why the curtains jammed after the Herod scene and have not been used since.

The children take their curtain call bowing stiffly from the waist, as instructed, and grinning at their acclamation. Lady Flemington steps forward to say how jolly an evening we have all had and aren't the children jolly good and don't they jolly well deserve a round of applause. Then by a contrivance she steers her little speech towards decorating our homes for the Festive Season in a responsible manner and hints at an objection to villagers pillaging the holly trees up her drive.

Morag who has been peeping from behind the curtain suddenly disappears behind it and John guesses precisely where his holly came from.

In more generous mood, Lady Flemington produces a bag full of sweet bars of various kinds and gives one to each child. She does it every year yet the children still make a fair show of being surprised. Then she announces mince pies and tea. The doors to the back hall are flung open to reveal tables of them, plate upon plate of them, with Wanda, Susan, Dot, Spot and others waiting to serve. There's tea, coffee and orange juice for the bairns. We had better hurry or we'll end up with those big rock-like mince pies at the end; Wanda brought them. Go for those on the cake stand with the open tops, they're Dave Pallin's (the scone man), made to a secret recipe; he makes the mincemeat himself. If he was anything like as good a fisherman…. shh…. don't be like that, it's Christmas! The sparkling, decorated hall fills with the clatter of cups, the banter and laughter of adults, the murmur of gossip and intrigue, and the skirling delight of children running, dancing, screaming. In the racket, the raffle is drawn and ten prizes are awarded; Helen wins the cake; she put it in. John, free of the anxieties that have plagued him and open to the spirit of the season feels the warm comfort of the event, feels the affection, feels at home. An encounter, however, an overshadowing encounter, many miles away, is, at this very moment, bearing down upon his dream.

John's deceit, as we know, is conscious but not vicious. There would come a time when it could be revealed without risk; but not yet and not now. Yet a circuitry of circumstances had already decreed that now will be the time. Had John not recruited Ian, had Ian not gone to work for Jacqui, had Fiona and Marion not been friends or had not remained friends, had GANY not preferred a married man, or had not mentioned it to Jacqui and Jacqui to Ian, had Ian not been close enough to Fiona to talk to her about his work and about John's chances, then John and Marion would have gone to Grodwice and consummated their rekindling love. But the signal tracked unerringly through this labyrinth, taking always the route to danger. Yet still there was a chance that the switch would not be tripped.

Then at the choir practice on the eleventh of December, six days before the Grodwice trip Marion mentioned the trip to Fiona, mentioned it to her friend with pleasure. Fiona at the gate of all these circumstances opened it. The spark leapt, she jumped to the wrong conclusion, the conclusion that Ian and she had longed for and wrongly imagined: that GANY's desire for a married man had brought them together again. Fiona's relief loosened her tongue.

"Ian said that when John heard that GANY wanted a married man he would come to his senses."

"What do you mean?" asked Marion.

Fiona realised immediately what she had done, but she could not undo it. She tried to explain that she may have misunderstood Ian, that even if she had not, she was sure that GANY's preference was just that; a preference, nothing more. She tried to convince Marion that John would not be so calculating as to pull such a stunt. She pleaded with her friend to take John at face value, that he had told Ian that more than anything else he wanted them to be together again. It proved futile. The spark detonated the suspicions that Marion had so assiduously battened down. The explosion flared and spread. Fiona caught it first, and from Fiona, Ian; from Marion, Rebecca felt it and from Rebecca, Robert.

It was Ian that conducted it to John; he rang him the following day. John shuddered at the shock but did not panic. He immediately set out for York. Marion, he assumed, would not be at work, but he underestimated his wife. Marion would tackle this sickener the way she had tackled the others. When he arrived at Poppleton shortly after three, she was not at home; she had gone to work. Rebecca had called off college, but Marion had gone to work.

"You pig!" cried Rebecca when she opened the door to her father, "you unscrupulous pig!"

Her eyes were red with crying. Never before had she spoken to her father this way. She did not invite John in, but he walked in anyway. He sat down and for a long time accepted the abuse Rebecca heaped on him. His daughter had not yet mastered guile so she used no logic, deployed no arguments, she simply let loose the anger surging within her. John had rehearsed his reasons and his explanations but they were no match for this. He painfully and painstakingly tried to explain to his daughter what he thought and felt, but his words sounded contrived, his thoughts pre-packed. He tried to be completely honest. He could not have been so with anyone else. The sight and sense of his distraught daughter, the evidence of her betrayed trust, his shattering of her dreams, dug out from him that which he had always known but never admitted: the crushing knowledge of what his ambition had done. He protested that he would give up the job at Grodwice if that would win Marion back; he had offered it, that the job meant less to him than his family. As he said it, he knew it was not true. He wanted Marion but equally desperately he wanted the top job at Grodwice. He wanted both and, for all his rationalising and protestations had not given up the conviction that he could have what he wanted.

It hit him then that arts of deception learnt in his career had seeped into his life and corrupted it. That what he called persuasion was lying; that what he counted leadership was cheating; that his positive thinking was simply fraud. All his absorbed techniques of bending the truth and finessing lies that kept the team together, the workforce sweet, and the directors off his back had become instinctive. As he tried to convince his daughter of his integrity, he learnt that he no longer possessed it. He had wandered into a far country and no longer knew where he was. In the end he stopped speaking; in the middle of a sentence, he stopped speaking.

Rebecca detected the change and softened. She did not resume her tirade. They sat for fully half-an-hour without speaking; Rebecca no longer capable of attacking her father, John no longer able to defend himself. Then they heard the door and Marion walked into the room. She showed no surprise at her husband's presence. John stood up and moved towards her.

"I can explain," he said urgently.

"Save your explanations, John," she said firmly, "You use too many."

She turned and walked away.

"It is not what you think," he said desperately following her to the door. She walked upstairs. John turned back into the room.

"She won't listen," he complained to his daughter.

"It is too late for words, dad, and too great; words are no use."

John looked at her, struggled to speak and then not to speak. Then left.

Marion, when she heard the door slam came downstairs. Rebecca told her mother what had happened between them and told her that she thought she knew why her father had given up so easily. But she could not explain it.

'Dad has lost himself,' she said.

Marion had no heart to push her further.

CHAPTER FIFTY-TWO

If you believe in God or the Devil, you might attribute what happened in the next two days to divine intervention or satanic influence. If you believe in neither you will find support for the principle that when things are bad, they can always get worse.

The day after he came back from York, John made his way down the brae to complain to JP and Rachel about what had happened. He was, as you might expect, in a foul mood not least because he knew he had created the mess himself. But (as we all do when we fall into our own hole) he looked for someone to join him in the blame. JP had urged him to ask Marion to go to Prague; if he had argued against it, he might not have risked it. JP must take his share, but what John saw at JP's door compounded his complaint - not of bad advice only but of bare-faced duplicity. As he approached, he noticed a car, a top of the range Jaguar. JP must have a visitor. He hesitated, then continued towards the door. As he drew near, the door opened and out stepped a tall man dressed in a baggy suit. He looked towards John and John saw his face, the face of a farmer, round, rough, with the eyes of a ferret, small, darting. He recognised him immediately: The Knight, Sir Frank Wantley. Both men froze. Then Sir Frank unlocked his car, got in and drove away, passing John without a glance.

John stood for a while then, confused and dismayed, he turned from his friend's door and walked back up the brae. By the time he had reached Braeshiel he had figured it out. It had been a fix! He saw it now. JP all along had argued against his pursuing a case against Loyalty, had tried to distract his attention to Gainslaw Globes, had tried to keep him in Birsett where he wouldn't embarrass the Loyalty Board.

'Who had first recommended Sir Frank to Loyalty? JP! Who had recommended Belinda Boyd to me? JP! What had she advised? Settle! And lately, JP's antipathy to Grodwice; he didn't want me loose in the business world. He wanted me here in Birsett, cooped up with fishermen and peasants. It all fitted. Then this latest fiasco: he had deliberately urged me to take Marion because he knew, he *knew*, it might scupper the whole deal; that Marion would find out and would refuse to go and I wouldn't go either. It would sicken me so I wouldn't go.'

Now if we were able to tap John on the shoulder, we could point out to John that these interventions by JP could be reckoned as kindnesses. But we are not able, and even if we were, we would be ignored for John is in no mood for reason. He wants someone to blame, and who better than a friend. He scrabbled around in his memories for material of JP's deceit and found it everywhere. He picked up all the dark threads and wove them into a sombre cloth of his own design. The world had turned nasty; he would stitch it up as he saw it.

Then he got caught up in an event that seemed not to concern him at all. Yet it disturbed him profoundly and counselled him at a level deeper than reason. It had to do with Wanda, Marvin and Rott.

Dave Pallin, who we met in the company of scones and mince pies, skippered the Boy Peter, a crabber sailing out of Birsett. Dave had a canny streak and from experience knew that in the week before Christmas the price of lobsters soared.

Mysteriously for the past few years he had been able to land a bumper catch in that week after three or four weeks of poor returns. Not mysterious at all, according to Delightful who had discovered his secret: Dave had strung a fleet of net cages just behind the Carr Rocks about half-a-mile offshore with a dhan to mark the spot. For the weeks of December, at the end of each fishing trip, Davie transferred some of his catch to the cages. The unknowing identified it as a fleet of ordinary craves. The week before Christmas, Davie raided the cages and reaped his harvest of higher prices. However, others had heard of the Boy Peter's treasure. Rott had heard.

No one knew Rott knew until Marvin went looking for him on the Friday after John's Wednesday trip to York. This day is one of those dull cold December days that never lightens, but Armitage Antiques in Hecklescar is bright and inviting as Marvin enters just before closing time. He is there to buy Wanda a present, a very special Christmas present, something Wanda has always wanted: an engagement ring. He has scraped together six hundred pounds, partly from what Wanda has given him as pocket money, partly from under-the- counter sales of cooked clawless lobsters (fish merchants won't buy lobsters without claws), and partly from off–balance-sheet activities organised by Delightful.

Do not underestimate this gift he is buying, the huge amount he is prepared to pay, the sacrifice and discipline that has gone into saving it, or the magnificent waste of money for a crab fisherman with four mouths to feed. He has spotted a ring in the window; a large green stone that he hopes might be an emerald surrounded by clear ones that he thinks might be diamonds. He feels foolish. He isn't dressed for buying engagement rings having just offloaded the day's catch of crabs and lobsters at SeaNorth fish processors.

He brings the smell of shellfish and diesel into the shop but Nigel behind the counter serves him as if he were Lady Flemington herself. He spreads a velvet cloth on the counter and lays the chosen ring on it. Marvin picks it up and examines it. It is a ring, a gold, emerald and diamond ring. It is what he wants. He is sure Wanda will like it. How much? Six thousand five hundred pounds! How does he say he cannot afford it? He does not need to. Nigel suggests it is rather big; would he not be better with something less showy? He produces another, emerald too, a smaller emerald, less diamonds. Two thousand! Still suppressed alarm.

'What about this one, sir? A lovely ring, not an emerald, but dark and beautiful, a garnet with a diamond on each side, restrained, elegant, refined'.

How much?

'To you: eight hundred pounds.'

He has his six hundred pounds - and the other two hundred in his pocket, part of his week's share that he must hand to Wanda when he gets home tonight. But his cousin Rott owes him, not two hundred, not eight hundred, but a thousand or two over the years never paid back. Now is the time.

"I'll take it," he says. "Would you put it in a box please, one of those little ring boxes?"

Marvin went straight to Rott's door, his singles flat in Linkim Square. He wasn't there. To the Flemington Arms; not there: The Old Barque; not there: The Legion; not there: Hill's Turf Accountant in the High Street; not there: Rowena; not there: The Basking Shark; in the bar.

"Hallo, our kid, what'll you have?"

Money, Dermot, is what your cousin will have; what you owe him; he'll take two hundred for now.

Rott, if he had the money didn't want to give it to Marvin. But he could not shake him off, tempt him away; could not threaten him or divert him, so he told him about the Boy Peter's treasure. Told him that there must be close on a thousand fucking quid crawling around in the cages; told him that he could offload them to a man up the Forth and they'd share the takings; told him there was more than two hundred quid there. Marvin would not hear of it. Rott reminded him they had robbed craves before. Marvin refused. All they needed was a boat. The Aurora would do and you have the key. Marvin refused. He didn't have the key anyway; it was in the house. Marvin demanded his money, threatened to beat it out of him. Marvin beat Rott! Then, to Marvin's surprise, Rott relented.

"I have two hundred up the house. I'll need to go and get it."

"I'll come."

"No, no need, I'll be straight back. You stay here and have a drink. OK if I take the van? An export for our kid, Geoff."

Five minutes later, Wanda doing Quentin's homework in No 13 Upper Birsett heard the front door slam and expected to see Marvin. She saw Rott.

"Hello, darling."

"Where's Marvin?"

"At SeaNorth in Hecklescar. I've come for the key to the boat. Usual place?"

He walked into the kitchen; Wanda followed him.

"Why are you taking the key?"

"Marvin wants it."

"Why?"

"How the fuck would I know? He told me to come and get it."

Wanda stood in the doorway and blocked it.

"I don't think you should take it."

"Marvin wants it."

"Then Marvin should come for it."

"But Marvin hasn't come for it, I have."

He moved to confront Wanda. He smelt of drink and smoke. She did not move. He put his face into her face. Then she felt the change, saw it in his eyes and sensed it in his body: a shift of purpose. He grabbed her and forced his mouth into her mouth and his body against hers. His hands grabbed her buttocks. She broke free and ran into the room beside Torquil and Quentin. The two boys started up. Quentin went white. Rott stormed in and seized Wanda.

She screamed, "No, no." Torquil squealed.

"Come here, you slag," said Rott groping at her trousers.

"This is rape, rape!"

Rott paused.

"Rape?" he sneered, "You? Me? Everybody knows about you and me. You're a slag, Wanda, and your boys are bastards. Rape! No-one will believe you. Come on, enjoy it!"

"Run," she shouted to Quentin, "Run, get Auntie Helen."

The little boy ran for the door. Rott let go of Wanda to stop him.

"Come back, you little bastard."

Quentin did not come back. He ducked under Rott's flailing arms and shot out of the door into the night.

"Run, Quentin, run!" his mother shouted.

Run, Quentin, run! You are all the hope your mother has. The society that should protect your little family has conspired against it; has left your mother defenceless. It has bred the likes of Rott and encourages him run free; his instincts must be expressed and his behaviour not inhibited. Run, Quentin, run! Before your mother becomes a footnote in a novel with Rott as hero, or as a half-naked extra in a movie with Rott as star, for such a life is celebrated nowadays. Run,

Quentin, run! Your mother fights for decency, but decency is mocked. If Rott succeeds, some will blame her, some will laugh, some will snigger. Only a few will pity her shame and disgrace. Run, Quentin, run for Auntie Helen for she is such a one! Run, Quentin, run! You are all the hope your mother has. Run, Quentin, run!

But the little boy did not need to fetch Auntie Helen. His escape switched Rott back to his original intention. With the key of the Aurora in his hand he ran out of the front door. Wanda heard the van start. She rang SeaNorth, then The Basking Shark and called Marvin home. When Helen arrived. Wanda told her the story, but they did not understand the significance of the boat key until Marvin stormed in and discovered that Rott had taken it.

"You find Del; I'll try to stop him. The Aurora's lying inside the Boy Peter; he'll have a job getting her out."

"Don't go, Marvin," pleaded Wanda. But he shot out of the door.

"Don't fight," she shouted to the wind as he ran along the street. Then she went in and pulled her bairns to her. Helen rang Delightful but failed to raise him. She rang Kit: no answer. Del will be at Birsett Inn; he always goes on a Friday night. Helen ran to fetch him.

Twenty minutes later in Braeshiel John was moaning to Alex about the weather and …. well, about everything else, when Del burst in.

"We need the Silver Cord," he cried, "Rott has taken the Aurora to raid Davie's cages. Marvin's gone after him but he'll not stop him."

The three men ran out into the darkness and down the brae to the harbour. There, the sight of familiar things out of place made it strange. Under the cold orange lamps the Boy Peter swung loose, bobbing, turning, slewing in the middle of the basin. Aurora's empty berth expressed a presence more significant than the boat. Alongside the berth a confusion of fish boxes and craves disordered the quay. A cold drizzle blew across the lights and an uneasy swell chattered among the boats as if excited by happenings just witnessed.

"The boat's gone," said Del, "There's been a fight."

"Poor sod Marvin," muttered Alex.

John instinctively glanced down into the dark water and saw half-submerged fish boxes swirling and heaving in the swell as if in a ghastly dance. He shuddered: what else, who else, might be down there? Alex caught his eye and read his thoughts.

"Nah" he said nervously. The swell clanged one of the boxes against the iron ladder. Both men started.

The three men boarded the Silver Cord then captured and secured the Boy Peter. Alex nosed the Silver Cord out into the long swell; into the black night beyond the wall; into the narrow channel between the rocks that menace the harbour mouth. As the lights of the harbour fell behind, their senses, diminished in scope, increased in intensity. They became acutely aware of the looming sky above, the cold drizzle around, the restive sea beneath, and of all these together and more as if they had entered some other dimension. They took comfort in the familiar steady throb of the engine; it masked the sea sounds of the night. Delightful and John went forward but they could see little. The quarter moon that had half-lighted Rott's way through the rocks now hid in clouds leaving his pursuers to grope forward in darkness. John marvelled at Alex's ability to thread his boat through the channel.

"He can't see," he hissed to Del.

"No," replied Del, "but he kens."

They cleared the growling rocks.

"He'll be laid up behind the Carrs," shouted Delightful

from the bow.

"Or on them," muttered Alex to himself in the wheelhouse.

The mention of Rott increased the men's apprehension: he is not the sort of man you seek out on a dark night. Del rummaged in the spare box in the bow and produced two lengths of heavy rubber hose. He gripped one like a truncheon and gave the other to John: John trembled as he took hold of it: he doubted if he could use it. The boat probed forward through the brooding water yard by yard, until suddenly a white wraith of surf materialised just off the starboard bow.

"West Carr," shouted Del. Alex swung the boat away and hove to. The swell surged over the rocks and clacked along the side of the boat. There was no sign of the Aurora. Alex edged his boat to East Carr; nothing. They found the dhan on the end of Dave's fleet of cages and followed it along to the other end; nothing. Wherever the Aurora was, it wasn't here.

"Shut the engine down," suggested Del, "See if we can hear anything."

At first, they heard nothing but the slap of the waves against the boat, the hiss of sea over rock and the low rumble of breakers along the shore. Then Del heard it.

"I can hear her,"

"Where?"

"North! No, in, in! She's further in!"

John listened and heard the dull beat of an engine. The hair on the back of his neck stiffened. Alex nosed the Silver Cord towards the shore; the night enveloped them; the wheelhouse searchlight searched but caught only the rocking foremast and the rolling bow. The rumble of breaking swell grew louder.

"Switch her off again," Del shouted.

The boat bucked sullenly under their feet. The grumbling sea-sounds occupied their ears once more; the boat creaked and complained, water slopped and chattered along the hull; not far off, waves growled and hissed on the shore. Then the disembodied throb of an engine.

"She's not far away. North a bit. Stay out though; we're close in to Breeches Rock."

Alex restarted the engine and edged the Silver Cord towards the phantom boat. They strained their eyes forward into the blackness; lumpy waves surged and soughed all around them. Alex shut off the engine. The throb of the Aurora lay closer. He powered up again and swung the Silver Cord towards the sound: in a hundred yards then stop; pick up the beat; chase the sound; switch off; stop; listen. The engine pulse sounded faint but distinct against the long low rumble of swell tumbling into the base of the cliffs; the Aurora was close. The Silver Cord bucked and reared in troubled water.

"Ye'd better pull away," shouted Del to Alex through the wheelhouse window, "We're too close in; pull away."

Alex, silent and intense, drove the boat on. The low thunder of wave on rock filled their ears. John could no longer hear the Aurora. But the fishermen could - both of them.

"Back off," yelled Del, "She's gone."

"I can hear her," said Alex.

"Pull away," yelled Del.

At that moment the veiling clouds drew back from the moon. Immediately in front of them towering cliffs reared up into the night sky; at the boat's bow a tumult of white water. Away to starboard Breeches Rock leapt white mouthed from the sea. But off the port bow, something moving: a pallid blur dancing in the darkness. It resolved into the white flash on the Aurora's bow lifting and falling in the swell. The wheelhouse appeared, then the whole boat, materialising from the gloom like a bowing ghost, not a hundred yards away. Her engine was running but not engaged; she sailed only at the whim of wind and tide. Del gripped the length of hose and motioned to John to do the same. John's heart pounded in his chest. Alex eased the Silver Cord towards the Aurora.

"What's he doing here?" John whispered to Del.

"He's not here," Del mumbled, to convince himself if no-one else. "There's nobody on the boat. She's adrift."

Alex brought the Silver Cord alongside the Aurora. He raked the dark boat with the searchlight on the wheelhouse. The three men scanned her from bow to stern. Nothing living moved on her.

"Alloa" shouted Del.

No reply, no living movement.

"Be careful," said John, "He might be hiding."

Conscious of their danger, awe-struck by the scene before them, they fell dumb. They were close under the cliff now; its rugged and contorted flanks thrust upward to dissolve in brooding darkness above them. Less than fifty yards away breakers shattered in turbulent fury among the reefs and rocks at the cliff's foot; glowing spray leapt high in the air then fell back hissing and cascading into the sea; the roar filled the men's ears and battered their senses; hungry white water licked at them from the shore; spindrift hung in the air and drifted, billowing, up the cliff face. Breeches Rock crouched close by, now lurking beneath the waves, now snarling above them. And amongst all this, like flotsam in a maelstrom, the puny throbbing Aurora, lunging, powerless, helpless.

"There is no-one aboard," Del roared over the tumult. "Bring her alongside and I'll board her."

The Silver Cord eased forward, lurching and rolling in the shallow water. The gap between the two boats narrowed then closed. Del leapt aboard his boat, truncheon in hand:

John leapt after him, scared, a knot in the pit of his stomach. Del crept to the wheelhouse and kicked open the door. The wheelhouse was empty. He switched on the navigation lights then the lamps that lit the deck. They lit up an empty boat. Wherever Rott was he wasn't on the Aurora. Nor was Marvin.

Del engaged the engine and swung the boat away from the rocks into deeper water. Then a sound above the noise of the engine attracted his attention: he motioned to John and pointed forward to where Kit normally stood to haul the creels.

"The hauler's running."

John caught the circles of reflected light as the winch trundled slowly and patiently, round and round, rumbling and tumbling, round and round in obedience, but in obedience to no-one, hauling nothing. For a moment neither man moved as their eyes searched the space behind the hauler for a presence they could not see. Then Del stepped out of the wheelhouse and forward to the controls. He pulled out the clutch; the hauler stopped. Although the engine throbbed on, it created a silence; as if a life had been cut off.

"He must have been hauling when........."

When what?

Del did not need to say.

"We'd better call out the lifeboat," he radioed to Alex.

"Are we looking for one or two?"

"One only.... I hope."

Until the lifeboat arrived the two boats searched the sea, the shore and the rocks and circled round and in and out and back. Even after the lifeboat arrived, they stayed, quartering the sea, motoring close into land, searching. But they did not find Rott; nor did the lifeboat, nor the coastguards with their lamps and the torches along the shore, among the shadows of the rocks or dark down in the gullies. They called off the search at ten o'clock and resumed at dawn.

Next day Rott was found not by the coastguards, the lifeboat, the Aurora or the Silver Cord. Dave Pallin took out the Boy Peter early in the morning to see what damage had been done to his hoard. Lifting the first cage the winch whined and strained with extra weight on the line. When the cage rose out of the sea the body of Rott rose with it, his hand tangled in the netting.

CHAPTER FIFTY-THREE

But where was Marvin? Who found him? Wanda! She could not sit worrying in the house, so Helen stayed with the boys while she ran down to the harbour. By the time she reached it, the Silver Cord had left. She ran onto the pier and along to where the fish boxes and craves tumbled in chaos on the quay. She did not look into the water; dare not look into the water. She scrambled and heaved and threw the boxes aside, screaming, "Marvin". Then she came to a foot, with a seaboot on it she recognised, then a leg, then a body, then Marvin, with a battered face, empty and unmoving. She slapped it and shook his head and doused him with water, but nothing would bring him round. She groped for a pulse and could not feel one. Where do you feel? What does it feel like? She ran sobbing to the emergency telephone on the wall and rang 999. When she got back Marvin was stirring.

"Marvin!"

"Wanda"

"Are you all right?"

"Where's Dermot?"

"He's gone in the boat."

Marvin slumped back. Wanda sat beside him and cradled his head in her lap.

"The ambulance is coming," she murmured.

Marvin pushed a fish box out of the way and attempted to sit up. But he cried out as a pain shot down his arm. He tried to put his hand in his pocket, but again the pain and the cry.

"Wanda," he said, "In my pocket, that one, there's a present for you."

"Never mind that now."

"No, hen, find it, take it."

Wanda fished in his pocket and pulled out the little box from Armitage Antiques.

"Open it, hen, it's for you."

She opened it, took out the ring and gave it to Marvin. He couldn't push it on her finger, but he held it and she pushed; it was far too little and wouldn't go past the first knuckle. Nevertheless, there on the cold quay at Birsett in the freezing drizzle of a winter's night, lit by cheerless street lights, surrounded by fish boxes, craves and the dried viscera of miscellaneous sea creatures, serenaded by squawking herring gulls, Wanda became, in her own eyes at least, a respectable woman. In our eyes too, hen, in our eyes too.

* * * * * *

Jimmy Possum has long since given up any hope of winning the National Lottery but every week travels to Hecklescar to buy a ticket for fear his chosen numbers will come up the week he stops. In John's attitude to Grodwice lay the same desperation. It had cost him any hope of saving his marriage yet still he must go. It is called addiction, and like many an addict John rationalised his actions. He had to go to Grodwice for he must not let GANY down after they had been so fair. For Jacqui and Ian too; they had backed him, so for their sake he must go. But addiction had drained purpose from his ambition. He still craved the big job, but he no longer knew why.

John had to be in Prague by teatime on Monday. On Sunday, JP called him to wish him luck. John did not believe him but said nothing of his suspicions about Sir Frank; no, not suspicions, they were much more solid than that - conclusions. He replied to JP in monosyllables; JP noticed, understood, but did not comment.

Like a deprived smoker drawing on his first fag for a fortnight, John found his spirits lifting as he entered the Business Class Departure Lounge. He settled into a cosy armchair and pulled out his Financial Times. He was back in the groove, wasn't he?

The plane leaned into the sky away from a drab dissonant world. Here sings a chorus of living: bright, clean, clear, quiet, controlled. Most of the people on the flight were people like him - businessmen and a woman or two. He did not have to wear a business suit, but like them he wore one; he did not need to carry a brief case but his lay in the rack beside theirs; no one would ring his mobile phone, but he placed it on the table in front of him, like some of the others. The seat beside him lay empty; they had not been able to reallocate Marion's ticket. The vacancy intimidated him so he took down his brief case and put it on the empty seat. He left the case there for a while, then opened it and took out the notes he had made on GANY and on Grodwice. Others were reading business papers too. Unseen and unnoticed cabin staff brought coffee, drinks, lunch. Like ministering angels, they had no faces and no form; labelled, they had no names; no nicknames like Possum or Delightful, certainly.

Prague was what Prague is supposed to be in winter: cold, bright, elegantly austere. Flecks of snow fell listlessly as if paid by the hour by the tourist board. But none fell on John. Chosen from the crowd by the sign, 'Mr Swansen of London', he was driven by the uniformed sign man in an air-conditioned cab to the TransContinental Praha. For two days he would occupy a spacious room on the second floor decorated in gilt baroque to give it a feel of old luxury. A restrained Christmas tree in the corner by the bookcase acknowledged the season, another brightened the marble bathroom. He unpacked then walked to the window and looked out into the Old Town. He saw the Old Town Square, with its haughty buildings, bright shops and busy cafes. People wrapped up against the cold moved in and out of the stalls of the Christmas Market. He reminded himself he was in Prague just before Christmas, but he didn't feel it; he felt he closeted in a hotel room, any hotel room, anywhere in the world. He went downstairs and was met by Dwight Graf in whose pleasant and assiduous company John took comfort for the rest of the evening. The American explained the itinerary. Tomorrow they would fly to Grodwice in the company jet with the Head of Manufacturing, Europe, Gordon McAllister, tour the factory, meet some of the local managers then return to Prague for dinner in the evening. Jochen Muller, Vice-President, Europe, would join them for the meal; so would the other candidate, Peter Metier.

"Peter is visiting Grodwice on Wednesday so we thought it would be a good opportunity to all get together. Jacqui Boutelle will also be with us. I believe you know her."

This came as news, this dinner; John had thought the selection games were over but plainly they were still comparing and contrasting and wanted them in the same room together again. This sounded encouraging, for it meant that Peter Metier had not established a commanding lead – and Marion's absence had apparently not done too much damage.

The king-sized bed that night seemed large, empty and uncomfortable. He slept fitfully and at two o'clock awoke with a start. Something had startled him in his sleep, but he could not remember what it was - a dream, perhaps, or a spectre. He rose, switched on the lights and made himself a cup of something out of the cupboard, (cocoa, was it, with a fancy name?). He sat on a gilt chair, looked round the room and told himself that this was the life. He took his cup to the window and looked out onto the sleeping snow-dusted square and told himself that to-morrow he would land an international appointment; that when he flew in and out of Prague on his way to the UK and the States he would stay here.

But try as he may he could not connect with his surroundings. They seemed artificial and pretentious - and wafer thin, for whatever his dream had been it had broken through it. He had brought something from Birsett with him, something that disturbed him to which he could not give a name or a shape. He opened his briefcase, took out the stuff on Grodwice and forced himself to read it. Then he worked his way through his ideas on how the operations might be set up and run. He made notes. His composure returned. He went back to bed and slept until the waiter arrived with his early morning tea.

Had you been Dwight Graf, Human Resources, GANY Europe, on that Tuesday morning you would have looked across the breakfast table at a confident, articulate John Swansen and complimented yourself that you had selected a prime candidate for Head of Operations at the new plant at Grodwice. You would have found him pleasant company and would have believed that he was relishing the day in front of him. You would not have thought that he had been frightened in the night and therefore you would be surprised by what happened at dinner that evening.

Had you been Gordon McAllister Head of Manufacturing, GANY Europe, you would have welcomed the ebullient John Swansen that came aboard the company jet at Prague airport and you would have thought that he, like you, enjoyed the luxury of the private plane. You would have been impressed as you travelled to the new plant by the man's knowledge of Grodwice and its culture and by his understanding of its place in the global strategy of the Corporation. When you were walking round the plant you would have found yourself under pressure to keep up with his questions, comments and ideas. His enthusiasm and expertise would have been obvious to you as he discussed with local site managers the layout of the factory and the placement of the plant. You would have been pleased by his ability to communicate with them and charmed to see him putting them at their ease by greeting them in their own language. As you talked with him in the half-furnished office of Head of Operations you might well have concluded that here was a future Chief Executive as well as the present Head of Operations. You too would be very surprised by what happened a few short hours later.

Had you been Jacqui Boutelle, Lead Consultant of Sumner and Frieburg, you would have been gratified when, over an aperitif, Graf and McAllister of your client company GANY complimented you on the quality of the senior candidate from York you had persuaded them to consider for the position at Grodwice. But, although it was unexpected, you would not be wholly surprised at what happened at the ensuing meal. For when you passed on the compliments to John Swansen you found him off-hand. This puzzled you, for the first time you had a meal together you thought he was trying to flirt with you.

There were ten at the dinner. Muller, McAllister and Graf had brought their wives to Prague at Christmas by way of reimbursement for leaving them at home so often during the year. Peter Metier had, since the colloquium, acquired a fiancée, a blonde and beautiful Austrian fluent in four languages including German and English. Jacqui unworthily suspected she was on hire for the week. The wives were in good humour because they had spent the afternoon (and a fair amount of dollars) at the Christmas Markets and their husbands were in good humour because their wives were treating them well.

Jochen Muller proved an attentive host commenting on everything from European Affairs to cat food with a loquacious and perceptive wit. Jacqui fed him his lines; Graf and McAllister led the laughter and made their own suitably subordinate contributions; Peter Metier spoke cleverly when spoken too and his partner had the good sense not to outshine the older ladies. In all then a comfortable and genial party apart, that is, from the dour and brooding Scotsman. Jacqui, embarrassed, tried to bring him into the conversation. Had enjoyed his trip? Yes. What did he think of Prague at Christmas? Christmassy. What did he think of the Grodwice plant? Impressed. Then back to surly silence. In the end Muller had had enough.

"Something wrong, John?"

John glowered at him. Jacqui feared for what he might say.

"Yes," he said, "there is something wrong. But not with you - with me. I should not have come. I do not want this job."

"Goddam it," spat Muller, "You might have told us, we have spent...."

John cut him off. He no longer cared what they thought of him.

"Last Friday a man drowned in the sea off Birsett. I was in the boat looking for him. We found the boat at the foot of the cliff, adrift like a ghost ship, almost on the rocks. But he wasn't on board. We looked for him but we couldn't find him."

"Poor guy," said Graf and McAllister together.

"Dave Pallin found him the next morning. He had been trying to rob Davie's lobster creels. He had opened the creel to take out the lobsters when the creel toppled back into the water. His hand tangled in the net of the creel and he was dragged into the water; he tried to struggle free but he couldn't; he had almost wrenched off his hand. But he could not save himself. His ambition had dragged him to his death.'

John stopped suddenly, stared at them all, then stood up and walked out of the room. Jacqui made to follow him but Muller called her back.

"Leave him, I'm sure he wants to be alone," he said. Jacqui sat down.

John was sure he had explained why he could not accept the job at Grodwice, that ambition would drag him under, but he was wrong. They put it down to PTSD (posttraumatic stress disorder). The label allowed them to file it and proceed with the business in hand. They enjoyed the rest of the meal.

When Jacqui went up to look for him an hour and half later, John had booked out and gone to the airport.

The day before the day before Christmas, a De Luxe Festive Hamper from Fortnum and Masons, Piccadilly, arrived at Braeshiel with a note:

John Swansen,

Thanks for your interest in the GANY Inc. Get well soon.

Dwight Graf, Human Resources, Europe

CHAPTER FIFTY-FOUR

There were no flights from Prague to the UK that evening so John stayed in the airport all night and managed to find an economy class seat on the 9.10 the following morning. He could have gone back to the hotel but he did not consider it. He wanted away. On the plane he accepted the comparative discomforts of Economy Class because there he felt out of the company of successful people. Unexceptional, he sat among other unexceptionals. He sat in Economy Class but could not shut Business Class out of his tired mind. It somehow attached itself to Sir Frank: swanning off to the Far East: leering at Asian secretaries; lauding it in his office at Pinkerton: cracking crude jokes with the board at Loyalty. Then with severer bitterness he saw him with JP, talking, laughing about John and his fall from grace. Sir Frank had out-manoeuvred him. He hated the man - and JP too, the weasel. These thoughts plagued his dismal journey back to Birsett.

By the time he was back in Braeshiel on Wednesday the sun had set. Mechanically he checked his answering machine. Two calls: one from Kate at Gainslaw Globes saying she had good news but if he didn't ring back, she would see him on Friday as promised; the other from JP asking him to ring back. He returned neither call. Instead he rang Helen to say he was home, made a light meal which he didn't eat and after a few hours not watching the screen that flickered in front of him, went to bed.

John had long since given up bedtime prayers but this night he said one: "Welcome to the rest of my life," he prayed; a bitter prayer, but a prayer nevertheless?

John now entered the ranks of those who see that the Christmas bonfire casts shadows as well as light. Mr Scott, for instance, whose friend Willie had cheered him last year, blind Emily who had lost Mrs Dryden's company and eyes; and, of course, poor Susan bereft of her little boy. But these and all others like them rallied to the great conspiracy to make Christmas bright. In defiance of their troubles and griefs they would take from the season what they could. They decorated their homes, put up trees, sent cards, bought presents, ordered the turkey and wished each other Merry Christmas. Thereby they saw into the heart of the mystery far more clearly than those who approached it only from the light.

Not John; he thought his problems so immense, his life so decimated, his prospects so crushed that he had the right not to make the best of it. For most of Thursday he brooded at home. He spoke to no-one and returned no phone calls, particularly that of JP who left another message on the answering machine saying he needed to speak to him.

Life, however, with blessed impatience, particularly life at Birsett, does not wait for instruction from our plans; it rushes us on, tumbling us into what comes next. At teatime that day the four Halloween black cats turned up at Braeshiel. Now masquerading as cherubs, they had come to sing him carols. He made it quite clear that they were not welcome but Morag and Louise were used to his moods. They barged past him into the lounge as soon as he opened the door. They were horrified by what they saw: Uncle John had no Christmas decorations; no streamers, no danglers, no plaques, no displays, no lights and, worst of all, no tree. Well, he had a tree -it was propped up in the hall but stood as it had been delivered, wrapped up in a plastic bag. John protested that he didn't want carols and gave them a pound each to go away. But they had promised him carols and carols he would get. They sang three: 'While Shepherds Watched', 'Once in Royal David's' and a stray from the Hoity-Toity Angel: 'It was on a Starry Night'. John deafened himself against the songs, and ushered them out of the door as soon as they finished. Morag and Louise went straight home and reported Scrooge to their mother.

Helen rang John to check on the children's story. John said it had nothing to do with her. Helen thought it had and told him she would be down later. At seven o'clock she arrived accompanied by Louise and Morag. Calum, thinking there might be a fight, had come to watch. John let them in but repeated that he did not want Braeshiel decorated; there was no point. Helen listened to his orders then took the children upstairs. They emerged a few minutes later each carrying a box of Christmas decorations. Helen flanked by her children confronted John.

"Do you have any ideas," she said, "or should I do it the same as last year?"

"Helen, I think I have made it clear I don't want the house decorated. There is no point."

"It has always been decorated; all the time your father was here it was decorated. I helped him and I will help you."

"I don't want any help. It is not being decorated. It is not my father's house now, it is mine."

"No," said Helen, "It is mine - and it is not going to be black at Christmas."

Holding their boxes like usherettes with hand grenades the children tracked the dialogue from face to face and waited for the command from their mother to launch operations.

"Helen," said John, almost pleading, "What's the point? Marion isn't coming."

"Did she say that?"

"No, she didn't need to."

"If she didn't say she wasn't coming, she might still come."

"You don't know Marion."

"I think I do. You'll have to ring her up and ask her if she's coming."

"You must be joking."

"Does Rachel know she's not coming? Have you told her? She'll be getting ready for you all and you say she's not coming. Have you told Rachel?"

The children enjoyed this assault by their mother. They almost cheered.

"I'll tell her," mumbled John from his foxhole. Helen adjusted her aim and prepared to shoot him out of it.

"What will you tell her?"

"That Marion isn't coming."

"But you don't know that."

"She won't come," snapped John, breaking off the engagement, "and I don't know if I want her to."

"Try her," said Helen, firmly but softly, "she might like you better without a big job and a big opinion of yourself."

John looked Helen in the eye and saw a truth he had not recognised. He fell silent for a moment. Helen filled the gap.

"Rebecca might come; she told David she was coming for Christmas."

"She'll not be here; you'd better tell David."

"You'll be here, and the bairns will come."

The bairns smiled and nodded their heads: 'surely we can thaw him out'. But their Uncle stayed cold.

"Right, we'll get started."

They hauled the tree from the hall and Louise and Morag decorated it. Calum fetched the ladders and strung up gold, green and red streamers across the room. Helen looked out a miniature nativity set and candles and arranged them on the mantelpiece. She placed Santa and Merry Christmas plaques in the window.

And what was John doing the while? He sat in a chair, tried to look indifferent and felt foolish. He was almost glad when Morag asked him what he had done with the holly she had brought him. She'd find it in the shed. Where? She went out to fetch it and came back saying the shed door had jammed. John came to free it and helped Morag carry in the holly.

"Thank you, Uncle John. Now would you help me put it up, it's high?"

Thus, John was inveigled into helping.

When they finished, the bairns stood in a circle waiting to be thanked. John balked. Helen asked him what he thought. Then he relit the fuse.

"What's the point?" he repeated.

"What's the point?" exploded Helen, "I'll tell you what's the point! The point is that everyone else is trying to enjoy Christmas and you must join in. That's the point. There's not a woman in Birsett this night who couldn't see Christmas far enough but they're hammering away at it because winter would be gey driech without Christmas. That's the point."

"That's a poor argument," said John almost sneering.

"It's not an argument, it's a fact. OK, so you didn't get the job you had set your heart on. Why punish the rest of us for that?"

"I turned it down."

"Turned it down; that's nice! How nice to be able to turn down a job. But you have a fat pension and thousands in the bank. How many in Birsett have that? You moan about losing a job you don't need. Fishermen here are worried sick that jobs they do need will be taken from them in the New Year. But they'll still enjoy Christmas. You moan about Marion not coming. What about Susan who lost her little boy to the sea? What kind of Christmas morning d'ye think she is facing? But is her house dark. No! She has a tree in the window and streamers on her ceiling. What about Cecil from Surrey? His wife's gone ga-ga now and he's had to put her into The Towers home at Beanston. It will be the first Christmas for 51 years they have been apart. But go and look at his house. He has lights on his tree outside and a wreath on his door. And your father, in this house, the Christmas after your mother died. 'Deck it out, Helen,' he said, 'we'll keep the feast'. You've been spoiled, John, you've had too much. You have nothing to moan about. Welcome to the real world. Come on, bairns, we're wasting our time here."

The children glowered at him and left. But they had brought Christmas to the shadows of Braeshiel - and to their Uncle John - by force.

On Friday morning before he had finished breakfast JP walked in and told him they were going to Gainslaw Globes.

"Kate has good news," he said, "we need to go and talk to her about it."

"I'll go later," snapped John.

"We'll go now," insisted JP, "as promised. I'll wait until you get ready. We'll go in my car."

John slung himself into JP's car but JP made no attempt

to start it.

"I think I know what all this is about," he said, "It's about Sir Frank, is it not?"

"Yes, and a lot more," exploded John and would have shot all his compounded anger into his companion's face had not JP cut him off.

"Before you say anymore let me try to explain. You know Sir Frank has been to see me."

"Yes," snapped John.

"But do you know why?"

"I can guess!"

"And you would be wrong."

"Sir Frank is trying to raise five million pounds. That's why he came to see me. He needs it to buy his daughter back from a militant group in Bainan – if he can. They say they are not interested in money; they're against western investment. They want SEAC Corporation (Sir Frank's on the board) to hand back the companies they have bought up in Bainan. SEAC, of course, won't do that but they are playing for time. Sir Frank hopes they can buy them off. But time is running out. If SEAC doesn't announce by New Year's Day that they are pulling out they have threatened to kill his daughter."

"He arrived out of the blue; he had driven all the way from London and went back the same day. The man is frantic. He thinks if he can offer them five million, they'll release her. Apparently, he had wheedled a job for her in Bainan, PA to a government minister, a sinecure, part of a deal of some sort. She disappeared last month. They don't know what is happening to her or where she is being held."

"I haven't seen anything in the press," muttered John

"The Foreign Office has imposed a news blackout to give Sir Frank a chance to raise the money. They think that once it's in the news, it'll be more difficult for the terrorists to back down. They think they'll be forced to stand by their threat to kill the girl. He just arrived on the doorstep. I don't like the man any more than you do. He wanted me to promise quarter of a million."

"And did you?"

"Yes," said JP, "Her name is Monica; she's twenty-one. He had a photograph. She reminded me of Rebecca."

CHAPTER FIFTY-FIVE

The news of Sir Frank's distress washed through John like a cathartic stream. By the time JP had finished the story John no longer loathed The Knight. He had not forgiven him but he no longer wanted him punished. Leave vengeance to God, Belinda Boyd had said. John felt with a shudder that God had answered a prayer he thought he had not prayed. He had not wanted this. He asked JP's forgiveness for distrusting him. JP shrugged it off.

"You've been through a lot," he said and made it clear he did not want to hear any more of it.

"What is Kate's news?" John asked. "If it's good news I want to hear it; I could do with some good news."

"It's too important for me," laughed JP. "She must tell you herself." He started the car.

After a fortnight of dour, dull, blurred days, this day dawned clear, fresh, cold. Under a duck egg blue sky, the land lay at peace under a powdery overlay of frost; the blue-green sea shone like a polished shield. It was as if God had relented and had half-decided already on a white Christmas. On their way to Gainslaw the two men enjoyed the fine morning and their repaired friendship. JP asked about Grodwice and heard John's story with interest and concern.

"You turned it down."

"Yes."

"And do you know why?"

"I realised it would pull me under."

"What now then?"

"I don't know. I suppose I will have to make my life from what I have here."

"Can you do that? Will it be enough?"

"It will have to be."

"I am glad to hear it. I would have missed you, John. So would Rachel and Kate. I'm glad you've decided to join us drop-outs."

"I made no decision," said John, flatly. "I seem to be boxed in."

JP smiled and changed the subject. He enquired about the Christmas arrangements. Christmas Day lay only five days away; Rachel had been enquiring. John told him that story too.

"You think Marion will not be coming?"

"No."

"Rachel will be disappointed. Ben will be disappointed. I will be disappointed. Is there no chance?"

"I don't think so. Helen says I should ring her up."

"Maybe you should."

"I dare not."

"Why"

"She would say, 'No'"

"But you think she is not coming anyway."

"No, but I couldn't bear to hear her say, 'No' and if I rang, she would be bound to say it. That would be the end of it."

"What will we do?" said JP and John thought he meant

about the meal on Christmas Day.

"It's not fair on Rachel," said John, "but can we just leave it? I'll come anyway and with Rachel's permission I'll bring Mr Scott. And if Mar...." He choked on his wife's name.

"That'll be OK," murmured JP. "I'll arrange it with Rachel, but not until after the weekend; she worries about change. We need to go down south to-morrow for a couple of days, delivering and collecting presents. I'll tell her on Monday when we get back."

Then they went into Gainslaw Globes to hear Kate's good news.

"I'm pregnant," she announced.

John complimented her.

"Due next July. But I'm worried about what will happen here. I don't think Colin is up to it."

"Don't worry about that." replied JP testing John. "John will look after the shop while you're away."

John shrugged his shoulders and said to JP.

"See what I mean, another nail in the coffin."

Then he smiled.

"I thought you were going away," said Kate to John.

"Not now," said John.

Then Kate smiled too.

You may not think from this conversation with John that JP had plans to play peacemaker for John and Marion, but if you listen again carefully you can hear that that is his intention. Not him alone; Rachel will lend what help she can give. What this generous couple fear is that their friends will lose each other in a standoff of fear: John afraid that Marion will have nothing more to do with him: Marion afraid to trust. We have seen Jacob try and fail with John; he will therefore see what he can accomplish with Marion. The trip south with presents is genuine enough, but without their peace mission they would have returned on Monday morning; now they will delay their return north to see Marion at teatime on Monday. They have told her they are calling in.

Without a conjunction of circumstances their chances of success, not high, would have been hopeless. Marion, as you have gathered, is not a sentimental person and normally the songs she sings with the choir are just songs. But one verse in one of the songs this Sunday Evening will enter her heart and make her open to counsel. It would not have done so if circumstances had been better.

The false re-start with John had undermined her confidence. She had ventured against her reason and had fallen hard. She had battled on; that was her way, but this time it seemed pointless and she now understood that her reaction had been born of expectation, the expectation that something better would come along. But that hope had been cruelly crushed. She felt weary and defeated. The feeling intensified during the short dark days of December, and by the shadows cast forward by Christmas.

For the first time since she came to York, she felt a stranger in a strange land; she longed for her own people. This arose partly from the knowledge that, early in the New Year, Fiona would return to Glasgow with Ian. This, of itself, would not have loomed large had her own family not been fractured. She had anticipated Christmas would be painful and had laid careful plans to prevent some of the pain. But these plans had been ripped apart by John's intervention and now she could not cobble them back together again. She did not have the heart for it.

Rebecca harried her every day, asking what they were doing for Christmas; were they going to Birsett? She wanted to go to Birsett. 'Swallow your pride mum.' But mum didn't want to go and she didn't want not to go. Like John what she wanted most was to not make a decision. All this battering had weakened her defences, but still the song would not have found its way to her heart. Her vulnerability arose from the memory that this concert had been an assignation - with John. They had talked about it, had joked about it, had basked in the warmth of it; of her singing in St Martins-le-Grand at York while he sat at The Messiah in The Queens Hall in Edinburgh. You may think it strange that in this assignation the parties are two hundred miles apart. But love has no odometer. They were doing this together and they both knew it.

Then, of course, there was the song itself. By what destiny had this song been chosen for this concert?

John set off for The Messiah reluctantly. He had promised Mr Scott so he must go. He would have preferred to sit at home and try to reassemble his life; work out where all the parts fitted; make a plan. Planning is the essence of good management. But he had tired of planning and, as we have already seen, life has had its own plans for him. He picked Mr Scott up at half-past five on a cold clear night and in the moonlight drove over Coldingham Moor and up the A1 to Edinburgh. As they went John talked to Mr Scott about his future. If he could not brood on it alone, he would brood on it in company. Mr Scott let him run on, asking questions, nodding agreement, murmuring reassurance. Then John asked him what he thought.

"Since I came back from Prague, I have been asking myself what have we to look forward to."

He had forgotten he was addressing a man in his eighties. Mr Scott let out a quiet, thoughtful laugh.

"For me," said the old minister, "The Messiah to-night! Then Christmas. That's as far as I can see. I think I'll make it now. What is it? Three days. Yes, that's achievable!"

He turned to John in the dark.

"Do not be deceived, John, by all my philosophising. I stagger from one milepost to the next. For the moment, Christmas. After that, New Year; then I would like to see the sun up before seven, then the aconites. After that I'll try for the equinox, then Easter and the first swallows. Away, away, on the distant horizon I speculate on the Fisher Queen in July. A far country. I am not sure my leaky vessel will carry me that far."

"I'm sorry," said John, "It was a tactless question."

"Not at all," said the old man. "'It is circumstance that shapes our ends, rough-hew them how we will'. That is true for us all."

"I thought it was '*destiny*' that shapes our ends."

"'*Divinity*', actually. I used to think that once," replied Mr Scott, deliberately. "But that is too theological. It is circumstance."

"I don't think so," said John, "If that were true, we'd still be in the dark ages. Look at what science, commerce and industry have accomplished."

"And what is that? Make things happen by plans and projects! Politicians too! Can they can choose? No! They tweak circumstances, that's all."

"It sounds a fatalistic creed," said John humouring the old man by keeping the debate going. Mr Scott took him up.

"Better that than the modern heresy: that you can have whatever you want. Planning - the great hope! Plan your education, plan your career, plan your family, choose lifestyle, choose children or not, and when, choose whether to bear them or destroy them, choose to stay or choose to go. Worst of all: believe that choice brings happiness. Ignore the fact that people are miserable. Why? Like Russian Roulette, choose wrong and you blow your head off - and it's your own fault. What a burden! Who has choice? Who doesn't? Think of Betty

Brison, the lassie that fell over the cliff. Did she plan that? Did she choose it? Would it have featured in her life plan? No! Yet look at what she made of it. She's an expert at, what is it, computers?"

"Relational databases."

"That's it! Would she have done that if not paralysed? Would she have lived such a fulfilled life? Jacob and Rachel - would they have wanted a son like Ben? Did they plan it? Did they choose it? Would they change it now? Would their lives be better if they did? It is academic. Charlatans - these chatterers that sell planning and choice! Look at Del and Dot, or Alex or Helen. What choices do they have? Scarcely any, but to do what they are doing; where circumstance has stranded them. Do they waste their years grieving after something better? No, they make their coat out of the cloth they've been given. None of us are any different."

"You make quite a case, but I still don't believe it."

"It's not a matter of believing. Can't escape it. It is the way the world works, the way life works; if you like, the way God works. Scientists recognise it: Chaos Theory. A butterfly flapping its wings in Tokyo triggers a hurricane in New York. I believe it; everything is connected and events beyond our control are always knocking us sideways. There are no great plans. We knit it up as we go; pick our way through circumstances, enjoying what we can, and helping others along the road."

"That's more or less what Helen says."

"Did she really?" Mr Scott sounded impressed.

"Yes," muttered John, "but in fewer words."

Mr Scott laughed.

"You're beginning to sound like yer fither," he said. He meant it as a compliment.

The Messiah is sung at Christmas in the Queen's Hall by twenty singers, some of whom step forward to sing the arias. Mr Scott preferred it to the large choruses and part-time soloists of traditional performances. John heard harmonies and melodies that he had not heard before in the great productions he had heard in Leeds Town Hall. But he heard them through a mist, for everything seemed to draw his attention to that other group of singers in St Martin's-le-Grand and to one singer in particular. Mr Scott sensed it and as the choir stood up to sing '*His yoke is easy and his burden light*' he turned to John to add a footnote to his thesis.

"Have faith," he whispered, "Who knows what is happening now elsewhere that will affect us all profoundly."

Just then, in St Martin's-le-Grand, York, Marion fell silent in the verse of the song she could no longer sing.

The song is The Rose; the verse, second verse:

'It's the heart afraid of breaking that never learns to dance.
It's the dream afraid of waking that never takes a chance.
It's the one who won't be taken who cannot seem to give.
And the soul afraid of dying that never learns to live.'

The following day at teatime, Marion opened the door to Jacob and Rachel glad to see her friends from Birsett, but unaware that they were on a mission.

CHAPTER FIFTY-SIX

In the lounge at Poppleton, Jacob and Rachel accounted for their presence by playing the daft lad about the Christmas arrangements: were they still as arranged? Should they leave the presents now or keep them for Christmas Day? Marion expressed surprise that John had not told them. Told them what? About her calling off the trip to Prague. They knew she had not gone but did not know the details. She gave them the details. They listened with attention to a story they had already heard, listened to hear not the narrative but the low music of the heart. And they heard it; Rachel more clearly than Jacob.

"I must bear some of the blame," said JP, "I encouraged him to ask you to go with him. If I had not done so, I believe he would not have asked you."

"I think John knew what he was doing," said Marion flatly, "He is still trying to have it all. He still wants the big job and the little wife."

What Marion felt was far muzzier than this soap opera soundbite, but we all reach for clichés when we're confused. JP recognised it for what it was.

"I think more than anything he wanted you back. I believe he still does. You know he has given up the job at Grodwice."

Marion studied JP. She saw sincerity but doubted it.

"You mean he didn't get the job."

"No," said JP, "he gave it up; he withdrew."

"Is that what he told you?"

"Yes."

"And you believe him?"

"Yes."

"He must have withdrawn because he believed he wouldn't get the job. He told me he wasn't the preferred candidate."

"No, he walked out and I think I know why."

The image of Rott entangled in the crave leapt into his mind. He hesitated, dismissed the image but held the allegory.

"I think he thought he would be trapped again in a life to which he was addicted. I believe he found the job too attractive; that it would drag him under. You see, Marion, top managers live in a rarefied atmosphere. People in the organisation become dependent on you and strive to make you feel successful, for your success is their success. They agree with your ramblings until you begin to think that you are all-wise; they manipulate the results so the wins are down to you and defeats to someone else. Although you are under considerable pressure, life is essentially very simple. Everything is at a remove from reality; filtered, processed, cleaned up ready for one of three possible solutions presented on a single sheet of A4. Every complication is smoothed and tamed, every eventuality reduced to a clear statistic, every problem capable of resolution. Then you come home to a child crying over a broken toy you can't mend or a tired wife complaining about a neglect you do not recognise."

JP glanced at Rachel when he said this. Rachel smiled and glanced at Marion. Marion smiled and shook her head gently acknowledging that JP touched sore sentiments long unshared. JP continued.

"If you are not careful you begin to prefer the pre-processed life of business; prefer it, then choose it; choose it then surrender your life to it. Many never discover what a hold it has on them until it is too late, until they have destroyed everything else that is worthwhile in their lives. But John was lucky enough to lose his job. Yes, lucky enough! Over the past few months, Marion, I have seen the cords that bound him to that fantasy life snap one by one: the job, the title, the perks, the status, the Mercedes, worst of all, the Mercedes."

JP laughed. The women, for relief, joined him.

"At the same time, John has become attached to Birsett, or, rather, he has become tangled up in it. He did not want that and fought against it. But I believe he now feels what we, Rachel and I, feel. A couple of weeks ago, I was complaining only half-seriously to Jimmy Possum about having to go down to London. Quite seriously he commiserated with me, then said, 'Aye, a day out of Birsett is a day wasted.' Most people would laugh at him but I am horrified to say I knew exactly what he meant. I repeated it to Rachel when I came back and she too understood it. We have been all over the world, lived in great cities, have met thousands of people, important people, movers and shakers some of them, yet now we find our happiness depends on an obscure fishing village and a handful of ordinary people who live there. Yet not ordinary – they are precious to us, irreplaceably precious, unique: Helen and Alex, Louise, Morag, David, Delightful, Jimmy Possum, Mr Scott, Susan that lost her little son (Ben found him, you know), Kate, Colin, ... Each name triggers a face, each face a life. Is that right, Rachel?"

This simple question distilled a lifetime's searching. JP looked at his wife, longing for her agreement. Rachel smiled and nodded. But the question did not spark a smile in Marion. She knew precisely what JP meant but could not share the pleasure. She was bereft of her folk, and her family had broken. JP saw the distress and moved on.

"But I think what proved more important to John than the pull of Birsett, was the thought that if he accepted the job, he would finally lose you and Rebecca. In the end he knew the trade-off was not worth it. He realised that if he got what he wanted he would lose what he most desired. I believe that the thought he might land the job frightened him; what he would lose by gaining it. No, no, he made his choice, I'm sure of it: he turned it down."

JP stopped speaking and waited for Marion to take up the conversation. For a while she said nothing, wrestling with hopes and doubts.

"I have come to conclusions too." she said, "I don't think John could live without his job, and I think his job will always take first place. I find that hard to accept. Even as I say it, it chokes me. And it's not selfishness. It's just that I thought John and I .... Oh, it's all a mess, it's all broken; it can't be mended."

She looked at JP, confusion and resentment burning in her eyes. The look silenced JP. But not Rachel.

"It is selfishness," she said quietly but firmly. "Of the worst kind; for it masquerades as love. John and Jacob and people like them have work to do in the world. The world needs to be fed and clothed, sheltered and furnished, healed and made comfortable. Someone has to do it. People like John and Jacob do it because they are good at it. They are able to do it so they must. That means commitment, a commitment every bit as demanding as the vocations we respect, like doctor or clergyman. It absorbs their time and their energy; it wears them out and wears them down. I have come to it that it is selfish to think that it should not be my husband, that my husband should be exempt, that he should work just enough to keep us in comfort then should come home and pass the buck to some other man or some other woman."

Rachel glanced at Marion afraid she might offend her. But she had to take that risk for she is speaking to her husband as well as to her friend. She is demonstrating that she understands, or, at least, is trying to understand how the world works and how she accounted for her husband's place in it. She could thereby reckon the account for her own life, for her hours of loneliness, frustration and despair. There had to be some purpose in them; they amounted to more than money in the bank, surely. She continued.

"Jacob says that John ran the plant at York well; kept at it when others might have given up and moved on. John was not as wrapped up in himself as Jacob claims. He did not think only of himself – not like those two that came from Loyalty. What did they call them, Jacob? One of them is something big in the government now. "

"Tom and Jerry," confirmed JP, "Not in the government; Tom Curtis is an adviser to the President of the Board of Trade, and Chairman of British Communications. Gerald Hopkins is the other one, Chairman of E&L Finance now."

"I remember them," said Marion, attempting a cold humour, "John talked to me then. Happy Days!"

"Well, John is not like them," Rachel continued; "they were only interested in themselves – the size of their package and their own prospects. And they moved on before they were caught. Isn't that right, Jacob?"

"It's slander," smiled JP, "but it's true and there's a lot like them. But not John."

"He is too honest for that," continued Rachel, "and loyal. He stuck by the folk there as long as he could. He showed great courage, Jacob said."

This praise for John strangely warmed Marion for it contradicted all those chilling thoughts of John's indifference and calculating coldness that had so chilled her in the past year. It opened a channel back to the days when she admired John for what he had achieved and what he was attempting. Back then she had shared in it, just as he shared in the life at home, in raising Robert and Rebecca. They might work separately but their life's work was whole, bound together by mutual interest and affection. She had felt this again at Durham; and it had betrayed her into trusting once more; it touched her now. She became aware that Rachel was still speaking, asking a question.

"You will come for Christmas, won't you? If you do not want to go to Braeshiel, come to us. It will be a lonely day for us without you."

Marion smiled. She could not accuse Rachel of conspiracy. She spoke to JP.

"Did John put you up to this?"

"No, he does not know we're here speaking to you, and never will unless you tell him. I did try to persuade him to ring you. But he wouldn't."

"Why not?"

"He was afraid you would say no."

"And if you felt what I feel would you not say no?"

She looked at JP. JP looked confused; he was out of his depth. Rachel replied.

"No," she said, "I would say yes. Why? Because you only know what you feel, not what John feels. He says he loves you and wants you. You can either trust that or suspect it - and trust is always better than suspicion. Trust walks with love, suspicion trails behind. If you want John, if you want your family back together again, you must trust; you have no alternative. You must come for Christmas; you must take a chance."

'*Take a chance*'! Had it not been for the song Marion did not sing the night before, the last phrase would have had stood silent outside her door, but the song had unlocked it. Rachel's words entered and excited her. Could she take a chance on the dream? Was she afraid to live again?

For a while she sat studying the hands in her lap. Then suddenly, surprisingly, Jacob and Rachel heard her say that she would come. Could they tell John? No, she said, he must ring and invite her. She had things to say to him.

CHAPTER FIFTY-SEVEN

That Monday evening, the day before Christmas Eve, at half-past nine, scarcely five minutes after JP left him, John rang Marion and invited her to Braeshiel for Christmas. She had prepared her answer, and the questions before the answer, but in the end simply said she would come. She found it much easier than she had expected because John put up no defence, offered no explanation. He just said he wanted her to come - as if it were their first date, as if they had no history and nothing to regret.

They made arrangements. Marion would be at work until lunchtime but Robert and Rebecca would be ready for her whenever she arrived home. They would take a quick lunch then set out. John would prepare a meal for them when they arrived at, what, about five. Marion laughed at the thought of John making a meal for her. John took no offence. She had forgotten that he had fed himself for over a year. He had in mind his speciality, a safe ham salad.

John had another invitation: would Marion come with him to the Christmas Eve Service at midnight in The Priory? They had gone once or twice during their courting days and when the children were young. The ancient and beautiful sanctuary is the place to welcome Christmas and who knows what else may be ushered in. Robert and Rebecca could come too, of course. But they would have to go in their own car; John had invited Mr Scott before... well, before... Marion said she would like to go to the Priory; it would be nice; she remembered the old church.

About the ham salad. When John told Helen, she changed it to steak pie from the butchers, potatoes and peas; it could be heated up in the microwave when they arrived; a warm meal after a cold journey.

Chaos, however, had not yet finished with our family: somewhere a butterfly flapped its wings and conjured up a snowstorm for the Scottish Borders on the afternoon of Christmas Eve.

It was not a particular spite. The butterfly disrupted many other journeys to and from Birsett that Christmas Eve: mothers and fathers heading for new families of sons and daughters in Edinburgh, Aberdeen, Darlington, St Helens, even Hawick. Lizzie Mitchell flew Batman out to Toronto to let her son take a closer look at her admirer. Alex reckons it will put paid to Batman's ambitions. Incoming families arrived from Scotland and furth of Scotland: up from England, across from Europe and in from Chicago and Singapore, to see parents and grandparents; some to stay for Christmas Day, some for two days, some over into the New Year. A nephew of Cecil from Surrey motored all the way from Basingstoke one day and back the next to deliver presents to his grateful aunt and uncle. The son of Mr & Mrs Smith left his own family in Glasgow for Christmas Eve to stand between his warring parents on Christmas Day.

Other gift-bearers turned up that day, among them Margaret and Roddam. They came into Braeshiel a bickering pair, so forlorn that a busy and excited John felt obliged to spend more time with them that he wished. He invited them for lunch and gave them ham salad. They left straight afterwards to avoid the threatening snow. The first flakes drifted in as they walked down the path.

"I hope it doesn't prevent Marion from making it," commented Margaret from the window of the new BMW. This was gracious considering she half-wished John's Christmas would be spoiled the way theirs had been by Abigail.

Because of the sea, Birsett, Hecklescar and Prior's Cross see little snow in winter. But to the north snow often blocks the road over Coldingham Moor and to the south, forty miles to the south, south of Alnwick, Newton Moor heaves the Great North Road into the path of any blizzards blowing in. And it was on Newton Moor at four o'clock in the gathering darkness that Marion decided she should not drive any further in the drifting snow. They pulled into The Chef and Skillet at Newton-on-the-Moor, to take a break and consider their options.

"It's Okay at this end," said John when she phoned, "But don't move until it is safe. Wait till the plough has been through; the snow is to ease later on; you have plenty of time. Take care, Marion. Ring me when you are leaving."

John heard again at nine. The hotel, anxious to close, had offered to put them up for the night. John's heart sank, but lifted when Marion told John that Rebecca had said, 'No way!'; they would make it. The snow was easing; they would be together for Christmas. Just after ten a call to say that the snow had stopped, the plough had been through and they were setting off. Then another call, faint and distorted, from near Wandylaw. They had skidded off the road, but were alright; they were pressing ahead; not to worry if you don't hear again - the mobile's batteries are failing. John said he would cancel the Priory service and wait for them. No, said Marion, it will be after midnight anyway before we get there. Go to the service; don't disappoint Mr Scott.

'Take care, Marion, take care Rebecca, look after your

mother and sister, Robert; take care.'

John had set his heart on them all going to the Priory. He did not know why, but it had become important. He wanted them there to see in Christmas, to be there together. He hung on until the last minute but heard nothing more. He picked up Mr Scott and travelled four miles along clear, quiet roads to Prior's Cross and The Priory.

The Priory is the chancel of the old cathedral and all that is left of the Benedictine Monastery once fought over by Scots and English, archbishops and princes, reivers and avenging armies, Covenanters and Cromwell. But on this tranquil night its rich red stones warm the hearts of the folk who gather in peace to await Christmas.

The first hymn is being sung as John and Mr Scott enter. They make their way forward to the only pew left unfilled - at the very front of the church. A face pokes out from a pew on their way. It belongs to David; converted for the night to church attendance. His face brightens when he sees John but darkens when he sees no-one behind him but Mr Scott.

The service proceeds unannounced: Carol then Lesson: four recorders played by four children: Carol then Lesson: then three violins and a flute: Carol then Lesson. No one speaks but the Authorised Version, read by the undertaker, the headmaster, a retired colonial officer and the woman from the caravan shop. No message but what the music brings: *'O Come, O Come Immanuel'*: *'Away in a Manger'*: *'Still the Night, Holy the Night'*: *'Love came down at Christmas'*.

This last is one verse through when the door at the back rattles, opens, and three figures walk softly down the aisle to the front. John turns to see his family coming to him: Rebecca, his daughter, Robert, his son, Marion, his wife. Mr Scott makes room; they step in beside John, Marion next to him. He leans to her and grasps her hand.

Lesson then Carol: then all lights are extinguished; the

Priory sinks into darkness: a single candle flickering beside the crib draws all eyes to it: light in dark places; unspoken prayers in every heart, of hope and expectation. Then the midnight toll of the old bell: Welcome Christmas! Children light tapers from the single flame and carry it to the candles on each pew; a soft light spreads through the church and a quiet joy runs through those that will receive it: the organ, the hymn: 'O Come all Ye Faithful'.

"Happy Christmas, Robert," a handshake. "Happy Christmas, Rebecca," a kiss and a hug. "Happy Christmas, my love," a lingering close embrace; tears in the eyes. "Happy Christmas, Mr Scott. See, they have come."

"Robert, would you take Mr Scott? Your mother and I will follow on. Do you mind, Mr Scott?"

They stepped out into the cold night air, and walked along the snow-dusted path to the cars. Mr Scott went with Robert, Rebecca with David, leaving John and Marion to find their own way home on a long, lovely journey. The gibbous moon drew them along the road to the top of Hallydown and for their delight threw a glittering silver ribbon across the sea. They turned away from the brash streetlights of Hecklescar and meandered inland under the great stars of Orion. They did not say much and what they did say was trivial and comfortable: the journey, the snow, the service, the coming day. But they said nothing of the tangle that had enwrapped their lives. Mutually but by no conscious agreement they had decided to discard it. They drove up the snow-covered lane to the top of Chester Law, where Willie and Jane used to come and where they themselves came for solitude in their days of courtship. They stopped the car and walked towards the moon along the quiet lane, their steps crunching in the frosty snow. Their eyes became accustomed to the soft moonlight; they stopped and looked out over the sleeping land, slate grey under a star-studded sky. Then they turned to each other and they kissed.

The kiss extracted from the past all the goodness their love had ever brought them; it sloughed away all the hurt their pride and foolishness had cost them. Yet it was their first kiss for here are a couple about to step into the unknown. All the old life maps have been thrown away: John has rejected life as a big boss but has no idea of what might take its place: Marion's year of confusion is over but still she is not sure of what she must settle for.

They are venturing, these two. They do not even know where they are going to live, have not yet discussed it. (But do not pity them over much: they have a pension of thirty thousand a year a year, cash in the bank and an expensive house to sell. Many fisher families will have to settle for a lot less than that this coming year.)

Nevertheless, the kiss is an act of trust, the beginning of life together again, of prospects and dreams, of closeness and of love fully restored. They clung to each other and embraced the wonder of it all.

They drove home slowly, not wanting the journey to end, seeking to distil from this holy night the essence of what they felt, to draw from it the last drop of exquisite joy. Rebecca and Robert greeted them at Braeshiel when they eventually arrived and John served them with steak pie from the butchers, potatoes and peas. If you think this is unromantic what can I say but that John had prepared it and that they were hungry. Besides, how could he explain it to Helen if he had not fed them?

During the meal Rebecca asked them if they had seen the lights on the Aurora. David had shown her the boat. They hadn't, so when they had finished, at half-past one in the morning, they walked arm in arm down the brae to the harbour. There lay the boat living up to its name, bright with starbursts and streamers, festooned in fairy lights strung from masthead to wheelhouse to stern; the gunwale and wheelhouse picked out in light strings. A Santa glowed on the wheelhouse roof and a snowman clung to the very top of the mast. It looked gloriously ridiculous.

As they turned away laughing, who should they see weaving his unsteady way down the brae but Delightful, decked out as Santa Claus. They complemented him on the boat and wished him Merry Christmas. He explained his presence and the uniform.

"I'm away to Susan's, ye ken, Johnny's mother. She's frantic. The bairn won't go to bed until she sees Santa - and I had the suit."

He set his face towards Susan's house, stepped a few unsteady paces then stopped. He turned round and slowly staggered his way back to them. They gathered around. He leaned forward as if he had some deep secret to share.

"It's guid tae see ye all thegither again," he whispered. Solemnly he shook hands with each of them in turn, gazing intently into their eyes as he did so.

Then he mumbled, "Christmas, aye, Christmas; it's an awfu' thing" and set off again on his kindly mission.

They laughed all the way back to Braeshiel. They did not want the night to end so they stoked up the fire and sat down in front of it. But one by one they fell asleep, until Marion woke them and said it was time to go to bed. And they did: Marion and John together.

THE END

Printed in Poland
by Amazon Fulfillment
Poland Sp. z o.o., Wrocław